**Praise for Dinah Lampitt**

## THE KING'S WOMEN

'A meaty dish of lust and medieval intrigue'
*Daily Mail*

'Ingenious and highly readable'
*The Times*

'Best writer of her kind'
*Kent Messenger*

## AS SHADOWS HAUNTING

'She has a strong sense of history and an uncanny ability
to bring it to life'
*Daily Mail*

'Sympathetically told, and the lives of the twin heroines
touch and part in a very convincing manner'
*The Times*

*Also by Dinah Lampitt*

SUTTON PLACE
THE SILVER SWAN
FORTUNE'S SOLDIER
TO SLEEP NO MORE
POUR THE DARK WINE
THE KING'S WOMEN
BANISHMENT

# As Shadows Haunting

## Dinah Lampitt

**CORONET BOOKS**
Hodder and Stoughton

Copyright © Dinah Lampitt 1993

First published in Great Britain 1993 by New English Library
a division of Hodder Headline PLC

Coronet Edition 1994

The right of Dinah Lampitt to be identified as the author
of this work has been asserted by her in accordance with the
Copyright, Designs and Patents Act 1988.

10 9 8 7 6 5 4 3 2 1

A CIP catalogue record for this title is available
from the British Library.

ISBN 0 340 60402 6

Typeset by Hewer Text Composition Services, Edinburgh
Printed and bound in Great Britain by
Cox & Wyman, Reading, Berks.

Hodder and Stoughton Ltd,
A division of Hodder Headline PLC
338 Euston Road
London NW1 3BH

*For the elegant gentleman I met at
The Society of Authors Annual
Reception upon whose suggestion this
book was written.*

# Acknowledgments

My sincere thanks are due to Lorna Fulford, the musician, in whose company I spent an entire evening discussing the career of Sidonie Brooks. Lorna gave me tremendous help, encouragement and insight into the classical musician's world and I could not have written about Sidonie without her. I would also like to thank Stephen Devine, who played the harpsichord especially for me during the summer season of 1991 at Finchcocks, Goudhurst, Kent, the instrument being part of their Historical Keyboard Instrument Collection. Stephen was only sixteen years old at that time, yet he played with a stunning brilliance that was quite unforgettable. My thanks are also due to Deborah McMillan, Deputy Manager of the King George VI Memorial Youth Hostel at Holland House during the spring of 1991. Deborah not only very kindly showed me round the interior of the building but also told me the legend of the ghost of Holland House, supposedly a former Lady Holland. On this occasion I was accompanied by the poet Beryl Cross, whose usual good humour made the research project most enjoyable. Thanks are due, too, to fellow author Derek Nicholls for supplying me with background information on the life of Sir Charles Bunbury. As always heartfelt gratitude to my agent Shirley Russell and my editor Anna Powell, not to mention the back-up team, Anna Foinette, Geoffrey Glassborow, Erika Lock, Rohini Patel, and Peter Jeffrey, whose retirement from Barclays Bank is yet another nail in the coffin of the good old days of considerate and friendly banking.

At length burst in the argent revelry,
With plume, tiara, and all rich array,
Numerous as shadows haunting faerily
The brain, new stuff'd, in youth, with triumphs gay
Of old romance.

THE EVE OF ST. AGNES
John Keats, 1795–1821

# One

How strange is memory! To a child the elm avenue had seemed so tall, so gigantic, that Sarah had been prone to giddiness when she had bent her head back to stare at the tops of the trees. But now, similarly craning her neck to look out of the window of the coach that bowled along the avenue's impressive length, she could see that, though magnificent, the elms were actually no higher than any others nor, indeed, more imposing. How odd, then, that she had for so many years been convinced that the tree-lined approach to the mansion was quite the grandest she had ever beheld.

Early that morning she had left London in order to reach the village of Kensington before it grew dark, for it was November and gloomy, and the muddy tracks that connected the sweet place with the metropolis were shadowy with footpads, haunted by highwaymen and dangerous to traverse once the light grew dim. So it had been with a sense of relief that Sarah had seen the wrought-iron gates loom up beyond the fields and felt the sway of the carriage as it turned off the road and started up the two-mile, elm-lined drive towards Holland House. Yet that very relief had been tinged with a certain apprehension at the thought of the future ahead of her, for Sarah was about to take up residence with an older sister whose face she could only recall as a dim memory from her early childhood.

With a crack, one of the carriage wheels dipped into a rut and at exactly that moment the first distant glimpse of Holland House came into view at the end of the avenue's sweeping lines. Even though it was barely two o'clock in the afternoon there was something about the light that already held a hint of dusk and the cloisters which ran on either side of the east and west wings were full of shadows. But despite this, the towers and balconies which soared above them were bathed

1

in the sharpness of autumn sunshine. The girl was instantly overwhelmed by the warmth of the house's red brick, the many gleaming mullioned windows in both the wings and central block and the whiteness and grace of the steps leading to the front door. She knew at once that in this instance her memory had played no childish tricks; the house was as she remembered it, gracious and charming yet at the same time overwhelming in its size and splendour.

As Sarah Lennox gazed in admiration at her future home the carriage turned through the small wicket gate into the sweep and she saw that at the bottom of the flight of steps leading to the courtyard a liveried footman hovered, ready to open the door of the coach as soon as it came to a standstill. With a swift movement, Sarah pulled a mirror from inside her muff and rapidly checked her appearance. But there was no time, they were drawing to a halt, and she was left with only a fleeting impression of an unruly mass of black hair fast escaping from her hat, a pair of long-lashed eyes more green than blue in this autumnal light, and a complexion of poppies and snow made fine by the wild damp climate of Ireland, the lilt of which land was in her voice as she stepped out of the equipage and thanked the servant for his trouble.

He bowed low. "Welcome to Holland House, Lady Sarah. If you would be good enough to follow me, Lady Caroline awaits within." And with that he bowed again and led the girl across the courtyard, flanked on either side by the arched cloisters, to the semicircle of steps that rose to the main entrance. The door opened even while she stood at the top, not so much catching her breath as collecting herself, and Sarah went through, vaguely aware of the vast paintings on the walls, the chandelier already ablaze with candles against the coming night, and the ornate ceiling, scroll-enriched in low relief, the letter H and a coronet decorating the square panels. But it was to none of these that her gaze was drawn. Instead, Sarah looked at the tall thin woman who stood waiting, suddenly remembering the angular features and brilliant eyes set beneath straight dark brows which made her sister's countenance so arresting.

"Caro!" she exclaimed, and flung herself into the older woman's arms.

It was almost a Dutch face that Sarah first stared into, then kissed, and indeed Netherlands blood ran in the family. Caroline and Sarah, amongst many, many others, were the daughters of the Duchess of Richmond whose mother had been of sober Holland stock, and it was to this grandmother that Caroline had thrown back in appearance. Sarah, for her part, had inherited the dark vivid looks of two far more interesting ancestors, namely the girls' great-grandfather, King Charles II himself, and Louise de Querouaille, his witty, clever mistress, a Frenchwoman endowed with all the style and grace of that country.

La Querouaille had openly become the King's lover in 1672 and he had created her Duchess of Portsmouth as a reward. When her son was born in July of the same year, Charles had attended his baptism in person, giving the boy the surname of Lennox and his own Christian name. And three years later this fruit of royal lust had been ennobled, little Charles Lennox being created Earl of March and Duke of Richmond, Duke of Lennox, Earl of Darnley and Baron Methuen of Torbolton. Louis XIV, not to be outdone, had bestowed on the Duchess of Portsmouth the title and estates of Aubigny in France in gratitude for her faithful services to her country!

It had been this particular royal bastard who had founded the Lennox dynasty and whose son had been the father not only of Sarah and Caroline but eighteen other children as well, quite a few of whom had survived to adulthood. And it had been the dark looks of both Charles Stuart and his French lady that had passed through the generations to Sarah Lennox, making her, at fourteen, already one of the great beauties of her day.

"You've grown lovely," said Caroline, holding her sister away and looking at her intently. "But then you always were. Such an adorable little creature."

Sarah pulled a face. "A forward brat, you mean." Her expression altered. "Oh, Caroline, *you* haven't changed at all. I had this terrible feeling on the way here that I wouldn't even recognise you, but I *do*. You look *just* the same. I would have known you anywhere."

Her sister gave a delighted laugh. "No older?"

"Not a day, not an hour, not a minute. I feel as if I have just stepped outside for a moment, not been away eight years."

"But, sweetheart, you were a little child when you left here and now you have returned to us a Beauty. But enough of that or I'll turn your head. Would you like to see your room straightaway or would you prefer to take tea first?"

"Tea, please. I'm famished for a cup. And anyway I want to greet the others."

Caroline smiled, the angular features lighting with an inner radiance which made her suddenly attractive. "Alas, Mr Fox is in London and the two older boys are both at Eton until Christmas."

Sarah looked wistful despite herself. "Then it will be just the two of us?"

Caroline smiled again, this time a little impishly. "I had not thought, my darling, that you would relish an empty house after Emily's entourage in Ireland so I have taken the step of inviting Mr Fox's niece to join us. She tends to vegetate in Somerset and prefers Kensington as somewhere nearer to town."

"Is she pretty?" asked Sarah, without meaning to put the thought into words.

"Not so much as you, dearest, but lively and vivacious. I promise that you will either love or loathe her, and if it be the latter then I shall send her home on some pretext."

"La, Caro, you have not changed a bit," said Sarah and tucked her arm through that of her beloved sister, her earlier fears allayed, her excitement mounting at the prospect of dwelling once more in Holland House. So, turning to follow the arched corridor towards the east wing, the pair of them went to find Mr Fox's niece.

In after years, Sarah thought of her first meeting with Susan Fox-Strangeways and wondered if there were indeed such a thing as predestination, if the hand of fate really had been at work to bring her together with someone who would prove to be as close as any sister of the flesh.

Tea had been served in Caroline's sitting room, the fire glowing, the candles already lit. And into that splendid light, the gloom without, the luminosity within, had walked Susan, small, demure, with a round almost childish face, a soft mouth and clear steadfast grey eyes bright as crystal. She had looked round and appraised the newcomer, afraid of rebuff, wanting so hard to be friends.

"Lady Sarah, may I present my niece, Lady Susan. Lady Susan, my sister Lady Sarah Lennox," Caroline had said formally.

But there had been no need. The two girls had looked at one another and both had felt that extraordinary sensation of recognition experienced so rarely, yet with such utter clarity. Pretty curtseys had masked other, deeper thoughts.

"I am sure we are going to be friends," Sarah said, and really meant it.

"May I show you Holland House later, my Lady?"

"Please call me Sarah, I much prefer it. And yes, I would love to see all those half-forgotten places again. I have not been here since I was five, you know."

And conversation flowed at that, giving Caroline a chance to sit quietly and study her sister, observing the sculpted arches of her cheekbones, the sweeping dark lashes, the amusing but attractive Irish accent that the girl had acquired during her eight years in that country.

The Duke and Duchess of Richmond, Caroline and Sarah's father and mother, had died within a few months of one another and their three youngest children, Louisa aged eight, Sarah, six, and Cecilia, only a tiny tot, had been sent to join yet another sister, Lady Emily Kildare, to be brought up in her household. Emily herself had been barely twenty years old at the time of the deaths but had earlier, at the age of sixteen, made a brilliant match with the Earl of Kildare and was thus able to offer the girls a good home. So it had been in the carefree atmosphere of elegant Dublin society that Sarah had been educated – and with what results! Even listening to her now, Caroline could hear the freshness of her approach to life, the sharpness of her wit.

'She will cause a sensation when I take her to London,' she thought, and could already imagine the hordes of suitors pressing for the hand of this most eligible of young women.

Caroline stood up. "It is high time we changed for dinner. Mr Fox should be home within the hour."

"Is he still as big a rogue as ever?"

Susan looked slightly shocked at Sarah's forthright question but Caroline only smiled.

"He is the kind of man who never loses his fascination for me."

"Then you are lucky indeed, dearest."

"I am truly. Now, little sister, I have given you a bedroom in the east wing next to Susan's apartment. Go with her now and discover whether you like it."

"I'm sure I shall," Sarah answered, pleased even before she had seen her new room. She turned on the spot, her eyes taking in every detail of Caroline's parlour. "Oh, how I *love* Holland House. Sure, Kildare House and Carton were magnificent but there's something quite fascinating about this place."

"Then let it be hoped you will always feel the same."

Leaving Caroline's sitting room, situated at the most northerly end of the wing, the two young women made their way through an adjoining chamber, used by Mr Fox when he wanted to relax away from the world, into a smaller hall out of which rose the east staircase. Climbing this they came to a passageway from which led Susan and Sarah's bedrooms. Throwing open the door of hers, Lady Sarah exclaimed with pleasure.

It seemed that there were windows everywhere, encompassing the entire far wall and also that on the left, all overlooking the parkland which stretched as far as the eye could see, to the village of Kensington itself several miles off. Behind the west wing lay the terrace and the formal garden, geometrically arranged and separated by straight paths, a warm brick wall running its length. Beyond the formal lay the Iris Garden, with a pool and fountain, the icehouse standing nearby.

"Do you like it?" asked Susan from the doorway.

"It's even nicer than I had hoped."

"Then I shall leave you to prepare for dinner."

Sarah turned away from the window. "Lady Susan, forgive

me if I have not given you my full attention today. The journey from Ireland to London and thence to here has filled my thoughts, added to which has been the excitement of seeing dear Caroline again. But I feel most certain that we will grow like sisters."

"I believe it. I have a houseful at home in Somerset but somehow, Lady Sarah, you are more *interesting*."

And with that the crystal eyes twinkled and the seventeen-year-old whirled away to her own quarters.

Sarah stood stock-still for a moment then went to the writing table, glad to see that her journal, leather bound and clasped in brass, had already been unpacked by the invisible army of servants who had seen to her luggage as soon as the coach had gone to the stables. Opening it, she drew up a chair, picked up the waiting pen and wrote importantly:

> This day, the 15th November, 1759, I took up Residence in Holland House, the home of my Sister Lady Caroline and her Husband the Rt. Hon. Henry Fox, Politician and Paymaster. I shall miss all in Ireland but cannot wait to enter London Society.

This done, Sarah called for her new maid, Lucy, hovering eagerly outside the bedroom door, and the business of getting into "full dress" for the evening began.

Sarah had often heard it said in conversation that while children of a very elderly sire were often born genius or mad, Henry Fox was quite indubitably a mixture of both. For, looking at him where he sat on her left at the head of the long dining table, studying those large expressive eyes beneath his full white wig, watching the mouth that barely suppressed a smile and frequently twitched at the corners, listening to the elegant voice full of notes and nuances, Sarah supposed that only such a divine lunatic as he could have wooed her sister and won her hand against all odds.

Sir Stephen Fox, Henry's father, had married twice, for the second time when he was seventy-six and his bride, who had been brought up with Sir Stephen's own daughter, twenty-five. From this extraordinary union had come four children, two boys and two girls. One child, Henry's twin sister, had died in infancy but the other three had survived to become adults.

Henry Fox's form of madness had been to fall in love first with a married woman many years his senior who had spitefully responded to her own hopeless situation by wedding her only daughter to her youthful lover's brother. Thus, Stephen Fox had become the husband of Elizabeth Strangeways-Horner, and these two, in their turn, had produced Susan Fox-Strangeways. But whether any feelings of guilt racked the enigmatical Mr Fox as he looked at his niece, presently sitting on his left and regarding him with a clear cool gaze, it was impossible to tell. He had forgotten all about his affair with the girl's grandmother the moment he first cast eyes on Caroline Lennox.

Caroline had been ten years old and Henry twenty-nine at that first fateful meeting. But wild though he might be, Mr Fox was a gentleman. He had not started to court his love until she was twenty.

Only a man of his charm, Sarah thought now, could have succeeded in winning such a young and attractive woman. Forty years old, inclining towards stoutness and double chins, those liquid eyes and magnificent voice of his must have done the wooing for him, these assets combined with his witty, immensely fine personality. For fall in love with him Caroline most certainly had. When Their Graces, her parents, had refused permission for her to marry, introducing her to another more suitable suitor, Caroline had cut off her eyebrows in protest. And when, in May 1744, they had announced their intention of removing Caroline from London she had slipped out of the house on the morning of the 3rd and married Henry Fox at a secret ceremony. Then she had returned home and waited for her husband to break the news to his father-in-law.

The Duke and Duchess had gone wild with fury. Indeed the whole of London had been suitably shocked, even the King growing angry and taking the Duke's side. Walpole had roundly stated that the elopement of Princess Caroline could not have caused a greater sensation. Then, in 1745, just before Charles Edward Stuart landed in Scotland and gathered the clans to march south, Caroline had given birth to her first baby. Yet still her parents had continued to ostracise her. They finally relented three years later and through Stephen Fox, now elevated to the Barony of Ilchester, sent for the erring couple and at long last made their peace with them.

"And what are you thinking about, Sarah? You look mighty serious." And with that Henry Fox broke the train of thought of his young sister-in-law.

He was leaning forward on the table, a glass of claret in his hand, his large eyes smiling lazily. "Will you be happy here, do you believe?" he added, almost as an afterthought.

"I am sure I will, Sir. And to be honest I was contemplating your marriage to Caroline and remembering how extremely romantic it all was."

Fox burst out laughing. "It was indeed. Well, there's time for you yet, though I wouldn't recommend a runaway wedding. Which reminds me, an old admirer of yours has been asking after you, in fact was delighted to hear you are taking up residence as one of his neighbours."

Sarah shook her head, puzzled. "An old admirer? But I have none. To whom do you refer, Mr Fox?"

He chuckled again, a deep inviting sound. "Why, your old flame, goose. The one whose heart you stole when you were only five years old."

His sister-in-law stared incredulously. "You don't mean the King?"

"Of course I do. His Majesty was overjoyed to hear you are returning to us and has asked me to take you to Kensington Palace when he is next in situ."

"What's this?" put in Susan.

Sarah grimaced. "A childhood tale and a horribly precocious one. I was taken to the Broad Walk one day by my French governess in company with my sister Louisa, and when the King passed by I broke away and rushed up to him."

"You did *what*?"

"I was only five but such a little prig. Would you believe your ears that I spoke to him in French?"

"What did you say?"

"*'Comment vous portez vous, Monsieur le Roi? Vous avez une grande et belle maison ici, n'est ce pas?'* Oh, I blush for shame to think of it now."

"His Majesty considered it sweet," Caroline interrupted. "He insisted that Sarah be taken to Kensington Palace when he was next there."

"And did she go?"

"Many, many times. He liked her, you see. He said that Lady Sarah was always cheerful, and to test it, on one visit he snatched her up and put her in a large oriental jar, shutting down the lid."

"How cruel!"

"Ah," said Henry Fox, "but Sarah won. Instead of crying she sat down inside and began to sing *'Malbruk s'en va t'en guerre'*."

Lady Susan's eyes grew large and round and her mouth opened in surprise, like that of a nesting bird. "How brave of you! I should have panicked."

"Nonsense," answered Fox benignly.

Caroline's angular face glowed at the memory. "The King could not do enough for Sarah after that. No wonder His Majesty hasn't forgotten you from that day to this."

"Well, I can scarce remember him. Except to know that he's a little red-faced cock bantam of a man, all struts and stares."

"That, my dear sister," Fox put in drily, "will be enough of that kind of comment if you want to get on in Society."

"Don't worry, Sir, I'll watch my manners I assure you. Unless King George tries to put me in a jar again; in which case, look out!"

The Paymaster laughed and after a while, the meal being done, the family left table together, not standing on ceremony, and retired to the Crimson Drawing Room for a while before going to bed. Outside the night was raw but Holland House stood solid and warm, ablaze with candles, fires glowing in all the principal rooms and bedrooms. The feet of the night watchman crunched on the gravel of Night Walk as he did his rounds, reassuring those within that all was well.

Squeezing close to Caroline on the giltwood sofa, sinking into the long comfortable cushion covered with crimson velvet, Sarah took her sister's hand in hers.

"Thank you for offering to look after me. It's going to be wonderful here."

The bony Dutch features made their usual transformation as Caroline smiled in the firelight.

"I know it, dearest."

Unsuccessfully fighting off a yawn, Sarah said, "And now if you will forgive me I would rather like to go to bed."

Caroline stood up. "I'll take you to your room. Lucy is already there with the warming pan and there's a good fire, so you won't be cold."

"This house could never be that," Sarah answered gallantly.

But indeed there was a chill as the sisters left the Crimson Drawing Room by a far door and traversed the next room, a comfortably large den which Caroline had given over entirely to the use of her three sons, Stephen, Charles James and Harry, only the youngest of whom was at home, though by now comfortably asleep in his nursery in the west wing. This Boys' Room opened onto the passageway which connected with the east wing and the bedrooms, and Caroline and Sarah now made their way along this to Sarah's room at the north end.

"It has such beautiful views," said the younger woman as they went in. "I saw them just as the sun went down."

"I hope you'll find the room comfortable as well."

Sarah gazed round at the elegantly draped bed, at the shining mirror lit by two large candles in silver sticks, at the cheerful fire, the dancing light of the flames reflected in the rosewood furniture.

"I could not ask for more." She threw her arms round her sister's neck as exuberantly as her sudden state of fatigue would allow. "Goodnight, Caroline dear." And Sarah gave her a kiss that was both grateful and affectionate.

"Good night, my love, sleep well and long. I will see you at breakfast which is served in the Oak Room."

And with that Lady Caroline Fox left the room. Sarah

turned to look round her appreciatively once more and then called to Lucy who stood by the bed vigorously applying the warming pan.

"You can help me undress now."

"Yes, my Lady."

The long process began. First the open robe, lavishly embroidered and with a border of braids, frills and flowers, was removed, then the many petticoats beneath, followed by the bodice cut with a downward point and trimmed with pleated lace, then the great hoops made of rods of osier came off, until finally Sarah stood in her stays, longing for the moment when they would be undone and she could breathe freely once more.

"Shall I unlace you now, Lady Sarah?"

"Yes please, Lucy. I feel as if I'm about to expire."

And then the daily torture was over and, slipping into her night-rail, a comfortable loose gown worn over her shift, Sarah sat down before the dressing-table mirror while Lucy unpinned her hair and brushed it through with long, infinitely soothing, strokes.

She was a fine country girl, born in Kensington and brought up away from the stale air of London. Yet despite her peasant stock she had a bucolic grace, there being a lithe, natural, almost sensuous movement about everything she did.

"How old are you, Lucy?" asked Sarah idly.

"Sixteen, my Lady."

"I shall be fifteen next February, on the 25th to be precise."

"Then we're much of an age," Lucy ventured, shooting a quick look at her new mistress to see if she had gone too far. But Lady Sarah was smiling through her yawns.

"Yes, indeed," she said. "And now you can go. I am quite capable of getting into bed on my own."

"Do you have everything you need, my Lady?"

"I shall ring if I require anything further."

"Very good, Ma'am."

And then, for the first time since she had caught the packet boat for England, Sarah was at long last alone with her thoughts, experiencing all the anguish of one who has been uprooted from her childhood home and thrown into a strange world. Yet what was there to fear? She was in the safe and capable hands of her sister and her husband, one of the wiliest politicians of his day. A dazzling future seemed assured.

The room grew quieter, the only noise the ticking of a small clock that stood on the mantelpiece and the crackle and spit of logs burning low in the grate. The silence of Holland House suddenly seemed both enormous and ominous and Sarah found herself straining her ears for any sounds of life. With a sense almost of fear the girl half rose from the dressing table to go towards the bed. And it was then that she saw as a reflection in the mirror that the door to her room was slowly opening behind her. Too nervous to turn round, she gazed into the glass and into the eyes of the woman who stood in the opening.

It was an elegant face that stared at Sarah over her shoulder, quite pointed at the chin and with wide high cheekbones beneath a pair of tilting golden eyes. The mouth was full, almost large, and looked as if normally it would be curving into a smile. But now it was open in an attitude of fright while those usually laughing eyes were dilated and full of fear, tempered by a certain curiosity. The woman wore no cap or pinner on her head and as she moved slightly, Sarah saw the sheen and bounce of hair the colour of a red setter's, of the dark long-headed poppy that waves in the cornfields and waste places of Ireland.

Just for a second the eyes of the two women met and held, and then as quickly as she came the intruder was gone and Sarah was left wondering who on earth it could have been who had wandered into her bedroom without knocking at this hour on a winter's night. But then, she considered, it wasn't really so late, it was only that she had retired early. Obviously her sister's or Lady Susan's maid had mistaken her door for theirs. Yet, if that were the case, why was she breathing quite so hard and why was her heart thumping as if she were afraid?

"Tiredness," said Sarah sensibly, and putting her night cap firmly on her head, blew out the candles and climbed into the large and comfortable bed.

13

# Two

The first Christmas at Holland House, the Christmas of 1759, proved to be by far the most exciting Sarah had ever enjoyed. Certainly the festive season in Ireland, always celebrated by Lord Kildare at his country seat Carton, situated in County Kildare, Leinster, had been uninhibited and joyful, but this particular occasion, perhaps because of the fact that she was growing up and made aware of it by one memorable event, was far more special than any other that had gone before.

In the second week of December, Caroline's two elder boys returned from Eton. They were, of course, Sarah's nephews but their ages made a nonsense of this relationship and the great house was at once alive with the laughter and shrieks of the young people as they danced and played cards and organised amateur theatricals, preparing for a Christmas performance. The eldest of the group was Susan Fox-Strangeways, who had celebrated her seventeenth birthday. Then came Stephen Fox, born on 20th February, 1745, followed by Sarah, born exactly five days later in the same year and Charles James, who had come into the world on 24th January, 1749. The youngest was Harry, born several years afterwards.

Stephen, known to the young set as Ste – much to the annoyance of his mother – was already showing signs of the portliness which had early engulfed his father. His face was plump, his lips heavy, his brows dark, and Sarah considered him the ugliest boy in Christendom. But for all that he had his parents' charm and Henry Fox's trick of endearing himself by means of his mercurial personality.

Charles James was a very different creature. At ten he had the dark Dutch appearance of his mother and, unbelievably, in that closed and clever young face there was a definite resemblance to Charles II, most strikingly so about the eyes. His father, who adored and spoilt him, as he did all his sons, called him Mr Thumb.

And now Mr Thumb was in high fig, leaping about the room wearing one of Susan's petticoats, a small transvestite piping, *"Comment vous portez vous, Monsieur le Roi?* How are you, my dear fellow? Is that what you're going to say to him, Sarah? Is it? Is it?"

"Oh shush, Thumb, do," his young aunt answered, rushing at him in mock attack. "You know very well that I shall comport myself nobly and as befits my station. I shall make a deep curtsey, so – ", she demonstrated " – and afterwards engage His Majesty in polite conversation."

"Do you think he'll stick you in a pot again?" Ste wondered aloud.

Like many fattish boys he had rather a plummy voice and this remark, made so seriously, sent both Sarah and Susan into fits of laughter.

"I do hope so," his aunt answered. "I'll be the talk of London for weeks if he does."

"You will be that anyway," observed Charles acutely, "with those handsome black looks of yours."

"I suppose *I* shall just pale into insignificance by comparison," said Susan, with just the slightest touch of petulance.

"You," answered Charles smoothly, "are the beautiful rose to Sarah's tiger lily. How could you pass unnoticed?"

"Now there's a silver-tongued brat if ever one sought one," commented Ste fruitily. "Shall we dance?"

And with that the quartet formed up for a minuet, laughing even more as Mr Thumb fell over in his improvised gown.

Spirits were high that day and small wonder at it. That morning, that very morning, had come an invitation from George II himself for both Lady Sarah and Lady Susan, in company with the older Foxes of course, to attend him at a Drawing Room to be held at Kensington Palace, where the King had taken up residence in order to celebrate the Twelve Days.

Drawing Rooms were a weekly gathering given by His Majesty to which were invited only select guests. Sometimes such occasions could be crowded and uncomfortable but in general consisted of a well-regulated and elegant assembly of the best company. And now the two young ladies of Holland House were to go and make their curtseys, and as this was deemed the moment when they finally stepped forth into Polite Society the occasion could not be paralleled for excitement and anticipation.

"Do you think the King will recognise me?" Sarah whispered to Susan.

"Of course he will, goose."

"But I've changed."

"Only to grow beautiful and no man, even an old one like the King, could complain about that."

The distant striking of a grandfather clock in the Saloon on the floor below broke through the strains of the minuet which all four young people were humming loudly in order to dance.

"'S'blood," said Ste morosely. "Three o'clock. We'll have to change for dinner soon."

"One more measure," pleaded Charles, but was promptly outvoted and the four reluctantly went their separate ways to be dressed for the main meal of the day, due to be served in an hour's time. Once in the privacy of her own bedroom, however, Sarah hugged herself with pleasure. After all the years that had passed since the funny little man had played with her so childishly, tickling and squeezing and crawling on all fours, he had not forgotten her. Instead His Majesty had paid Sarah the great compliment of insisting that she be brought to meet him as soon as he returned to his Palace at Kensington.

"Good old King George," she said, and jumped when Lucy stepped out from beside the great bed, wagging her finger in playful reproof.

"That's no way to speak of the King, my Lady."

"It's every way. He's a kind soul to think of me so."

"And what excitement, eh Ma'am? The dressmaker's taken on two assistants to get the gowns ready in time."

"Mine is to be of gold brocade with fine lace and silk for trimming."

"I know. I've taken a peep at the material."

Mistress and servant laughed together, then Lucy said, "Oh dear, I must start on your *toilette* if you are to be ready in time. Now, sit at the dressing table, do."

Still smiling, Sarah did so, staring into the mirror at her reflection, remembering the night when the strange woman had stood in the doorway behind her, a woman whom she had not subsequently been able to identify as a member of Caroline's household.

"Is Holland House haunted?" she asked idly now, wondering about it.

Lucy stopped her tortuous twisting of Sarah's hair and stared at her.

"They do say an old man in Jacobean dress walks through the library at night. It used to be the Long Gallery once on a day."

Sarah shook her head impatiently and some of Lucy's handiwork fell back into its natural dark waves.

"No, not an old man. I meant does a woman haunt the place?"

"Not as I've heard of, my Lady. Why do you ask?"

"Oh, for no reason really. It's just that one night, the very first night I was ever here to be precise, I was sitting where I am now and I thought the door opened behind me and a woman stood there and looked in."

"It must have been one of the maids."

"That's what I thought at the time but when I asked there was nobody answering her description, and I most certainly haven't seen her since."

"What did she look like?"

"She had wonderful hair, very rich in shade and texture. A colour like autumn leaves. Not brassy or coppery but subtle, if you understand me?"

"I understand all right," answered Lucy. "And I understand that if you don't sit still I'll never get *your* hair done and then what trouble will I be in?" She added, "My Lady," to show that cheeky though she might be she had not forgotten her place and would never seriously overstep the boundary that lay between her and the daughter of a peer of the realm.

Particularly one who had been remembered by that most kindly of monarchs, George II.

"Well, if you don't do it properly I might set the ghost on you, Lucy Bell."

The girl shrieked. "That'll be enough of that, Lady Sarah. I'll never sleep at nights."

"Of course you will. It was only a dream I had. There wasn't anything there in reality."

"I expect that's the truth of it. Now hold still. I do hope Lady Caroline isn't expecting me to put up your hair for the Drawing Room."

"No, my sister has arranged for a man to come from London."

"A man!" shrieked Lucy, clapping her hand over her mouth and giggling frantically.

"And why not? It is considered *de rigueur* in France for a *friseur* to do a lady's hair."

"Oh, my soul!" said Lucy, and laughed all the more.

She was still laughing when, three days later, Monsieur Claude arrived early in the morning having set out from London at daybreak by coach, his pale rather silly face peering anxiously out of the window all the way for fear of being set upon by thieves. Caroline, who was nothing if not practical, had him cut the two elder boys' hair while he was there, much to the annoyance of Ste who was trying to grow his long, Eton style.

"If I run late I beg I must stay the night, Lady Caroline. The highways are simply *crawling* with both foot and rum padders."

"Have no worries on that score, Monsieur. We will not put you in any danger."

"*Très bon*," said the hairdresser, much relieved, and crammed a vast purple ostrich plume into Caroline's already elaborate headdress.

But with the girls he worked a delicate miracle. There being few fresh flowers available he used artificial, weaving wild poppies into Sarah's ebony coiffure, while on Susan, whose hair was much lighter, the colour of barley, he put a simple wreath of rosebuds. These decorations enhanced their new dresses, both of the gown and coat variety, which meant a robe worn open over a petticoat itself extended on hoops. Sarah's petticoat was of the same material and decoration as her gown but Susan's contrasted, both styles being highly fashionable. Caroline wore purple, looking like an inverted tulip as she swept down the steps and into the waiting coach, and Mr Fox complemented her in a deep pink topcoat and breeches made of silk, heavily embroidered with silver lilies-of-the-valley, his silver waistcoat bearing the same motif.

There was a cheer as the equipage bowled off down the elm drive, Monsieur Claude waving a lace handkerchief and shouting "Huzzah" several times.

"Do I look presentable?" asked Susan nervously.

But though Caroline nodded Sarah did not reply, intent on staring out of the window, gazing at a distant figure the sight of which, though innocuous in itself, laid a sudden cold finger of fear along her spine. For standing in the Green Walk, which ran parallel with the drive and consisted of a long pathway alongside the fields leading to the east wing of Holland House, was a woman, a woman whose hair gleamed brightly in the winter sunshine. Even at this distance and across the parkland, Sarah was convinced it was the same creature who had stood in the doorway of her room on the night she arrived. She strained to see, half rising from her seat, and realised that the woman was turning to watch the coach go by.

"Sit down, Sarah, do," said Fox sharply, "your hoops have just knocked my cravat flying."

And he would not be placated until Caroline had rearranged the lace neckpiece to his complete satisfaction. But though Sarah took her seat meekly enough she kept her head slightly turned, perturbed that something she had dismissed as a dream, a figment of her overtired imagination, should after all be a creature of flesh and blood, visible in the broad daylight, standing in the Green Walk as bold as you please.

"Does one of the farm hands have a wife with auburn hair?" she asked despite herself, despite the grand occasion to which she was going and should by rights be thinking about.

"Auburn hair?" repeated Caroline in astonishment. "Yes, I expect so. Why do you ask?"

"Oh, just because I've seen such a woman round and about," Sarah answered casually. "It's mere curiosity."

For not even with her sister, that most trusted of people, could she discuss the extraordinary impact the sight of the stranger had had upon her, the fearful lurch of her heart, quite disproportionately violent when all she was seeing was one of the many people working round the Holland House estate.

But even this inexplicable feeling of fright was forgotten as the carriage arrived at Kensington Palace and swung through the archway beneath the Clock Tower into the courtyard. Ahead of them lay a line of coaches and chairs awaiting entry.

Mr Fox laughed, "Every exquisite in London is here, my dear girls. This will be a great opportunity for you to be seen."

Now Sarah's heart thumped for a very different reason and as the Fox conveyance finally came to a halt at the head of the queue and a liveried footman helped the passengers out, she and Susan exchanged a glance of genuine anguish. And then there was a queue of another sort as a crush of magnificently dressed ladies and gentlemen started a progress up the King's Grand Staircase, through the Presence Chamber towards the Drawing Room where His Majesty was receiving his guests that night.

It seemed to Sarah as she walked on that she passed through "three great staring rooms full of men" – or so she wrote to her sister Louisa afterwards – before she got to the door of the Drawing Room. But small wonder that the fashionable world stared, for tonight the girl's special beauty was immense, the deep set blue-green eyes vivid in a face the colour of whipped cream, wild flowers blooming in both her cheeks and hair.

Craning her neck past the shoulder of the liveried major-domo who was sonorously announcing, "Lady Caroline Fox, Lady Sarah Lennox, Lady Susan Fox-Strangeways and the

Right Honourable Henry Fox," Sarah gazed at the scene that lay waiting for her.

The King, stouter and shorter than she remembered him with a vivid complexion the colour of port, sat in a gilded chair, a grim-faced middle-aged frump whom Sarah identified as Princess Amelia, his unmarried daughter, on his right. On His Majesty's left sat his granddaughter, the Princess Augusta, named after her mother in the usual confusing manner of the times.

This particular princess, the Prince of Wales's elder sister, claimed the dubious privilege of having nearly been born in a coach. Poor Prince Frederick, her father, was so loathed by his parents, George II and Queen Caroline, that the Queen in particular had become convinced he would try and foist a spurious child, a creature smuggled in a warming pan, on the nation, that her son was too odd or too incapable to sire his own progeny. Even when Frederick had announced that his wife was pregnant, Caroline had remained unconvinced, so much so she had announced, "At her labour I positively will be . . . I will be sure it is her child."

To spite the Queen the young couple had decided the baby would be born at St James's, and not at Hampton Court as the King had ordered. Twice they had hurried off in a coach and twice it had proved to be a false alarm. On the third occasion, therefore, they left it rather late and poor Augusta had nearly been caught short, only just managing to struggle into the palace in time where she was "delivered of a little rat of a girl, about the bigness of a large toothpick case". The furious Queen on seeing the child had declared that such a "poor, little, ugly, she-mouse" could be nothing but her son's child. And that had been that. The young Princess Augusta had arrived in the world to be followed eleven months later by her brother, George.

Behind this fairly unprepossessing trio hovered a young man, looking about him and smiling. Not quite sure if she was right, Sarah guessed that this must indeed be the Prince of Wales and gazed in frank admiration at a tall, slim creature with fresh colouring and large, very gentle, china-blue eyes set beneath sweeping well-defined brows. Just as fortune would have it the Prince chose this very moment to glance up, presumably sensing that someone was staring at him intently, and looked straight across at her. Invisible arrows flew as the two fine young people instantly became aware of one another.

"God's mercy," said Fox beneath his breath, "the Prince is givin' Sarah the eye!"

Fortunately nobody heard him, for the next moment they were propelled into the mêlée and his wife was making as gracious a curtsey as anyone could wish. And then it was Sarah's turn.

"May I present my sister, Your Majesty?" Caroline asked clearly, and on the monarch's nodded assent took Sarah by the hand and led her forward amongst the now silent circle of onlookers.

The girl's curtsey was deep, executed just as she had practised it with her dancing master at home, but all she could think as she rose, straight-backed and dignified, was that the Prince of Wales's eyes were fastened upon her, a look of obvious admiration in their depths. Slowly, Sarah stood up and shyly glanced at her King.

"Cooee," said George, leaning forward in his chair and pinching her cheek rather too hard. "'*Marlbruk s'en va t'en guerre*', eh what? Chook, chook, chook."

And with that he got to his feet and danced a few steps towards the horrified girl, bowling an imaginary hoop as he came. There was a titter of polite laughter and the information that His Majesty used to play with the female in question when she was a child was passed round in a loud whisper. Not knowing quite what to do, Sarah stood motionless as the King approached.

"Well, little Sarah," he said, stopping in front of her. "Do you remember how you used to sit on my lap, eh? And how I would cuddle you and sing songs?" And His Majesty put his arms out roguishly as if she were still five years old.

Horrified, Sarah felt a horrid red blush sweep her face and neck and involuntarily took a step back, not saying a word and hanging her head in total embarrassment. The

King chucked her chin then held on to it forcing Sarah to look him in the eye.

"Don't you want to play any more?" he said, obviously rather hurt.

She would like to have answered then, at least to have had the courtesy to say something to her sovereign. But the press of people round her, the fact that every pair of eyes in the Drawing Room was turned towards her, overcame the poor girl completely.

"Pooh," said the King, releasing Sarah and walking away from her, "she's grown quite stupid!"

And with that he returned to his chair looking thoroughly put out.

Into the awful silence that followed, Princess Amelia spoke, her voice gruffer and even lower than her father's.

"No manners, what?"

Sarah wanted to die, for the floor to open up and allow her to descend into the cellar, for everyone to stop staring at her. Caroline saved the day by saying loudly, "And if Your Majesty permits, this is my niece, Lady Susan Fox-Strangeways," thrusting the unfortunate girl into the arena in Sarah's place. All eyes turned to examine the next victim and for the moment at least the pressure was off.

And then the miracle happened. A voice at Sarah's elbow said, "Seasonably cold weather, is it not?" and she found herself looking up into the bright eyes of the Prince of Wales. Blushes came again but this time the delightful sort. Almost as a reflex action, Sarah swept her very best curtsey and gave a charming smile.

The Prince was really very good-looking indeed. Both his great-grandfather and grandfather had been and were short, unkindly known as the Strutting Dwarfs, but this George was long and gracefully lithe. Sarah, who at five foot four inches was considered tall for a woman, had to bend her head back to look at him, admiring as she did so the straight nose, passionate mouth and large china-blue eyes. Even better, in an age of rotten teeth his were excellent, strong and white.

'What a very agreeable and mighty pretty sort of man,' thought Sarah, and promptly lost her heart.

"It *is* indeed cold, Highness," she answered, "but I quite like that. In fact I love snow. We used to play in it when I lived in Ireland. The winters are quite severe there, you know."

"I thought I detected an Irish brogue," he said, smiling so that his perfect teeth were even more noticeable.

"Is it very pronounced? I'm trying hard to lose it."

"Oh don't," George replied earnestly, and actually laid a hand on her arm in mock restraint. "It's very attractive. It enhances your beauty, if that were possible."

Beyond the singing in her ears Sarah was aware of a sound in the room like that of the incoming tide and glancing under her lashes saw that, once again, a bevy of quizzing glasses was flashing in her direction. Just for a second she glimpsed her brother-in-law, his mouth very slightly open and his eyes starting from his head.

'God's mercy,' she thought with amusement. 'I've triumphed after all!'

But it was only the Prince's intervention that had done it and now she gave him another grateful smile. "Thank you for coming to my rescue, Sir. I was somewhat flummoxed at that moment."

"I," answered George unexpectedly, "am frequently flummoxed. Adieu, Lady Sarah, I do hope that we will meet again."

This curtsey was even better than the last and Sarah held it respectfully as the Prince walked away. But as soon as he was safely out of earshot Fox was at her side, and a few moments later several other people came up, asking to be introduced to his sister-in-law.

"Well done, child, well done," he hissed as just for a second the two of them were alone. "What did His Highness say to you?"

"We talked about the weather," answered Sarah, her face completely straight.

"The weather?"

"Yes, Sir."

"Nothing else?"

Sarah frowned, looking for all the world as if she were trying hard to remember. "Oh yes, he told me I was beautiful."

And with that she went to join Caroline and Susan, both covering their excitement with a thin layer of calm, leaving her brother-in-law for once in his life quite speechless.

But in the coach home Fox's wits had most certainly returned.

"Damme, Sal, it's the consensus that you made a hit with Wales. Newcastle stated firmly that he had never seen the boy so animated."

"Boy?" put in Lady Susan. "Surely the Prince is in his twenties?"

"He's twenty-one but everyone's a boy to Newcastle."

And they chattered on. But Sarah was not listening, thinking instead of that pair of china-blue eyes whose owner had not even tried to conceal the fact he found her fascinating. It was then, on her way back to Holland House from the Drawing Room at Kensington Palace, she was certain that she had indeed finally grown up.

With two young women in the house, both beautiful and of marriageable age, it occurred to Fox he should start to entertain more and that a fifteenth Birthday Ball for Sarah would be a splendid plan. So on 25th February, 1760, Holland House opened its doors to the cream of Society. Everyone of note was there and the guest list included the Earl and Countess of Kildare (born Emily Lennox), the Countesses of Coventry, Holderness, Stafford and Hillsborough, the Ladies Betty and Diana Spencer, the Earl of March, the Dukes of Bedford and Marlborough and Mr Horace Walpole, always worth inviting because of his viperish tongue and high command of the latest gossip. All in all there were some seventy guests and Ste and Charles James had been fetched back from Eton by their father, a hopelessly indulgent parent, in order that they might attend. The one person missing who should perhaps have been present was the Prince of Wales.

"Should we invite His Highness?" Fox had said to Caroline in January, when the gold-edged invitations had gone out.

"No," she had answered emphatically, sipping her early morning chocolate.

"But damme, Caro, he fancies the girl."

She had looked at him reprovingly. "How coarse you can be on occasion, Mr Fox."

"You don't always object to that," her husband had answered, and given a wink.

"If you don't mind we are discussing the Prince of Wales and Sarah."

"How well those two names sound together."

"Henry!" Caroline had exclaimed sharply. "You are beginning to scheme and that is dangerous. If His Highness fancies Sarah – to use one of your unpleasant words – let him seek her out for himself. No good will come of forcing the issue."

Fox had sighed heavily. "Very well, my dear; like a dutiful husband I accede to your command."

But secretly he had known that Caroline was right, that to push his sister-in-law at this delicate stage of the proceedings could be fraught with hazard. But, in his inimitable style, he had immediately started to plan how he could get Sarah back to court and there, most casually of course, make sure that the Prince not only saw but conversed with her.

Most fortunately for Caroline, who very much hoped to copy a highly successful house warming she had given in May some years previously, that particular February was delicately mild and it was decided that the balconies above the two cloistered arcades of the east and west wings could be used as places on which the guests might promenade. Torches were made and fixed to the outer walls, giving the house a theatrical and exciting look, and a thousand extra candles were ordered, many to go in the first floor Gilt Room where there was to be dancing. On the floor below tables were set up for supper in both the Saloon and the Dining Room, these two rooms leading into one another. Additionally, three card tables were put up in Caroline's dressing room which opened off the Great Staircase.

Behind the scenes, lacking the assistance of Monsieur Claude, Lucy fought nobly with Sarah's hair, eventually having to beg Lady Susan to hold the green feathers with which the maid was trying to create a fashionable arrangement.

"La, but I'm in a twit of nerves," said the birthday girl, visibly excited that such a very grand occasion had been arranged especially for her. "Thank God, say I, that His Highness is not coming."

"I don't think you really mean that," answered Susan, her crystal eyes sparkling at the patent falsehood.

"Oh yes I do." Sarah grinned defiantly at their two reflections in the dressing-table mirror.

"Hold still, my Lady," said Lucy, her usual plea.

"What's he like?" asked Susan curiously.

"The Prince? You saw him as plainly as I did."

"Don't mince. I meant what is he like as a person."

"Well, he don't talk nonsense and pester one with music. He talks the same as other people."

"I think you have taken kindly to him, Sarah Lennox, despite all you say."

The younger girl smiled. "He's pretty, both in nature and looks. Yes, I think perhaps you're right."

The distant sounds of musicians tuning up cut across their conversation.

"Oh, God, the orchestra's here. Hurry up, Lucy, do."

"I'm trying my best, Ma'am."

"Here let me," said Susan, and seizing hold of the thick dark hair rapidly twisted it into a knot which she fastened on top of Sarah's head, pulling another piece free to form a ringlet over one shoulder. "Now, Lucy, let's get those feathers in quickly. Madam's keeping still just for once."

"That'll be through thoughts of the Prince of Wales," the maid commented slyly but the two young ladies chose to ignore this remark.

The ball was due to begin at nine o'clock and punctually as the great clock struck in the Saloon, Mr Fox and Lady Caroline, the Ladies Sarah and Susan, Ste and Charles, plus the Earl and Countess of Kildare, who were house guests, formed a receiving line in the entrance hall. Already there were the sounds of carriages and chairs coming up the elm drive and, it being safer for the conveyances to travel in convoy, those who had driven from London arrived together. Within half an hour all seventy guests had made their entrance and dancing began in the Gilt Room, those not wishing to cavort sitting down to cards or simply to converse.

The magnificent chamber in which the ball was being held was, as its name implied, one of the most spectacular of its kind. Lined with panels decorated with the family devices, with dancing figures, with coronets and the initial H, it boasted Ionic pillars set at intervals along the walls, each adorned with a classical bust. The room had two entry doors, two fireplaces and three enormous windows, one of which was set in the turret which rose from the ground floor and housed the main front door. The overmantels above the fireplace bore painted medallions containing the heads of Charles I and his Queen, Henrietta Maria, and family legend had it that the room had originally been decorated for a festivity to celebrate their marriage.

Whether that were true or false, the opulence of the surroundings was quite breathtaking, and seeing all the dancers stepping out Mr Fox again had a pang of regret that the Prince of Wales had not been on the guest list. But Sarah had almost forgotten George's absence, almost but not quite, as she danced every dance with her partner for the evening, Captain Carlton, only stopping occasionally for a negus in the adjoining Tapestry Room where liquid refreshments, including tea, were being served.

Meanwhile, the Duchess of Bedford, Lady Pembroke and the Duke of Marlborough had cut in at whist; Lady Albermarle and Lady Yarmouth, with two partners, were playing two pools at Quadrille; and Lord Bury, Lord Digby and Mr Dicky Bateman were intent upon cribbage. Others again wandered upon the balconies, taking the air and admiring the splendid way in which the rout had been organised. But by one o'clock in the morning all were ready for a cold collation and went down the Great Staircase to the tables already prepared in the Saloon and Dining Room. Sarah sat with her family, a mound of birthday gifts banked on a smaller table behind her, and thought she had never enjoyed herself quite so much.

"A speech," called someone gaily.

"Hear, hear," said somebody else, and the guests in the Dining Room crowded into the doorway to listen.

"My Lords, Ladies and Gentlemen," Sarah began, "I thank you all for coming to honour me on my fifteenth birthday

29

and as I detest long speeches myself I intend to make mine brief. Therefore I shall very simply propose a toast to my delightful guests coupled with my splendid family. I drink to your health."

She raised her glass and everybody laughed and applauded, some concealed person saying quite audibly, "What a pity the Prince ain't here to see her."

Fox himself proposed the toast to Sarah's birthday and then the supper was ended with a dessert and ice.

"More dancing, my Lady?" asked Captain Carlton attentively.

"I think if I may, Sir, that I will just take the air alone for a moment or two. I'm flushed with the fun of it all."

He laughed aloud. "You have a quaint way of speaking, Lady Sarah."

"I expect I learned it in Ireland. When I was first taught to ride by an Irish groom he told me to 'sit tight and feel the baste's mouth'. No wonder I've grown up maddish."

"Maddish, but beautiful," said Captain Carlton, and bowed.

Sarah smiled, leaving the Saloon quietly so as not to disturb the party. Crossing a passageway beneath the dome of the central tower she went into the Entrance Hall and out through the small vestibule to the front door with its delicately moulded fanlight. Liveried flunkies sprang to attention as she appeared, but the girl merely nodded to them and went to stand on the marble steps, looking out to the drive and parkland.

In front of her lay the square entrance court, lit to a gleaming white by the torches burning on the balconies above. Beyond it lay steps leading down to the carriage sweep and beyond that again were the Inigo Jones entrance portals, an iron fence the width of the house which stopped the cattle wandering onto the lawn, stretching between them. Sarah could just make out the man who operated the wicket gate, at that moment standing open lest any carriage should wish to leave, snoozing on his little portable seat. And then, almost against their will and somehow frighteningly slowly, her eyes were drawn to Night Walk which lay on the far side of the fence.

Even before she had seen who stood there, the girl had experienced an ice-cold thrill of fear and so was not surprised to glimpse a figure, shadowy in the torchlight, its burnished hair glowing in the dimness.

'Why does she stand so still?' thought Sarah. 'Why does she stand so damnably still?'

She took a step forward, straining to see more clearly, and just for a second one of the torches above spluttered and flared so that everything was brilliantly illuminated. Sarah gazed at clear eyes, wide open almost as if in wonderment, the lips of a quizzical, smiling mouth parted in surprise.

"Who are you?" she called. "What do you want?"

The wicket keeper woke with a start. "Eh? What? Oh, it's you, Lady Sarah!"

"Huggins, go and tell that woman to come to me at once. She's always loitering about the place and I won't have it."

He jumped to his feet, running along the fence, but Sarah knew that the intruder had already gone, had vanished into a pool of darkness beyond the east portal.

"She's over there somewhere, I believe. Do try and find her, there's a good fellow."

"Anything wrong, my Lady?"

It was Captain Carlton standing right behind her. Sarah was suddenly filled with a great desire to tell him the whole story but decided against it, thinking she might spoil what was proving to be a truly perfect occasion.

"No, nothing at all. I thought I saw a poacher but Huggins is sorting it out."

"Then shall we return to the ball?"

"That sounds enchanting."

And Lady Sarah Lennox dropped one of her impeccable curtseys, took the arm of the gallant military man, and returned to the Gilt Room to enjoy what was left of the night.

The last of the carriages went down the elm drive at five o'clock in the morning and it was only then that the Foxes, exhausted, elated and fit to drop, finally said goodnight and went to their bedrooms. And yet Sarah, tired though she was, still felt she would not sleep unless one question was answered. Going down by the East Staircase which connected with the Servants' Hall, she went out through the side door and hurried round the house to where Huggins was finally closing the wicket and packing away his little folding chair. She rushed up to him impetuously, not caring that her behaviour was strange and extremely unmannerly.

"Did you find her, Huggins? That woman I saw?"

He scratched his head, looking at her curiously. "I searched and searched, my Lady, but there weren't no one there. Strange, like." He smiled, his rough outdoor face looking like a cheerful ham. "Sure it weren't your imagination, my Lady?"

"Of course not. Why do you say that?"

"Because I never saw nobody."

"That, my fine fellow, is because you were asleep," answered Lady Sarah Lennox haughtily and, turning on her heel, she went back into the comfortable familiarity of Holland House.

# Three

It started to rain during the night, at first very gently, a fine light spray which merely moistened the parched earth. But then in the hours before dawning the delicate veils of drizzle turned to a downpour and began to drench the street, all the refuse and litter sweeping along the gutters, blocking the choking drains with yet more garbage.

Sometime between three and five, the fact that it was raining hard impinged itself on her consciousness and Sidonie woke, gazed at the alarm clock, said, "Oh God," and buried her head beneath the bedclothes, not wanting to start what promised to be a long and stressful day. But sleep had gone, her mind already racing over all she had to do, her tensions beginning to mount as she lay in the darkness listening to the deluge and wondering why after a summer in which the words "Greenhouse effect" had become positively boring, the weather had to choose this day of all days to break.

Ahead of her stretched the dreary and depressing prospect of moving house, listed amongst her six pet hates. The very sight of removal men armed with tea chests and newspaper was guaranteed to send shivers down Sidonie's spine and yet, as if through some awful twist of fate, she had moved many times since she had left her childhood home.

"But this one will be the last," she muttered into the darkness. "Never again," realising even as she spoke that she was being utterly ridiculous to hope for such a thing.

Another glance at the clock showed that it was half past four, too late for rest, too early to rise, yet just to lie there thinking until the alarm went off at six seemed a grim idea. Very slowly, moving rather as if she were walking in her sleep, Sidonie got up and made her way through the darkness to the kitchen. There, eyes half-closed, she switched on the

light and stared round. The kitchen stared back coldly, devoid
of its trappings, the cupboards empty, only the kettle braving
the empty space that had once been a crowded work top.

Returning to the living room, Sidonie thought that it, too,
seemed angry with her for betraying the flat by selling.
Stripped of all her pictures and ornaments the room was
bleak and bare, while the light bulb hanging down, its shade
gone, did nothing to soften the effect.

"Sorry," she said aloud, "but the new people will be in by
tonight."

And she herself, when the move was finally over and the
last thing put in place, would be in such a splendid home that
the agony of it all would have been justified. Sipping her tea,
wishing she had had the nerve to make it something stronger,
Sidonie thought back to her very first glimpse of the Garden
Flat, Phillimore Gardens.

She had never imagined in her rarest moments she would
ever have had enough money to buy an apartment in
Kensington – what her grandmother would have termed a
"good" address – let alone one that was actually a maisonette,
occupying both the ground and basement floors. But the result
of a highly successful and exhausting concert tour of Japan,
combined with a legacy from that very same grandmother,
had boosted Sidonie's bank balance sufficiently not only to
consider such a thing but even to go and look.

A cool spacious room leading onto the garden had greeted
her eyes in the basement, and just for a moment she had visu-
alised it furnished with her clavichord and two harpsichords,
the little spinet tucked into a corner so that when she sat at it
she would see nothing but the lawn and flowerbeds enclosed
by a warm brick garden wall. Also on that basement floor
had been an adjoining room, perfect for watching television,
listening to recordings and generally relaxing.

On the floor above there had been a dining room and
kitchen, a superb bedroom above what was already des-
ignated to be the music room, and another small room for
guests. But the selling point had been the fact that the garden
would be entirely Sidonie's, that none of the other flats had
any claim to it.

"I can't meet the price," she had told the estate agent. "Will the owner take £2,000 less?"

"It's a buyers' market, Miss Brooks. He might."

And much to her amazement and pleasure the deal had been struck. The flat in Phillimore Gardens – maisonette seemed too precious a word somehow – had become hers, with only the dreaded move to live through before she took possession of it.

At eight o'clock sharp, Sidonie long since ready, the pantechnicon arrived and after cups of tea and fags all round – "You don't mind do you, luv?" – the loading began.

"Careful with them pianos," shouted the foreman. "They're valuable."

"They're not pianos actually, they're early instruments. Two harpsichords, a clavichord and a spinet to be precise."

"You don't look the type to play those."

"Oh," Sidonie answered vaguely, not really wanting to get into a discussion as to what type would.

By noon the first stage was all done, the entire contents of the flat in Highbury aboard the furniture van, the cat, the plants and Sidonie in her car.

"Away you go, dear," said the foreman cheerfully. "We'll just have our spot of dinner then we'll catch you up."

And so she was off through the traffic of London in the rain, plunging into the tunnel at Knightsbridge, down past Kensington Palace, then the High Street, turning right into Phillimore Gardens itself. Just for a moment after she had switched off the engine, Sidonie sat staring up at the house's white facade, mentally dating it as Victorian and probably built at around the time of the Great Exhibition. Then, relishing every second, she put her key in the lock of the main front door and went into the hall.

The door to the Garden Flat lay immediately opposite and getting out yet another key Sidonie opened it. In that microcosm of time as she stepped over the threshold into her new apartment she felt that fate was suddenly singing in her ears, that somewhere a comet was born. She was simultaneously excited and daunted as the place appraised and then consumed her. Rushing down the small flight of stairs to the basement, she unlocked the garden door and stepped out in the rain to a small terrace from which three steps led to the walled garden.

A door in the far end of the wall gave access onto Holland Walk but for obvious reasons of security this was both heavily bolted and locked, and try as she would to push back the bolts, Sidonie found them stuck fast.

'I'll get that fixed,' she thought, being somewhat obsessional about things that did not work.

But, even in the downpour, the garden itself was charming. Sidonie imagined the terrace with her white iron furniture on it, bright geraniums in terracotta pots, two director's chairs side by side beneath the apple tree.

'Why two?' she wondered silently, then screwed her face up. 'Must be old habits dying hard.'

But she would not let her thoughts go down that path, would not spoil the first few minutes in her new home by thinking about Nigel and the past. Instead she ran indoors as the deluge became even heavier and poured herself a glass of wine from a bottle she had brought with her.

"To the Garden Flat!" she toasted and raised her glass to the empty spaces around her.

By five o'clock those spaces had been filled, all the tea chests carried in and deposited in the middle of the living room floor, the plants put to stand in the bathroom until permanent places could be found for them.

"Well, luv, that's it," said the foreman. "I reckon you'll be happy here. You've got yourself a right cosy pad if you ask me."

"Very nice," added Darryl, one of the crew.

"Thank you," said Sidonie and reached in her handbag for a suitable tip. "Have a drink on me."

"Oh ta, luv. You'll be all right will you?"

"Yes. I won't unpack much now. I'll probably have an early night."

"Very wise. Well, we'll be off then."

"Thanks for everything. Goodbye."

With the men gone, the silence plunged inwards as Sidonie, following an age-old piece of advice given by her mother, made the bed as her first priority. Then, feeling suddenly exhausted, she went to the kitchen, fed the cat, got some tea and toast and took the tray to her bedroom. Climbing into bed, she was too tired to eat, but she drank the tea, then closed her eyes. Almost at once a dream came, quite the most vivid she had ever had.

Sidonie dreamt that she walked in the garden in the darkness and saw that the door in the far wall now stood open wide. Drawn compulsively to go through it, the dreamer found herself in Holland Walk, the long avenue separating Holland Park from the houses in Phillimore Gardens. Not knowing why, she made her way up the Walk towards Holland House, and it was then that a beam of moonlight pierced the dark sky, clearly illuminating the scene ahead of her.

Sidonie realised to her astonishment that the great mansion had not been destroyed by an incendiary bomb during the war as she had thought. She gazed with admiration and a certain awe at a huge courtyard flanked on two sides by arcaded cloisters, airy balconies above them. Behind the third part of the court lay the main building, all towers and turrets and glinting mullioned windows. The Inigo Jones gateway no longer existed, the two portals set at some distance apart, an iron fence separating them one from the other.

As Sidonie stared it seemed to her that every candle in the place was lit simultaneously, for all at once the house was ablaze with light. There was the sound of music and laughter coming from within. And at that the dreamer became afraid and turned to go. She wanted to run but found she could not. But worse was yet to come, for when she got back to the garden door Sidonie saw that it was closed once more. She started to bang on it with her fists, calling "Let me in." And that was what she heard herself shout as she finally awoke.

At first she had no idea where she was, staring at the high Victorian ceiling with its moulded rose and cornices, not recognising them. And then the memory of the move and the Garden Flat returned and Sidonie smiled wryly.

"Longing to live here and when I do I have nightmares," she muttered.

But it hadn't really been a nightmare. In its way, the dream had had a haunting kind of beauty. Sidonie stared at the alarm clock, much as she had done much earlier that day. It was half past eight in the evening and still light. Thinking that this inability to sleep was getting ridiculous, she heaved herself out of bed.

In the bathroom she caught sight of her face in the mirror left by the previous owner. Her eyes, so full of hazel flecks that they appeared almost golden, had dark shadows under them, and her hair hung limply like the coat of a sickly fox. Her skin, too, had lost its normally healthy look and was pallid and drawn.

"Not a pretty sight!" Sidonie remarked to her reflection, which grimaced back.

After a long bath she went into the bedroom again and, going to the window, looked over in the direction of Holland House. The garden wall obscured the view completely and even though she tried standing on a chair, Sidonie still found it impossible to get a glimpse of the place.

"I wonder if it has been restored," she said to the cat, who had curled up on the end of the bed and was fast asleep. "I'll have a look at that tomorrow. But meanwhile some sleeping pills. I'm getting an undisturbed night tonight if it kills me."

This decided, she read and listened to the radio until eleven and then took the capsules, used mainly when she was on tour and found it difficult to sleep in overheated hotel rooms. Within ten minutes she was unconscious and this time not a single dream came to disturb her.

The first morning in her new home went well. Sidonie had got up at seven after a good night's sleep and started to tackle the packing cases, then at midday had gone to do the weekend shopping. Having put this away she had had a snack lunch and left the flat to explore the neighbourhood, heading almost automatically towards Holland Park.

The rain of the previous day had stopped in the night and the sun was out again, enhancing the colours of the many lovely flowers in the Dutch and Iris gardens. But as it was Saturday there were people everywhere, a fact which Sidonie rather resented as she made her way up Holland Walk staring in the direction of the house and giving a slight exclamation of surprise as it came clearly into her line of vision. For where in her dream had stood a beautiful and magnificent mansion now only the ground floor and arcades remained, with the exception of the east wing which had been more fully restored. A German bomb had cruelly done what four hundred years could not and brought the great house to its knees.

Following the sign 'To Holland Park Theatre' Sidonie turned into Nightwalk, which ran in front of the building, though slightly distant from it, and then stopped short. From this angle it was almost impossible to see the place as a flight of steps and a brick wall obscured the view.

"Damn," said Sidonie and climbed upwards.

What had once been the entrance to Holland House was now obviously used as the theatre, the archway, windows and steps serving as the backdrop, the space in front which had been the courtyard, the auditorium. Longing to get closer, Sidonie pressed closely to the iron-railinged gates which had been set between the Inigo Jones stone portals, now as close as goal posts. And then she saw that the only thing stopping her from going in was a small portable sign saying 'No Entry' standing to the left of the gate. Pushing it to one side and trying to look as if she were acting with the necessary authorisation, Sidonie stepped into the courtyard.

Close to, the house looked even sadder, crumbling and neglected, only the east wing remotely resembling the stately edifice Sidonie had seen in her dream. Smiling at a pair of workmen who stared at her curiously, she approached for a better look.

The cloistered arcades threw pools of purplish shadow where once must have walked bewigged and fashionably dressed people longing for a little shade. Sidonie could imagine the click of high heels, the swish of hoops as they paraded the length and breadth of the arched walkways taking the air without being exposed to the elements.

'Useful for rainy days too,' she thought – and then she saw the door. It stood in the arcade of the east wing and looked very much to Sidonie as if it could have been original. Not knowing why she had suddenly changed into such a lawless individual her hand was out to push it before she could stop herself and she watched as to her enormous surprise it slowly swung open.

She stepped into the coolness of a paved passageway and experienced a horrible moment as something like a black spiral seemed to whirl towards her. But it was gone as quickly as it came and Sidonie put the mirage down to a moment's faintness brought on by the fact she was now flagrantly trespassing. Despite feeling weak, despite the fact that she could be caught at any moment, Sidonie looked round her curiously.

Whoever had restored the east wing had done a brilliant job for not only was the interior absolutely authentic looking, it was also furnished with period pieces. Furthermore, a great and antique staircase leading off a larger hall into which she had now wandered, was hung with beautiful Georgian mirrors that appeared to be worth a fortune.

'It's been done as a museum,' Sidonie concluded, and wondered that the place wasn't swarming with tourists on a Saturday afternoon in high summer. But there was nobody about and she made her way slowly up the stairs, looking at all the lovely things that lay casually around for anyone to steal.

At the top of the flight a passageway led off to the right, then turned left, and as Sidonie followed it she saw that it was lit by candles, most of them attached to mirrors which reflected their light.

"What *is* this place?" she said out loud, and then stopped at a door on her right, the temptation to look at the room beyond, utterly overwhelming. Very gently she pushed it open and stared inside.

It was a bedroom, a fire burning in the grate and the whole thing done as if it were a reconstruction of a Georgian room. Sidonie gazed at the draped bed, the rosewood furniture and at the girl who sat with her back to her looking into the dressing-table mirror.

She was like something from a Joshua Reynolds painting, her gown loose, flowing and beribboned, her dark hair hanging to her shoulders. For a moment or two she wasn't aware of Sidonie's presence and then she looked at her in the glass.

Sidonie saw the girl's eyes, shining and deep as the sea, and a lovely startled mouth, before she took to her heels and ran, down the staircase, across the two halls and out through the door into the daylight, knowing that she had for the first time in her life undoubtedly seen a ghost.

Afterwards, of course, when she was once more in the harmonious atmosphere of the Garden Flat, Sidonie took herself to task for being an utter fool. What she had obviously seen was an actress from the Holland Park Theatre in one of the dressing rooms which also doubled as a props room, hence the period furniture, all made no doubt in a theatrical workshop somewhere.

"I'm a fool," she said to the cat, who arched his back and purred, hoping for food. He had settled in well and was already using the flap which led out into the garden. "I think you'll definitely like it here," Sidonie went on, stroking him. "But there's still the problem of the neighbours to overcome."

The cat cocked an ear.

"Yes, I know. I should try and see them tonight. It's not easy living above a musician and I've got to explain about the noise."

The cat appeared to nod, not relishing it much himself when Sidonie was preparing for a concert.

"I ought not to let this silly fright I had put me off. I'll call on them in the next half-hour. Promise."

The cat lost interest and went downstairs.

The bedroom was by now looking quite presentable, make-shift curtains at the windows and all Sidonie's things out on the dressing table. She sat down before the mirror, making herself ready to go calling and thought of that other creature, so intensely beautiful yet with such a look of another age.

"Costume and make-up," Sidonie said very firmly, and then started to apply her own.

It was an interesting face she worked on, quite bony and pointed. She had been told once that she had a passionate mouth and Sidonie supposed she probably had. Except when she was extremely depressed it curved upwards and this, added to the wide setting of her eyes, gave her an amused look. But without doubt it was her hair which was her best feature. She was called Foxy in certain musical circles, as that was the nearest her fellow musicians could get to describing her mane, for it had many shades in it, though nothing of ginger or copper. It was a true deep red.

Sidonie applied lipstick for the finishing touch, a deep strawberry which suited her. She was not of the school of thought that believed certain colours were prohibited to auburn heads, and wore exactly what she liked.

"Will I do?" she said to the cat, who had come in again. He yawned and went straight to the kitchen. "Thanks for the compliment!" Sidonie called to his vanishing tail and stuck her tongue out, thinking that if anybody could see her they would think she was quite mad.

"Oh well," she said as she went out of her front door and started up the main staircase. "That's what comes of living alone."

She had seen from the bells in the entrance that the house was divided into four separate apartments, hers being the largest and, no doubt, by far the most expensive. Immediately above her in Flat One lived someone called O'Neill, in Flat Two was a Parker and in the attic flat, which Sidonie noticed with a certain amusement had been renamed the Penthouse, were Mr and Mrs Rupert Carruthers-Greene.

'Them first,' she thought.

There was no reply to her ring and Sidonie dropped through a note she had already written.

"Dear Neighbour," it said, "I have just moved into the Garden Flat and thought perhaps I should warn you that I am a professional musician specialising in early keyboard instruments. Because of this I am obliged to practise for several hours a day but I do confine this to working hours, 10 a.m. to 6 p.m. in my case. Very occasionally, when I am preparing for a concert, I might continue until eight in the evening but would advise you of this in advance. I do hope that my playing will not inconvenience you in any way but if you do have any problems please do not hesitate to let me know. Yours sincerely, Sidonie Brooks."

The door to Flat Two was opened after a slight pause during

which a player self-consciously belting out Vivaldi was turned down. There was also a scuffling as if clutter were being thrown about. Then came the rattle of a chain, the turning of a key and there stood Parker.

"Yes?" she said.

Sidonie cleared her throat. "Good evening. My name is Sidonie Brooks and I'm your new neighbour. I moved into the Garden Flat yesterday."

There was a flashing smile revealing a set of rather small teeth.

"Oh, do come in. I heard someone arriving. Mr Beevor, he was the previous owner, recently gave a little drinks party and broke the news that he was going. We're all very friendly in this house, you know. I'm Janet Parker by the by, generally known as Jannie." She giggled in a way which suggested she thought she had a silvery laugh. "You must excuse the mess, the flat's a tip. I usually tackle it at weekends but it's been so fine I've been in Holland Park nearly all day. Now, what would you like to drink – G and T or dry white wine? Or sherry perhaps?"

"Wine please."

Jannie pushed several old copies of the *Guardian* out of an armchair and onto the floor. "Do sit down. I'll get the bottle."

She whirled into the kitchen in a flurry of ethnic skirt, leaving Sidonie a few moments to look around. The room was large with two big windows overlooking Phillimore Gardens and was furnished with several old chairs and a sofa. A portable CD and tape player, still playing Vivaldi, stood on an old sideboard nestling next to a man's head sculpted in bronze. Sidonie thought it quite the most repellent thing she had ever seen.

"Good, isn't it?" said Jannie, returning with a tray. "One of my girls did that. I'm a social worker, you know. It's so draining I simply can't tell you, but rewarding of course. I took them to a concert at the Festival Hall recently. Do you know, some of them had never been into a concert hall before, let alone listened to Mozart."

"Did they enjoy it?"

Jannie meditatively rubbed her head. "One or two, I think one or two." ·

She paused to take a sip and Sidonie studied her curiously. Her new neighbour was small with tiny scuttling hands and feet that flew about like birds. It seemed quite impossible for her to sit still for more than a moment.

"In a way it's about music I came to see you," Sidonie said cautiously.

"Oh yes?"

"I'm a musician, you see, and have to practise for quite a while every day. I promise you that I only play during working hours. If you're out, it shouldn't be a nuisance."

Jannie's eyes lit up and she stroked the crown of her head with enthusiasm. "A musician? What instrument?"

"Early keyboard, mostly harpsichord."

"Gosh, how marvellous. What did you say the name was?"

"Sidonie Brooks."

"I'm sure I've heard you at the Wigmore Hall. Oh what a thrill. I shan't mind a bit." Her minute hands flew up in excitement. "Play on, give me excess of it." She took a gulp of wine. "I must tell my friends you're here. We're *all* into the arts and I know they'll be dying to meet you. If it's all right with you I'd like to arrange a little get-together."

Sidonie finished her drink and stood up smiling. "You are very kind. Look, I'd love to stay chatting but unfortunately I've got to visit the flat below."

"Ah, the dashing Dr O'Neill." Jannie laughed tinklingly. "Very dishy, as they say. Full of bedside charm."

"I look forward to meeting him."

"Who wouldn't?" Jannie's manner changed again. "It's a pity you must go. But please do call again, soon."

"Thank you for being so understanding," Sidonie answered, and swiftly made her escape.

There was music coming from behind the front door of Flat One as well, this time what sounded like a CD of Callas singing *Norma*. Accompanying "Casta Diva", Sidonie was rather amused to hear, was a male voice joining in an octave lower. It stopped abruptly as Sidonie rang the bell and after a moment or two a man in an apron answered the door, a tall energetic creature with a mass of black curling hair.

"Good evening," he said. "And what can I do for you?"

"Dr O'Neill?" asked Sidonie, holding out her hand.

"Yes. And you must be my new neighbour. I saw you this morning from the balcony. Not spying I assure you, but interested."

He was as Irish as they come with that soft lovely lilt associated with the deep south.

"May I come in?"

"Please do. Would you like a drink? I was just going to have one myself."

"I've already had some wine with Miss Parker but, yes, I'd love one."

"Good. By the way she's a Ms and resolutely so if you know what I mean. Will it be gin this time?"

"Sure, but it will," answered Sidonie, meaning no offence.

He took none. "Do you like my accent? I always swore when I left Ireland that I would be more Irish than the Irish."

"And quite right too. I can never understand these people who go to America or Australia and come back with a twang."

O'Neill handed her a large glass. "Well cheers, Miss . . . er . . . Mrs . . ."

"I can hardly say Ms after your last remark. I'm Sidonie Brooks, a Mrs once but thankfully no longer."

"As bad as that, eh?"

"As bad as that."

"Well I'm Finnan, as in haddock. I'm a consultant at St Mary's so your practising won't disturb me. I'm out most of the day and don't usually get back till about seven."

Sidonie stared at him. "How did you know I was calling about that?"

"Well I come from the land of the leprechauns and have second sight. But actually I was working at home yesterday and saw the harpsichord going in. It's a handsome one, surely."

"I bought it at auction in Ireland about a year ago. It's

eighteenth century and actually has the original owner's initials carved beneath the name board. S.L. I often wonder who he or she was."

"The auctioneers didn't have its history?"

"Only a recent one. All they could tell me was that the instrument came from a house near Dublin."

"What a coincidence." Finnan downed his drink. "Talking of the Irish, we have a reputation for being hospitable. Will you be staying for supper? I'm just knocking something up and there's plenty for two."

Sidonie hesitated. "I was going to have an early night."

"I would hate to ruin your beauty sleep but on the other hand I'd appreciate company."

What was it about an Irish voice, Sidonie wondered, that made everything it said sound so utterly charming.

"When it comes to willpower," she answered, "mine's nonexistent. I'd love to stay."

"Then come into the kitchen. You can talk to me there."

"May I see over your flat? I'm so interested to find out how the original house must have looked."

"Let me just get this thing in the oven and then I'll give you the guided tour."

It was a very beautiful apartment, spacious and light, with a wonderful bay window in the living room which had two French doors leading onto a large creeper-covered balcony. Stepping onto it, Sidonie exclaimed delightedly.

"You've done this beautifully. It's like a little garden."

There were tubs and troughs everywhere, all bursting with flowers; even an old hip bath had been painted white and filled with crisp red geraniums. On the shady part of the balcony, where the wisteria grew thickest, Finnan had put a lounger, while on the sunny side he had two iron chairs and a small table.

"Would you like to eat out here? I often do."

"What a wonderful idea. Yes, please."

He went back to the kitchen and Sidonie leaned over the rail and looked down. Her terrace, directly below, was hidden but there was a good view of the lawn and flowerbeds.

"You won't mind me being down there?" she asked as Finnan came back armed with cutlery and mats.

"Not a bit. You won't mind me above? Though I promise not to look when you're sunbathing. Well, not much that is."

She laughed. "I'll try to be discreet."

The preparation of the meal progressed while Sidonie sat on the balcony sipping a drink and Finnan made forays in and out of the kitchen. He was a very peaceful person, she decided, and wished that she could be more so herself, instead of suffering great bouts of tension before she played, then pouring her feelings into the music until she was left exhausted.

The sun began to set over the park, drenching the south face of Holland House with rose-coloured light. From this distance and height Sidonie could only get glimpses of the building so it was not easy to tell that it was merely a shadow, not much more than the restoration of a shell.

"I wish I could have seen it in its heyday," she said, to herself as much as to her host.

"Holland House?" asked Finnan, gazing in the same direction.

"Yes." She turned to look at him. "Have you ever been to a performance in the theatre there by any chance?"

"Several times. They're very good."

"Where do the actors change?"

The Irishman looked amused. "What an odd question. In the house I imagine. Why?"

"I wandered in today by accident and came across one of them."

"Were you accused of trespassing?"

"No, I got out while the going was good."

"That was very wise of you," Finnan answered, and laughed.

"Why do you say that?"

"Because they're doing Jack the Ripper there this week. You might have found yourself in danger."

"Oh!" Sidonie answered, and wondered what it was about that remark that somehow struck her as wrong.

But afterwards, when the meal was over and she had said

goodbye to her new acquaintance and returned to the Garden Flat, it suddenly occurred to her what it was. Jack the Ripper was the story of gruesome murder in the East End of Victorian London; the girl she had seen was wearing the costume of an earlier time altogether.

"Well, even doctors can make mistakes," she said, smiling in the dark, remembering Finnan's eyes and voice, happy that she had moved into the company of such an extremely interesting neighbour, intrigued that not far from her own garden lay the remains of one of the greatest houses of the eighteenth century.

# Four

The long and luscious summer was over at last, for though September was hot, the sky held a purplish tinge as Holland Park basked in the last golden hazy days. Then came October and the evocative smell of bonfires, leaves crunching beneath the feet and park keepers sweeping the paths with long-handled brooms.

Sitting on his balcony reading the Sunday newspapers, Finnan O'Neill put on a sweater for the first time and looking down into the garden below wondered when Sidonie would be returning from her European tour, hoping that it wouldn't be long, that the brightness of her hair and spirit would soon be around the place again. Then the doctor laughed with genuine surprise when, as if in answer to his wishes, he heard the French doors open beneath him and a second later saw her, dressed in a smart blue suit, somehow contriving to look professional and vulnerable simultaneously, the cat struggling in her arms.

"You're back," he called, and waved.

"Hello," she shouted, "how are you?"

"I'm well. And yourself?"

"Exhausted but elated."

"It went well?"

"Very."

"Come up and have a drink before you crash out."

"How did you know?"

"I come from the land of the leprechauns – "

"And are the seventh son of a seventh son! All right. I'll just change, then I'll be up."

The autumn sunshine was clearer suddenly, the day bright as blueberries. Whistling to himself, Finnan went to put Callas on the CD player and polish his best wine glasses. For the first time after three long years he felt he was finally starting to come back to life.

Sidonie was dramatically pale, the golden eyes shadowed and heavy, but the foxfire hair blazed as ebulliently as ever and the amused mouth was curving upwards.

"Top of the morning to you," said Finnan. "Do you know, I've never actually heard anyone say that in Ireland now I come to think of it."

"Begorrah, neither have I," she answered.

Then they laughed, Sidonie with pure exhaustion, Finnan with the certain feeling that a slow thaw was taking place somewhere near his heart.

"I can't stay long," said Sidonie. "I really am dropping."

"Ten seconds will be enough," answered Finnan extravagantly. "You've cheered me up already."

Sidonie looked surprised. "Do you need cheering?"

"From time to time."

They went onto the balcony and sat companionably together neither saying a great deal, listening to Callas, until Sidonie eventually broke the silence by asking, "How's everything been? Did the man come to repair the door in the wall?"

"Yes, I gave him the key and he dropped it in afterwards."

"Is it working all right?"

"I don't know. I didn't presume to try. But he said he'd renewed the bolts on the garden side and put in new Yale and mortice locks on the Holland Walk side."

"Excellent. You've earned your bottle of duty-free, Doctor."

And Sidonie produced a litre of Irish whiskey from the depths of a handbag that looked more like a haversack.

"I take that very kindly, Ma'am."

"Not to be consumed all at once."

"I'll make a note."

It was superficial banter, conversation that needed no concentration, though beneath ran something as yet not identified, not even born, which might indeed never see the light of day. But though Finnan was aware of this Sidonie was not and so was able to part from him with ease some half-hour later. He watched her go down the stairs to her flat, then turned back into his own, happy to spend the rest of the day alone, to wait until he should see her again in the natural course of events, as yet too overshadowed by the past to look for involvement.

And she, as she undressed and snuggled beneath the duvet, pretending that autumn had deepened and outside it was cold, wondered about him, considered how a man so vital and attractive could spend so much time by himself. Determined one day to find the answer to this intriguing question, Sidonie went quickly and easily to sleep.

When she woke it was dusk and the garden was full of shadows. Deciding to spend the evening up so that she could sleep again that night, Sidonie got out of bed and went into the twilight for some air. The garden had grown dishevelled in her absence but was still pleasant to walk round, and there in the brick wall was the newly repaired door simply calling out to be opened. Going back into the flat, Sidonie fetched the keys from the kitchen where the workman had left them.

The bolts on the garden side now slid back easily and, grasping the latch, she clicked the lever of the Yale lock and pulled it down. Just for a second Sidonie stood gasping, overcome by a moment's weakness, caused no doubt by so many recent hours of travel. And then the feeling was gone and she went through.

She knew immediately that she was dreaming again, that none of this was happening and she was really lying in bed asleep. For not only was Holland Walk no longer there but the entire landscape had changed. Even the sky was lighter, the colour of a winter's afternoon, the autumn evening having completely vanished.

Because she knew this couldn't possibly be real, Sidonie looked about her with interest. She was standing in the midst of a grass pathway which lay, lengthy and straight, alongside a stretch of fields. About a quarter of a mile distant, the east wing facing towards her, was Holland House, fully restored and in all its splendour, a formal garden descending to a lawn behind it; beyond, planted rows of trees. Leading from the house and running parallel with the walkway in which Sidonie stood, the breadth of a field away from her, was a magnificent elm drive which stretched into the distance and looked at least two miles long to her inexperienced eye.

Despite the fact that it was a cold afternoon the colours of the landscape were pleasant, interspersed here and there with dark green plantations. A farm with outbuildings lay to the south and enclosed within the confines of the brick wall which surrounded the area of the mansion house she could see barns and stables, an orchard, various yards and courtyards, and formal gardens which bore some resemblance to those still in existence in Holland Park.

Sidonie felt like Dorothy in the Wizard of Oz, lost in a wonderland which had no reality or substance and yet was incredibly beautiful to look upon. And then she drew her breath in wonderment as round from the stable block which lay beyond the west wing of Holland House came a coach drawn by six stamping, neighing, glistening black horses, plumed in gold, harnesses gleaming in the weak winter sunshine, hooves crunching the gravel, mettlesome and ready to go.

In the midst of a bevy of liveried footmen four people appeared on the marble steps of the entrance and walked in a dignified way across the courtyard to the second set of steps leading down to the carriage sweep which the coach had now entered by way of the wicket gate. The man of the party stood back to allow the three ladies in first and Sidonie caught sight of wide swinging hoops, of flounce upon flounce of lace, of feathered headdresses and high square-heeled shoes. Then, when all were settled, he climbed up himself, an elegant portly figure with, even at this considerable distance, a decidedly stylish air. Sidonie watched delightedly as the postillion called to the coachman who then cracked his whip before the entire equipage moved off through the other wicket which stood open to let them through.

Having left the half-moon of the sweep the coach turned into the elm drive and began the journey down drawing ever closer to Sidonie as it did so. She stared in amazement as the head of the Joshua Reynolds girl, the girl she had thought to be an actress, suddenly appeared at one of the windows, obviously looking across in her direction. Over the distance, Sidonie saw the sheen of lustrous dark hair woven with flowers, the heavy elegance of the girl's costume, the oval of her face turning to gaze over her shoulder as the coach passed and began to move away. And then, very faintly, a bell began to ring somewhere.

She must have staggered to the telephone straight from her bed, Sidonie thought afterwards, for the next thing of which she was consciously aware was picking up the receiver and saying, "Hello."

"Is that the surgery?" asked a distant voice.

"What?" she gasped stupidly.

"Is that Dr Smith's surgery?"

"No, you must have got the wrong number."

"Oh, sorry. Are you – "

But Sidonie had already hung up, suddenly feeling nauseous and faint, clinging to a chair as if it were a lifeline.

"What a dream, oh what a dream," she repeated out loud and then, without any control at all, burst into tears and flung herself down on the bed where, eventually, she slept once more.

A week after Sidonie's return from Europe, Jannie gave a get-together which, in many ways, turned out to be a thoroughly extraordinary evening. Hours before the appointed time a great deal of Mozart combined with frantic vacuum-cleaning noises and the sight of Jannie rushing about with armfuls of shopping gave the guest of honour feelings of guilt that so much trouble should have been taken on her behalf. And, climbing the stairs, Sidonie made a vow that however terrible the people present were she would be charming.

But though she had feared the worst, having several times in the past met earnest groups keenly interested in the arts, nothing had quite prepared her for the reality of Jannie's friends. As she went through the front door and into the living room it was almost like stepping back into the sixties. Sidonie had a sense of *déjà-vu* as she cast eyes on a collection of "beautiful people", alas grown middle-aged, gathered together as if for some reunion.

They were all there: the lady with the ample bosom and

pink hair who sculpted, the man with an enormous beard who looked like one of those Victorian pictures in which the head could be turned upside down yet still made a face, the elderly woman in a sombrero, the angular confident man who was writing a book and immediately launched into a conversation about it.

"It's a thriller with a really unusual plot. Though I say it myself the film potential is enormous. That, or a television serial. Made on location of course. It's an absolute winner."

"Who is your publisher?" asked the woman with the pink hair.

He promptly became furtive and walked away.

"Gracious!" Sidonie murmured faintly, looking round for help. A movement in the doorway caught her eye. "Oh, there's a friend of mine," she said thankfully. "I really must go and have a word with him if you'll excuse me." And she headed for Finnan as a sailor would a raft in a shipwreck.

"Ah, Herr Doctor," boomed the man with the beard, appearing from nowhere. "Good to see you again. I would like if I may to continue the conversation we had when last we met."

"Which was?"

"The social and sexual aspects of being a widower to which category we both belong, do we not?"

Everything was suddenly crystal clear, the reasons why Finnan lived alone, why his flat seemed to have the woman's touch. The fact that he could talk so easily to her, Sidonie.

"I didn't know," she said simply. "Finnan, I'm very sorry. How long ago did your wife die?"

"Three years. In a car crash. She must have fainted at the wheel then fallen because the driver of the car she hit said ours seemed to be empty. Fortunately there was no one else with her."

"How terrible. What a tragedy."

"I'm getting over it but it's taken a long time."

Black beard cleared his throat noisily. "Of course one is in a state of shock. My wife died in hospital after lingering some while so I had more time to prepare myself. None the less it is a trauma – " he pronounced it trowma " – of quite monumental proportions. If it had not been for my ex – " he waved vaguely in the direction of Jannie " – I simply don't know what I would have done."

Sidonie stared. "Were you married to Jannie?"

He smirked slightly. "She is the mother of my children. Yes."

"Heavens," said Sidonie. "I had no idea."

Surprise was following surprise and she felt at a loss for words, especially now that Finnan was appearing in a completely new light. Fortunately Jannie came to her rescue at that moment by shouting, "Food's ready in the kitchen, folks. Hope you all like curry."

"Oh, God!" said Sidonie involuntarily.

Finnan smiled. "Never fear. Just pick, then concentrate on the cheese."

"But cheese is fattening."

"I wouldn't have thought you have any need to worry on that score."

And for the first time in their relationship he gave Sidonie a look that had something else hidden in its depths. Without knowing why, her heart quickened its beat.

"You'll turn my head, Doctor."

"And about time too. I've got a feeling you don't realise quite how stunning you are."

Without wanting to think about Nigel, a picture of him flashed into her mind. "Perhaps not. My divorce hit me a bit hard. I've kept a low profile since then."

"You, my dear Sidonie," said Finnan, laughing, "don't know the meaning of the words. Now, what's all this I hear about you playing at the Wigmore Hall next month?"

"How did you know?"

"I saw a poster. Why didn't you tell me?"

"I was going to. In fact I was going to ask you – and Jannie of course – if you'd like complimentary tickets."

"Only if you let me take you out to dinner afterwards, minus Jannie I might add."

"How cruel you are. Yes, I'd like that."

They laughed joyfully, both aware that they had crossed

some vital bridge in their understanding of one another; that their friendship was about to progress.

"Let's go," said Finnan suddenly. "As soon as we've eaten and it's polite, let's leave."

"What about poor old Jannie? She's worked so hard."

"She'll be all right, she's with all her mates. They'll be talking about the books they're going to write and the paintings they're going to paint until the small hours."

"Yes, Doctor," said Sidonie meekly, as they went into the kitchen.

After they had left they went through the door in the wall and out into Holland Walk, Finnan taking Sidonie's hand and putting it in his coat pocket to keep it warm. Over to the left the lights were just going out in the Holland Park Theatre as it closed down for the night.

"I had the strangest dream about this place recently," said Sidonie, suddenly longing to confide.

"What was it?"

"I saw the park as it must once have been, all rural and spacious. Holland House was there, standing in its entirety, and I watched a coach go down an elm drive that's no longer in existence."

"Perhaps you stepped back in time," Finnan answered lightly.

"Perhaps I did. It certainly felt like that." She looked at him cautiously. "You're not laughing, are you?"

"No, I'm not laughing. I'm an Irishman and believe there are lands beyond the mist."

"Lands beyond the mist? How poetic that is."

Finnan smiled. "I was that once, and perhaps will be again."

"Do you still miss her?"

"Rosie? My Rosie, my little wild rose? No, not any more. She has slipped gently into the past and taken her place in my memory. Yet I still bear the scar."

Sidonie shivered in the cold wind that suddenly blew down the Walk. "But I dreamt of the past, of memories."

"We're getting introspective," said Finnan, deliberately breaking the mood. "Let's go back and have a brandy."

"I musn't be late. I've got a lot of work to do before the concert."

"Are you nervous?"

"Finnan," said Sidonie, turning to look at him, "I am absolutely petrified."

"I'll be there to cheer you on," he answered.

And though, normally, she would have made some trivial reply about not being able to manage without him, Sidonie unexpectedly found herself saying seriously, "I'm counting on it."

The engagement at the Wigmore Hall had been booked some eighteen months earlier by Sidonie's agent, Rod Rees, the unlikely product of an Italian prisoner-of-war and a Welsh girl from the valleys who had "got into trouble", as Rod liked to tell it, rolling his big Italianate eyes and passing a hand over the strangely ginger hair which had been inherited from his mother's side.

"*Pwy sy'n fel ni?*" he would say whenever Sidonie, or any other of his clients for that matter, was waiting anxiously in the wings.

"Who's like us?"

"That's what I said, Sid bach. That's what I said."

Rod was not only a fluent Welsh speaker but also had an excellent command of Italian, German and French. Furthermore, he was the only person in the world that Sidonie allowed to call her Sid. He was also a famous lover, but though his amorous pursuits were spoken of with bated breath in musical circles, Rod made it a rule never to have an affair with a client nor to marry any of the many women who chased after him.

"Love 'em and leave 'em, that's my motto," he would say cheerfully.

"You'll be lonely when you're old."

"I don't intend to get old. I shall content myself with being a *grand seigneur*."

"You're incorrigible," Sidonie would reply.

"If that means I don't need any encouragement, you're quite right."

But for all Rod's amorous intrigues – his affectionate nickname amongst the musicians for whom he acted was Randy Roddy – he was a fine agent, tough and capable, and a man who became a personal friend of everyone he represented.

Now he stood in the Green Room of the Wigmore Hall with Sidonie, who felt that her face was probably the same colour as her long emerald dress, as she stared miserably at the photographs of all the eminent people who had performed there in the past.

"Now, now, Sid bach. *Pwy sy'n fel ni?* There's no need to be afraid, you know, you were a smash hit last time you played here, remember?"

"But I was barely out of nappies. Now I've a reputation of sorts!"

"Oh give over! You caused a sensation and you've been building steadily ever since. Anyway, your new harpsichord will bring you luck."

It already stood on the stage. Delivered to the Wigmore Hall that very afternoon, then freshly tuned.

"If only I could have it," Sidonie wailed. "I've had to warm up on a piano."

But it was just at that second the two-minute-call came and Rod said his famous last words of encouragement, always the same, almost a talisman, before he joined the audience.

"Give the buggers hell, bach."

"Oh God," answered Sidonie, knowing that she was about to die, probably in public.

And then she was on, standing in the spotlight, bowing, her beautiful hair falling forward as she did so. In the audience Jannie gave an audible sniff and Finnan O'Neill felt tears in his eyes as Sidonie's gallant heart and his met in his imagination and all her tension conveyed itself to him. Then the moment passed. She took her seat at the harpsichord and allowed herself to become the medium through whose fingers poured the sound of a sparkling piece by the Spanish composer, Soler. There was utter silence in the hall and Finnan's tears dried on his cheeks as he saw his neighbour and new friend pick up the audience and take them with her into another world. He had never witnessed anything quite like it nor had he ever felt such a surge of pride. Then, when wave upon wave of applause came and he saw the bright flame of a girl bend her head in acknowledgment, he clapped till his hands grew hot.

"Exquisite," said Jannie, clutching his arm. "Isn't she superb!"

"I didn't know," answered Finnan truthfully, "I honestly didn't know. I'd expected she would be good, but nothing like this."

"She almost seems possessed."

"I suppose every great musician must be."

"That she most certainly is. A great musician. I must tell the others."

But Finnan was no longer listening, ready for the next piece as Sidonie put her hands to the keyboard once more. Very vaguely, the doctor was aware that the man behind him gave a deep sigh as she started to play again, but paid no attention to it.

Sidonie though, looking into the audience for the first time as her programme drew towards its end, was horrified to see that her ex-husband Nigel Beltram was not only amongst the crowd but sitting directly behind Finnan and Jannie. Just for a second she felt herself lose concentration as she registered the fact but then, like the true professional she was, gave even more to her playing and ended the evening triumphantly with a fiendish piece of fireworks by Scarlatti.

The applause was truly rapturous. To hear a brilliant soloist was really all the audience wanted but to have one so good to look upon was a bonus. At least half those present rose to their feet, Jannie and Finnan amongst them. Amidst the sound of cheers, Sidonie gave them an encore and then left the stage, suddenly drained of energy, dreading the inevitable meeting with the man to whom she had once been married.

"Nigel's here," said Rod, meeting her in the dressing room, picking his way amongst the bouquets of flowers. "Do you want me to keep him out?"

"You can't," Sidonie answered wearily. "I don't think he'll

make a scene. Remember he's got a junior ministerial post now."

"That wouldn't stop the bugger. You know my opinion of MPs. All a load of crooks and creeps."

"Which is he?"

"Both, bach, both."

And as if that were a signal the door opened at precisely that moment and the man whose wife Sidonie had been for three extremely wretched years appeared wearing his stars-in-the-eyes expression. Without saying a word Nigel put his hands on her shoulders, held Sidonie at arm's length, and stared deeply into her face as if the secret of her talent lay there and he might somehow unlock it. It was a pose, as everything he did was a pose, and his ex-wife wriggled out of his grasp. But not before he had said, "I had forgotten how lovely you are," and kissed her swiftly on the brow. Over Nigel's shoulder Sidonie could see Rod miming the act of vomiting and was forced to stifle an hysterical giggle.

"I was in raptures," Nigel went on. "What a wonderful performance, my love."

"Thank you for coming," she answered coldly.

"Nothing but a three-line whip would have kept me away. I am your most ardent supporter and admirer – still," he added in a heavy undertone.

Sidonie turned away, not wanting to look at him any more, loathing the way his early Greek-youth appearance was running rapidly to fat, how his breath smelt faintly of whisky.

"I still care," Nigel continued, right beside her ear.

In the dressing-room mirror Sidonie saw both their reflections, hers alight with the triumph she had scored, though somehow made gaunt by Nigel's presence; his, large and pale, over the hill at thirty-five, yet the fact that he was still sexually aroused by her made obvious by the shaking of his plump white hands.

"Well I don't," she answered firmly, and turned to face him.

The door opened again and several people erupted in simultaneously, two of whom, Sidonie was delighted to see, were the Irish doctor and Jannie, who wore a vintage purple evening dress which did not become her.

"I think you had the fairy's kiss in your cradle," said Finnan, coming over and giving her a peck on the cheek. "For sure I've never heard anything like it. You're a genius, so you are."

"You enjoyed it?"

"Enormously. I felt so proud."

"Beltram," said Nigel, interrupting and offering his hand. "Nigel Beltram. I'm the ex-Mr Brooks, if you see what I mean."

He laughed boyishly and Sidonie noticed that his expression had changed again, this time to his all-lads-together look, a stance adopted a great deal at election times.

"Finnan O'Neill," the doctor answered, shook the extended hand and turned back to Sidonie. "You haven't forgotten that we're going to dinner?"

"Of course not."

"Then I'll leave you to your fans. Shall I bring the car round in fifteen minutes?"

"Make it twenty and I'll be ready."

"Fine. Goodbye, Mr Beltram. No doubt we shall meet again."

"No doubt," said Nigel, and nodded curtly, his bonhomie abruptly vanished. "Who the hell was that?" he asked of Finnan's departing back.

"It's really none of your business but actually he's one of my new neighbours. There's another one over there." And Sidonie waved to Jannie, who waved back enthusiastically.

"You've moved?"

"Yes, to Kensington. And now, Nigel, you really must excuse me. There're some people I'd like to talk to."

And with that she walked rapidly away, leaving her ex-husband to the mercies of Rod Rees, who descended on him like an avenging Welsh angel, his dislike of parliamentarians in general second only to his dislike of Nigel himself.

It took nearly an hour for the dressing room to clear by which time Finnan had returned, his car parked somewhere illegal. But eventually he and Sidonie managed to retrieve it and make for Brünnhilde's, a restaurant owned by an ex-opera singer who specialised in after-theatre suppers. By the time the meal was finished and that most exciting of evenings eventually over, the elated musician at last ready to go home, it was past two o'clock in the morning.

"Thanks for everything," she said as the Irishman saw her to the door of the Garden Flat.

"Thanks for being so talented," he said, then kissed her rapidly on the lips and vanished up the stairs to his own apartment.

Sidonie stared after him, part of her slightly disappointed that he had made no attempt to seduce her, another part glad that this most pleasant of relationships was not about to become complicated. And yet her vanity was piqued despite the fact that even if Finnan had suggested he spend the rest of the night with her she wouldn't have had the energy to do much about it.

With her thoughts re-enacting the concert, her meeting with Nigel, her meal with Finnan, Sidonie went out into the garden for a last breath of air before she went to bed. And then a need to stroll came over her and she went through the door in the wall and out into Holland Walk. Drawn as always by some inexplicable compulsion she found her footsteps turning in the direction of Holland House, and in the inconstant moonlight went up the avenue towards the house.

As with all London parks, Holland Park was closed at night but Sidonie had discovered on her many trips of exploration that there was a secret way in. The path leading to the youth hostel which was situated both in the east wing and in some new buildings just beyond it, was never closed and by going up this and into the courtyard that lay beside the wing, an ornamental pool at its centre, it was possible to get through to Nightwalk. This she now did without knowing why she felt drawn to do so.

And then she stared in amazement. From where she was, directly opposite the house, she could see that it was ablaze with light, that somewhere musicians, playing on what sounded like original instruments, were rendering a lively air.

'A concert,' thought Sidonie, 'a late night concert.'

But who would be making such a noise at three o'clock in the morning? And where was the audience if this was a theatrical event?

The moon had just gone behind a cloud yet it seemed in the half-light that the steps leading to the courtyard were not in their usual place, that the Inigo Jones gateway had vanished. Instead, it appeared she stood at an iron railing fence which came up to her chest in height, so that she was able to see above it without difficulty.

To her amazement Sidonie realised that Holland House was brightly illuminated by torches which lit the upper balconies above the arcades, while every window was alight with candles. She could distinctly see the shapes of people passing to and fro, their shadows thrown up in silhouette. It was almost as if she were having the dream again, the dream in which she had seen the house restored, but this time Sidonie knew she was awake. There was no question of it. She had not even sat down since the concert but instead gone straight out for a walk. There was no conceivable way in which she could have fallen asleep. And yet she was seeing the past as clearly as if it were actually happening.

And then, without warning, the Joshua Reynolds girl became visible on the steps leading to the front door, looking over in her direction. Sidonie stood stock-still and stared in a kind of terrified delight, aware that this was a psychic phenomenon yet too enraptured to be afraid. She saw the texture of jet hair in the torchlight, the sway of a hooped dress made of some heavy silver material, the toss of green feathers as the girl moved her head. Then came the sound of feet crunching on gravel and out of the darkness the musician saw a man in a tricorne hat and cloth topcoat running towards her.

Her trance-like state came to an end and Sidonie shot off in the direction of the path through to the east wing, praying that she would find it, that the entire topography had not changed, that she could get back to the Garden Flat and away from this house in which the ghosts of the past were holding a Ball in a ballroom that had long, long ago ceased to exist.

# Five

"I do vow and declare," said Lady Sarah Lennox roundly, "that I shall never wear black again, so I won't. It don't suit me."

"Nor I," answered Susan, "I look a regular pale little milksop in dark clothes."

"Well goodbye and good riddance to it say I. Tonight I shall wear crimson."

"Won't that be considered a little extreme?"

"I don't give a fig," Sarah replied carelessly. "It's Twelfth Night after all."

"Whatever you wear *he* will only have eyes for you."

"*He* can look where he pleases."

"You're a liar, Sarah Lennox," said Susan knowingly. "Were His Majesty to gaze at anyone but you you'd go into mighty high stirrup."

Sarah grinned. "You read me too well, that's your trouble."

And with that the two young ladies of Holland House burst out laughing, then grew serious again as the extremely important matter of what shoes, fans, headdresses and jewellery should be worn at the Twelfth Night Ball came under earnest discussion.

Nine months had passed since Sarah's fifteenth birthday, a nine months during which the fate of the entire nation had changed. On 25th October, 1760, King George II had risen at six, looked to see if all his money was in his purse – according to the waspish Horace Walpole at least – and called for his chocolate. An hour later he had gone into the water closet and there he had dropped down dead, hitting his head on the wooden seat as he fell.

"What a place to end it all!" Fox had commented wryly to Caroline.

"A little undignified indeed."

"Ah well, the old man had had a good run. Had he lived another sixteen days he would have been seventy-seven."

"And now we have a boy of twenty-two in his stead."

"Plus that boy's mother and her lover," Fox had answered darkly, and drawn his black brows into two straight lines as he scowled.

For no one knew, as yet, just how influenced by Princess Augusta the new King would be, and this unknown factor was of great importance to the Foxes.

While still Prince of Wales, George III, as he had now become, had not tried to hide the fact that he was attracted to Sarah. Indeed on the half dozen or so occasions he had seen the girl since their first meeting, the young man had paid her as much attention as was allowable within the confines of royal etiquette. And now to this, his very first private Twelfth Night Ball, with the period of mourning just over and everyone allowed to dress in bright colours once more, but still with only a limited company of guests, Sarah and her family had received their invitations.

"Significant, what?" Fox had said speculatively.

"As long as His Majesty's mother doesn't think so," Caroline had answered with asperity, putting all their concern into words.

"That meddlesome woman!"

"The King will have to watch he's not petticoat ruled."

"Unless it be by a petticoat that dwells beneath *this* roof."

"Mr Fox, you're scheming!" Caroline had said accusingly. "I've told you before, you are to let things take their natural course."

"I'm all for nature, my dear, as you should know." He winked a large and brilliant eye. "But I am also for giving it a helping hand from time to time."

"What do you intend?"

"Wait and see," replied her husband. "Wait and see."

So it was with certain trepidation that Caroline handed her black gown and coat – her open robe and petticoat – to her maid for storage in her clothes chest and, after bathing in her bedroom, put on a rich and elegant lilac satin outfit. Just as glad as the younger people to be out of mourning for the late King, Caroline surveyed herself solemnly in the mirror as purple ostrich feathers were placed on her head and fastened into place with two silver combs. But her serious Dutch features still stared back despite the finery and Caroline sighed.

"La, I vow I'm getting old. What a dullard I appear."

She picked up a little brush, dusted some coloured powder onto her cheeks, then rouged her lips as well. After this, feeling a little daring, Caroline stuck a patch in the shape of a heart high on her cheekbone.

"You're very in looks tonight," said Fox, appearing from his dressing room.

"I had thought just the opposite."

"Nonsense." He came over and kissed her, his white wig so close that it tickled her nose. "You're as lovely as the day I married you."

"If only that were so," answered Caroline, sighing a little. "If only it were."

For truth to tell, it was a little daunting to be seen constantly in the company of two such attractive young women as Sarah and Susan, different though they were one from the other. With the Prince of Wales's obvious interest in her, Sarah had become more and more the centre of attention wherever she went, and now that he was King, if his affection continued and was not diminished by the fact of his elevation, Caroline could envisage the situation getting quite out of hand. Tonight, she thought with yet another sigh, was going to be quite an ordeal.

His Majesty was at last beginning to show signs of a certain independence, an excellent portent to all those who feared the domination of his mother, the Princess of Wales, born Augusta of Saxe-Gotha. This German princess had some years previously married George II's son Frederick, the heir to the throne, who had predeceased his father and, to make matters more painful, been loathed and detested by both his parents while he was alive.

"If I was to see him in hell," Queen Caroline had said of her own child, "I should feel no more for him than I should for any other rogue that ever went there." But his sad and early death had solved it all. Frederick's young son George had become Prince of Wales in his father's place.

But now, despite the fact that he had set up his own establishment, there were those, Fox amongst them, who feared for the future. Augusta still tried to rule with a rod of iron through her favourite, the Earl of Bute, formerly a close friend of Prince Frederick's but who, so gossip said, had consoled his widow only too well. Infatuated with Bute, though clearly not sexually so, George turned to the older man for advice as he would have done to a beloved father.

Emulating his grandfather, His Majesty was keeping Christmas at Kensington and it was with some relief that Fox observed, as his party entered the receiving room, that not only were there very few guests, literally about thirty people in all, thus making the compliment to Sarah even more marked, but also that neither Princess Augusta nor Bute were amongst those present. Tonight, at least, the youthful monarch would be free to do what he pleased.

The new King looked splendid. Dressed in deep purple, possibly an extension of his personal mourning, George stood tall and handsome, his white wig, tied with a smart black bow, only serving to enhance his blue eyes and fresh skin. He smiled broadly as Sarah Lennox came into view, showing his strong and even teeth, while she curtsied in front of him in a manner which suggested intimacy as well as respect.

'He's in love with her,' thought Fox, watching narrowly. 'I'd stake my life on it.'

And, indeed, when the dancing began, and after the King had led out the most senior lady present as a mark of politeness, it was Sarah's hand that he claimed as partner for the next dance. There may not have been many guests at the Ball that evening but those who were there had plenty to think about as the King bent his head close to Sarah's and murmured what looked like a string of compliments, judging by the way she smiled and lowered her lashes. And then, at around ten o'clock, His Majesty actually left the dancing with his partner and was observed going alone with her into the room where tea, negus and other drinks were being served.

"Do you see that?" said Fox to Caroline, positively jigging from one foot to the other.

"They are only going out for refreshment."

"Yes but *alone*, my dear. For the first time ever they are *alone*."

And so they were, for the room was empty except for the two women presiding over the cups and glasses.

"What may I fetch you, Lady Sarah?" the King asked as they sat down side by side, something of the novelty of the situation obviously appealing to him, for his eyes were very lively.

"It is not seemly, Sir, that you should wait upon me."

"But nothing would give me greater pleasure," George insisted. "Would you like tea?"

"No, negus, if you please. It's a cold night and I adore the warmth of it."

"So do I," he answered, glancing round quickly in a way that suggested to Sarah his mother did not approve of him drinking. "I'll get two."

He got up and she did likewise, it being considered the height of rudeness to remain sitting while royalty stood.

"Please, Lady Sarah, let us be friends and not ruled by ceremony. I beg you to take your seat and be comfortable," the King said, looking at her very tenderly.

He crossed the room to get two glasses of the hot port punch, sweetened and spiced and quite the most delicious drink ever made, Sarah watching his shapely back as he did so, trying to take in the fact that the King of England was actually fetching her a drink, while she sat like his sweetheart and let him wait on her.

"There," he said, returning and bowing slightly, "now let us converse."

"What would you like to talk about, Your Majesty?"

"You," said the King very definitely, and crossed one elegant silk clad leg over the other.

"Me?"

"Yes, you. First of all let me say that I'm so delighted you have done nothing to lose your Irish accent. I told you when we first met that it enhances your many charms and it most certainly does. So remind me how you acquired it. You went to live in Ireland when you were very young, did you not?"

"I did, Sir. My mother died when I was little more than a tot and I was sent, in company with the two sisters nearest to me in age, one older, one younger, to be brought up with Emily, yet another sister who had married the Earl of Kildare."

"I see," said the King, nodding, though Sarah knew that he wasn't really concentrating, his blue eyes too busy staring at her hair, her mouth, her own eyes, deeper in colour than his by far.

"It was a happy time, very boisterous and amusing. Dublin society is quite *bon ton*, you know."

The King smiled. "Your sister must have had a good heart to surround herself with so many children."

"Fortunately both Carton, the Earl's country seat, and Kildare House, in the capital, are very large so we did not get under each other's feet. But what helped most was that my brother-in-law was so supportive to us all. My sister loves him greatly for it. She declares that he is the best and kindest of husbands."

George sipped his negus. "And who takes the lead in this happy household? Is it Lady Emily or Lord Kildare who rules the roost?"

Wondering why he was asking such an odd question, Sarah lowered her eyes. "My sister is a clever woman, Sir. Therefore it is Lord Kildare who governs."

"And do you approve of that?"

"I think women who appear to rule can be overbearing."

The King nodded sadly. "Indeed, indeed."

Draining her glass, Sarah said boldly, "I have heard it said, Sir, that you are under the maternal thumb."

The handsome face paled and an expression of utter amazement crossed George's features.

"Do people really believe that?"

"Yes, Sir, they do."

"But surely parents are the best people to govern a child."

It was out of Sarah's mouth before she had time to think. "Not when the child is King of England and the mother a German princess."

70

He stood up, turning slightly away from her, and the girl knew she had gone too far, that encouraged by the negus she had made an utter fool of herself by repeating the views of Mr Fox, frequently expressed at considerable length but always in the privacy of Holland House.

"I hope I have not offended, Sir, but you asked that we might be friends and converse as friends do. Yet in obeying I believe I have upset you," she said contritely.

He spun round, looking down at her from his considerable height and taking both her hands in his.

"On the contrary. I admire the honesty in you, Lady Sarah. In fact I would go so far as to say I love it. You would not have been capable of saying that parents know best and leaving it at that, would you?"

"No, because it would have been telling an untruth."

"But you would not mind telling a white lie presumably?"

"Oh yes I would, Sir."

"So then I shall always know where I stand with you?"

"You will, Sir."

He drew her fingers to his lips. "Lovely Lady Sarah, how very happy that makes me. Will you honour me with the next dance?"

Sarah curtsied delightfully. "I will indeed."

They were falling in love, exhilaratingly so, and both of them knew it. Nor did they care who noticed for when the couple re-entered the ballroom, smiling secretive smiles, there was an audible murmur of interest. Fox caught Caroline's eye and winked his own while Lady Susan thrilled with silent jubilation. She, above all, by the very way her friend responded when Susan teased her about the King, knew that Sarah was more attracted to him than she was prepared to admit. And now they danced as if there were not another couple present in the place.

"A pretty sight," said the Duke of Bedford drily, within earshot of Fox.

"Pretty be damned," snorted his Duchess. "I'd rather the King were given time to look round other English beauties."

"Meaning her own wretched daughter," Fox whispered audibly and was rewarded with a piercing glance.

But the young couple danced on oblivious to all, Sarah teaching George the steps of Betty Blue, an Irish country dance.

"I have plans," said the King softly as they whirled around, "for extending the grounds of Kensington Palace."

"Have you, Sir?"

"Yes, I thought it might be both pleasant and convenient to take them as far as the parkland of Holland House. Then, perhaps, we could meet as we rode out."

"I am entirely at Your Majesty's command," answered Sarah.

The blue eyes grew ardent and the pressure of the King's hand tightened.

"I will not forget that, Lady Sarah. Be sure I will hold you to such a promise at some time in the future."

"It will be an honour, Sir," answered the girl and the couple indulged in exchanging warm glances before George said, "Reluctantly I feel I should mingle amongst my other guests though I would far rather stay at your side all evening."

"Of course, Sir." And Sarah dropped one of her spectacular curtseys as he kissed her hand.

The company, small and select though it might be, was positively buzzing with gossip by now and the Duke of Newcastle, a seasoned old cynic with a hard shrewd eye, said to Fox, "Odds on your sister-in-law, what!"

"Meaning, your Grace?"

"You know what I mean. She's obviously destined for great things, damme."

"You think so?"

"I most assuredly do."

Fox smiled secretly, as wily and cunning as his name. But as soon as the carriage door was closed for the journey home he lowered his guard, quite unable to resist asking questions despite Caroline's tuts of disapproval. Sarah pulled a face in the darkness, disliking the inevitable interrogation which followed a meeting with her royal admirer.

"If you must know, dear brother, we talked about the park, Betty Blue and Princess Augusta," she said sulkily.

"I beg your pardon?"

Sarah grinned. "I taught His Majesty a new dance, discussed his proposed alterations to the grounds of Kensington Palace, and told him that in your view he was completely governed by his mother."

"You did *what*?"

"I said that in your opinion, Sir, a King of England has no place being told what to do by a German woman."

"Are you serious?"

Sarah relented slightly. "I did say it but in truth omitted the fact they were your words and actually pretended they were mine."

"Sarah!" remonstrated Caroline, stung into action. "How could you? Not only will you have hurt His Majesty's feelings, you will also have put yourself completely out of favour."

"On the contrary. The King told me he loved my frankness of speech and lack of guile. He said it was quite one of my most attractive features."

"Then by God he's smitten," announced Fox loudly. "No man would stand for it lest he be in love. 'Zounds but this puts a new complexion on the matter." He banged on the carriage roof with his ebony stick. "Make haste, Hawkins! I declare I need a bumper of champagne. Holland House at speed, man."

"Very good, Sir."

And with a crack of the coachman's whip the equipage rushed through the night as the first snow of the year 1761 began to fall.

It snowed for three whole days, transforming the park into a fairyland which gleamed and glittered through the whirling flakes. On the fourth day it stopped and the young people of Holland House, well muffled against the cold, stepped outside and began to explore the changed and beautiful terrain of their grounds.

Immediately behind the mansion lay the knot garden, created in Jacobean times when Holland House had first been built, and beyond this, below the formal terrace, were a series of wooded walkways known as The Wilderness. These paths had been created in a spoke formation and led to a central circle in which stood two stone seats and a classical statue of a partially nude girl. With a whoop of delight, Charles James slid across the snow-filled terrace on his bottom then, dusting the powder from his breeches, hurtled into The Wilderness and vanished amongst its trees. Shouting excitedly, the others ran to find him.

The colonnades of the woodland had been planted with hornbeam, now piled high with coronets of snow, their branches stooped and laden with white. Shaking the lowest as he ran past so that he was constantly immersed in flurries, Charles James headed purposefully for the centre where he climbed up the plinth, hung his cap on the statue and started to fondle her snow-clad breasts.

"You're a very rude boy," said Susan, catching him up and attempting to look stern.

"I'm only keeping her warm," he answered, then winked, clambered down again, missed his footing and fell into a drift, from which he emerged like some arctic elf, grinning and covered in white.

"I think a snowman to keep her company is a better idea," announced Ste plummily, and scooping up a handful threw it at his brother.

In seconds a snowball fight had broken out, the two young ladies involved against their will, not relishing the thought of icy snow going down their backs.

"Oh do stop it!" shouted Sarah, at odds with the boys already, the stirrings of love she felt whenever she thought of the King's adoring glances putting her out of countenance with childish games, awakening in their stead strange sensations which the girl did not fully understand.

"Spoil sport," Charles called back. "What's the matter with you, Sal? Don't be elderly and boring. Please!"

She rushed to him, suddenly guilty because he, too, loved her in his way, and this time they both fell over, giggling and tickling as they did so. And then, even before she looked up, Sarah felt a sudden change in the atmosphere. In that fine bracing winter's day came another coldness, a tingling frisson, fearful and icy, which hastened her heartbeat and made her gasp for breath.

"What is it?" asked Charles James, sensing the tension in his young aunt. But she did not answer, sitting up slowly and staring straight in front of her, blind to everything else.

At the end of the row of trees immediately opposite, distinctly visible from where she sat in the snow, Sarah could see a motionless figure gazing up the colonnades as if transfixed. She recognised the sheen of red hair, the startled expression, with a remorseless sinking of her heart. She had not thought of the woman for months, had not seen her since the night of her fifteenth birthday, in fact had almost forgotten her. And now here she was, back again, standing in the snow and staring straight at her.

With a sudden burst of anger, Sarah struggled to her feet, sending poor Charles flying as she did so.

"Hey you," she called out, "I want a word with you."

And slipping and sliding as she went, Sarah ran down the avenue towards the still, motionless figure. The woman turned, as if in sudden panic, and began to hurry away through the trees, though this only added to her pursuer's resolve. Throwing caution to the winds, Sarah skimmed down the snow-filled colonnade, determined to catch the intruder up.

Bordering The Wilderness on one side was Green Walk, on the other Little Hill Field, and it was towards the field that the interloper now made her frantic way, gazing round her helplessly as if she had no idea where she was going. Glancing back over her shoulder, Sarah could see her three companions looking in her direction open-mouthed, for all the world as if she had suddenly taken leave of her senses. Regardless of them, Sarah rushed on and then, almost from a clear sky, it started to snow again – and everything vanished.

Gasping, the girl stopped short, realising that to proceed would be foolish. Before her lay a great stretch of fields and woodlands in which she could get dangerously lost. Angrily aware that her quarry must be well ahead of her but that there was nothing she could do about it, Sarah turned and slowly made her way back through the blinding flakes.

"What made you run off like that?" asked Susan as Sarah, somewhat shakily, limped up to the trio awaiting her.

"I saw that wretched spying woman and gave chase."

"What spying woman?" Ste repeated curiously.

"There's a female who loiters round the estate, even comes into the house. I've seen her two or three times."

"Who is she?"

"That I don't know. I gave chase to try and find out."

"How strange," Ste went on thoughtfully. "Have you told Father?"

"No, I don't like to bother him. Besides, she hasn't been around for a long time. I thought she'd gone."

"Well, I didn't see anyone," put in Charles James, "and I was sitting right beside you."

"I think it's a ghost," said Susan. "I did when you first told me of her, Sarah, and I haven't changed my mind."

"I didn't know ghosts walked in snowstorms." This from Ste who was obviously giving the matter weighty consideration. "How interesting."

"She doesn't look like a ghost to me," Sarah answered. "In fact she seems more startled than I am."

"Did you lose her in the snow?"

"Yes, she vanished from sight."

"That proves it," said Charles triumphantly. "The woman is a phantom; the ghost of Holland House."

"Oh, you," said Sarah, ruffling his hair.


The snow lasted for a fortnight and then cleared away dramatically, almost overnight, revealing early spring flowers. It was now the end of January and Charles James, delayed from returning to Eton by the treacherous roads, set off in merry fig, waving goodbye as his coach disappeared down the elm drive, leaving Holland House quieter and a great deal more calm. Ste, who had given up school a year earlier after a severe illness, now set off with his tutor to do the Grand Tour, so that only young Harry, aged six, remained to keep the older people amused. In this suddenly still atmosphere it was a relief to go to St James's Palace for a Drawing Room.

Strangely, even before she set out, Sarah had a feeling of unease. Her last meeting with the King had been so perfect, so exciting, in a way so provocative, that now she faced this next with a certain nervousness, fearing, perhaps, that

George might have reconsidered his feelings, might have taken offence with hindsight at her forthright statement about his mother, the Princess of Wales. Appearing composed but with her emotions actually in turmoil, Sarah left Holland House with her family, only for disaster to befall on the way.

Hyde Park, a notorious haunt of highwaymen, had to be traversed on the route as it was. And sure enough as the coach rumbled through on its way to St James's, two figures emerged from the trees and headed straight for the Fox equipage. Hawkins began to slow the horses but Fox would have none of it. Leaning out of the window he fired a warning shot from the pistol he always carried with him.

"Henry, for the love of God be careful," screamed Caroline. "You'll get killed."

"Not I," Fox answered stoutly. "Hawkins, speed up. I'll keep 'em at bay."

Bullets were whizzing through the air but with the aid of the postillion, also armed as a security measure, the villains were beaten off and disappeared as quickly as they had come.

"There," said Fox, blowing the barrel to hide the fact that his hands were shaking. "One has to stand up to these bastardly gullions. Damme, if I'll give in to 'em."

"You're very brave," Susan and Sarah chorused admiringly, though Henry's wife continued to look daggers, afraid, obviously, that he might have been shot for his pains.

This excitement delayed their arrival by some thirty minutes and it was in this way that the family missed the receiving line entirely and found the Drawing Room already in progress when they arrived. Trying to look unconcerned, Sarah stared round for the King, thinking to see him talking with, perhaps, one of the older gentlemen. Yet in this she was to be disappointed; George was in deep conversation with Lady Caroline Russell, daughter of the Duke and Duchess of Bedford, as sly a little baggage as ever saw the light of day.

"'Sblood!" exclaimed Sarah beneath her breath and from behind her fan studied her rival closely.

Caroline Russell was small, neat and fair, somewhat dull of feature except for her nose which was large. However, her eyes were pleasant, a greyish blue, set slantingly above arched cheekbones. She had a winsome way with her too, and laughed delicately at everything His Majesty had to say, which was quite a lot judging by the animated way he held forth. Furthermore, a sideways glance at the Duchess of Bedford, who patently glowed with triumph, indicated that this conversation had been going on most of the evening and showed no sign of coming to an end.

"Oh dear," said Susan close to Sarah's ear.

Her friend shrugged a delicate shoulder. "If that is what pleases him."

"He probably got buttonholed, poor fellow."

"But is making no particular effort to escape it would seem."

They could converse privately no more as at that moment Fox launched himself into a circle, currently clustered round Lord Shelbourne, and began a spirited description of the excitements of his recent journey.

"La, Fox, you're always in hot water," drawled a familiar voice on the edge of the listeners and both Caroline and Sarah looked up in delight to see that their brother, George Lennox, younger than Caroline but seven years older than Sarah, had not only been invited to the reception but was there ahead of them.

"My dear," said his elder sister, drawing George to one side and kissing him. "This is a pleasure to be sure. I had no idea you were coming tonight."

"Neither had I," her brother answered quietly. "The decision lay, as always, with her Ladyship."

And with a twitch of his brows he indicated his wife, Louisa.

"Still the same?" whispered Caroline.

"God bless her, so she is. A determined little woman, that one."

With a certain amusement Sarah looked over to where Lady Louisa Lennox, known as Lady George, was obviously putting the world to rights, holding forth to a handful of women all of whom looked decidedly bored.

She was a plump waspish creature who, none the less, considered herself extremely desirable to men, having a highly overrated opinion of her charms. Not tall and decidedly buxom, Louisa had black hair and sharp matching eyes which missed nothing. Sarah was both repelled and fascinated by her but maintained a show of cordiality for her brother's sake.

"Ah, Lady Caroline, Lady Sarah," Louisa called now, seeing the sisters look in her direction. "How *very* nice. How are you both?"

Rather reluctantly, they went to join her, Susan very sensibly remaining with Fox and Lord George.

"Such gay company," Louisa burbled on, not waiting for their reply. "The King seems most taken with Bedford's gal, what? That'll put my brother's foot out of stirrup."

She smiled triumphantly in the way of all good gossips.

"Your brother?" said Caroline, not following her drift.

"Newbattle," Louisa answered enigmatically.

"Lord John?" asked Sarah, getting a glimmer of daylight. "Did I not meet him once in Kensington?"

Louisa turned a delighted smile on her. "The very same. Quite the most handsome creature in the universe, did you not think? La, but he's a wicked fellow. Why, my brother has broken more hearts this season alone than most men do in a lifetime."

Caroline's angular features presented a mask of bewilderment and Sarah felt an overwhelming desire to giggle.

"But what has that to do with Caroline Russell?"

"He's set his cap at her, so he has. Decided she was the best catch I dare say," Louisa added in an undertone. "But now his ace has been trumped. For who could compete with the most eligible bachelor in the world?"

Looking over to where the King still conversed with the Duke of Bedford's daughter, oblivious of the fact that she, Sarah, had so much as arrived, the girl felt a cruel pang of jealousy that demanded action.

"Did you say your brother was here, dear Lady George?"

"Yes, over there, surrounded by gals as usual."

Sarah followed her sister-in-law's eyes and recognised at once the young man whom she had met when out walking in the grounds of Kensington Palace.

Lord Newbattle was certainly handsome in a Greek youth

type of way, Sarah thought, his hair curling and dark as Louisa's, though there the similarity ended for her brother's eyes were blue and his features blandly babyish. He was obviously one of those young people who compensated for a singular lack of intelligence by smiling a lot and leaning heavily upon his charm.

"I would so like to meet him," said Sarah, fluttering her lashes.

Louisa immediately jumped to the wrong conclusion, being far from as shrewd as she liked to pretend.

"And so you shall, dear Lady Sarah." She raised her voice. "John, if you would step this way. There is someone to whom I would like to present you."

Very aware that the King had finally looked up and was staring in her direction, Sarah swept one of her special curtseys as the pretty youth joined the group and bowed before her.

"Lady Sarah," he said huskily, "we meet again."

"Lord Newbattle, it really is most pleasant to renew acquaintanceship."

"Most," he answered, smiling. "May I escort you to supper?"

"I can think of nothing nicer."

And Sarah flirted her way past the King, to whom she dropped a deferential but distant curtsey, as she went out of the room.

"And that is sauce for the goose," she murmured triumphantly as George stared helplessly after her, Lady Caroline Russell obviously forgotten.

"You said something?" enquired John Newbattle.

"Did I mutter? I did not mean to. La, it must be a sign of age."

"I would not imagine you to be possessed greatly of that, Lady Sarah."

She sparkled at him prettily. "I am a few weeks off my sixteenth birthday. And you, my Lord?"

"Twenty, Madam."

"And betrothed to Lady Caroline Russell if rumour serves me correctly."

The handsome face flushed. "Rumour serves you wrong, Lady Sarah. I am unattached."

Her smile grew mysterious. "But you have a fondness for her?"

"A fondness, yes."

It was enough, the challenge had been issued. To Sarah's budding emotions, full of hurt pride that the King had ignored her for another, another whose sweetheart was now gazing down at her, Sarah, with obvious interest, it instantly became a game – a game in which the prize was John, Lord Newbattle, the prettiest man in London, the man who up till now had loved and left every girl who had crossed his path.

"Frankly I think fondness dull," said Lady Sarah languidly. "For me only passion counts."

"Passion," answered Lord Newbattle, "is something I know little about."

"With a friend like Lady Caroline Russell," came the sharp reply, "I am hardly surprised to hear that, my good Sir."

And with that the little minx gave him a small but unmistakable wink.

# Six

In common with most empty-headed young men with little to commend them other than their fair features, John William Newbattle, son and heir to the Earl of Ancram, had an excellent eye for the main chance and a ruthless tenacity when it came to achieving it. Once having decided that an alliance with the Duke of Richmond's sister might be even better than a marriage with Bedford's daughter, and that Sarah Lennox was far more beautiful than Caroline Russell into the bargain, there was no holding the young man. He pursued the new object of his affections with an unwavering resolve which, in its way, was admirable.

From the very evening when they met, letters began to arrive at Holland House begging to see Sarah. And so it was that she started a series of daily walks in the grounds, meeting him where the park bordered on the main road from London to Uxbridge, which lay beyond The Wilderness and beyond the fields known as the Great Breaches. It was here, in the privacy of the woods, that Sarah experienced her first kiss and could not believe the wild breathless sensations it aroused in her. The blood of Charles II and his French mistress ran strongly in the girl. She was fiery with passion and the pretty lordling, who had already claimed a few virgin ladies for trophies, played her like a fish on a line.

Added to all this excitement was the thrill of creeping out of the house, coupled with the spicy feeling that she was stealing Caroline Russell's beloved from under her very nose, paying Bedford's daughter back in her own coin for having monopolised the King's attention. Yet perversely, His Majesty himself, her other admirer, was temporarily forgotten in the whirlwind of Sarah's first romance.

"You are in no circumstances to behave like a woman of

doubtful character," Susan admonished her friend sternly. "Once a reputation is gone it is gone for good."

"I'm too afraid to let John step over the mark. Oh but, Susan, he is so handsome and lively. I do love him so."

"Handsome is as handsome does in my view. And what about the King? Why, only a few weeks ago it was he who was all the rage."

Sarah smiled secretively. "I'll be honest with you. This affair started as a caprice, a whim to discomfort that horrid Caroline Russell. But when John kissed me, when he held me in his arms – "

"Oh stop it, do!" Susan interrupted crossly. "You sound like the heroine of a paltry romance."

"You only say that because you're jealous."

"Of John Newbattle? Don't make me laugh. I prefer men to boys."

And with that the usually mild-mannered Susan Fox-Strangeways had swept from the room. Yet angry though she was with her friend's arrant foolishness it was not Susan who betrayed Sarah's secret to Henry Fox. Rather it was the Paymaster himself, out exercising round his estate, who caught a glimpse of the erring couple entwined in a kiss and rode home in a cold fury, throwing his riding crop to the floor as he walked into his wife's sitting room.

"Where is Sarah?" he thundered in a voice that Caroline knew presaged trouble.

She looked up from her book, trying to stay calm. "Out walking. Why do you ask?"

"Because," bellowed Fox, "I want to know your complicity in her sordid affair."

"What sordid affair?" repeated his wife, rising to her feet, her feathers just beginning to ruffle.

"I speak of her liaison with Newbattle. I've seen them just now, over in the far plantation, kissing like farm hands. By God, Caro, I've a mind to take my whip to that young puppy. He's vain, inglorious, insignificant, and a fly in the poxing ointment. What the devil can she see in him?"

Caroline sat down heavily. "I can't think! She must have

taken leave of her senses. Oh, good heavens, what a coil! I'll have words with that young woman."

"*You'll* have words? *I'll* have 'em if you don't mind, Madam. I'm master in this house and *will* be listened to."

He had not been in such a fury for years and when, some thirty minutes later, there came the distant sound of the opening and closing of the great front door, Caroline positively trembled as Fox strode from her room, shouting, "Bring your sister to me immediately, if you please," and headed for his study. Torn between fury over Sarah's crass stupidity and a dread certainty that a monumental family quarrel was about to begin, Caroline rushed to the entrance hall to find Sarah already climbing the main staircase.

Normally very reserved, Caroline suddenly erupted at the sight of her sister's smug little face.

"Sarah Lennox, come here at once," she called in a tone of voice that Sarah had literally never heard before. "How dare you creep upstairs like a thief? Mr Fox wants to see you straightaway."

The girl went pale. "Why?"

"You may well ask. Your secret is unmasked. You have been seen sporting with your lover and now you must face the consequences."

"Who saw me?"

"Mr Fox himself. You have abused our hospitality, Sarah, by engaging in this squalid intrigue. Newbattle is a known rake, a debauchee." Caroline stopped as a thought struck her. "He has not robbed you of – ?"

"No, no," answered her sister, dramatically bursting into tears. "He has behaved like a gentleman throughout."

"A fine kind of gentleman," snorted Caroline, a rare sound for her, "who lures my sister out of doors to make love to her. Why does he not have the decency to call?"

"Because his parents believe him spoken for."

"And so he is. Now come with me. Mr Fox will brook no further delay."

And with that the older woman took the younger firmly by the arm and marched her to where Fox waited, sitting behind his desk, his face ashen with rage.

"You are a fool," he said, as Sarah walked through the door. "In fact I have never met a greater in all my years in parliament – and that is saying something, believe me!"

"Why am I a fool to fall in love when all the world does so?" his sister-in-law replied with a desperate attempt at spirit.

Fox made a contemptuous noise. "It is not the act of falling in love, girl, it is with whom you choose to do so that is the art of life. Newbattle is an empty-headed ass, not ugly, quite lively, I grant you that, but a known ladies' man. He don't love you, Sal, he loves the challenge of you."

"And what do you mean by that, Sir?"

"I mean that you represent the unobtainable. The Beauty of London, everyone's darling and quite obviously the King's current favourite. To a puff of wind like that boy you must be the ultimate prize."

"At least he has declared himself which is more than His Majesty has done."

Fox went purple before Sarah's eyes. "Christ's mercy, am I brother to an idiot? For a king to make a declaration thus is a matter of state. He is not free to propose without reference. Begone to your room, Sal. The sight of you is causing me to tremble."

The girl dropped a small curtsey and turned to leave.

"Wait!" thundered her brother-in-law. "Hear this and hear it well before you go. From henceforth Newbattle is forbidden to set foot in this house or its grounds. Furthermore you are prohibited from communicating with or seeing him again. If you disobey me in this I shall despatch you to your brother at Goodwood away from all mischief. Do you understand?"

"Yes, Sir."

"Very well." His tone softened. "Sal, I beg of you not to throw yourself away on someone unworthy. You have too much beauty, too much brain, to squander your splendour on a wastrel."

His sister-in-law did not answer but merely raised her chin as she walked through the door. But once outside, the tears came, gushing and warm, stinging her eyes as she rushed up the stairs and into the privacy of her bedroom.

"I'll not be told what to do," she muttered furiously. "Fox

is only angry because of his own monstrous ambition. It is the King who is trifling with me, not John, if he did but know it."

Yet deep down, too deep for the thought even to be acknowledged, Sarah knew that the owner of such honest china-blue eyes as King George's, would be hard put to it to hurt or deceive a living soul.

"He's too gullible," said the Princess Augusta firmly. "My son is an innocent abroad. It is your duty, my dear Bute, to see that he does not fall into the hands of that scheming Lennox girl."

"But Madam," answered the Earl, raising her hand to his lips and kissing it delicately, "he has already confided in me and given his solemn promise not to marry an Englishwoman."

"Be damned to that," the Princess replied sharply. "I still don't trust that Fox clan."

Bute sighed silently, knowing his assurances were about to be ignored. The Princess of Wales had loathed Fox from the moment he had opposed her Regency should the old King die before the heir to the throne attained his majority. As things had turned out, of course, George had been of age when his grandfather had finally gone, but the Princess had none the less remained unrelenting. As far as she was concerned Fox was as self-seeking and wily as his name.

"No," she went on forcefully, "we must have a decent German girl as we always have. Bute, find some suitable names. I believe he is still drawn to Sarah Lennox and it is high time we acted."

"Very good, my dear," he answered, and this time kissed her on the mouth.

The rumour that he had been Augusta's lover since the death of her husband was absolutely true. For John Stuart, Earl of Bute, born into the impoverished Scottish nobility, made up for his lack of funds by an overweening ambition, and his obvious stepping stone to advancement had been the bed of the Princess of Wales. Four years after the death of Prince Frederick – lovingly known as Fritz to his intimate circle – the nonentity who hovered in the shadow of the

Princess had become one of the most important men in the country, promoted Groom of the Stole to the new Prince of Wales. Furthermore, he had risen to be George's friend and adviser, a father figure of enormous influence.

"You are very naughty," admonished Augusta now, "we are discussing George's future."

"You may safely leave His Majesty to me," Bute answered lazily, fondling the Princess's breasts with a long and elegant hand.

"How dare you," said Augusta, but she was smiling.

"I dare because I love you," he murmured smoothly. "Does Madam have a spare hour this afternoon when I may prove it?"

"If I say yes will you get rid of that awful Lennox girl once and for all?"

"Consider it already done," replied the Earl of Bute as he led the Princess of Wales, not protesting at all, towards her bedchamber.

The shadow of the disagreement between Henry Fox and Sarah Lennox hung over Holland House for several days, days during which she kept to her bed, declaring a cold, and he stumped about the mansion or rode round the estate with a bevy of servants looking for signs of an errant lover. As is always the case in such circumstances it was Caroline, his wife, who bore the brunt of the situation, attempting to run the household and heal the breach simultaneously. But in these strained conditions Lady Susan Fox-Strangeways showed her true worth and offered to take over all day-to-day business while Caroline concentrated on being a full-time peacemaker.

"They are both such strong personalities," sighed the older woman, returning from Sarah's room with an untouched tray of food.

"Yet Mr Fox is right. I have no time for John Newbattle."

"Ah, but the more we tell Sarah that the more determined she will get."

"That is the way of the world," answered Susan, and smiled wistfully.

"I hope she will not be foolish and refuse to come to the February ball."

"I hope so too. For that will be my last sortie with you, dear Lady Caroline. This morning I heard from my father that he wants me to return home for the summer."

"Well, you have been with us a long time. I am sure they are all missing you at Redlynch House."

"I dare say they are. But perhaps the fact that I am leaving could be my excuse to get Sarah to join us."

It was, in a way, a form of kindly blackmail, but whether Sarah saw through the ruse or not was not certain. In any event, she graciously agreed to accompany Susan on her very last rout of the season and rose majestically from her sick bed to the great relief of her elder sister. Mr Fox, for his part, consented to remain tactfully at home having extracted a promise from Caroline that she would faithfully report back every look and gesture that passed between Sarah and the King.

"I'll see that beastly puppy boy put out of countenance if it's the last thing I do," he whispered in his wife's ear as she left the house.

"Well, he won't be present. One can only attend by special invitation and he won't have one for certain."

"Surely you don't think rumours about Newbattle and Sarah have reached His Majesty's ears already?" asked Fox fearfully.

"It wouldn't surprise me. I'm positive Bute would be only too agog to pass on tittle-tattle."

"Oh pray God no," Fox groaned, and rolled his eyes heavenwards.

But for once the face of that tall, most elegant of kings, was unreadable as George III stood in his receiving room while the line of guests paid their respects then made their way past him into the ballroom. Watching with narrowed eyes and feeling like a court spy as a result, Caroline Fox could see nothing between the young couple that could be interpreted as anything more than ordinary friendship as Sarah swept one of her spectacular curtseys and the King graciously inclined his head. Just for a second, though, it suddenly occurred to Caroline that His Majesty *was* up to something, for momentarily those bright-sky eyes of his darkened then dropped. But a minute later he was as normal and she put it down to her overeager imagination. Gathering the ladies of her party round her, Caroline made her way in to the ball.

Obviously every effort to dazzle had been made this evening for a brilliant sight greeted the eye of the beholder. A thousand candles shone in glittering chandeliers, each prism washed especially for the occasion, covering the dancers with rainbows as they moved to the sound of the musicians, who sat in the gallery above. All Polite Society was present and as a result high fashion was much in evidence. Velvets and satins, rich with embroidery, transformed even the plainest of men; while the ladies, powdered, patched, and rouged, sparkled with jewels, some even having diamonds scattered in their hair.

"Pretty company," remarked Lady Albermarle, Caroline and Sarah's aunt, who was staying in town.

"Everyone who's anyone is here, as they say."

"Vying for the King's attention, no doubt."

"No doubt," answered Caroline and had the good grace to blush, thinking of the recent *contretemps* at Holland House about which Lady Albermarle knew nothing.

A round of applause brought her attention back to the evening ahead and she saw that the dance had just ended and partners were being engaged for the next. Almost immediately, the Duke of Marlborough and Lord Barrington's nephew were asking permission of the two older ladies to lead out Sarah and Susan and, with her aunt gone to join old friends, Caroline found herself alone. So it was that she saw the King quietly enter the ballroom and stand for a moment looking round.

Fox's wife knew everything then; knew that he was in love with her sister, that he had made up his mind to do something of moment about it, that he was wrestling simultaneously with a problem which was making him wretched. Caroline's heart went out to the young man and she took a guess that somewhere in the coil lay the heavy hand of the Princess of Wales and, slightly more subtly, that of the Earl of Bute.

The music ended once more and there was an audible swish as the ladies spread their skirts and took their seats, preparing to flutter and flirt behind their fans. The gentlemen began to stroll and it was at this moment that Lady Susan, quite unprepared for what was about to happen, went to join Lady Albermarle on the opposite side of the ballroom to Caroline and Sarah. But no sooner had she sat down than everyone round her rose and Susan saw that the King, smiling and charming, had sought her out. Somewhat flustered as she had never before had a conversation with him, Susan curtsied and smiled.

"My dear Lady Susan," he began, drawing her to one side so that they were out of hearing range of Lady Albermarle, who was craning forward, one hand actually cupping her ear.

"Your Majesty?"

"I hear that you are going back to Somersetshire."

"Yes, it's true, Sir. I leave town in a few days time."

She was dying to ask him how he knew this but didn't quite have the nerve.

"That is a great shame for I am sure you will be missed. When do you plan to return?"

"Not till the winter, Sir. But when exactly I'm not certain."

The King smiled mischievously, a trait that Susan would not have associated with him. "And is there nothing that would bring you back before?"

The girl stared at him blankly, wondering where this line of chatter could possibly be leading. "I don't know of anything, Sir."

"Would you not come to see the Coronation?"

"Oh yes. I hope I would be able to come and see that."

George's face grew mysterious. "I hear it is very popular my having put it off."

Susan nodded silently, fearing that she was about to get into political deep water.

"You see, the Coronation will be a much finer sight when there is a queen," the King continued meaningfully.

Wondering if she was starting to see the thread behind the words, Susan answered, "To be sure, Sir."

His Majesty narrowed his large eyes. "I have had a great many applications from abroad but to be honest I don't like any of them. Yet strangely I have had none at home which, of course, I should like much better."

'So that's it!' thought Susan frantically. 'It's like a dream. He wants to marry Sarah. Oh, good God!'

The King stared across the room to where the Beauty sat, laughing and talking, unaware that he was looking at her. "What do you think of your friend?" he said in a lowered voice. "You know who I mean. Don't you think her fittest?"

"Think, Sir?" repeated Susan, terrified of putting a foot wrong, stalling for time.

The King looked her straight in the eye. "There will be no Coronation until there is a queen, and I think your friend is the fittest person for it. Tell her so from me."

With those words he crossed the ballroom and bowed his head to Sarah, who shot to her feet in consternation. Looking over in Susan's direction he spoke in Sarah's ear and after a few moments she, appearing immensely surprised, nodded and curtsied. His Majesty, obviously satisfied, then walked away.

'*Was* that a proposal of marriage I heard just now?' thought Susan wildly, 'or have I lost all reasoning power? And if it was an offer, why was it made through me? Oh dear, oh dear. I can think of nothing worse than playing a king's Cupid.'

But she had no further time to sort out her ideas. The music had begun again and the Master of the King's Horse, the Duke of Rutland, was making his way over, asking Lady Albermarle's permission for Susan to dance with him. Burning with impatience, Fox's niece hardly knew how to contain herself as she plodded through a minuet, the Duke unquestionably being the most terrible dancer in the world. A private conversation was obviously going to be out of the question from now on. However, Susan did manage to whisper, "I must talk to you about the King," only to be answered with a supercilious smile from Sarah which the older girl found intensely annoying.

And this annoyance was doubled when, on arriving home, her friend announced that she was vastly tired and made

straight for her bedchamber without waiting to hear a word
of what Susan had to say. Indeed it was Caroline, her straight
features lit by curiosity, who said, "What did His Majesty say
to you so earnestly this evening?"

Susan hesitated, then decided she was too young to handle
such a weighty matter alone. "I think that perhaps, dearest
Caro, I should tell you all before Mr Fox."

"The light is still burning in his study. Do you wish to speak
with him now or can it wait until morning?"

"I believe it would be better at once. I feel heavy with
responsibility."

"Gracious!" said Caroline, gleaming with anticipation.

"I can't understand it," said Fox, shaking his head as
everything was told. "Is it a joke? For, if so, it's a very
bad one. I wonder, can His Majesty possibly be serious?"

"I felt that he was," Susan answered truthfully.

"But it's such a strange way of going about things. Why
use you as his ambassador? Why not come directly to me?"

"Because he is afraid of Bute's spies," Caroline put in
with certainty. "They're everywhere, watching any move
the poor creature makes. If he was seen talking to you in
a serious manner, Henry, it would be all round Court in five
minutes."

Fox looked thoughtful. "You may well be right, my dear.
His Majesty has been tied to his mother's apron strings so
long he might at last have grown weary of them and be
pulling at the knot. I believe he may be learning guile and
cunning."

"What shall I do?" asked Susan. "Should I tell Sarah?"

"Oh yes, you must. It is your duty. But there is one
thing that we must all watch for in the face of these new
events."

"And what is that?" asked Caroline.

"We must be extra vigilant for any sign of Newbattle. That
beastly boy could ruin everything."

"He's hateful," said Susan, very violently for her. "I much
prefer the King. He's altogether nicer."

"But there's none so blind as those who think they're in
love," Fox said gloomily.

"Perhaps Sarah will come to her senses soon," Caroline suggested hopefully.

"I'm not so sure. Newbattle made such a set for her she is puffed with vanity as a result."

"Think of preferring him to His Majesty," said Susan, shaking her head. "It's like comparing a monkey to a lion."

"But monkeys perform tricks," countered Fox solemnly. "I'll swear we've not yet heard the last of that poxy fellow."

"I hope you're wrong," sighed Susan. "I would so love to see Sarah as Queen of England."

"Sister to the Queen!" said Caroline, and laughed joyously at the very thought of it.


"If I may speak boldly, Sir, it is my view you are now being made a fool of," said the Earl of Bute succinctly.

"Why?" asked the King, his voice strangely quiet.

"Because the object of your affections, whom I long since warned you against if you remember, Sir, is playing you false."

There was no reply and Bute wondered if he had gone too far with the royal puppet who sat, back turned, gazing out of the window, averting his face and the china-blue eyes that revealed all from the man he termed "dearest friend". And there was indeed a long silence before George spoke.

"Why do you say this?" he asked eventually.

"Because Lady Sarah Lennox, who obviously still fills your thoughts, Sir, is being courted by Lord Newbattle, Ancram's son."

The King's shoulders twitched but he said nothing.

"No good can come from hankering after the girl," Bute persisted. "You promised that you would put her from your mind but still have not done so. And your mother is firmly of the opinion that you should now be choosing a German bride, Sir."

George turned violently. "I don't want one, Bute. I am not drawn to anyone but Lady Sarah. I know what promise I gave you but I fail to see your objection to an English queen. I'm damned if I do."

The Earl stood silently, thinking that he had never seen

his malleable charge quite so angry or so strained, and just for a moment panicked, wondering if his vast influence might be diminishing. Then he rallied like a true Scot and came in on the attack.

"There is no Englishwoman well born enough. As King it is expected that you marry a princess. This motley collection of minor nobles' daughters cannot provide a fitting consort."

"May I remind you," hissed George furiously, "that Lady Sarah's great-grandfather was Charles II."

"And may I remind *you* that *your* great-grandfather, George I, was begged by the English people to take the place of the Stuart dynasty? How could you marry one of their blood, Sir? You would be a laughing stock."

"As I am already," His Majesty muttered.

"What did you say?"

"I said as I am already for being under the influence of both yourself and my mother. I'll choose my own bride, I swear it."

"Have it your way," sighed Bute wearily. "But it seems foolish to me to bring about a constitutional crisis over one who does not love you."

"I know the mood of the people better than you," George retorted sharply. "There'll be no crisis. An English queen would be a popular choice. Anyway, Lady Sarah cares for me. I know it."

"If I can prove to you that she is having a liaison with Newbattle will you change your mind?" Bute asked, the slightest note of desperation tingeing his voice.

"If I thought I had no chance of winning her, obviously yes."

"Then such evidence will be found."

"Dear friend," said the King, more firmly than he had ever spoken to Bute in his entire life, "tittle-tattle and gossip will not suffice on this occasion. I shall want proof positive before I ever believe ill of Lady Sarah Lennox."

And with that he got to his feet and left the room, leaving the Earl to stare after him, realising for the first time he was in the grip of a dangerous situation, that someone with equal power to himself was making a rival bid for the loyalty and affection of the King of England.

Driven underground by the edict of Mr Fox, John Newbattle's courtship of Sarah Lennox predictably became even more intense. Banned from the house or even from communicating with her, the feckless youth went complaining to his sister, Lady Louisa, whose husband George was Sarah's brother.

"What? Does the wretch say you are not good enough for her? The jumped-up fool! I'll see his nose out of joint. I shall be your go-between, dearest. Leave everything to me."

Unfortunately, Lady George not only attitudinised constantly but championed causes into the bargain. And now the cause became Young Love. Sarah, like the heroine of a romantic novel, was the victim of a callous guardian who stood in the way of her happiness because of his own inability to recognise true passion. Lord Newbattle, so very handsome, was Sarah's soul mate, her ideal husband, sinned against by those in authority. It became Louisa Lennox's quest to unite the pair in the face of all the odds.

At once she began to call on her sister-in-law, Caroline, and leave notes for Sarah behind a loose brick in the garden wall, a place prearranged by the two of them during a whispered conversation when no one else was in the room. This frequent visiting was facilitated by the arrival of Emily, Countess of Kildare, the sister who had raised Sarah. Obviously, family gatherings were arranged and so it was little problem to take Sarah to one side before dinner and murmur that her lover would be waiting for her in the Home Park early on Saturday morning and that she, Lady George, and her husband would see to it that the girl was able to leave the house undetected. Feeling rejuvenated by the intrigue, the arch plotter then went in to dine.

Sarah, equally elated by all the secrecy and the fact that she had stolen the heart of the most dashing rake in London, hardly knew how to contain her excitement. In comparison with this adventure the fact that the King was attracted to her faded to nothing. A longing to elope had come over her and Sarah could concentrate on nothing but thoughts of her gallant young man.

"But the King said you were the fittest person to be Queen," Susan protested vigorously.

"It was a joke," Sarah replied. "If he had really meant it he would have spoken to me direct."

"But he asked me to repeat it to you. That's as good as saying it."

"No it isn't. If he's not man enough to declare himself face to face I'll swear I am no longer interested in him."

And with that she refused to discuss the matter further, leaving poor Susan to depart for her family seat, Redlynch House in Somerset, feeling that she had not obeyed her sovereign's commands correctly.

Since the ball ten days earlier at which the King had made his extraordinary statement, Sarah had not been to Court. Terrified that, infatuated as she was by Newbattle, she might say something out of place, Fox had deemed it necessary that his sister-in-law remain at home. The public excuse for her nonappearance was the visit of Lady Emily Kildare to Holland House, but it had not escaped Bute's attention that the Fox family were conspicuously absent from all gatherings. Master manipulator that he was, the Earl made it his business to ask Lady Louisa Lennox to cut cards with him when next he saw her at the house of a mutual friend.

"I do trust, my dear Lady George, that the visit of Lady Emily is going well," he said whilst dealing.

She looked at him sharply, wondering how it was that no detail, however trivial, escaped the attention of this suavest of creatures.

"Very pleasantly, thank you, Sir."

"Good, good," Bute answered, and played a card.

He really was a most attractive man, thought Louisa, preening and simpering as he gave her a delightful smile, and recalled how, when the Earl had been penniless, trying his hardest for recognition, it had been his superlative legs which had finally brought him to attention. At amateur theatricals and masquerades, Bute had displayed his greatest asset in well-cut costumes, and it had been while playing the part of Lothario in *The Fair Penitent*, organised by the Duchess of Queensberry's private theatre group, that he had been seen by Prince Frederick of Wales and his climb to power and riches had begun. Rumour had it amongst the ladies that it was not only the Earl's legs that were amazing and at this thought Lady George felt the colour come into her cheeks.

"Tell me," Bute said now, "is it just her sister's visit that keeps the lovely Lady Sarah at home or is she trying to avoid someone at Court?"

"Who might you mean, Sir?" asked Louisa archly, having heard every rumour there was about her sister-in-law attracting the King.

"Your brother perhaps," Bute replied unexpectedly.

"How did you know?"

"As adviser to His Majesty I make it my business to be *au fait* with all that goes on," Bute said with the merest suggestion of a wink.

"La, are you aware of everyone's *affaires* then, my Lord?"

"But of course," he said, and patted her hand.

It occurred to Lady George then that it was as well they were playing bezique so there were no other players at the table to eavesdrop on their conversation. Slightly emboldened by this privacy, she said, "It is actually Mr Fox who has interfered. He has had the gall to ban my brother from his house, nor will he let John and Sarah meet outside. Perhaps the Paymaster feels he has bigger fish to fry."

The Earl raised his eyebrows. "Perhaps, indeed. Ambition is Henry Fox's middle name."

"I can't say that I care for the man, now you mention it. To me there is something *déclassé* about his antecedents."

"Then you personally are not against a match between Lord Newbattle and Lady Sarah?"

"Not at all. I think it insulting to our family that he is not considered good enough." Lady George took a good swallow of champagne and added in a whisper, "In fact I am doing all I can to aid and abet the young couple."

"That must be very difficult when they are not allowed to see one another."

Lady George looked slightly shifty. "It may be wrong of

me, of course, to flout the wishes of Sarah's guardian but they are in love. And who has not been? How dare Fox, with *his* reputation for a rakish past, stand in their way?"

"So you help them meet secretly?" said Bute, studying his cards.

"Yes, I do," answered Lady George defensively. "This very Saturday morning at dawn they are to see one another in the Home Park of Holland House and there, or so I believe, my brother intends to ask Sarah for her hand in marriage."

The Earl raised his brows. "Really? So the relationship is a serious one?"

"Most serious. I would not assist them if they were indulging in a grubby little affair."

"Of course not," Bute replied soothingly. "What woman of honour would?"

And with that he changed the subject, talking instead of the latest fashions at Court and congratulating Lady George on the beauty of her gown and the width of her hoops. He was one of the most charming people alive and by the end of the evening Louisa Lennox could understand perfectly how both the King and the Princess of Wales relied on the Earl of Bute completely.

"A nobleman of substance," she remarked to her husband as they drove towards Holland House.

"Bute?"

"Of course."

"A scheming devil more likely."

"George, how could you?"

"With ease, my dear. I wouldn't trust the man as far as I could spit."

"You're excessively churlish," said Louisa furiously and relapsed into an angry silence.

"Not so damned churlish that I won't help you tomorrow morning."

George's wife relented. "You are good-hearted, Sir. I apologise. Tell me the plan again."

"As we are staying at Holland House tonight it will be simple. I shall rise before dawn, awaken you, and together we shall help Sarah creep out of the house."

"Is it wrong of us?"

"Too late to think of that now, my dear," answered her husband briskly. "Your brother is standing by and will be at the rendezvous as arranged, and if my sister has set her heart on him then so be it."

Lord George Lennox believed firmly that people should be free to marry whom they chose, but even he felt guiltily that he was betraying Caroline's trust as he stole out of Holland House with his younger sister into the frosty February morning. Yet the look on Sarah's face as she spied Lord Newbattle waiting beneath some trees at a discreet distance from the house, his horse tethered nearby, went a great way towards reassuring him. Tactfully, George turned away and went back inside, leaving the lovers to share their illicit tryst alone.

"I've missed you terribly," declared Lord Newbattle ardently, smothering Sarah's flower face with kisses.

"And I you," she answered, thinking him the most romantic figure in the world and so handsomely dashing.

"I can't bear this separation much longer, nor is it right that we be made to endure it."

"No, it isn't. Oh John, my own dearest, what are we going to do?"

He grinned triumphantly. "I know the precise answer. Sarah, I formally intend to ask for your hand in marriage. I beg you, will you be my wife?"

And the pretty young nobleman dropped on one knee before her, both hands clasped over his heart.

"My first proposal," gasped Sarah, turning the colour of a peony. "Oh how thrilling!"

"But what is your answer to it? Will you have me?"

"Of course I will. I can think of nothing more delicious than being married to my own beloved John."

Lord Newbattle stood up again. "Then that is settled. I shall go at once and ask for my father's consent to the match."

"Will he give it?" Sarah asked anxiously.

"Of course he will. He let his daughter marry a Lennox, there is no reason why he should not let his son do likewise."

And John kissed her in a way that made Sarah's body fill with longing for him. But as she pressed against her lover, closing her eyes, Sarah thought she heard the distant whinny of a horse. Starting and pulling away from him, she looked over her shoulder to see if they were observed.

"What is it?"

"I thought I heard something. I had the sudden feeling we were being watched."

John stared round him. "There's no one in sight. But it's best we don't linger. The household will soon be up and stirring. I'll get home quickly."

"I can't bear to leave you."

"We must be sensible." He took her face between his hands. "Goodbye, my beautiful love. I shall send word to you tomorrow of what my father says."

And without any further delay the young man crossed to his horse, untethered it and mounted. Sarah ran to him, sighing theatrically.

"I can't bear this parting."

"You must," he answered with just the faintest hint of irritation. "Now, farewell. It's not safe for me to stay any longer."

And with that John Newbattle dug his heels into the sides of his mount and went off at considerable speed. Sarah gazed after him, dabbing her eyes with her handkerchief, and feeling exactly like a deserted heroine in one of the theatrical performances so well loved at Holland House. Then she braced herself and began to hurry through the grounds and gardens to the safety of the mansion.

It was just as she had left the protection of the trees and drawn level with the Lady Well that Sarah clearly heard the sound of distant hooves and turned, wondering whether John had come back to her for some reason. Over in the Little Breaches, heading in the direction of the Uxbridge Road, was a horseman, his back towards her. Yet even at this distance there was something familiar about that tall elegant figure. With a lurching heart, Sarah realised that the King of England was abroad in the dawning and might well have witnessed all that had taken place between herself and her lover.

Instantly she was torn by warring emotions. Vivid memories of how kind George had been to her, how he had tolerated her criticism of his mother, how his clear and sincere eyes had gazed into hers, came back to torment her. Sarah Lennox suddenly felt cheap and shabby, a worthless drab who had unkindly dropped one lover to make way for another. She also remembered Fox's description of John Newbattle as a vain inglorious insignificant puppy and wondered momentarily if there was any truth in it.

And then every other thought was banished from Sarah's mind as to her immense horror she saw that the King was not alone, that beside him, outlandish in loose pink trousers, a creature was running, its red hair gleaming in the first rays of the sun. The sinister woman, last seen when the January snows had lain upon the ground, was also abroad in the early light.

It occurred to Sarah then, though it made little sense, that the stranger might be a spy, sent to watch her, hired perhaps by the Earl of Bute or even the King himself. With a shudder the girl hurried in through an open door leading to the servants' hall, and scurried up the east staircase towards her bedroom and sanctuary, wondering what the consequences of this eventful daybreak might turn out to be.

# Seven

It snowed after Christmas, very swiftly and very thickly, so that Holland Park and the remains of the magnificent dwelling that once had stood there were swathed in the most beautiful of coverings. Paths and walkways were blotted out, ankle-deep, and all the age-old trees were bowed beneath the sparkle of white that decked their branches.

It had started to snow as Sidonie drove back from Wiltshire, leaving behind her the mystic village of Avebury and the sixteenth-century farmhouse in which her parents lived. By the time she reached the outskirts of London it was falling quite fast, and when she had put her key in the main front door of her home in Phillimore Gardens it had been still and shadowy because of the silence in the streets. The fact that the place was empty, everyone away for the festive season, had only added to the general air of desolation.

Finnan had flown to Ireland on the day before Christmas Eve, while Jannie had gone to stay with the owner of the black beard, Max, and their three teenage love children. The couple from the Penthouse, Rupert and Fiona Carruthers-Greene who, as Sidonie had discovered, only used the flat as a pied-à-terre and actually lived in a large house in Sussex, had spent the holiday in their country home. And so now, in those odd few days between Christmas and New Year, the entire building was deserted.

To combat her solitude, Sidonie practised ferociously, playing long into the night, knowing that she wasn't disturbing anybody. She ate out a good deal, mostly at the little Italian restaurant round the corner, then would hurry home to talk to Catty Scarlatti, her feline companion, called Carl for short. He was currently very affectionate as he had been boarded out while his owner was away from London.

But by the third day of isolation Sidonie was beginning to realise how much she missed having other people around. Even without seeing the doctor or Jannie it was somehow reassuring to know that they were only a flight of stairs away if she should need them, particularly in the case of Finnan.

"I wish they were back," said Sidonie to Carl, who flicked one ear. Getting up from the keyboard she walked to the glass door of the music room and looked out.

The garden was full of snow – there was even a large ball of it, which Sidonie had rolled for fun, standing in the middle of the lawn. A sudden desire to be outside engulfed her, to breathe the crisp stinging air deep into her lungs, to run about and make a fool of herself in all the wonderful whiteness. Without stopping to worry about wasted time, Sidonie put on a big hat, a coat and scarf and headed off for Holland Park.

It was gloriously deserted, the weather obviously keeping people indoors, and it was with a tremendous feeling of ownership that Sidonie crunched through the snow-filled ornamental gardens and made her way round that shell of what once had been. Remembering the night when the mansion had been lit by candles, and ghostly dancers had thrown their nonexistent shadows against the windows, Sidonie thought now, when everything was normal and innocent, that she must have been mistaken, that it must have been an optical illusion caused by the intense fatigue following a concert. And yet in a part of her mind that she used very little because it made her afraid to do so, she knew there had been no mistake, that she had actually experienced something beyond rational explanation.

Turning away from the house, Sidonie made her way over what was known as the north lawn and into the rose walk, barely recognisable in its thick covering of white powder. It was more heavily wooded than she remembered, great rows of trees standing on either side, clumps of snow falling from their branches as she walked beneath. Everything seemed so different beneath its bleached covering that she could almost have sworn she was in a planted woodland, yet there was none in the park, as far as she knew. And then Sidonie stopped, frozen in her tracks, as she saw what lay ahead of her.

The wooded path led to a central clearing in which stood

two stone seats and a statue. And though there was nothing remarkable about this it was to the people who stood within its enclave that Sidonie's eyes were drawn. The Joshua Reynolds girl was there and with her three other creatures who could have stepped straight from the painter's canvases. An awareness of time slipping out of rhythm, of ghosts from the past appearing as once they did in life, filled Sidonie's mind as she gazed and gazed at the delightful vision of two boys and two girls from another age playing merrily in the snow. Then suddenly there was a distant cry and Sidonie realised that the girl who had been haunting her ever since she first came to Holland House had not only seen her but was about to give chase. Fear replaced pleasure and Sidonie turned to run.

Now a sense of nightmare overtook her for, as it had done once before, the landscape changed. Ahead of her lay fields and parkland, all white with winter's drapery. The whole terrain seemed treacherous and heavy with drifts, and nowhere in sight was there a familiar path or turning. She was trapped in another age, falling and floundering in snow so deep that it seemed likely to drag her in and bury her. Frantically, Sidonie blundered on, aware that the girl was still behind her. And then she tripped and plunged downwards into the sinister softness.

She lay panting for a moment or two, her heart thumping, the sound of her blood roaring in her ears. Then she heard, quite distinctly, the chatter of excited young voices close at hand and knew that they had caught up with her, that something that was impossible had taken place. But when Sidonie raised her head, tears stinging her cold cheeks, she saw that it was only a group of schoolchildren, well muffled up and wearing woolly hats, determinedly throwing snowballs at one another. A black child, more friendly than the rest, approached her.

"You all right?" he said.

"Yes, thanks," Sidonie panted. "I've fallen over, that's all."

He tried to heave her to her feet but fell beside her, giggling, his ebony face spectacular in such white surroundings. Then with a great deal of grinning he struggled back up again as Sidonie did too.

"You'd better go home. Ain't no good getting wet at your age."

Sidonie laughed, then the sheer relief of being back in familiar surroundings overwhelmed her so greatly that she wept again.

"'ave you 'urt your knee?" said the boy, simultaneously embarrassed and concerned.

"Yes. I'll be all right in a minute. Here, this is for Christmas." And she gave him a pound coin from her coat pocket.

"My mum said not to take money from strangers."

"I'm not a stranger really. You helped me get up." And Sidonie plodded away before he could argue further.

But even the safety of the Garden Flat could not allay the emotions that this most recent experience had aroused. For now Sidonie was forced to admit finally that those other occurrences which she had dismissed as dreams or delusions could no longer be explained away, that they had been genuine psychic phenomena in which she had glimpsed Holland House and its inhabitants as they once had been in another age. The very concept opened a floodgate of bewilderment as to why she who had never seen a ghost should be the one to glimpse such mirages, such echoes from the past.

Desperately trying to be sensible, Sidonie looked at the clock to see how long the experience had lasted. She had left the flat at a few minutes past noon; now it was four o'clock. What had seemed to happen in only a brief space of time had actually taken some considerable while. Resolutely, the musician noted down the fact at the back of her diary.

But no amount of being orderly, of trying to be calm in the face of such tumultuous events could help her. Feeling spineless and silly, Sidonie wept again, though this time with a sense of confusion rather than abject terror. With tears streaming down her cheeks, the ring of the telephone was a harsh intrusive sound. Almost before she picked it up, Sidonie had guessed who it was.

"Hello, darling," said Nigel's voice. "How are you?"

"Fine, thanks. How are you?"

"I thought I'd ring to remind you that it's New Year's Eve. Are you celebrating?"

"Yes," Sidonie lied. "I'm going to a party at Rod's."

"Oh, that's a pity. I was going to invite you to join me. The Chancellor's having a reception at Claridge's for his blue-eyed boys."

"That sounds different. Sorry I'm booked, though I'm sure you'll find somebody to go with."

"I have no lack of partners," Nigel answered angrily. "I just thought my wife would be the most fitting person to accompany me on such an occasion."

"Your *ex*-wife," Sidonie countered. "We have been divorced a year, you know."

"It seems more. I still miss you – a lot!"

The very way he spoke brought back bitter memories of her marriage.

"You miss having someone to act as hostess, that's all."

"You're a bitch, Sidonie. That remark was entirely uncalled for."

"Oh, go away," she said, only just in control of herself. "You have no right to ring up and harangue me. Leave me alone."

And with that she banged the receiver down, feeling thoroughly fraught. A moment later the phone rang again and, snatching it up, Sidonie barked, "It is an offence to make nuisance calls in case you didn't know."

"Well, I'm not making one," answered Finnan's voice, "though I can if you want me to." Sidonie stood gasping, unable to utter, and he went on, "Has someone been bothering you?"

"Only Nigel," she answered huskily.

"Oh! That's naughty goings-on for a junior minister. Anyway, other than him, how are you? Did you have a good Christmas?"

"Very relaxing. What about you? Are you phoning from Dublin?"

"No, Gatwick. I just wanted to know if you're doing anything tonight."

Sidonie smiled, letting the sound of his voice wash over

her, wondering why it was that simply hearing him made her feel so much better.

"I'm not actually. What did you have in mind?"

"Going to Brünnhilde's for dinner. I haven't booked a table but I'm sure they'll squeeze us in somewhere. Would you like to?"

"I'd adore it."

"Excellent. Can you get hold of a minicab for about eight o'clock, to bring us home at two?"

"I'll try. Oh, Finnan, thanks. I needed something like this."

"Good. See you at six."

His money ran out and he put the receiver down.

'Is this great attraction love?' thought Sidonie, and immediately started wondering what to wear.

Fortunately she was in the bath when she heard the doctor return and so was able to resist the temptation to rush into the communal hall and tell him all about the events that had befallen her earlier that day. Instead, she behaved impeccably and when he finally rang her bell answered the door looking composed and beautiful in a long dress of ice blue velvet which she had last worn at a concert in Vienna and which still had pinned to it a crystal brooch, not expensive but exquisite, which an elderly Viennese admirer had presented to her.

"You look marvellous," Finnan said in admiration. "I'm so glad you weren't otherwise engaged, as they say."

"It's wonderful to see you," she said, throwing caution to the winds and giving him a hug. "I wasn't expecting you back."

"I wasn't expecting to come back but the family scene began to pall a bit. The trouble with the Irish is that they tend to leave Ireland and then sing about it. My brother-in-law took to weeping into his gin as the nights drew on."

"Did *he* leave Ireland?"

"Not at all. What he found so moving was the fact that *I* had gone."

"Oh I see! Did you kiss the Blarney Stone while you were there?"

"Listen, from Dublin to Blarney Castle is a fair stretch but

I must confess that in my misspent youth I gave it a couple of goes."

"Is it true you have to hang upside down to get at it?"

"Like a bat," said Finnan and gave Sidonie a smile that warmed her heart.

"I'm so glad you're back," she said and squeezed his arm. "Did you miss me, then?"

"I certainly did. The house was quite creepy with no other tenants in it."

"Oh, so that's the reason."

"No, I missed you for you as well."

And after that she said no more, returning to her cool image as they made their way to the restaurant, got a table, and donned silly hats and masks in the true spirit of the occasion. Yet, despite this, there was a certain restlessness about Sidonie which she could not quite conceal, the extraordinary events of that day still weighing on her mind and worrying her.

"You're preoccupied," said Finnan. "Is it Nigel?"

"No, he's just a minor irritation really. There's something else."

"What?"

Impulsively, Sidonie stretched across the table and laid her hand in his.

"Do you remember me telling you about a dream I had in which I saw Holland House as it used to be, complete with a coach going down a drive that's no longer there?"

"Yes, yes I do."

"You said then that perhaps I had stepped back in time, that you believed in lands beyond the mist. Did you mean it?"

"What exactly are you asking me?"

"Finnan, ever since I moved here odd things have happened to me. I've seen the house restored to its former glory on several occasions. I've seen a girl in eighteenth-century dress. Today, in the snow, I found myself in a planted woodland in a landscape that had entirely changed. The girl was there with three others, all of them from about the 1750s. It frightened me because I knew they could see me too. And if it is all a hallucination, why? I'm not on drugs,

I only drink socially, and I am most certainly not having a nervous breakdown."

The doctor looked at her in silence and for the first time Sidonie had the feeling that he was regarding her with something of a professional eye.

"I could answer in one of two ways," he said finally. "I could tell you to see your GP and have a checkup or I could say that for some reason we don't understand you are being privileged to glimpse another age."

"But how can I be?"

"Which?"

"Seeing things from another time because I know I'm perfectly well." For a moment Sidonie seemed a little uncertain. "At least I think I am."

"You look the picture of health to me. And the other answer I can't give you, except to say that a stone thrown into a pond sends out ripples that go on and on. Perhaps you are seeing a distant ripple."

"So you don't think I'm mad?"

"No, I don't, I think you're beautiful."

The sound of Big Ben boomed into their conversation. It was midnight and everyone had risen to their feet and linked hands for "Auld Lang Syne".

"People can be beautiful *and* mad, you know," whispered Sidonie, laughing.

"Like Ophelia or Lucia di Lammermoor?"

"Two fine examples."

"May I wish you a Happy New Year, lovely loony?"

"And Happy New Year to you, Finnan."

They shared a briefly delicious kiss before turning to the people next to them and wishing them well. Then they were in each other's arms again and Sidonie realised with certainty that she was about to have an affair. A neat little particle of her brain stood back and looked critically at the situation, attempting to envisage any future pitfalls. But apart from the usual dangers of becoming involved with another person she could see none in particular.

"I'm more complicated than you think," said Finnan, reading her mind.

"And I see ghosts."

"What a lovely couple!"

Their happiness at that particular moment was superb and intense, full of the excitement that heralds the start of any new relationship, and when they came back in the small hours to the house in Phillimore Gardens there seemed little need for many words to be spoken.

"I would be greatly honoured if you would stay with me," Finnan said quaintly, meaning every word.

"And I would be honoured to do so," Sidonie answered, also speaking the truth.

Standing hand in hand on Finnan's balcony beneath a million icy stars, gazing out over the frosty park to the snow-covered ruin that had once been a great house, they kissed long and ardently, then went to his bedroom without haste.

"You're tired," Finnan said, looking at the shadows beneath the golden eyes.

"Yes, I am. Yesterday I wandered into the eighteenth century and it exhausted me."

"Then we'll sleep."

How comforting it was, she thought, to be naked in his arms yet still able to rest.

"Don't worry," Finnan murmured as Sidonie closed her eyes. "I've waited such a long time for this that one more night makes no difference at all."

"Has there been anyone since Rosie died?"

"A couple of superficial encounters. Nothing important."

"Am I important?"

"You could be, very."

"Oh good," Sidonie said, and fell asleep.

She woke to his kisses, very passionate, very Celtic, and instantly longed for him to make love to her. But Finnan took his time, caressing her pretty breasts, running his hands over the delicate length of her. But finally the awaited moment came and, caught up in his extraordinarily powerful rhythm, Sidonie cried out with pleasure.

"Good?" Finnan whispered.

"Very."

But those words did not adequately describe the feelings

that they aroused in one another nor the great burst of sensation as they came to the climax of love almost simultaneously.

"Oh dear," said Sidonie, when both of them had eventually grown calm again.

"What?"

"That was seriously marvellous."

"Personally I could become addicted to such delightful pastimes."

She laughed. "That's going to be difficult when I go on tour."

Finnan propped himself up on one elbow and looked at her. "We'll have to cross that bridge when we come to it. In the short term I've somehow got to avoid turning into a pest as far as you're concerned."

Sidonie stared at him seriously. "You could never be that. You're far too nice."

"You probably thought that about Nigel once."

"Funnily enough I didn't. And by the way it was never like this with him."

"Don't be too kind to me. I might fall in love with you and then where would you be?"

"Probably exactly where I am now," Sidonie answered, and putting her arms round the doctor kissed him most affectionately.

# Eight

Sidonie's love affair with Finnan was certainly made intriguing, indeed more fun, by the fact that she was away so much, her concerts constantly taking her to places as disparate both geographically and spiritually as Glasgow and Venice, to say nothing of various other ill-matched world cities. Yet, in a way this set-up, exciting though it was, had one great disadvantage. The couple never had time to be dull together.

'One month,' thought Sidonie, 'I wish I could have just one month when I wasn't off somewhere.'

But her schedule was too full for such luxuries and all she could do was count her blessings, be glad that she was so much in demand and that she had such a marvellous life when she was at home.

"Now, now, Sid bach," Rod said, noticing her frown as she looked through the list of engagements he had just handed her. "This is going to be a good year for you. There's no need to make a face about it."

"It's just that I have so little time to myself."

"You never worried about that before." Her agent's expression changed and he looked sly. "Here, are you up to hanky panky with that Irish boyo?"

"What do you mean?"

"You know perfectly well. Are you having an affair with the doctor?"

"Yes I am," Sidonie said defiantly. "And it's wonderful. I haven't been so happy for ages."

"Well don't get too involved. You've spent years trying to get as far as you have. Don't let another Nigel situation develop."

"It's not another Nigel situation," Sidonie answered wrathfully, "I can't think of two men more unalike. Anyway,

113

Finnan adores my music. He would never stand in my way."

"I hope not for your sake."

Sidonie had not replied, afraid of falling out with an agent of whom she was very fond. For in her heart she knew that Rod was only trying to protect her future, and that it took a considerable man to cope with a woman who had a highly successful career of her own.

"Do you resent my giving so many concerts?" she had asked Finnan tentatively.

"Only the fact that I can't attend them all," he had answered.

But still Sidonie felt uncertain and considered how much easier things must have been in the time of her ghost, as she now thought of the dark-haired girl. Then women had had the time of their lives, liberated from the yoke of arranged marriages prevalent in earlier centuries, yet adored by their menfolk, who cherished and protected them.

"No need for striving in those days," Sidonie said to Catty Scarlatti. "It must have been sheer bliss."

"Though of course it would have not been possible to have a career," Sidonie answered herself on the cat's behalf. "So how would you have liked that?"

"I honestly don't know," she said aloud, and went to sit in front of the mirror and stare at her reflection, trying to imagine living in another age when her life would, through custom, have been entirely different.

Sidonie had been born in hospital, in Swindon, which, of course, would have been impossible in the eighteenth century. Then, Jane Brooks, her mother, would have had a home confinement. The old house in Avebury, which had seen so many babies delivered into the world in its time, would have added yet another one to its list. So both her birth and education had been very different from those the dark-haired Beauty must have undergone. No home governess for Sidonie, no occasional study with a brother's tutor. Instead Primary then Grammar School, and the usual piano lessons when she had been seven years old.

'Those might have been the same,' Sidonie thought. 'I wonder if my ghost plays the harpsichord.'

But she stopped thinking about supernatural events at this point, remembering instead Mrs Miriam Jenner, whose husband had died in a Japanese prisoner-of-war camp, so that she had been forced to continue teaching music after the war. Sidonie had been like a daughter to her and as the pupil's talent had developed so had Mrs Jenner's affection. It had been with her that Sidonie had gone to the house called Silbury Abbas where a collection of early instruments had been housed and had seen a harpsichord for the very first time.

"Can I play one of those?" she had asked.

And with the owner's permission she had been allowed to do so, and Sidonie's inexplicable love for the instrument had begun.

"It makes me believe in reincarnation," Miriam Jenner had said to Sidonie's mother. "She came into the world with a gift for it, I'll swear to that."

"Do you think she should go on?"

"Oh, but she must! I have arranged for Dr Ralph Greville to hear her at Oxford. He is one of the foremost teachers in the country. I'm positive he will take her as a pupil." Mrs Jenner had looked apologetic. "I hope you don't mind."

It would have been too bad if they had, Sidonie recalled. She had started private lessons with Dr Greville on Saturdays and at eighteen had entered the Royal College of Music to do a three-year Performers' Course.

'No eighteenth-century girl could have done that,' Sidonie thought. 'The most that anyone with talent could have hoped for would have been a really good tutor who would have instructed her at home.'

Nor would what followed later have been allowed. When she had left the College she had gone to Paris to study with Madame Monique Amboise, living in cheap *chambres*, sharing the *lavabo*. Sidonie had also shared a workshop with others, where she had practised the harpsichord for hours. It had all been a far cry from the life of the black-haired girl who had lived in the eighteenth century.

Sidonie had met Nigel by then, a local boy who had

gone to Marlborough College and been handsome though decidedly thick-set. He would phone her, coming through on a telephone situated in a nearby launderette; but usually Sidonie phoned him and they would murmur trivialities at one another in a rather sentimental manner. She supposed now that distance had enhanced the view, that he had seemed far more attractive because he was on the other side of the Channel. Whatever the reason, Sidonie had married him at the age of twenty-three when she had returned to England in 1982, and Nigel had promptly been elected to parliament, standing for the Tories, at the next by-election. In a way they had hardly known one another and Sidonie thought now that it would have taken two very exceptional and adult people to make the marriage work.

"And that is where my little ghost would have triumphed," Sidonie remarked to Carl. "She would have had nothing to do all day but look after her husband, while I had to fit in hours of practice and the occasional concert with all he wanted to do."

They had been married two years, two years during which Sidonie had been expected to play the part of political hostess as well as everything else, when Nigel's somewhat liquid charm had got him noticed by the Prime Minister. Sidonie had done her best, trying to help him as much as she could, but he, typically, had not returned the compliment. The member for Midhurst had wanted his wife to give up her career and become strictly an amateur. She had been on the point of doing so when Roderick Rees had heard her play in Bath and everything had changed.

The natural antipathy between the two men had been instant. Rod had even gone so far as to call Nigel Beltram MP a selfish bastard in a very loud Welsh voice.

"It's music or me," Nigel had shouted when things had finally came to a head. "If you sign on as one of that Welsh crook's clients you can bloody well get out."

"Then I bloody well will," Sidonie had shouted back. "I didn't waste countless years of my life studying music just to make small talk at political cocktail parties. I'm off."

He had struck her so hard then that she had reeled through the front door, dizzy and hardly able to see.

"That's it," Sidonie had gasped over her shoulder. "Men who hit women disgust me. I hope I never set eyes on you again."

'Now that *could* have happened in the eighteenth century,' she thought, 'but I wonder how tied they would have been. Would a woman have been able to get a divorce or would she have been stuck?'

But whatever the answer to that question, Sidonie in her century had had no hesitation.

"Get rid of the pig," her mother had said forthrightly. "Violence is something that must not be countenanced."

Rod had put it a different way. "Tell him to piss off or I'll land one on him."

"One what?"

"One knuckle sandwich. Now don't think about the prat any more. Listen, I've got you a cancellation at the Wigmore Hall for 1990."

Sidonie had looked at him breathlessly. "Do you mean it?"

"Yes, Sid bach, I do. It's a Tuesday night, worse luck, but I'll get everybody there who counts. Trust me."

"I do."

"And as to the future, divorce that creep and concentrate on your playing. You are going to be a very big star indeed."

"Am I truly?"

"Yes, but no mixing with the wrong sort of men, mind. You can sleep with who you like but it's got to be love 'em and leave 'em. I don't want some half-baked idiot interfering again."

"But what happens if I fall in love?"

"Avoid it like the plague," Rod had said succinctly. "Chauvinism is alive and well and dwelling in the hearts of most European males. Don't trust any of 'em."

She had laughed, watching his great Italian eyes rolling in his head, but still there had been something about the words that had struck home. She had had one affair since the divorce, with a flute player in the orchestra of the Royal Opera House, but it had been doomed from the start. It had almost been a contest as to which one of them had the greater ambition, and had lasted only a few months.

'And now here I go again,' thought Sidonie, 'falling for the man upstairs and about to make a fool of myself no doubt.'

But what a beautiful man he was, and only available to her because of the death of some poor creature she had never met.

"Fate is very odd," she said to Catty Scarlatti, who opened one eye and then closed it again. "I wonder what will happen next."

She stared at her reflection, back in the present day, her reminiscences at an end, regarding herself critically. Her eyes were lively, shining, obviously much improved by the love affair. But it seemed to Sidonie that she was a little fuller in the face.

"Oh, God, I'm not putting on weight, am I?" she groaned, and pulled at her chin, looking for flab, then stood up and turned sideways. "I'm sure I'm getting a paunch. It's all that sitting."

Much as she disliked the idea it did seem to Sidonie that she was fatter and a quick leap onto the scales showed a gain of five pounds.

"Oh dear, it's diet and exercise time," she grumbled to the cat, and searching in her wardrobe unearthed an old pink tracksuit which she rather disliked. "Time this went to a jumble sale," she said, but put it on as there was nothing else handy.

Sidonie had, in common with quite a few musicians, never really liked exercising, while still being aware that it was vital she took a fair amount. Hours of practice, in her case sitting down, quickly took their toll on even the slimmest, and the recent tour when she had crammed in as much hotel food as she could to keep her energy level high had not helped at all. Added to this was the fact she felt under no strain, that she bloomed in Finnan's company, that when they were together they cooked for one another.

"I've got to jog," said Sidonie determinedly and let herself out of the front door.

It was Wednesday and it was March, a sharp day with clear

definition of leaf and bud, a day of high bluster and needling showers. But, as always, none of this was apparent in the roaring abyss of Kensington High Street and it was not until she had turned into Holland Park, feeling a little foolish in her blancmange-coloured gear, that Sidonie seemed capable of taking a deep breath and running freely.

Having sped past the Commonwealth Institute, a building that everyone was supposed to like but which she actually detested, Sidonie ran up the grass slope towards Nightwalk, the pathway in front of Holland House where once the night watchman had done his rounds. It went through her mind just then that she had not seen her Joshua Reynolds girl, her dark-haired ghost, since New Year's Eve, that she had been away so much her extraordinary trips into the past had not been possible. And it was even as Sidonie thought this that a horse suddenly and rather shockingly loomed in front of her.

She had been running head down, concentrating on her feet, on making her metabolism rise with her heartbeat, and so had not actually been watching where she was going. In this way it was something of a surprise to see four equine legs stand directly in her path and realise that there was a rider abroad where she had never realised such a thing was allowed. Instantly Sidonie was suspicious, aware of mysteries which allowed supernature to catch up with her at any time. Panting for breath, feeling dishevelled, she looked up.

A man sat astride the horse, a man with whom for no reason at all she felt an instant empathy. He was young, in his early twenties, and had a fresh handsomeness which appealed to her. A wide pair of bright blue eyes stared towards Holland House and a clear healthy skin, quite unblemished and unspoilt, flushed as a consequence of what he saw there. Sidonie followed his gaze and realised it had happened to her again. The mansion stood whole and splendid, while the surroundings looked as they had done over two hundred years ago.

In the past Sidonie had been either afraid or alarmed, but now she took a deep breath and tried to conquer the panic that seemed an inextricable part of any experience she had into the unknown. Though she had been barely able to grasp its complex mathematical formulae she had recently studied Einstein's Theory of Relativity, particularly with regard to the concept of lapses of time being different in different frames of reference.

In the encyclopaedia she came upon the example of the pair of twins, one on earth, the other travelling in a rocket to Proxima Centauri, the nearest known star. Eight and a half years would elapse on earth between the launch of the spacecraft and its return, but on the vehicle itself only fourteen and a half months would pass because of the speed at which it travelled. Therefore, so Sidonie understood, if the twins had been ten at the start of the journey, the earthbound one would be eighteen and a half when the rocket returned but the travelling twin just over eleven.

If time truly could elapse at different speeds for different people might this be the explanation of Sidonie's own strange experiences? But now, gasping from her exertions in the cold clear light of day, rational answers seemed to have little place. Only just keeping in control of herself, Sidonie studied the rider who sat his horse so close by, unaware that she was only a few feet away from him, observing everything he did.

She recognised the man at once as somebody famous, somebody whose face she had seen before and yet who, for the moment at least, she could not identify. Fascinated but irritated by her loss of memory, Sidonie scrutinised his appearance.

The man was tall and slim, with fine broad shoulders and a simply excellent carriage. Beneath his tricorne hat he wore a short wig but, close as she was, Sidonie could glimpse traces of his own hair, cut close to his head and fairish. His nose was long and straight, the mouth passionate, full-lipped and loving. He was, even measured by modern standards, a very good-looking young person and Sidonie experienced again that strange feeling of empathy, so much so that it distressed her to see he was shaking with emotion and seemed almost on the point of tears. And, looking once more in the direction that he did, it was not difficult to see why.

The ghost, the Joshua Reynolds beauty, was creeping back

through the park towards Holland House in a most furtive manner while, in the distance, another young man, dark and dashing, was cantering off in the direction of the farm buildings. So the girl had two sweethearts and one had caught her in the act of keeping an assignation with the other!

The rider wheeled to go and Sidonie saw the girl look up, startled. For no reason the musician started to run alongside wanting, perhaps, to tell him not to upset himself. Gazing up at him, she wondered if he had finally noticed her. If, momentarily, time had gone mad for him too, for he seemed to stare at Sidonie and mouth something. But then he was gone in a great drumming of hooves, the sound of which rang in her ears long after he had vanished from view and Sidonie found herself, somewhat perturbed, jogging in Holland Park as if nothing unusual had taken place at all.

The identity of the horseman puzzled her throughout the rest of the day, and though she practised a new and complicated work, and also had to concentrate on giving a lesson to one of her private pupils, the mystery of him would not go away.

"I knew his face," she said to Finnan O'Neill later that evening.

But for once the Irishman was not receptive. He had been giving a lecture on haemophilia to medical students on top of a day dealing with children suffering from leukaemia and his patience was understandably short.

"Could we talk about it another time," he said, slumping into a chair. "I'm not feeling particularly bright at the moment."

At once Sidonie was suffused with uncertainty. "I didn't imagine it. Honestly, Finnan, it *did* happen."

"Yes, I'm sure," he answered, and closed his eyes.

Stung, she reacted in the silliest way possible. "I think I'd better go," she said huffily. "It's obvious you need an early night."

And with that she left his flat and went downstairs to her own despite the fact she could hear him calling out for her to come back. Once inside her front door Sidonie fought back a terrible urge to cry but instead broke her diet by pouring herself a glass of wine, then switched on television. Briefly looking at the programme guide she saw that a late film had just started and, as it was about the life of Handel, decided to watch. The story was fairly standard and somewhat glossy, the actor playing the name part far too handsome, one or two of the minor characters speaking with pronounced American accents. But it was the last scene in the film that riveted Sidonie's attention. It showed the great man's funeral in 1759, Westminster Abbey packed with three thousand people, the combined choirs of the Abbey, St Paul's and the Chapel Royal soaring out his beautiful music and, walking behind the coffin as a mark of respect, old King George II, supported by his tall handsome grandson. The make-up department had obviously done their stuff with these two characters for they looked very like the portraits of the monarchs concerned.

Sidonie leant forward in her chair, unable to believe her eyes. "George III," she breathed. "Of course!" And despite the lateness of the hour rushed to her set of encyclopaedias.

There was no doubt about it. The painting of the King in his Coronation robes was identical to the man she had seen in the park earlier that day. So George himself had somehow been involved with Holland House. Hardly able to take it all in, Sidonie began to read his biography.

"George William Frederick, King of Great Britain and Ireland, and Elector of Hanover, was born in London on 4th June, 1738, son of Frederick, Prince of Wales, and grandson of George II." There followed a paragraph about the Prince's education and then something of enormous significance. "The young Prince of Wales feared the burden of kingship and relied heavily for advice on his mentor, the Earl of Bute. This handsome, easy man ruled the life of the heir apparent and when the Prince fell in love with the fifteen-year-old sister of the Duke of Richmond, he turned to the Earl for advice."

Sidonie put the book down slowly. Were the Joshua Reynolds girl and the fifteen-year-old one and the same person? And, if so, who was the dashing rival who had galloped off at such great speed?

'Tomorrow when the library is open I'll check on this,' Sidonie decided, and went to bed so full of excitement that she only spared her quarrel with Finnan the merest passing thought.

They made up the argument simultaneously, he appearing at her front door with a bunch of flowers, she opening it to go upstairs and tell him what she had discovered.

"I'm sorry about last night," Finnan said. "I was very depressed and tired into the bargain."

"And I'm sorry too. I behaved like a spoilt child. Please forgive me."

"I do. Shall we go out to supper?"

"Why don't I get it? I've so much to tell you. I think I know who my ghost is."

"Let me have a bath and then I'll be with you."

While he was gone, Sidonie, who had been hoping he would come all day and so had little preparation left to do, remonstrated with herself about being selfish.

'He was obviously dying to talk about the hospital and all I could do was waffle on about seeing things. This is not the way to make friends and influence people, Sidonie Brooks.'

Deliberately keeping the topic of conversation away from herself, she said over dinner, "Have you had another terrible day?"

"Not as bad as yesterday. It's the children with haemophilia who are also HIV-positive that I find so distressing." Finnan paused, then added, "By the way, there's a chance I may soon be able to see some very interesting work on that condition in Canada."

Sidonie looked at him blankly. "Are you going there, then?"

"Yes. That is if it comes off. There's nothing definite yet."

Sidonie suddenly felt cold, realising how much, in a short space of time, she had come to depend on his companionship.

"Do you hope you will?" she asked, speaking rather slowly.

Finnan leant forward over the table and Sidonie saw that his eyes were alight with enthusiasm. She realised then that he was as much in love with his profession as she was with hers, and felt that up to this moment she hadn't fully understood him.

"Of course. It would be a wonderful opportunity." Finnan smiled at her. "You're looking a little distant. I suppose having a haematologist for a friend can be a bit daunting. In future I'll try and spare you the gory details."

"Was that a pun?"

"Yes. I've been making it since I was a student."

"Well, it's terrible. You ought to be ashamed of yourself." Sidonie's voice changed. "I'm sorry if I looked far away. I was trying to imagine living here without you."

"Oh, glory be. You're always touring. You won't even notice I've gone."

If she said anything further, Sidonie thought, he might well mistake it for a heavy approach, so with a certain effort changed the topic of conversation.

"Do you want to hear about what happened yesterday?"

"Of course."

"Time slipped again and I saw a man on horseback in the park. Finnan, it was George III."

The doctor's face changed curiously. "George III? How do you know?"

"I identified him from his portraits. He was young, about the same age as the Coronation painting. Do you know, I liked him. He seemed so human. I wonder if that was what finally sent him mad."

"He didn't go mad in my view," said Finnan.

Sidonie stared at him. "What happened to him then?"

"Well, this is only an opinion, but I think he suffered from a metabolic disorder called porphyria. I became absolutely fascinated by that particular king when I was a medical student and made a study of his symptoms."

"But wasn't he treated for lunacy?"

"Of course he was, and I believe it was that that sent him over the edge and gave him a nervous breakdown. Two evil bastards got their hands on him, a pair of quack doctors, father and son. They invented what they called the strait-waistcoat and put the poor bugger in it. Do you realise that even the

Prince Regent, not exactly his father's champion to put it mildly, didn't approve of them or their methods?"

Sidonie shook her head. "I knew none of this. Too busy sticking my nose into music books."

"Horses for courses, my love. It's the way of the world." Finnan put his hand over hers. "Are we terribly different?"

"Terribly," answered Sidonie, then laughed to show she didn't really mean it, though by that time the Irishman had frowned.

"I think my ghost was probably his girlfriend," she rattled on to cover the awkwardness.

Finnan looked sad. "The one he wanted to marry?"

"Yes, that's her. Sarah Lennox by name."

"If only things could have been different regarding that situation I think we might have been able to rewrite English history."

"Why?"

"She'd have thrown those wretched quacks out even if she'd had to do it physically. There were no flies on that little baggage. Why do you think it's Sarah? Did she live at Holland House?"

"That I haven't yet found out. Her brother was the Duke of Richmond and his seat was at Goodwood. But where she lived I don't know."

"If my recollections serve me correctly I think she may have been brought up in Ireland. There's some Irish connection about Sarah Lennox, I know."

"Then she must have been nice," said Sidonie, "because you are, Finnan."

He smiled at her. "Even though I ramble on about medicine?"

"But it fascinates me."

The doctor smiled again, this time a little quizzically. "Let's forget it. Come here and kiss me."

"Gladly," said Sidonie, getting up from her place and going to sit on his knee.

"I please you in bed, don't I?"

"You please me as a person too," she answered, but Finnan

125

was no longer listening, intent on making love to her, and the musician was left with the unmistakable feeling that though they were drawing closer their worlds remained still very much apart.

# Nine

Still clad only in his embroidered night-rail, a crimson turban on his closely shaven head where usually sat his full-bottomed white wig, Henry Fox picked up his pen with relish and made an entry in his journal.

> The Commerce of Vanity is at an end, the Puppy has been finally leashed. Lady Sarah is in an Hysteric but so be it. Yesterday, being Saturday, Lord George Lennox and his Lady, forgetting or despising all honour or regard to their sisters, take Lady Sarah out of Lady Car. Fox's house (without telling her or Lady Kildare, then with her) into the Park by appointment to meet Lord Newbattle. It was here settled he should ask his father's consent. This morning (Sunday), Lord Newbattle by his father's and mother's direction writes a letter to Lady Sarah, lamenting that this must be at an end etc. etc. etc. This hurt the lady's pride and surprised her!

"And serve the silly creature right," said Fox with satisfaction, and going to the window surveyed the day with a merry eye.

It was pouring with rain, sheets of water obscuring the park and the outbuildings, even the iron fence and Inigo Jones's portals scarcely visible through the drenching flood. But to the Paymaster the vista looked fresh and clean, there not being one thing that could possibly dampen his spirits on this most triumphant of mornings.

Almost as soon as it had been light and while the family had been sipping their chocolate, a messenger had come, wearing the Earl of Ancram's livery, and had handed in a letter addressed to Lady Sarah Lennox. Fox, alerted by his valet, had lurked nearby to glean what information he could. A cry of triumph or the sound of a sob would reveal all, and his politician's heart had rejoiced when from behind his sister-in-law's closed door had come the noise of tears.

"Odds my life, Caro!" he had crowed triumphantly. "The little cock bantam has turned her down. I'll wager m'Lord Ancram has thickened his son's ear for him. What a glorious ending to such an inglorious coil." And he had danced his wife round by the waist.

Caroline had looked grim. "It's as well it's finished. But not for want of others trying to assist the wretched liaison."

"What others? Who do you mean?"

"George and his wife were seen escorting Sarah into the park yesterday where an assignation with Newbattle had obviously been arranged. Oh, Mr Fox, such villainy! My own brother has betrayed me."

"He probably doesn't think so," her husband rejoined drily. "No doubt Lady George filled his head with romantic nonsense. What a trull that woman is. I've a mind to ban her from the house."

"Oh, please not," Caroline answered hastily. "Family rifts are so *exhausting* and I swear I haven't the strength to cope with one at present. I have drained all my reserves trying to deal with Sarah's follies."

Fox had grinned. "You're a shrew, Caro. Always getting your way. But don't expect me to be polite to 'em. Why, I'd like to freeze off George's – "

"Henry, really! You grow coarser by the day."

"You're right, I do," he had answered, and kissed her nose.

But now, with the Newbattle affair safely at an end, Fox felt ready for action. Closing his Journal and putting it in a drawer which he locked securely, Henry left his study and went upstairs to dress. As he thoughtfully put on his hose, knee breeches and shirt he considered the situation, thinking it had reached a delicate and difficult stage which might yet be brought round to the family's advantage. It was Fox's view as a man of the world that the King would undoubtedly have heard something about Sarah's flirtation with Newbattle. The Earl of Bute could be relied upon for that.

"But how will he react, that is the question?"

"Sir?" said his valet, brushing a minute speck of dust from Fox's mulberry coloured waistcoat.

"Nothing, I merely muttered, wondering to myself whether a fellow would be spurred on by having a rival in love or whether he would give up all hope."

"That depends on the man, Sir."

"Yes, so it does," answered Fox, "so it does. But what manner of creature is he beneath it all?"

"Who, Sir?"

"The King of England, that's who," Fox answered succinctly, and went downstairs to break his fast.

Sunday or no, there was to be a Drawing Room at St James's Palace and as the morning passed and the time to leave drew nearer, Fox found himself growing nervous as a cat. In the manner of all females, in his view at least, Sarah was behaving as awkwardly as possible. She had locked herself in her bedroom ever since the letter arrived, ministered to at various intervals by Caroline and Emily Kildare, but seeing no one else. George and his wife had earlier on left Holland House in a huge huff, Fox having openly challenged them with interfering, calling Lady George a senseless jade to her face. There was an atmosphere fraught with hazard hanging over the place and the servants were noticeably talking in whispers.

"You've got to get her up," Fox had said grimly to Caroline as the clock struck midday. "She's going to Court this afternoon if I have to carry her there."

"And that you may yet have to do. She is refusing to eat or drink and is in a high lather, weeping and wailing like a banshee."

"Tell her I'll lather her arse if she don't come downstairs. I won't put up with this arrant stupidity a moment longer."

And he meant it. Beneath his white wig, Mr Fox's face had gone ruby red and Caroline recognised the danger signs.

"She will be downstairs in an hour, I promise you."

"Good. And I want no long face nor puffed eyes, mind. She is to look as sweet and demure as once she used before that rapscallion jackanapes came upon the scene."

"I'll see to it," said his wife, and hurried away.

Caroline estimated, after staring moodily at the gilt clock in her bedroom, that Sarah had now been crying for four hours, and that something drastic must be done if the girl was indeed to accompany herself and Fox to Court. Composing her bony face into the sternest expression possible she sailed into her sister's bedroom like a small but serious man-of-war.

"Enough!" she said forcibly. "Sarah, enough. You are to wash and dress and prepare yourself for the Drawing Room."

"But I don't want to go. My heart is broken."

"There'll be more than that broke if you don't obey your sister's orders," bellowed Fox, suddenly looming in the doorway, the colour of his clothes and cheeks making him resemble a fruit. "Go to, Lady Sarah, before you try my patience any further."

His sister-in-law shot him the most evil glance but slowly rose from the bed on which she had flung herself face down and made for her dressing room where her maid awaited, all eyes.

"One word more," said Fox, beckoning her back. "You disobeyed me, Sarah, by continuing to consort with Newbattle when I had warned you I would not tolerate such behaviour. Let me make it quite clear that if there are any further transgressions on your behalf I shall do what I have threatened. You will be removed from London and sent to your brother, the Duke, at Goodwood."

"And quite right too," put in Caroline. "I am sick and tired of your goings on."

But though she had really meant what she said she regretted having spoken as Fox's coach began its rumbling progress towards St James's Palace. For with every passing mile Sarah's face grew longer and longer while she sat in a corner glowering and refusing to utter a word.

'One false move,' thought Henry desperately, 'one action

out of place and the family's fortunes are done for! Oh God, don't let the little wretch spoil everything.'

But the sulky expression worn by his sister-in-law as she made her curtsey to the King did nothing to reassure him. His Majesty, however, obviously noticed nothing amiss for he smiled very charmingly and said, "How nice to see you, Lady Sarah. Will you walk with me?"

The young couple immediately moved out of earshot and nothing was left for Henry Fox but to stare after them, wondering whether George knew about Newbattle and what effect it had had upon him if rumours had indeed reached him.

But across the sparkling surface of the King's Gemini mind, full of currents and eddies and strange little patches of cold, had come a childlike certainty that the object of his affections must be fought for and won. He had been dreadfully hurt by his glimpse of a rival secretly meeting Sarah Lennox, but by the same token had grown more determined to have her. Quite unbeknownst to Princess Augusta and the Earl of Bute, their little stratagem had failed. His Majesty was about to make a proposal of marriage.

"Tell me," he said, drawing Sarah into the privacy of a large window recess, "has your friend Lady Susan left for Somersetshire?"

"Yes, Sir. About two weeks ago."

"And before she went did she say anything to you?"

'Here it comes,' thought Sarah. 'He's harking back to that extraordinary conversation he had with Susan and I've no patience with all this hedging. Why the devil can't he come out with what he means?'

Out loud she said, *"Say,* Sir?"

"What I mean is did your friend tell you of my conversation with her?"

"Yes, Sir," answered Sarah, staring at the ground.

"All?"

"Yes."

"And do you approve? Tell me, for my happiness depends on it!"

She looked him in the eye, cut to the quick that he to whom

only recently she had felt so drawn, had not the courage to come out into the open like any other man.

"I thought nothing, Sir," Sarah said evenly.

George drew himself up, pale with rage that he should have been treated so badly.

"Nothing will come of nothing," he answered, quoting King Lear and feeling similarly betrayed, "Good day, Madam," and with that he strode away, not only from Sarah but out of the room.

"God's wounds," groaned Fox, observing all. "This is the end. She must go tomorrow. I'll strike that smug face of hers if she is not removed from my sight forthwith."

"But tomorrow is only two days from her birthday," answered Caroline.

"I care not a whit. Your sister has overstayed her welcome."

And with that Mr Fox went gloomily to the refreshment room in order to consume a great deal of liquor.

It was not that his wife didn't agree with him; she did. But the next morning, despite all Sarah's foolish and contrary ways, she could not help but feel sorry for her sister as she and her belongings were packed into a post chaise bound for Goodwood in Sussex. Particularly as a letter had arrived but an hour before saying that Susan was unexpectedly returning to Holland House with her parents, Lord and Lady Ilchester, Fox's brother and his wife.

"I shall miss all the fun," whispered Sarah as Caroline handed her into the carriage.

"Nonsense. Charles's house is always gay. Anyway I should think you've had enough excitement to last you the rest of the season," the older woman added coldly.

"Are you *very* cross with me?"

"Very. Now go away and behave yourself. It really is not clever to antagonise Mr Fox, you know."

Sarah sighed. "Shall I see you again soon, dear Caro?"

"No doubt. Give my love to our brother."

"I will."

And with that the chaise was off, trundling down the elm drive until it vanished from sight. An hour later Caroline, who

132

was busy organising the rooms for her brother-in-law's visit, thought she heard it return and went to the sweep of steps that led to the main entrance of Holland House to see what was afoot. But the vehicle approaching was not a carriage but a smart wagon of the type used to convey furniture from one house to another. Tied on to the wagon, draped by a protective sheet, was what looked like a harpsichord. Caroline stared in surprise at the crest denoting that the conveyance belonged to the royal household, and also at the equerry riding beside it, smart as paint in the morning sunshine, obviously carrying a letter.

"Is Lady Sarah Lennox within?" the horseman asked, giving a small bow and blushing slightly, for he was young and pompous and trying hard to act with enormous unsmiling dignity.

"She left town this morning. But I am her sister, Lady Caroline Fox. Can I be of assistance?"

"His Majesty asked me to give this letter and birthday gift directly to Lady Sarah."

"Well as that is not possible, will you entrust them to me? I shall see that she gets them as soon as she returns."

The equerry frowned and went redder. "His Majesty was very insistent . . ."

"But surely it would damage the harpsichord – that is a harpsichord is it not? – if it were sent on to Goodwood. It would be far safer to leave it here."

The young man looked relieved. "Very true, my Lady. May I ask the carters to bring the gift in?"

"Certainly."

It was set down in the music room and the protective drape reverently removed. Caroline gazed in wonder at one of the most beautiful instruments she had ever seen. Made of mahogany and walnut it was a two manual harpsichord, the name board bearing the words, Thomas Blasser, London, 1745.

'The year of her birth,' realised Caroline. 'How very thoughtful.'

There were two notes accompanying the gift, one sealed with His Majesty's personal seal, which Caroline locked away in her desk. The other was attached to the harpsichord itself and quite open for anyone to read. It simply said, "Look beneath the name board."

Thoroughly intrigued, Caroline unscrewed the board, a simple task even for her, and there underneath, inlaid in that glorious wood, were the initials S.L.

If King George had made an open declaration of his feelings he could not have said more; a great deal of care and kindness had been expended on this particular gift.

"Oh dear," Caroline murmured, "I do hope Newbattle really has finished with her. He is so utterly worthless and, no doubt, because of that, all the more attractive."

And then Sarah's elder sister knew with horrid certainty that the Fox family had not heard the last of that particular rakish fellow, that he was just of the type to rebel against his father's wishes and cause further trouble.

"Rot him!" said the normally reserved and decorous Caroline, then, having gazed once more at the harpsichord, its warm wood glowing in the midday sunshine, went to take a stroll in the gardens and think her gloomy thoughts.

The chaise made good time over the rough roads lying between the village of Kensington and that of Goodwood, tucked away in the gentle hills of the Sussex Downs. Bowling through the sunshine, Sarah stared pensively out of the window, wondering when she would see London again, yet in a way relieved that two of her immediate problems had been alleviated by going out of town. For the thought of running into John Newbattle at one of the season's many routs or balls was too terrible to contemplate after his hideous snub. And as for coming face to face with the King . . . Sarah cringed at the very idea.

'Everything is in total disarray,' she thought disconsolately and, closing her eyes, tried to blot out the visions of John Newbattle and His Majesty which constantly plagued her waking hours.

It was the sudden sound of hooves that made her open them again abruptly. Not the beat of the pulling team ahead but another four pounding down the track behind the chaise as if all the devils of hell were in full pursuit. Sarah tensed, aware that this was no ordinary traveller overtaking them on the highway, and cautiously peered out of the window, only to fling back against the padded wall gasping for breath, her heart leaping as if she had just run a mile. John, Lord Newbattle, astride a great black horse, looking incredibly romantic, was about to draw level with the equipage. With great presence of mind, Sarah rapidly composed her features into an expression of icy disdain. And only just in time, for a second or two later the dashing young nobleman drew alongside.

"Sarah," he shouted frantically to her rigid profile, "I cannot believe that your guardian has sent you from town. Oh, my darling, how could he do such a cruel thing?"

"How could you, more like?" she answered, without turning her head. "When I read your letter you may believe I was only too willing to go."

"My father threatened to cut me off without a penny if I didn't break with you. My parents stood over me while I wrote the accursed thing. But it was all lies. I love you – "

His voice trailed away as Tannes, Sarah's coachman, realising that she was being courted by a jackanapes, put on speed and shot ahead, only for John to thrash up behind them, gasping for breath.

"Sarah, I – "

This time she turned to look at him, her deep eyes wide. "Do you mean it? Do you really love me? Was your hand truly forced?"

"Yes, to all three, my own dear – "

He was gone again as Tannes, grim-lipped now, applied the whip to his team. Sarah suppressed a wild desire to giggle as John, looking thoroughly exhausted, hastened to catch her up once more.

"Do you unsay all you put in the letter?" she demanded of the flagging young man as he yet again came into her line of vision.

"I unsay it," he panted. "I unsay it."

"So you still want to marry me?"

"Be damned!" swore Tannes audibly and roared his horses ahead as if it were a chariot race.

"Yes," came Newbattle's distant voice and, leaning out of the window, Sarah saw that the pretty lordling had finally given up the chase and was doffing his hat in farewell.

"Write to me," she shouted. "I'm to my brother's at Goodwood."

He nodded and waved and Sarah sat down again, a smile of triumph on her face. So there were two men in love with her after all and both of them had made a proposal of marriage. By anyone's reckoning this was a most satisfactory state of affairs for someone still two days off her sixteenth birthday. It seemed to Sarah Lennox as the post chaise went on its way that a bright and beautiful future was undeniably opening up before her.

When the second Duke of Richmond, grandson of Charles II, died, he had left behind him a large family. Caroline had been the eldest and Cecilia the youngest, while between them lay Emily, Lady Kildare; Charles, Duke of Richmond; Lord George, Lady Louisa and Lady Sarah. The new Duke Charles – all the heirs carried that name in order to remind them of their kingly, if bastardly, descent – had been seventeen when he succeeded to the title and was at that time undoubtedly one of the wildest young rips in London. The handsome boy had not only inherited his great-grandfather's dark and gleaming looks but also his love of pleasure.

At the age of fifteen he had written to Henry Fox, one of his guardians, much beloved of the naughty youth, "I was at Vaux Hall tother night with Miss Townsend, when she began to tell me I was troublesome; but I told Her I knew it and would be so and persisted, as she calld it, teasing her the whole night especialy after I Drunk her health in six half-pint bumpers in Champagnne, beside some super numeral bumpers which made me damnably drunk, but not stupidly so." In the same letter Charles had described another visit to Vaux Hall during which ". . . after supper I diverted myself with Patty Rigby in the dark walks as well as I could wish. Very well, I think, for the second time I ever saw her. I was again last night at Ranelagh, where I could do nothing but kiss Miss Rigby in the box, as there were no dark walks there. The Devil take it for having no dark walks. For God's sake never mention Miss Rigby's name to any mortal, nott even to Lord Kildare. For one should never kiss and tell. Besides you know, if it was known, what would be the consequence. Hi! Ho! But all my jollity is over. For the day after tomorrow I march off to Goodwood for the rest of the hollyday. However I shall divert myself as well as I can."

Henry Fox had chuckled at his young brother-in-law's mischief but had to admit to a sense of relief when, in 1757, the Duke had married Lady Mary Bruce, only child of Charles, Earl of Elgin and Ailesbury. Walpole had gushed over the union, "It is the perfectest match in the world; youth, beauty, riches, alliances, and all the blood of all the Kings from Robert the Bruce to Charles II. They are the prettiest couple in England, except the father-in-law and mother!" Charles's bride had in truth been excessively beautiful and was known in the family as the Lovely. But, tragically, the Lovely had so far been unable to produce a child and rumour had it that her naughty husband had already taken a mistress.

Now, though, neither of them were thinking of themselves or the state of their marriage but rather were agog as Sarah's chaise came into view down the long drive and they prepared to receive her in the entrance hall. Correspondence between Fox and his brother-in-law had been flying and Richmond, for all his own erring ways, could cheerfully have strangled his younger sister.

"To turn down a lover is one thing," he had said to the Lovely that morning. "But to turn down a King for the sake of a Pimple is another!"

"But you are to be the soul of tact," his wife had replied.

"I shall do my utter best."

And with that not very reassuring statement the Duchess had had to be content.

Sarah, she thought, as the girl made her way into the entrance hall was looking unusually bright on all her troubles. In fact there was almost something suspicious about the way her eyes sparkled and her cheeks bloomed peonies.

"Greetings, my dear," said Richmond, his saturnine features lit by the entire situation.' "I hear you have caused a sensation this season. What larks!"

"I've been sent from town as a result," Sarah answered ruefully.

"So was I – many times!" the Duke replied, then added. "Mind you, that is something of an accolade in the case of a man."

"And why not in the case of a woman?"

"For obvious reasons. Lest she lose her good character," Richmond replied primly, then threw his arms round his sister in a great hug.

"We'll be dining soon," said the Lovely, smiling at the new arrival. "Would you like to go to your room straightaway?"

"Yes, please. I must get rid of the confusions of the journey," Sarah said significantly, though neither of the two other young people understood what she meant. "But tell me first when you will be sending back the chaise?"

"Not till tomorrow. Why?"

"I would like to pen a note to Caroline to go with it. And also one for Susan Fox-Strangeways."

"Has she returned to town?"

"Yes. She is to go to Court with her parents, I believe."

"Ah, an ambassador," said Richmond, and stroked his chin.

"He's plotting something," said his wife, laughing. "Sarah beware."

"Nonsense," retorted the Duke, though his wicked face was creasing into a grin.

And he grinned on throughout dinner served punctually at four o'clock, until in the end several glasses of good claret loosened Charles's tongue and he conveyed the source of his amusement to the two ladies.

"Damme, Sal, I cannot recover from the fact that His Majesty has taken a fancy to you. He seems such a *sensible* dull fellow I can scarcely comprehend it."

His sister looked at him with twinkling eyes. "He is dull and sensible. Far too much so for me."

"Then you're all kinds of an ass," Richmond answered

sharply, his grin vanishing abruptly. "For is it not known that the right woman can make even a dolt turn bright? You've no spirit of adventure, I fear."

She flushed. "My affections have been engaged by another."

Richmond stared at her swiftly. "Have been? I thought *were* would have been more appropriate. Did not Newbattle write to break off your association?"

Sarah looked at her plate. "Yes, he did."

"Umm," said the Duke, and thought his thoughts. Eventually he ended the silence by saying, "And how was His Majesty when you left him?"

"Angry."

"I see. I wonder is he still?"

"There's no way of knowing that."

"Why not ask Lady Susan to find out," put in the Lovely.

"A splendid notion; well done, my dear," Richmond replied, beaming at her as if he had not already thought of it himself. "When you send your letters back with the chaise be so good as to ask Lady Susan to speak with the King and gauge his mood."

"Very well, Charles," Sarah answered with just a hint of asperity. "If that would please you."

She considered that her brother, a reckless scamp if ever there was one, had grown pompous. And the fact that even he did not approve of her love affair made Sarah more determined than ever to have John Newbattle for husband, even at the cost of an elopement and a split within the family. Yet there was one great worry that she had to deal with immediately. Tannes, the coachman, was a loyal creature of both Fox and Caroline and sure as fate would be bound to tell them of her encounter on the highway. The only thing to do was to make a clean breast of the meeting to Caroline and beg her not to tell Mr Fox and instruct the coachman likewise.

In the early hours of her sixteenth birthday, 25th February 1761, Sarah Lennox rose from her bed and went to the writing desk by the window. There, sitting in the pale light, she gave Caroline an honest account of all that had taken place on the journey to Goodwood, though omitting to say that John

Newbattle had once again asked her to marry him. This done, Sarah wrote to Susan.

"I have but just time to tell you that my sister Caroline will tell you, if you ask her, what has passed between Lord Newbattle and I upon the road. Adieu, yrs, S. Lennox."

She was just about to seal the letter when Sarah remembered what the Duke had said at dinner and added a hasty postscript. "My brother begs you'll go to Court, and let me know what *he* says to you."

This done, Sarah rang for her maid and told her to give both pieces of correspondence to Tannes to take back to Kensington with him. Then she went to the window again and stood gazing out over the spring parkland wondering what her seventeenth year would bring and whether she would be a bride by the time it came to its end.

Unbidden, His Majesty's honest face flashed before her, rather than that of her pretty lover, and Sarah felt a stirring of the heart.

"I mustn't feel sorry for him," she said. "It truly is a most dangerous emotion."

But was it pity that brought a flush to her cheeks and made her whirl round the room in a merry dance?

'I wonder what he'll say to Susan,' Sarah thought, and all at once felt she could hardly wait for her friend to answer what suddenly seemed an all-important question.

# Ten

Sarah Lennox was dreaming a sad evocative dream in which she relived her secret meeting with Lord Newbattle in the grounds of Holland House. It was strange. For, unlike what had really happened, this time both the King and the unknown woman turned to look at her rather than hurrying away with their backs turned. Sarah gazed incredulously on their beautiful smiles, His Majesty's so loving and tender with much pure kindness in its depths, the woman's humorous but friendly, as if she understood Sarah's plight and would help if she knew but how.

In the dream, John Newbattle was a vague figure, almost indistinct, but the King and the woman were crystal clear. Feelings stirred again, of love and friendship, of harmony and accord, of sorrow and loss, and when Sarah woke in the dawning, in painful discomfort, she found she had wept as she slept and her cheeks were moist with the dew of her sadness.

The high and elegant ceiling at which her damp eyes gazed was not that of her bedroom at Holland House, nor indeed the one at Goodwood. Sarah was looking at her room in Redlynch House, near Bruton in Somerset, home of Mr Fox's elder brother, Lord Ilchester. The girl sighed, thinking of the events that had brought her here and how one simple fall from a horse had changed the course of her entire life.

Within a few days of her arrival at the Duke of Richmond's Sussex home who should appear there to join her but Lord and Lady George, the latter buzzing with secrets, rolling her eyes and whispering behind her fan that her brother still loved Sarah, that she was playing Dan Cupid and was there to help the thwarted couple. Lovers' meetings were arranged and Sarah and John had exchanged kisses and declared undying passion. It had all been highly romantic and the secrecy extremely exciting but, of course, they had reckoned without the arch cynic, Sarah's brother.

Having been totally untrustworthy himself and not greatly reformed by his marriage to the Lovely, Richmond had suspected his sister from the start. Rather than order a groom to follow her when she rode out on the Downs, simpering Lady George dubiously acting as chaperone, the Duke had done so himself, an escapade he had greatly enjoyed. Slipping like a shadow through the beechwood trees, he had spied Sarah locked in an embrace with a vacuous youth, pretty but also pretty stupid, as Richmond had thought at the time. The fact that Lady George remained at a studied distance from the couple proved that this ardent young man could be none other than the beastly boy, Newbattle himself. The Duke of Richmond had slipped quietly away and written a letter to Fox.

"Lady George is carrying on the love in Richmond's very house," the Paymaster had exploded to Caroline. "What's to be done?"

His wife had gone white. "I thought something like this might happen. I knew the wretched fellow had not given up. Let Sarah be sent to Susan's immediately. Goodwood is only two days' ride away but he'll think twice about journeying to Somerset to do his courting."

"You've been found out," the Duke had said laconically to his sister. "And on your guardian's instructions you are to go to Redlynch at once. How sad for you. But then, Sal, if you intend to misbehave you must make certain never to be discovered."

"Who did discover me?"

"Myself of course. By the way, Newbattle's a waster. Written all over him. The sooner you forget him and concentrate on someone else, preferably someone who wears a crown, the better it will be for all of us."

Furious with her brother, feeling betrayed and bitter, Sarah had had little choice but to accept her fate. By the middle of March she had been removed from Sussex and had taken up residence in Somersetshire.

"What did His Majesty say, by the way?" Sarah had asked as soon as she and Susan were alone in their adjoining bedrooms in the older girl's home.

"He said he hoped you liked your birthday present but I replied that you had not been home to see it. The King looked disappointed at that."

"But I wrote to thank him after Caroline told me of it, explaining that I had not yet received the gift."

"He did not refer to your letter."

"Oh."

"It was almost as if he had not seen it."

Sarah shook her head. "Did he say anything else?"

"No, nothing."

And that had been the end of a somewhat disappointing conversation. Yet, in a way, Sarah had felt happier at Redlynch than she had at Goodwood, despite the absence of her admirer. Susan's company was always good and there was so much riding to do and visits to make. Remote from London though she might be, country life was not dull, and Sarah was just beginning really to enjoy herself when disaster had struck.

Returning from a visit to Longleat, she had fallen from her horse in the town of Maiden Bradley. The accident had been simple enough, her mount treading on a cobble which had broken beneath him, causing the animal to fall. Sarah had gone tumbling down too, but as the horse had risen he had pressed his shoulder against her leg and broken it against the stones. A coach had been sent for which had taken the girl, experiencing considerable pain, to Sir Henry Hoare's house at Stourton where her leg had been set by Mr Clark, a surgeon from Bruton. The next day the invalid had been carried upon men's shoulders, in a very pretty bed made for the purpose, home to Redlynch. With pain now dulled, Sarah had sung most of the way and Mr Clark had been so impressed by her cheerfulness that he had declared she was the most agreeable and merry patient he had ever had!

And then had come the long weeks of confinement, relieved by a stream of visitors to help pass the time. By day, Sarah rested on a couch in a spacious room overlooking the woodland, by night she had the adjoining bedroom to Susan. And now in the light of dawning, the sixteen-year-old lay in her bed, the power of the dream only just fading, and thought how the fall had changed everything.

The message coming from her family, most of whom had hastened to see her, had been abundantly clear. The King had trembled when he had heard of her accident, had barely been restrained from leaving town and hurrying to her side, had wondered aloud whether she should stay in the care of a country surgeon or whether he should send Mr Hawkins of London to attend her, had actually grimaced and winced in sympathy when Henry Fox had described her initial pain. By contrast, if her brother and sisters were to be believed – and Sarah felt that they would hardly dare lie on such an important issue – Lord Newbattle had tittered when he had heard the news and said that the accident would do no great harm as Sarah's legs had been ugly enough before.

It had been such a terrible remark to make, hinting as it did that he had seen her legs, that they had been physically intimate, then adding the insult of ugliness.

"I know you hate him but I beg you, Sir, please tell me the truth," Sarah had asked Fox when they had been alone together in her day room. "Did Lord Newbattle *really* say that?"

"He did, Sal. He's back under his father's thumb and furthermore up to his old tricks, flirting with the girls. I do earnestly enjoin you to forget him. There is another who loves you far better. Take my word for it."

"You mean His Majesty?"

"I do. No man could act out the genuine concern he showed when he heard the news of your mishap, believe me."

In the faint light, hugging her pillow, Fox's words came back and with it a thought that had been plaguing Sarah for days. It would seem that the man for whom she had refused a crown had made a brutal joke of her calamity. Whereas he who had offered that crown, and whose happiness her rude refusal and stupid behaviour had for the time destroyed, was all heart, sorrow, and more attached than ever.

It was then, thinking about her dream, realising how eagerly she had awaited Susan's report of what *he* had said and how disappointed she had felt that the King's words had not been of a more personal nature, that it occurred to Sarah she had simply mistaken infatuation for love and now, for the very first time, was facing the real thing.

She hauled herself up in bed, moving awkwardly but smiling for all that. The most pleasurable sensations of a fluttering heart, the quickening of breath, a ridiculous desire to laugh joyfully, were sweeping over her.

"What a fool I've been," said Sarah Lennox aloud. "I've missed what was right under my nose. Oh hurry up leg and mend. I must get back to Court. I've got to make it up to him. Oh my poor George, I've been a regular little bitch."

But she felt confident, as she sank back against the pillows again, that she knew perfectly well how to put matters right and could imagine the kiss she and His Majesty would exchange at the very first precious moment they had alone together.

Sitting behind his desk in Holland House, the tips of his fingers together, his eyes gently closed, Henry Fox's calm exterior belied the thoughts that were most unpleasantly racing through his agile mind. Never, in his opinion had it been so vital for outside interference to be minimised, for never had the forces against him seemed to be massing so strongly.

The first thing which had given the Paymaster cause for unrest had been the elevation of the Earl of Bute, plotter extraordinary and he of almost sinister influence over the King, to the rank of Secretary of State in the place of Lord Holderness. And not only Fox had been disturbed by this. A thrill of unease had run through the entire Court at this sudden extension of the Scottish nobleman's power and, accordingly, that of Princess Augusta of Wales.

As if that had not been enough, rumours had followed. Everyone who was anyone was saying that the King's mother had selected a bride for him, that a fifteen-year-old Princess of Brunswick had been picked and would soon be coming to

England. It had been a horrifying thought and yet, when Fox in his usual cunning way, set enquiries in train there seemed to be no basis for the gossip. Yet still the Paymaster was not easy. Wedding talk seemed in the air and surely must have started somewhere.

Opening his eyes, Fox drew a piece of paper towards him and wrote the words New Battle Plan, then beneath started to make a list.

1. Go to Court tomorrow and finally ascertain whether the Rumour be true or false.
2. Write to Redlynch and discover how quickly Sarah will return.
3. See H M and speak of Sarah, judging his looks and replies.
4. Scotch the antics of Lady George for once and for ever.

Having done this, Fox closed his eyes again. For all the setbacks in the world he was still a politician and a fighter. If the house of Fox were to receive a slap in the face over the question of the royal marriage, at least it would not be for want of his trying to turn events in its favour.

Twenty-four hours later Fox felt that the Battle Plan had not been devoid of success. First of all, despite his most rigorous enquiries, there seemed to be no basis in fact, other than the uncomfortable belief that Princess Augusta was up to something, for the rumour that a German bride had been chosen for the King. Secondly, an urgent letter had been sent to Caroline, who was staying at Redlynch House in order to nurse Sarah back to health, asking for a firm date on which her sister could return to town. Yet again, in the same letter, Fox had stressed the importance of allowing neither Lord George nor his wife near the patient nor of letting Sarah out of Caroline's sight. Finally, he was due to attend a Drawing Room that very afternoon and had every intention of dragging Sarah's name into the conversation, then narrowly watching His Majesty's reaction.

Actually, as things transpired, it was the King himself who first mentioned Fox's sister-in-law, thus giving the Paymaster an ideal opportunity for setting his scheme in motion.

"Good evening, Mr Fox. I am so very glad to see you. I have been meaning to enquire after Lady Sarah. Does she continue to make progress?" was the opening gambit.

'Right, my lad,' thought the politician. 'This is where you reveal all.' Bowing, he said, "Indeed she does, Sir. In fact she will be returning to London within the next two weeks."

This was both a guess and a gamble but it paid off. The King's clear complexion grew slightly pink and his eyes literally started to shine.

"But that is wonderful news. I am looking forward so much to seeing her."

"Let it be hoped that she does not experience too much pain when she starts to walk again."

George visibly winced and the close observer suppressed a small sound of triumph. "I pray she does not. Do you know, Mr Fox, I still wonder whether I did wrong in not sending Hawkins to attend her. I feel I would only have myself to blame if she were to suffer unnecessarily."

Fox allowed himself a smile. "Be assured, Sir, that she has been well treated. Lady Caroline tells me she is in excellent health and, unbelievably, more beautiful than ever."

The King looked positively radiant. "I am delighted by that news. When did you say she was coming back?"

"Towards the end of the month, I believe."

"Splendid," said the King, and Fox, who knew exactly the moment when to stop talking, bowed as if he had been dismissed.

"There's a man in love I'll stake my life on it," he murmured to himself. Now all that was left was for Sarah to recover quickly so that the wheels could be set in motion before Bute and his royal mistress made a move that would ruin everything.

As luck would have it the patient co-operated. The young strong limb knitted together and on 22nd May, Sarah Lennox's three-month stay in the country finally came to an end. She left Redlynch House with Lady Caroline, bound for Holland House and all the adventures that lay ahead.

Henry Fox had given a great deal of thought as to exactly how and where he would relaunch his beautiful sister-in-law into Society and finally decided that the playhouse was the best possible venue for putting her on public display. Having ascertained that the King was definitely attending a performance that night, the politician saw to it that Sarah, arrayed in the most glorious new gown money could buy, was placed in a loge virtually opposite the royal box.

The King, as was customary, made his entrance only a moment or two before curtain-up and *en masse* the audience rose to its feet and stood as a mark of respect. George looked round, smiling, and then – oh triumph of triumphs! – caught sight of Sarah and practically fell into the stalls below. To say that he gazed was an understatement. His Majesty positively stared, while Sarah, a born coquette if ever there was one, looked at him from beneath lowered lashes and dropped a small curtsey in acknowledgment of his attention. It was at exactly that moment that the theatre lamps were put out and the King sat down, the rest of the audience doing likewise.

Henry Fox wondered afterwards how much of the play His Majesty could possibly have seen. From the Paymaster's vantage point it seemed to him that George's eyes were fixed on Sarah throughout the performance and she, whenever she looked up, could feel that china-blue gaze on her and flushed with delight in the semidarkness. If she had doubted at all that the King was in love with her, these thoughts were now dismissed. Separated by the audience as they were, she could still sense his adoration as if it were tangible. He had eyes for no one and nothing but her and did not care who saw it.

If she had had more than a moment to spare them a thought, Sarah Lennox would have felt sorry for the actors who bravely struggled on despite the fact that every quizzing glass and lorgnette in the place was fixed on the King and the beautiful girl in the box opposite, not on the stage. Furthermore there were constant little sounds of "Ooh" and "Aah" as someone caught His Majesty smiling at the object of his affection. It was, in every way, an extraordinary evening and Sarah, her heart lifting with each passing second, felt she could not wait for next Sunday and the weekly Drawing Room when she would have the chance of speaking to the King withdrawn from the rest of the world.

Eventually the play came to an end and everyone stood again while the King left the theatre. He bowed handsomely to his subjects who, overexcited by the evening's events, let out a hearty cheer. To Mr Fox's jubilation there was another smaller cheer when Sarah swept out.

"Well, Sal, what did I tell you?" he said as the family climbed into their coach.

But she did not answer and when he looked at her closely the Paymaster saw that she had not heard him, too wrapped in her own thoughts to reply.

"What do you reckon on Sal for royal bride?" he said to Caroline as he blew out their bedside candle.

"I don't know," she answered, her voice close in the sudden darkness. "I wonder if a girl of Sarah's temperament would make a good Queen."

"Now don't start that. What I meant was, do you think the King is in love with her?"

"Oh yes," his wife answered firmly. "Of that I have no doubt whatsoever."

Talk of His Majesty's enraptured behaviour towards the beautiful Lennox creature in a place as public as the playhouse swept town in a matter of hours. Those who had been members of the audience and witnessed the *declaration des yeux* became the envy of others who had not. Invitations to the next Drawing Room were, of a sudden, prized possessions and by the time Sunday came only the very old and the very deaf were unaware of the buzzing excitement heralding what should have been a decorous and polite occasion.

Sarah had been in a twitter all morning, suffering the tortuous designs of Monsieur Claude, who had been urgently sent for, and simultaneously being pinned into a new ensemble which Caroline's dressmaker was literally finishing upon her. The entire staff of Holland House, having heard the rumours coming from London even in far-away Kensington, were treating Lady Caroline's sister with a certain new deference as if they already had the future Queen in their midst.

"Oh, Lucy, don't," said Sarah firmly as her maid almost fell to her knees in front of her. "There is no need for that. I am still your mistress and nothing more."

"But everyone says you will be the King's wife, my Lady."

"I think we had better wait until His Majesty asks me before we get too excited."

But for all that, it was hard to keep calm, particularly in view of her weather-cock emotions which had now swung violently away from Newbattle and towards the handsome young King who so openly adored her. Wondering whether she would get any opportunity to speak to George privately, the girl left Holland House in a flurry of nervous excitement.

Almost too tense for conversation, Sarah stared pensively out of the coach window towards the Green Walk that ran alongside the fields, remembering how once in the winter landscape a gleam of red hair had shown stark against the greyness when the unknown woman had stood and watched Mr Fox's coach go by. Now, just for a second, glancing in that direction, it seemed to Sarah that a row of tall houses, their backs clearly visible, towered above Green Walk, indeed overlooked it. But closing her eyes then opening them again rapidly, Sarah saw that they had gone and knew that it had been a mere optical illusion.

There was the usual queue of coaches in the courtyard of St James's Palace and the usual line of people waiting to be presented. Sarah was taken back in memory to her first Drawing Room in December 1759, when old King George II had embarrassed her so greatly and the Prince of Wales had taken pity and come to her rescue. Two thoughts struck her; first, that so much of moment had happened in the eighteen months since she had taken up residence in Holland House, and second, now she came to recall it, that the Prince had looked at her with admiration even then. Had it been love at first sight in his case, she wondered. Perhaps, very soon now, she would know the answer to that question.

It was immediately obvious that His Majesty had not been sure whether she would come or not, for as soon as he saw her he coloured up like a boy, a fact which Sarah found most endearing, and hurried up to her, his expression eager and pleased.

"My dear Lady Sarah," he said joyfully, "how wonderful it is to have you back at Court. Are you completely recovered from your fall?"

"All but for a certain stiffness in the leg, Sir, which alas spoils my curtsey to you."

And with that she lowered her eyes and made a reverence which obviously delighted him by its somewhat childlike clumsiness.

"Allow me to help you up." And His Majesty did so, much to the pleasure of everyone in the room, who, to a man was openly staring in delighted anticipation of the tittle-tattle that lay ahead.

"And you, Sir," said Sarah boldly, as he brought her safely to her feet and remained holding her hand a moment longer than was necessary, "have you fared well in my absence?"

A slightly sad look crossed George's features. "Mainly, yes, though there is a great deal to think about always. But everything will be brighter now you have returned. You will be coming to the Birthday Ball of course?"

"I think my newly mended leg will forbid me from dancing, but I shall be present, you can rely upon it."

"Lady Sarah," whispered His Majesty surprisingly, "do you get the impression that we are being observed?"

Glancing round at the scores of pairs of eyes fixed beadily upon them, Sarah whispered back, "I do, Sir."

"Then shall we step aside where we cannot be overheard?"

And with that the King headed for a window embrasure, taking Sarah firmly by the elbow, and sat down with her on the cushioned seat. Vividly reminded of the last time they had been closeted so, Sarah longed to make up for the many hurts she had given him for, in that moment, she could not see a king at all but an earnest young man, tall and elegant, with eloquent blue eyes in whose depths was written enormous tenderness.

Taking her courage in both hands, she said, "I think I owe you an apology, Sir."

The clear eyes clouded. "What for, Lady Sarah?"

"Last time we sat in this place I was grumpy and not civil. The truth was I had fancied myself attracted to a certain person but fortunately discovered before long that I was not. I believe, Sir, that we conversed on a bad day and I humbly crave pardon for it."

"I had forgot it," answered the King.

"Had you really, Sir?"

"I had put it from my mind as not being typical of the Lady Sarah I had grown to admire."

The object of his affection lowered her lashes, wondering if a declaration of some sort was about to be made, but in that she was to be disappointed for George simply added, "If you are able to dance at all on Thursday, Lady Sarah, I beg that the first shall be with me."

She looked at him flirtatiously. "I am yours to command, Sir."

"Then I command it," he answered, and smiled.

The Drawing Room, that is to say everyone in it, seemed strangely silent as the King's favourite returned to her family and he, obviously from duty, for his eyes constantly turned in Sarah's direction, went off to greet his guests. Fox noted with glee that there was a radiance about his sister-in-law that he had never seen before and concluded, without mentioning it to Caroline who suddenly seemed strangely anxious about the whole affair, that Sarah had finally grown to like her royal admirer.

And there the Paymaster was right. As Lucy, with much effort, brushed out Monsieur Claude's creation for the night, Sarah sighed but would not speak. And as soon as she was alone reached for her Journal that she might enter in it.

Tomorrow I will practise the harpsichord that *he* gave me and for which, like a Fool, I still have not properly thanked him. Did my Letter go astray, I wonder? Is it possible that it fell into the hands of Lord Bute? How I fear that Name, for it is certain if he and his *Lady* have their way I shall be sent from Court forthwith.

Downstairs, in Fox's study, the Paymaster, more optimistically, was entering in his record of events.

The Sunday after, as soon as his eyes found her in the Drawing Room, which he did not expect, he coloured . . .

". . . and came up to her eager and in haste," read Sidonie, curled up on the sofa in the Garden Flat, smiling at the sheer exuberance, the sheer joy and love of it all, ". . . and talked much and graciously. But on Thursday, at the Birthday Ball he had no eyes but for her, and hardly talked to any body else."

"Oh, dear George," said the musician, laying down the library copy of *The Life and Letters of Lady Sarah Lennox*, "if only it could have been different for you. If only it could. With Sarah beside you who knows what might have been achieved?"

She picked up the book again and read on, smiling at the pictures Fox's account of the King's first Birthday Ball so vividly conjured in the imagination.

He had done the very best possible with his appearance, that was certain. For someone who was not vain, who considered himself a bit of a dullish fellow, King George III had made the effort of a lifetime. Clad in a midnight blue velvet topcoat and breeches, copiously embroidered with a gold and silver floral border pattern in silk, and wearing a superb waistcoat of ivory satin, his silken hose a matching shade of cream, the young man stared at himself in the mirror as his valet slipped the blue riband sparkling with diamonds over his shoulder. Tonight even he had to admit that he looked a little like his fairy-tale counterpart, a King who had stepped from a storybook ready to meet a fair Princess.

But at that word George frowned, thinking of the endless list of lumpy German females that his mother kept thrusting under his nose when all he wanted was to have Sarah for ever in his life, in his arms and in his bed. Yet how to persuade his formidable parent and her resolute friend, Lord Bute, that he wanted to marry an Englishwoman, moreover an Englishwoman of Stuart descent, the King simply did not know. In fact he dreaded the thought of such a confrontation and shied away from the very idea.

Tonight His Majesty, who normally did not care for ostentation, sparkled not only with the diamond star. For he was wearing some of his grandfather's jewelled rings and had even pinned on a glittering ruby brooch which had once belonged to Frederick, Prince of Wales, poor Prince Fritz who had died before his time.

"You are truly magnificent, Sir," commented his servant. "Every eligible lady, if I dare venture such a remark, will be smiling in your direction."

In usual circumstances the valet would never have dreamed of saying such a thing, but the Palace was alive with rumours that Lady Sarah Lennox would be present at the ball and that His Majesty might well declare himself.

"You think so?" said George, just as if he were an ordinary and highly nervous young man.

"Tonight, Sir, you are Prince Charming come to life," the servant replied, and with those comforting words the King set forth to receive his guests.

Over the last few weeks every effort had been made that this, the first Birthday Ball since His Majesty ascended the throne, should surpass everything that had gone before, the arrangements for the festivities being, in the view of the Palace staff, sublime. Two orchestras had been placed in the gallery, both hidden behind a decoration of painted clouds, while the floor had been so highly polished it resembled glass. The banquet, to be served later, beggared all description – in fact the entire scene, as Horace Walpole delightedly commented, resembled the splendour of Hārūn-ar-Rashīd and the Arabian Nights.

For this most romantic of occasions, Sarah had chosen red and white for her theme, the only splash of contrasting colour the waves of her nightshade hair, woven with fresh rosebuds, the smell of which pervaded the air. Her ballgown was of rich white satin, the petticoat beneath embroidered with red flowers, at the heart of each flower a tiny scintillating brilliant. On the elaborate sleeves and also on the edges of the gown itself were stitched tiny silken scarlet leaves. The *tout ensemble* was stunning and Walpole, watching the lady's entrance along with everyone else in the room, wrote afterwards, "Lady Sarah is the ninth statue; and you will allow, has better white and red than if she were made of pearls and rubies."

On this occasion the demure Lady Susan, who had travelled from Somerset particularly to attend, was put completely in the shade and didn't care a jot. Already she felt like a Prime Minister, a King's confidante, the person to whom he had first spoken of his passion for Sarah. Fox's niece walked into the ballroom revelling in the stares and gasps, and basking in the sunshine of her best friend's glory.

Fox and Lady Caroline had entered the room first as befitted their status but had in no way attempted to vie with the star attraction. Fox wore sober black, laced and faced with silver, while Caroline had chosen a dark dull claret which toned beautifully with her sister's outfit but in no way detracted from it. Even the most jealous onlooker, and there were several present who fell into that category, had to admit that the Fox family outshone everyone present and that Lady Sarah was undeniably the most beautiful girl in London if not, indeed, the realm.

The arrangements for the evening were such as to give the greatest comfort to everyone there. Gilt chairs for the older guests were placed about the room and for the benefit of the dancers, when resting from their exertions, an elegant bench had been put to the left of the King's *fauteuil*. It was noted at once that the place at the head of the dancers' bench and nearest to the royal chair had been reserved for Lady Sarah Lennox.

It was obvious from the start, just as soon as the formalities of the receiving line were at an end, that tonight His Majesty was going to make no pretence, that he was going to devote himself to the delights of flirting and did not give a damn who saw it. Consequently, at the very moment the music began he was at Sarah's side.

"You promised me this dance if your leg was strong enough, my Lady? Tell me, is it sufficiently recovered?"

"My leg and I are at royal command," answered Sarah cheekily, and whirled away with him in a gigue.

Eyebrows shot up, someone muttered, "Beware the Earl of Bute," Mr Fox rubbed his hands in glee, while a hundred quizzing glasses flashed as they were simultaneously raised.

The King, oblivious to all that was going on, guided his partner to the middle of the floor and said without preamble, "I have never seen you look more beautiful. You are the Queen of Hearts, Lady Sarah."

"Then, Sir, you must be the King of that suit," she answered softly.

"As long as I am that in your eyes then nothing else matters," George said recklessly, not caring who heard.

Whether as a result of her recent illness or the speed of the dance or the feelings that were passing between her and the tall young man holding her so tightly, Sarah's head started to spin.

"I speak the truth," she answered breathlessly, then decided to risk all and hang the consequences, "and always will – to you," she added.

His Majesty did not reply but merely tightened his grip on Sarah's hand, which he continued to clasp until he had seen her back to her place at the head of the bench.

"Madam, may I claim every dance?" he whispered as she sat down.

"Sir, I have been told by the surgeon to be careful. I think I should rest for some of the time."

"Then if you rest, so shall I," George answered and took his place in his *fauteuil*.

Out of breath, fanning herself, aware that she was the centre of attention, Sarah could scarcely believe what happened next. Quite deliberately and with scant regard for how heavy it was or who was looking at him, George eased the royal chair a few degrees to the left, leant over and stared straight at her without saying a word. Catching his eye, the subject of his attention blushed then lowered her gaze.

"You are most becoming," whispered the King.

Sarah strained forward to hear him and the chair moved another few degrees. There was a scarcely audible ripple of amusement which His Majesty completely ignored.

"May I fetch you some wine?" he went on. "I long to serve you."

She looked at him boldly and saw that now it was his turn

to go a little pink. "I would rather accompany you, Sir. I feel somewhat *observed*, if you know what I mean."

"Only too well," he answered, and smiled broadly, his beautiful even teeth gleaming.

But if the couple had hoped to be alone in the refreshment room they were to be disappointed. Suddenly it seemed that every guest other than those actively engaged in dancing needed a drink, and a positive concourse set forth so that the women serving tea, negus and wine were inundated with custom. Out of the corner of her eye, Sarah could see Mr Fox and Caroline determinedly following in her wake.

The King actually laughed out aloud. "I had not realised this room would be so popular or I would have arranged for two."

"I think it is you who are the attraction, Sir."

"There is only one person with whom I desire to be so and I am looking at her at this moment."

Almost too overcome to reply, Sarah simply gazed at him and there passed a beautiful few minutes while the *langage des yeux* sufficed.

"Two guineas on a royal betrothal before the end of the month," whispered the Duke of Newcastle to Lady Diana Spencer.

"To a German princess you mean?"

Newcastle frowned. "No, I meant the delectable creature from whom H M cannot take his eyes."

Lady Diana shook her head. "I hear on the best authority that the Princess of Wales has already made her choice."

"Then heaven help the King for it would appear that he, too, has made his."

"He will never overrule his mother and Bute, that much is certain."

"I hope you are wrong," answered the Duke sadly, shaking his head. "But very much fear you are not."

Yet no one who saw the loving glances currently being exchanged between the King and Lady Sarah, and that included everybody in the room, could doubt the strength of his feelings. And as he helped her to her feet again, ever solicitous of her injury, it was noticed that his arm went round her waist and remained there.

"I truly believe the most private place for conversation is in the ballroom," George murmured as they left the refreshment room.

"I feel that perhaps we should dance again, Sir. My leg is rested."

The King beamed delightedly. "That is good news. If you will excuse me a moment, Lady Sarah, I will fetch my sister."

Somewhat bewildered the girl took her seat as the King threaded his way through the ballroom to fetch Princess Augusta who returned with him some moments later looking thoroughly put out.

As Sarah stood up and curtsied it occurred to her strongly that these days the Princess more closely resembled a frog than a she-mouse, as she had once been so unkindly described. The family tendency to protuberant eyes was in Augusta's case particularly pronounced and to add to the amphibian effect, the Princess's skin was so pale as to look positively greenish. She regarded the beautiful Sarah malevolently but gave a half-hearted smile as her brother's favourite rose from her mark of respect.

"I have been telling the Princess," said the King jovially, "about the dance called Betty Blue. I would very much like her to learn it. It is a dance, Madam," he went on, looking directly at Sarah, "that you are acquainted with. I am very fond of it because it was taught me by a lady."

So this was to be the game, was it? Sarah lowered her eyes. "A lady, Sir? Now who might that have been?"

"A very pretty lady," George answered, ignoring the glowering Augusta, "that came from Ireland a twelvemonth ago last November."

Sarah frowned, looking perplexed. "You say I know this person, Sir?"

"I am talking to her now. She taught it to me at the ball on Twelfth Night."

"Indeed, Sir, you're right. I fear I did not remember it."

"That may be," the King went on, ignoring Augusta, who puffed with rage, "but I have a very good memory for whatever relates to that lady. I had got a pretty new country dance of my own for the late King's birthday if he had lived to it, and I named it, The Twenty-fifth of February."

Her birthday! Sarah blushed with pleasure and as the hidden orchestras struck up the air Betty Blue, obviously having received some royal signal, she had the honour to be led out by the King to teach his sister the steps. As soon as the Princess had mastered the basic movements the other guests who knew the dance joined in and so, once again, Sarah found herself in George's arms.

"I want you to promise me something," he whispered, leaning close to her ear.

"What is that, Sir?"

"That you keep this secret. It is vitally important." He suddenly looked so serious that Sarah felt fractionally alarmed.

"I promise, Sir. I can be close if needs be."

"Then tell no one, not your sister nor even Lady Susan, that I am only happy in your company."

"Oh surely that cannot be true. So many exciting and pleasurable things must happen to a King daily."

"None of them mean anything to me if I cannot share them with you."

"Oh hush, Sir, please. You might be overheard."

"Then I shall remain silent when I have said one more thing to you."

"Which is?"

"That I am in love with you, Lady Sarah, and have been since first I saw your lovely face."

Everything spun again; the world, the ballroom, the chandeliers, and it was only the arms of the man who loved her which kept Sarah upright.

"Have you no reply?" he whispered urgently.

She could have simpered and talked about being honoured, alarmed, surprised, anything. Instead Sarah Lennox's honest Irish upbringing stood her in good stead and she murmured, "Those were fine words spoken by a fine man to whom I pledge my heart."

The King whooped with delight and lifted Sarah off her feet, then somehow contrived to make it seem as if it were all part of the dance. How many were deceived it was difficult to say, but

159

all the younger people copied him and there were shouts of joy from all sides as the ladies were raised, laughing and blushing, high into the air.

"She coloured, and in this *pretty* way did these two lovers entertain one another and the eyes of the whole ball room for an hour," read Sidonie, who suddenly found that for no reason at all she was crying. "He stopped very remarkably as he was going, and turned and spoke again and again, as if he could not force himself from her."

Sidonie flitted back a page and read Henry Fox's personal conclusion.

> . . . the next morning all tongues observing on the particularity of his behaviour, if it can be thought particular that a young King should not be able to avoid shewing the strongest symptoms of love and of desire for the prettyest creature in the world; for if possible, she looked prettyer that night than ever. Her Ladyship, with modesty very natural to her, and yet with looks as unaffected, returned the fondness of his eyes and gallantry of his discourse as much as ever he could wish. He is in love with her, and it is no less certain she loves him; and if she now ever thinks of Newbattle it is to vex and hate herself for the foolish transaction I before related.

Sidonie Brooks closed the book and looked at the clock. It was past midnight and already Sunday morning, and Finnan O'Neill could just be heard going up the stairs to his own flat, delayed at the hospital by a Saturday night emergency and obviously tired out. How wonderful, she thought, to have lived in an age when declarations of love came before people went to bed, when elegantly phrased words gave women all the reassurance they needed, when people knew exactly where they were going and were not prey to the doubts and fears that set in when a relationship, however good, became static.

"I wonder what will happen next," she said, and spoke just then not only for herself but also for Sarah Lennox.

# Eleven

There was, thought Sidonie, waking from a long and delicious sleep, something utterly different about Sunday sounds and smells. Normally by this hour, nearly ten o'clock, the other flats would have been silent but today she could faintly hear Finnan's CD rendering *Tosca* while, even more faintly, in fact little more than an occasional chirrup noise, Jannie playing Nigel Kennedy's version of *The Four Seasons*, attacked far too fast, at least in Sidonie's opinion.

The smells were sensual; bacon, eggs, Jannie's home-made bread, terribly health-giving and wholemeal. In fact it was lovely just to lie there, listening and sniffing, thinking about the book she had read late into the night, the book which had brought the story of Sarah Lennox and George III so vividly to life because it was told in the actual words of Fox, of Lady Susan and of Sarah herself.

Sidonie had seen nothing of that other age since the day she had gone running and had in some mysterious way passed out of her own time and into another. What had perturbed her about that particular experience had been the ease with which she had done it. There had been no black spiral, no feeling of faintness, not one thing to indicate that anything unusual had happened at all. It seemed to her that it was getting easier for these psychic occurrences to take place, almost as if there was some catalyst that drew them to her.

The telephone rang and Sidonie got out of bed to answer it, half expecting it to be her mother who usually phoned on Sundays when her daughter was not on tour.

"Top of the morning," said Finnan's voice in stage Irish. "Would the Lady from the big house be partaking of a little refreshment?"

She laughed. "Unfortunately Madam has not yet had her

bath, having sat up half the night reading. However, she asks me to tell you that she will see you in about an hour's time if that is convenient."

"The Master says that will be quite in order."

"I will pass that message on, sir," Sidonie answered and hung up.

Were Irish accents the most lyrical in the world or was it just this one in particular that she found so tremendously attractive? And it was not only the accent that fascinated her. Its owner had stolen into her affections and adamantly refused to go away. All alone on that Sunday morning Sidonie took herself to task for the hundredth time for having become too involved, for having allowed herself to feel more for the Irishman than he obviously did for her.

The telephone rang again and this time it was her mother.

"You sound a bit sad," said Jane Brooks perceptively. "Is anything wrong?"

"I'm just tired, that's all. Japan was rather exhausting."

"It looks as if it might be. All those people packing into the tube."

Sidonie smiled. "I didn't get involved with them, thank goodness. Anyway, the tour was very successful. One can't imagine the Japanese liking the harpsichord, but they do."

Sidonie's mother changed the subject. "When are you coming to see us? Why don't you come down next weekend and bring that nice Irish doctor of yours?"

"He may not be free. He sometimes works."

"Isn't he rather high up for all that?"

"He goes to see his patients because he cares about them. He doesn't have to but he does."

There was a slight pause, then Sidonie's mother said, "Why are you being so defensive? You could simply have said you'd rather not ask him."

At her end of the telephone, Sidonie sighed. "It's just that I don't want him to think I'm pushy. You know what I mean, Mummy. Strange interpretations can be put on invitations to meet parents."

Jane, in Avebury, nodded her head. "You're right. Let him be. But you come, darling. We're missing you."

"I'll be down on Saturday, about ten o'clock. That's a promise."

When they had finished speaking Sidonie walked slowly into the bathroom, wishing she could have said otherwise, that she could have told her mother she would have been happy to invite Finnan to join them for the weekend. It would have been easy if she hadn't cared about his answer, if he had just been a casual friend. But the truth was she *did* care, terribly.

"Oh bugger!" said Sidonie to the soapdish. "Why did I have to go and fall for him?"

It did not reply, nor did the cat who had wandered in on the off-chance it might be feeding time.

"Blast and damn," Sidonie went on, throwing her flannel about. "Of all the flats in all the houses in all the world, why did I have to walk into his?"

But then if she hadn't, she thought, if she had gone to one of the other places she had looked at when her grandmother's legacy had meant she could move to somewhere bigger and better, she would never have seen Holland House and become involved in its mystery.

Finnan looked well despite his late night, and it was as much as Sidonie could do not to hug him, saying how pleased she was to see him. But he saved her the trouble, swinging her off her feet as he gave her a smacking kiss of greeting.

"Well, how's yourself? And how was life amongst the Samurai? Did you have fun?"

"It was very hectic but they're very appreciative."

"You didn't get abducted by one of those big wrestlers?"

"I did actually but I wasn't going to tell you."

Finnan grinned. "I'm green with envy. I've always wanted to throw salt around and devote my life to putting on weight."

"They say the biggest one weighs over fifty stone. He's known as the Incredible Bulk."

"I believe you could be making this up," answered the Irishman, "so let me turn your mind to more serious matters. May I escort you to lunch somewhere and what would you like to drink?"

"Yes, please to the first and dry white wine to the second."

"Talking of weight," said Finnan, "you've lost some."

"Good. Last time I put it on I went jogging and ran into George III."

He paused, corkscrew in hand. "You've seen nothing strange since?"

"No, but I haven't been around much. Finnan, you *do* believe me, don't you? You don't think I suffer from hallucinations?"

For the first time that morning the doctor looked serious. "Do you remember the case of those two old girls at Versailles?"

"Miss Moberly and Miss Jourdain?"

"That's them. Well, I read a book that convinced me they were a couple of frauds, that they were always seeing things and that this particular incident was something so ordinary they did not even discuss it for several days after the event occurred."

"I thought what they witnessed was a dress rehearsal for a pageant in eighteenth-century costume."

"Yes, there's that theory too."

"But Finnan, where does that leave me? Do you think I'm like one of those gaga old ladies?"

"No, that's just the point. I don't. There have been other cases, well documented and well researched, which *do* prove that what you have experienced is possible. What about the crossword and D-Day business?"

"What do you mean?" asked Sidonie, shaking her head. "I don't know that story."

"Well, D-Day was planned with absolute maximum security and yet in the months leading up to 6th June, 1944, the words Overload, Utah and Omaha, which were the codenames of the actual invasion and two of the landing beaches, appeared in the *Daily Telegraph* along with several other relevant words. Everyone thought there had been a major secrets leak, but when they raided the paper's offices all they found was an erudite schoolmaster who had been creating the crossword for the past twenty years. He had never heard of D-Day."

"Good God, what a weird tale. He must have been glimpsing the future."

"And you the past. According to J.B. Priestley isn't it all one and the same?"

"You are very comforting, Doctor. You make me feel psychic and special."

"You *are* psychic and special, particularly if you're seeing dear old George. What a bad press the poor soul had."

"You think it was all the fault of the quack doctors?"

"The Willises? Well, not *all* but most of it."

"I've been reading about his love for Sarah. Oh Finnan, it's so evocatively put. I just adore Mr Fox."

"An old crook but an endearing one."

"Was he? I must find out more."

"Shall we walk before lunch?" asked Finnan, getting organised.

"Yes, let's. I'll go and get a jacket."

It was the last day of April, still showery, furry little clouds whizzing across a rather watery sun. The pavements were damp and inclined to be slippery and despite the fact that it was Sunday, Kensington High Street smelt of petrol fumes as traffic roared past on its way into central London.

"Why aren't we going to the park?" asked Finnan, surprised that Sidonie had led him straight towards the shops.

"There's rather a gorgeous evening dress in one of the windows. I thought it might do for my next concert. I'm going to attempt standing on my head to see the price ticket."

Finnan laughed. "I've heard that sort of thing before. It'll be me doing handstands, I can feel it in my bones."

And with those words he took Sidonie's hand in his and she was suddenly light-headed with happiness.

'I want commitment,' she thought wildly. 'I want to be with this man. Sleeping with him simply isn't enough.'

And there lay the crux of what could possibly endanger their future relationship, her desire to become more deeply involved, his to go along exactly as they were.

'Hell!' thought Sidonie, and concentrated on looking at the dress.

It was beautiful, a mermaid's garment, slimly cut to the knees where it ruched out into frills. A mysterious shade of sea-green, it was complemented by beading that looked iridescent.

"Glory be!" exclaimed Finnan Irishly. "But you'd look stunning in that."

Sidonie put the palms of her hands flat against the glass and peered closely, trying to see the price label which had got folded back and was barely visible. Behind her she could hear Finnan coughing as a particularly noxious car went past, and then the texture of the glass changed, there was an overwhelming smell of new-mown hay, and the doctor was silent. Sidonie's eyes jerked shut involuntarily then blinked open, her gaze fixed and immobile. She was staring at grass seeds while beneath her hands the feel of them pricked her palms.

"Oh God!" she exclaimed aloud and slowly, indeed fearfully looked about her.

She was in a place of rare beauty and as she inhaled in surprise could taste fresh clean air in her mouth. To calm herself, Sidonie breathed deeply and the smell was heady as wine. She stood by a wide track, large enough for two coaches to pass one another, albeit in close proximity. To her left stretched fields in which people were making hay and it was on one of these small ricks that she had been leaning. In one of the further fields stood a large haystack, while a smaller version was visible in the neighbouring. On the right-hand side of the track were the parklands of Holland House, the Home Farm buildings nearby, behind them a cultivated flower and vegetable garden which backed onto the track. Elated with wonderment, Sidonie stared closely at the haymakers.

Clearly visible amongst them, her black hair tumbling in curls from beneath the brim of a gypsy hat on which the flirt had pinned some real cherries, was Sarah. She was dressed as a country girl in a plain black skirt, a white blouse, over which was a red bodice laced with black ribbons, the top loop left casually undone to reveal a glimpse of rounded bosom, completing the ensemble.

'A beautiful figure as well,' thought Sidonie, and wondered whether the outfit belonged to Sarah or whether she had borrowed it especially.

That the King would soon come along Sidonie had no doubt

as it occurred to her she must be standing in the Great Road, which centuries later had become Kensington High Street, and that it was surely here the King had taken his daily exercise when resident in Kensington Palace. It was obvious that the beautiful creature in the hayfield expected him too, for she frequently looked over her shoulder towards the track then away again with a certain air of sadness.

A coach went past, then the post-boy, two sacks of mail tied to his saddle, a third strung across his back. He was going very quickly and had obviously read his instructions, "This Mail must be conveyed at the Rate of Six Miles in the Hour at least . . . And if any Post-Boy or Rider conveying this Mail is found loitering on the Road, he will be committed to the House of Correction, and confined to hard Labour for one month."

After a pause a shepherd appeared, blocking the way with his scurrying flock, and then a single horseman. Sidonie knew at one glance that the miracle had happened again, that she was in the presence of King George III of Great Britain and Ireland. Overwhelmed, she did not even try to hide herself, but stood and stared as he drew level with her, giving her one quick glance. Then His Majesty dismounted, holding the reins of his horse loosely in his hand.

"Lady Sarah," he called out in a quiet voice which none the less carried to the fields. "I'm here."

Sidonie saw the girl turn and hurry towards him, smiling and lively, unable to conceal her genuine delight in seeing him.

"Oh Sir, I am so *very* pleased," Sarah said breathlessly, and dropped a curtsey before the King, then grew very pink as he raised her fingers to his lips.

Nothing could have given her greater pleasure than to see him. The day before, delayed no doubt by matters of state, he had not come, and Sarah had waited forlornly until dusk before making her way home. She had worked in the fields since the beginning of the week, prompted by Mr Fox, who had gone to the Isle of Thanet, ostensibly for a week's bathing and rest, in reality to remove himself from the political arena at such a fraught time. At the Drawing Room three days after the Birthday Ball, the King had looked out of sorts and melancholy and, though he had talked most civilly to Sarah, there had been no exchange of fondnesses. Caroline had at once jumped to the correct conclusion. It was obvious that the Princess of Wales had been regaled with all that had taken place and was finally making her move.

"The King's been tutored," she had said to Fox, and his niece, Lady Susan, had agreed.

So the wily one had left London, reminding his sister-in-law of the King's daily riding habits and advising her to work in the fields alongside the haymakers. The plan had succeeded. On Tuesday the King had passed by, seen the object of his adoration, and stopped to speak.

"I will come back, tomorrow or the next day," he had promised as they parted.

"Come at midday, Sir. It is jolly then. The workers drink cider and eat cheese, and on Monday a fiddler played. It was fun," Sarah had answered, and seen his handsome honest face flush with pleasure.

"I will, I promise it."

And now he had kept his word. It was Wednesday, it was noon, and her royal lover stood beside her.

"I am so very glad," Sarah repeated.

"Not nearly as glad as I, my dear Lady."

And with that the King wove his fingers through hers, the most intimate thing he had ever done and, leading his horse behind him, walked with her into the fields.

It was idyllic, English pastoral beauty at its best. The June sun, splendidly hot, beat down on the golden hay which seemed to reflect in a sky so deeply blue that it was almost mauve. A heat haze lay over the park where the cattle swished their tails to keep off the flies and the sheep stood motionless in the shade of the trees.

"And is this my country?" said the King softly, gazing round.

"It is yours and more. And will you love it?"

"I shall – if they will let me."

They were speaking in whispers, the things they were saying too deep for normal tones, when the high bright sound of the fiddle broke across the lovers' reverie.

"It's time for the break," said Sarah. "Will you sit with us?"

The King smiled with pure pleasure and took from his saddlebag an apple and some cheese. "I have come prepared," he answered.

In all the after years, in every memory she had of him, that one above all others moved Sarah to tears. The young King's patent joy in the simplicity of pastoral life, and the pathetic fact that he had brought his own small bits of food for the noontime break.

The sound of the fiddle was unbelievable; a folk melody of such intricacy, such beauty, that Sidonie stood up behind the hayrick and listened wide-eyed. She felt that she had gone back to the age of gold, that she was hearing sounds, seeing sights that none before had ever been privileged to see.

A King sat leaning against the great haystack, his coat off, his horse tethered, his beautiful sweetheart dressed like a gypsy at his side. They were both so young, so vulnerable, that her heart lurched for them, and Sidonie felt a great surge of frustration that she could do nothing to help them, that she could only observe, knowing that what was to come must come and there was nothing she could do to stop it.

The music soared on, the old fiddler standing with his back to her, creating a melody so rare and sweet that the musician knew she would never forget so lovely a tune.

"How I love that sound," said George. "What is it?"

"A gypsy song, I think, Sir. I believe the old man is one of their race."

"He plays well. I wish he were at Court."

"He would never give up his life beneath the stars."

The King smiled fondly. "How beautiful you are and how beautifully you say things."

She smiled up at him in the demanding sunshine, not one drop of shadow to hide what she thought, and George knew then that she had grown to love him, that if he took her for his wife he need never be alone again. He leant forward and gave her that kiss which is a vow, the very first kiss and the finest of them all.

"I love you," he said.

"And I you," she answered, and putting her arms round his neck Sarah drew him to her heart.

It was over, all the despair and struggle. All that was past lay behind them, all that was to come ahead.

"We have enemies, my dearest," said George quietly. "My mother and Lord Bute wish me to marry a German princess."

"They berated you for your behaviour at the Birthday Ball, did they not?"

"How did you guess?"

"Because you were so restrained at the Drawing Room."

"I wanted to hide what I felt. I wanted no one to hurt us."

The King took great pleasure in saying *us* and watching Sarah's face as he did so.

"Nobody ever can if we are resolved, for you are King."

"Kiss me again or I shall die for lack of you."

And he felt such pain and passion in his chest that he really meant it.

"Can you stay this afternoon?"

"I shall stay with you come what may. Let them look for me. Just for once duty can go hang."

This speech was so untypical of him that Sarah could scarcely believe her ears.

"Then, Sir, do you truly love me?"

"I always will," answered George, and did not lie.

She saw them wander off from where she lay hidden and prayed, as if she were really there, a participant in those times, that all might go well for them, yet knowing, even as she did so, that there were too many forces stacked against them, that the King's very upbringing by a long-nosed and fearful mother would make himself the enemy he should most fear.

And then came faintness, harsh and sick, and the substance beneath Sidonie's hands turned from straw to glass. She let out a cry as everything began to dissolve and fade.

"What was that?" said George, pulling himself away from the splendour which was Sarah. "Who cried out?"

She looked round startled, for she too had heard something. "I don't know. It seemed to come from the Great Road."

"Should I go and see?" asked the King, half indoctrinated to run errands ordered by women, half wanting to please and impress his dark-haired darling.

"Let us both go."

They were in a mild state of disarray but were far from love's consummation. The King had undone Sarah's blouse and, for the first time in his life, kissed a naked breast.

"No, wait a moment more," said George, reluctant to leave such warmth and comfort as lay within the confines of the great haystack.

But the gypsy fiddler had gone to look, also hearing a sound and aware as only a Romany could be that something strange was afoot. Impassively he watched as Sidonie vanished from his sight, knowing that he was seeing a ghost but not afraid of this. In his own tongue he made a prayer for the dead and then by some extraordinary instinct that he did not understand, added a prayer for children, babies and those who as yet remained unborn.

"It's all right," said Sarah, looking across to the Great Road. "The old man has sorted it out."

"Has he?" said His Majesty absently and delighted once more in the sensation of running his lips over warm flesh that somehow seemed to grow ever softer beneath his touch.

This time – in a way reassuringly – the coming-to, the reawakening, was hideous. Sidonie found herself, at lunch time on a Sunday, slumped in a shop doorway in Kensington High Street as if she were a derelict, a vagrant, a tragic inhabitant of Cardboard City. As she made to stand up nausea gripped her and she had to cling to the window for support. And it was then that she saw Finnan, running like a man demented, peering into doorways, pale and desperate about the eyes.

"I'm here," she called. "Finnan, I'm here."

At once he was at her side, his arm about her, and was helping her as they walked back home, both too frightened to say much, extremely glad to be reunited, taking the shaky steps towards Phillimore Gardens. It was not until they were in his flat, a stiff drink in hand, that they finally spoke properly, looking each other in the face for the first time.

"It happened," said Sidonie, "a trip back. I saw them both,

Sarah and George. The whole thing was beautiful in its way, though I wish I hadn't frightened you."

"I'll admit that not since I was caught in a bomb explosion in Belfast have I been so bloody scared."

"Why?"

"Because you disappeared. I turned away to cough – ever the perfect gentleman – " he added wryly, "and when I turned round again you had vanished into thin air. I never believed I'd see the like of it. I thought at first that you were at another shop so I started to follow you. And then, hardened old cynic that I am, I guessed that you'd gone – "

"Walkabout?"

"Yes."

Sidonie swallowed her drink. "It frightened me, Finnan. I felt so nauseated, both going and returning. And yet what I saw was so immense, so captivating. I even heard a folk tune from a century long dead."

"I don't know whether to envy you or just be thankful that it doesn't happen to me."

"They were very much in love," Sidonie went on, hardly paying attention to him. "More than the history books realise. I think they tend to discount how genuine their feelings were because of what happened afterwards."

"You're talking about the King and Sarah Lennox."

"Yes. Oh Finnan, I wonder why it is she haunts me like this."

"Perhaps because you play the music of her century and are more in sympathy with the past than most." He looked at her closely. "You're still shaking. Come and lie down."

And he led her into his bedroom and, in what she could only think of as a professional way, undressed her to her underwear and put her to bed. It was tremendously comforting to be looked after like a child, to be cossetted and cared for, and when he brought her lunch in on a tray, Sidonie fell more in love with him than ever.

"It's worth the shock if I'm going to be treated like this every time."

"Well, I can't promise that but if I'm around you can rely on it."

She felt instantly sad, realising that he was finding a nice way to tell her he would soon be off on his research project, that she mustn't count on his being there for much longer.

However, she hid her feelings and said lightly, "I'll remember that."

He looked thoughtful. "If this was the last experience of a time slip you were ever to have would you be glad or sorry?"

"I think sorry though I can see that it could well become menacing. But that music, oh Finnan, that music. Here, lend me a dressing gown and I'll go downstairs and try to play it for you. In fact I want to write it down before I forget."

Clad in bright striped towelling, Sidonie sat at her little spinet and picked out the fiddler's tune, then added chords and played it through.

"Can you imagine this ringing out on a summer's day, the haymakers eating their lunch, the King and Sarah making love in the haystack . . ."

"Literally?"

"I couldn't see them. There are limits you know, even for a time traveller."

The Irishman laughed uproariously. "You are the quaintest creature that ever stepped out of a storybook. I have never met anyone like you, Sidonie Brooks."

"I should hope not indeed. I wouldn't like to think all your women friends are harpsichord players with a penchant for stepping out of this century and disappearing into the eighteenth."

"Come to bed," he said.

They seemed to flow, become part of one another the moment their bodies touched. Sidonie thought that her bones were melting as her breasts lifted against Finnan's chest and their thighs moved longingly together. Against her flesh, over which flew flame, or so it felt, she could feel the hardness of him, hardness within, the hardness without, every particle aching with sensation. She never wanted this divine carnality to end, for now, physically joined to him, Sidonie felt safe in her love, felt that even if he went away, Finnan O'Neill must return to her, so strong were the bonds between them.

The stroking of his hands grew reckless, his kisses consumed her lips. Sidonie believed that she would scream if the relentless beautiful throbbing did not end soon. And then it was over, an explosion of stars, each to the other, and they lay quietly, not thinking, barely breathing in a silence so intense Sidonie longed to whisper, "I shall love you always."

They parted at sunset, slowly and reluctantly, feeling that they should have stayed together all night, yet knowing that other people, other commitments, would not allow them this joy.

The King was shy yet deliriously happy. At the age of twenty-three he had done for the first time in his life what the naughty boys of town achieved many years earlier. In the great haystack, hidden from the world and from the haymakers who had moved tactfully away, he and Sarah had lain naked beneath the sun, and instinct, inexorable undeniable instinct, had had its way. Kissing and touching had turned to something more and George had found, to his intense delight, that he had known what to do. The fact that he was as passionate, as sensual, as his forebears had been denied to him by his mother and Bute, but in truth George was stirred by beauty and now to have it lying in his arms, joined to him by part of his body, was the most rapturous sensation he had ever experienced.

In its way it was an innocent seduction out there in that sylvan scene, but Sarah, other than for the fact she felt on fire with love, found the carnal act painful and wished that it would soon be over so that her loss of innocence could be forgotten and she could begin to enjoy what the *beau monde* so obviously delighted in. But as the evening shadows fell she and her lover parted and she was left to walk back to Holland House, feeling wicked and worldly now that he had gone, wondering what would happen next. Even in the height of ecstasy the King had not made a proposal of marriage and this gave her certain cause for alarm.

There was something else providing food for thought as well. As George had mounted his horse he had said, "Who was that woman who stood and watched me arrive? Is she one of your servants?"

"Who do you mean? What did she look like?" Sarah had answered, but already there had been a sinking of her heart.

"She was very distinctive. She wore strange clothes, like a boy's, and her hair was flame red. Furthermore, she stared quite rudely and gave me no salute."

"Have you ever seen her before?"

Her lover flushed. "I may have done. Why?"

"Was it the day you spied me with that ape Newbattle? Oh dear sweet, how you must have hated me for that."

"I could never hate you," His Majesty had protested hotly. "It made me all the more determined to see my rival off."

"I love you," they had chorused together, and the King had leant down in the saddle and kissed his sweetheart once more.

"Yes it was that day," he said some five minutes later.

"Then if you do not know her, neither do I. Oh, Sir, I do believe she is of supernatural origin."

"We must ask the gypsy," George had answered wisely. "For I am certain he saw her too."

"I will do so tomorrow. Oh, my darling, will you join me?"

"Yes," said George determinedly. "Even if my dear friend Bute should beg me not to I will come to you."

"But surely it would be better to keep our meeting secret?"

"In this instance, yes. But I shall have to inform him soon." George's face had clouded.

"Don't think about it now. We will deal with that problem when it arises."

And with that they had kissed and gone their separate ways. And now Sarah sat before the harpsichord he had given her, feeling that in a way she touched the King when she played it, and picked out the air that the old fiddler had played that day.

"What a lovely melody," said Lady Susan, coming into the music room. "What is it?"

"A tune the gypsy played when the haymakers stopped at noon."

"It's a love song, I think. Tell me, did *he* come?"

Sarah shook her head. "I really ought not to say, for things are getting towards matters of state. But it is so hard to lie to you, dear Suke. Yes, he did come and yes, he does love me."

Susan went very pink. "Has he asked you to marry him?"

"No, not yet."

"But he will?"

"I think so, in fact I'm sure of it. Oh Susan, everything is in turmoil."

"Get some sleep," said her friend soothingly. "Perhaps he will propose tomorrow so you will want to look your best."

"Yes, indeed." Sarah rose from the harpsichord and went to stand beside Susan. "Good night, my dear. I'll see you in the morning." And with that she left the room.

"Good night, darling. I'll see you tomorrow."

And with that Finnan quietly left Sidonie's flat and went back to his own to spend the rest of the night. She lay in the moonlight and wondered if she would ever sleep again, her mind so full of images and thoughts of the past and the present, of love fulfilled and love unrequited. Then, almost as if she were in a trance, Sidonie got out of bed and without putting the lights on went down in the silver radiance to the garden room.

The harpsichord looked almost ghostly, standing partly in shadow, partly lit by the rays coming through the garden door. Crossing over to it, Sidonie lifted the lid and from beneath her fingers stole out the sound of the gypsy fiddler's tune. She saw again, as she played, the pastoral lovers, the Daphnis and Chloe who had been King of Great Britain and Ireland and the sister of the Duke of Richmond. And she smiled a little wistfully in the moonshine at the thought that nothing ever changes.

# Twelve

He had done as he had promised. As the sun reached the meridian point the King had come at the canter, dressed sportingly, his wig short and tied back in a bow. The fiddler had scraped a few brave notes of welcome and Sarah had run through the fields to meet him while the other haymakers toiled on discreetly.

"So you were not stopped from coming, Sir," she said breathlessly as he kissed her hand.

George frowned. "The Princess of Wales wished to talk to me but I put her off until this evening."

"Was she annoyed by that?"

"Somewhat. But I said my head ached and I needed to clear it by riding forth."

"Does she suspect that you are meeting me?"

"I don't care," said the young King rashly. "Nothing matters if we are together."

They ate their midday repast sitting at some distance from the others. This day the King had brought a cake which he broke in half and shared with Sarah, a fact that moved her to tears. And then came an afternoon of love, sheltered from prying eyes by the great rick which stood, warm as a bed, beneath the midday sun.

At last Sarah knew the pleasure of passion, enjoying the sensations of naked limb upon naked limb, and this time the desires of such a sensual man as George had been even more aroused. She had felt his caresses grow wild, his body strong, his shyness vanish, and then had been born in her a sensation she did not even know existed. It was like a firework leaping towards heaven before bursting into a million coloured stars. Here, then, was true fulfilment for it seemed that George had experienced this wonderful thing at the same moment as she.

Sarah wept with ecstasy and surprise as the King mingled his joyful dew with hers.

"We must never part," he whispered over and over again.

"No never," she answered. "Oh, Sir, did you know such delight as I did?"

"Yes, oh yes. Sarah, make me be resolute, I beg you. Make me fear no one."

"Why should you? You are the King."

"But Kings are prey to more pressures than most other men."

"If you want me I promise we shall stay together always."

"I want you more than anything else in the world," answered His Majesty and kissed Sarah so ardently that she ceased to wonder whether or not she had just received a proposal of marriage.

"So," said Fox, unbuttoning his emerald satin waistcoat, removing his wig and letting out a sigh of pure satisfaction, "the stratagem worked. He rode past the hayfields and spoke to her."

"That is what Sarah said, yes," replied Caroline, who was growing distinctly uneasy about the entire situation.

"Good. And how many times did he do this, do you know?"

"Three I believe."

"And did he stay long?"

"Really Mr Fox!" his wife exploded. "All I was told was that His Majesty rode past the hayfields and on each occasion stopped for a chat with Sarah. That is the sum total of what I know and if you want my opinion it means absolutely nothing at all."

Fox put the tips of his fingers together and said, more to himself than anyone, "So there has been no proposal I take it."

"No, nor do I think there is likely to be. Everyone says that a German princess has been settled on and will soon be sent for." Caroline's bony features looked bleak. "And what price my poor sister then?"

Fox stroked his chin thoughtfully. "A princess may indeed

have been suggested, Caro, but it does not follow that His Majesty has to take her. He has the power to do what he likes."

"And stand up to Bute? I doubt he could summon the nerve."

"That depends on how much he has fallen in love with Sarah. And I see there's nothing for it. I shall have to ask her that question myself."

"You are not to browbeat her, Henry. My sister has enough to contend with at the moment."

Fox looked askance. "Would I do such a thing? Browbeat indeed!" And with that he plunged his nose into a book and refused to converse further.

His plan to interrogate Sarah was thwarted, however, by an urgent summons to London, for which the Paymaster left hurriedly next morning, having first firmly requested his wife to speak to the younger woman in confidence.

"Regarding what?"

"Regarding whether or not she expects an offer of marriage." Seeing Caroline's truculent face, Fox added hastily, "It is essential we know everything if we are to help her."

The elder sister had found the younger sitting on the stone seat in the middle of The Wilderness, idly turning the pages of a book on which she did not appear to be concentrating. Without saying a word, Caroline went to sit beside her, taking her hand.

Sarah had never felt so ashamed. For the first time in her life she was concealing the truth from her sister and was in torment as a result.

"Dearest, I would like to talk to you," came Caroline's opening gambit.

Despite her guilt, Sarah turned an open face towards her and said innocently, "About His Majesty, I suppose."

"Yes. You have probably guessed that I have reservations about the whole affair and it is Mr Fox who has enjoined me to ask you certain things."

Sarah blushed deeply and Caroline wondered why. "What things? And why do you have doubts?"

"My doubts are as to whether you would enjoy being a

queen, whether you are cut out for such a life. Mr Fox's queries are more specific. He wants to know if the King has asked you to marry him."

Sarah's mind went back to the passionate episodes in the haystack and she dropped her gaze.

"Not really, no. He said he always wanted me to be with him but that is all."

Caroline looked serious. "That is a commitment of a kind. Oh, my darling, would you really want such great responsibility?"

Her sister turned on her a glowing face. "Yes, if it meant being his wife. You see, I love him. His Majesty is gentle and sweet and all the things I admire in a man. I would take on the world if I could marry him, though I beg you to keep that to yourself." Looking away she said quietly, "Never tell how deeply I care for him in case the situation goes wrong."

"Why do you say that? Do you think it might?"

"I pray not, though I fear the power of His Majesty's mother."

"As do I," answered Caroline softly, squeezing Sarah's hand. "She has no love for the Foxes."

"I hope she doesn't hurt him because of it," her sister replied.

The storm had broken round his young, good-natured head when he returned to Kensington Palace, still warm from the touch of Sarah's body, his mouth bruised from the ardour of her kisses. He was deeply in love and the fact that he had expressed this physically only added to the depth of his feelings. For the King was a loyal, faithful soul, despite his innate sensuality, and in his mind had now committed himself irrevocably to Lady Sarah Lennox. Thus, thinking of her and smiling at the memory of all they had experienced together, George III walked into his apartments in Kensington Palace to find his mother and the Earl of Bute lying in wait for him.

"Where have you been?" said the Princess Augusta of Wales without preamble, as if her son were a nothing, a stupid child that nobody trusted.

"Out riding," replied the King, terrified but determined not to show it. "I told you I had a headache so I remained away till it had cleared."

The Princess gave a snort of contempt. "Six hours! God 'a' mercy, do you expect me to believe that? You have been with that Lennox girl and don't dare deny it!"

George did not answer, staring at his boots, and the Earl of Bute put in smoothly, "Sir, Madam is thinking only of the good of the realm. When you told me of your feelings for Lady Sarah some eighteen months ago I warned you then that the future Queen must be above politics. And, if you recall, you promised me on your honour that you would give up all idea of her for the sake of the nation."

The King stared at him obstinately. "Lady Sarah is not interested in politics."

"But her brother-in-law *is*," interrupted the Princess. "If you allied yourself with the house of Fox God alone knows what trouble there would be. Anyway, further discussion of the matter is pointless. Your future bride had been sent for. All we need is your consent."

Bute thought to himself that his mistress had gone too far this time, for the King lost all colour and stared at them stricken.

"What?" he gasped.

"I have sent for Princess Charlotte of Mecklenburg. You looked at her portrait, you said she was not unpleasing, so she has been chosen. And there's an end to it," Augusta added triumphantly.

"By Christ, it's not the end. It's not, it's not!" George shouted at her wildly, and threw his riding crop across the room so hard that it hit the wall behind his mother's head.

"How dare you!" screamed the Princess furiously, leaping to her feet.

"And how dare you!" her mild, obedient, dull son thundered back, and kicking over a chair that lay in his path stamped from the room, crashing the door behind him.

Augusta burst into loud and violent tears. "Mein Gott, he has gone mad. Bute, do something! The wretch is deranged I tell you."

Her German accent, always noticeable, now became

extremely pronounced and her long thin nose went the colour of a beetroot.

Bute looked lofty, a habit that many found heartily sickening. "Calm yourself, Madam," he said soothingly. "I shall go to him shortly when he has quietened a little. I shall point out to him that duty comes before all . . ." This was said with a roll of his fine eyes heavenwards. ". . . and he will soon see the error of his ways."

"I'm not so sure," Augusta answered, blowing her nose with a trumpeting blast. "The minx has obviously got some hold over him. Himmel, if she has taken away my boy's virginity – "

"Now, now, dear lady, do not distress yourself. All will be well, I assure you."

Red-eyed, she peered at him. "Do you promise me this?"

"I do."

But as the Earl marched purposefully towards the King's bedroom, his face was set in a frown. He had never seen his puppet, his infatuated pupil who adored his tutor above all others, in such a mood of furious determination. His creature seemed ready to slip from the iron fist.

'Pox on the girl,' thought the Earl as, with only the most token of knocks, he strode into the royal bedchamber.

The King lay face down, fully dressed, and he was weeping, though whether with rage, wretchedness or a combination of the two, Bute was not certain. Yet whatever the cause, the King was ashamed of his tears and wiped his eyes with his sleeve before glancing up.

"Sir," said the Earl, combining a look of concern with one of asperity, "what can I do to help you?"

"Let me marry Sarah Lennox," replied George surprisingly.

It was a classic case of a compliant child, always good, always dutiful, finally rebelling against its parent. But Bute stood his ground, knowing that his years of influence could not vanish quite so quickly, that all he must do was weather the storm.

"Indeed I am sure that would bring you much personal joy, Sir," he answered, and saw the King look at him, not expecting this tack.

"But that is not the lot of Majesty," Bute continued intoning grandly. "As you once wrote, Sir, you were born for the happiness or misery of a great nation and consequently must often act contrary to your passions. Now, alas, the truth of this remark has finally come home."

"But why?" said George, sitting up. "Why should marriage to the woman I love be disastrous for the nation? I've told you before, dear friend, a British woman would be a popular queen. I am the first truly English King. Born in London and proud of it. The days of German Queens of England should be at an end . . ."

"Only a foreign princess is of sufficiently high rank," the Earl persisted. "And only a foreign princess is above British politics. Sir, I put it to you, if you married a Fox your government would be in total disarray."

"But I love her," said George, suddenly pathetic. "I cannot face the future without her. She is my destiny."

"Your destiny is to rule wisely, Sir. You will never do that with the Fox clan pulling the strings."

"Nobody pulls my strings," the King retorted furiously. "Nobody, do you hear? Good night to you, Lord Bute." And he turned his back.

The Earl quite literally rocked on his feet, stunned that his compliant pupil seemed ready to break free of his fetters at last.

"Good night, Sir. I shall attend you in the morning to discuss what should be done about the Princess Charlotte," he answered stiffly. And with that Bute bowed and withdrew, much alarmed by the turn of events.

Since childhood it had always seemed to Sidonie that the standing stones of Avebury held a magic all their own, that they were warm to the touch whatever the climatic conditions around them. And today, sitting in the hot May sunshine, sheep grazing round her, her back against one of the stones of the inner south circle, she could feel a unique sense of wellbeing only to be found in her home village. Next to her daughter, Jane Brooks had set up her easel and was painting the stones in watercolour, not very well but gallantly, observed by two ladies in summer dresses and hiking boots. Looking at the scene, Sidonie smiled at the Englishness of it all and wished she could stay longer than just a weekend.

"I wonder what the stones were for? Do you know?" one of the visitors was asking Jane, while the other bit firmly into a bar of chocolate.

Sidonie's mother shook her head. "Nobody does, I'm afraid. But it is generally believed it was a temple or place of worship. It was enormous apparently, with great avenues leading to it. In fact it is the largest circle of its kind in Europe."

"Gracious, fancy that. I suppose it's very ancient."

"Again, nobody's sure, but it is thought to date from 2500 to 2000 BC."

"How *pagan*," said the chocolate-eater, steadily munching. "Has it anything to do with Silbury Hill, do you know?"

"I should imagine so."

"What is Silbury?" asked the first one.

"A burial vault," Sidonie put in dreamily, half asleep as she was. "I've always thought it must be."

"Oh how thrilling. Has it never been excavated?"

"An attempt was made some years ago to bore a tunnel to the centre but it failed," Jane answered.

"I like that idea," said the second woman, finishing her chocolate and starting another bar. "So there might still be someone lying in the middle."

Sidonie slowly opened both eyes. "It's a queen, I think. Lying in a gold sarcophagus, her skeletal hands crossed on her breast."

"Ooh, how romantic. You ought to write."

"I've enough problems without that," the musician answered, and laughed.

"You're in a funny mood," said Jane when the walkers had eventually moved on. "Where did you dream up all that queen stuff?"

"It's Finnan's fault," answered her daughter, closing her eyes again. "He's incurably romantic and believes in a land beyond the mists."

"Good heavens. How extraordinary."

"Oh, he's that all right."

Jane glanced at Sidonie shrewdly. "He's got you interested, hasn't he?"

"Yes."

"Do you want to tell me about it?"

"There's nothing to tell. He was happily married and would be now if his wife hadn't been killed in a motor accident. He's been on his own for about three years and I suppose he was getting lonely. I was in the right place at the right time."

"And that's all there is to it?"

"If you're asking if he's proposed marriage the answer's no. I enhance his life to a certain extent but no further. And to add to the general hopelessness of the situation he's off to Canada soon on a research project and that, I suspect, will be that."

"How very defeatist."

"Of him or of me?"

"Of both of you. If he's fond of you he ought to make a move. If you're in love with him why don't you tell him so? He might think you're strictly a career girl."

Sidonie was wide awake now, sitting up and hugging her knees. "I'm terrified of being rejected. I simply couldn't bear it if he said thank you but no thank you. I really have fallen for him, I'm afraid; hook, line, sinker, the lot. I know just how Sarah must have felt."

"Sarah who?"

"Oh, someone I once knew," Sidonie answered vaguely.

"Well, what did *she* do about it?"

"Got herself rejected, though not so much by the man himself, more by his mother."

"I didn't know that sort of thing still went on in this day and age."

Sidonie grinned mischievously, a lovely humorous smile which Jane adored. "It doesn't much."

"So you'd rather suffer in silence than risk the congé."

"What a lovely word that is. I must start using it more often. Yes, I'm afraid that's the truth. I am too smitten with Finnan to risk pushing my luck."

Jane sighed. "What complicated times we live in. Bring back the good old Debs Delights and arranged marriages I say."

"You're probably right. Into the cattle market at the beginning of the season and out again at the end of it leading a bull by the nose."

"Not quite how I'd have put it, but yes."

"You know," Sidonie said, suddenly serious, "I don't believe things are really any worse now even though they appear to be. I used to think it was easier in the past, particularly for women in the eighteenth century, but I don't any more. It was just as difficult for them to make a match with someone they really loved."

"But there was freedom of choice, wasn't there?"

"Within strict limits. There was hell to pay if they married anyone considered unsuitable. Look at the row that broke out when Caroline Lennox went off with Henry Fox."

"What makes you bring them up suddenly?"

Sidonie went slightly pink. "I've been reading up on them. They used to live in Holland House, which obviously interests me as the flat's so near it."

"And how is the flat?"

"Wonderful. When are you coming up?"

"Very soon. I'm dying to get a look at the Irish doctor."

"I'll invite him in, and Jannie. She really is amazing, straight out of a play."

"Terribly intense?"

"Terribly, but awfully kind and good. I'm sure she's a reincarnation of Marie Stopes."

"Heaven forbid," said Jane, as she began to pack away her painting things. "She sounds unbelievable."

"The whole place and everybody in it is. It's almost like living in a dream."

"What an odd description. Why do you say that? Is the house haunted?"

"Yes, in a way."

"By whom?"

"A girl like me who was a bit of a fool when it came to men."

"I agree that you have made one mistake, Sidonie," Jane answered severely, "but don't write yourself off for all time. If you *are* a fool about men, stop being one. It's as simple as that."

"Yes, Mother," said Sidonie, pretending to be chastened, "I'll mend my ways at once."

Rumour was flying everywhere. Palace gossips, purporting to be in the know, swore that the King had set his heart on Sarah Lennox and that a proposal of marriage was imminent. Others said that this was nonsense, that the Princess of Wales had already sent for a German girl, and that Mr Fox's hopes would soon be dashed. It was all highly intriguing. At the Drawing Room on 18th June, 1761, the atmosphere was electric with anticipation. One gentleman had even gone so far as to have magnifying lenses fixed in his quizzing glass in order that he might note everything of interest that took place.

That morning the two young people at the heart of all this speculation and conjecture felt they hardly knew how to conduct themselves. The King was frantic, informed by his mother that Fox had been ordered to send Lady Sarah out of town and that the girl would most certainly not be present.

In a frenzy of desire and despair the King dressed beautifully, hoping against hope that Sarah would come, determined that if she did he would settle things between them once and for all despite the obstacles his mother would most certainly put in their path. And yet, he realised, to converse privately with Sarah, should she be there, would be almost impossible for his sister Augusta and her lady-in-waiting, Lady Susan Stewart, hovered at his elbow, preparing to listen to every word he said.

"Go away!" hissed George, moved to rudeness by this arrant invasion of his privacy.

"Shan't!" Augusta replied, every inch her mother's daughter.

"I order it. If you do not stand aside I shall have you removed," he countered.

And her brother looked so angry that the Princess thought better of it and, though she continued to remain close by, behaved somewhat more discreetly.

Sarah, when the King finally saw her, seemed to have stepped from a rainbow, wearing soft shimmering colours, her dark hair woven with matching ribbons, her eyes radiant as she looked at him. George knew then that he could never be happy without her, that he must have her for his wife. Not caring that her sister, Lady Emily Kildare, obviously expecting a child but cheerfully flaunting it, was close enough to see and hear, he practically pulled Sarah from her curtsey and remained handfast with her.

"Oh, my dear," he said emotionally, "I am more than delighted that you are here. I was told you were to go out of town. If you had gone I should have been miserable. For God's sake think of what I hinted to Lady Susan Fox-Strangeways before you went to the country. You know what I mean, don't you?" he added in a whisper.

Sarah nodded. "I believe I do."

In the lowest voice she had ever heard, the King murmured, "Think of it if you love me."

Then that part of the encounter came abruptly to an end. The *beau monde* swept up, all craning necks, and even the quietest of conversations became an impossibility. His Majesty, obviously much put out, was seen to be drinking more than usual and Emily, whose child was leaping wildly, forcing her to sit down, became seriously worried as to the outcome of the day. She had never seen anyone more obviously in love than the King, and she had never seen anyone so frustrated at not being able to express it.

'There's going to be prodigious trouble,' she thought and laid her hand to her body to quiet the dancing babe.

The Drawing Room wore on, Sarah surrounded by sycophants, the King never taking his eyes off her, regardless of to whom he was speaking. He was clearly in his cups, albeit moderately, and getting more reckless with each passing minute. Yet even this mood could not come to his aid. As far as Sarah was concerned he could look but not speak as courtier after courtier, some deliberately, others not, crowded in on him seeking the royal attention.

'He'll explode in a minute,' thought Emily, but even she was not prepared for what happened next.

The Drawing Room was reaching its end and soon the King would depart, thus signalling that everyone else should go. A general farewell at this stage was all that was customary but most of those present presumed that this would not be enough in the case of Lady Sarah, and they were not to be disappointed. With his blue eyes blazing adoration, His Majesty swept up to her and caught one of her hands between his.

"For God's sake remember what I said to Lady Susan before you went to the country, and believe that I have the strongest attachment," he said loudly, his expression, or so Sarah's sister described it afterwards, both serious and fervent. Then, without another word, the King left the room to the sound of an audible gasp.

"Was that a proposal?" whispered Emily as they curtsied.

"I believe so."

"It was couched a mite obscure, if I may venture."

"I know. His Majesty just will not come out with the words."

"He had little chance today. That was probably the best he could manage."

Sarah blushed. "But he and I have been alone – "

Emily's eyebrows tilted up.

" – and still he said nothing."

"Then he must be made to do so," said Lady Kildare firmly. "I shall write to Mr Fox and tell him as much."

"Oh, Emily, where will this all end?"

"With you ascending the throne of Great Britain and Ireland if I have anything to do with it. Now, let's get to work."

Good as her word, Lady Emily Kildare, despite the lateness of the hour and the fact that she was extremely fatigued, wrote a joint letter to her eldest sister Caroline and Mr Fox and sent it round to Holland House by special messenger. It arrived at exactly thirty minutes before midnight, but Fox, on tenterhooks, was waiting up for it and took the communication to his study where he scanned its contents immediately.

"'. . . believe that I have the strongest attachment'," he read. "The last words were spoken extremely loud, and the whole with the greatest seriousness and fervour."

"'Zounds and 'Zoodikers," bellowed the Paymaster into the stillness of the sleeping house. "He *must* intend to go further. There can be no mistaking this!"

And he charged upstairs to wake his wife and tell her that, at last, the King was in good earnest.

"It's marriage, Caro. He wants marriage with Sarah."

"Then why doesn't he say so?"

"He will. Your sister has no option now but to pin him down."

And so it was decided, after much family discussion, that on the very next occasion when they spoke alone, Sarah was to ask His Majesty if he could explain himself more fully. It would have been an ordeal for a woman twice her age and the girl found the whole idea thoroughly distasteful and said as much to Susan in a letter which she wrote the day before the next Drawing Room.

"After many pros and cons it is determined I go tomorrow, and that I must pluck up my spirits, and if I am asked if I have thought of what he said – " She crossed the last three words out, " – or approve, to look . . ." She did not dare put his name for fear the letter might fall into the wrong hands. ". . . in the face, and with an earnest but good-humoured countenance say that, I don't know what I ought to think!"

Sarah sighed, wrote some more about all that she was expected to do to draw His Majesty out and then ended, "I am working myself up to consider what depends upon it, that I may *me fortifier* against it comes – the very thought of it makes me sick in my stomach already. I shall be as proud as the devil, but no matter . . ."

"Good for you," said Sidonie aloud. "These bloody men!"

She read Sarah's postscripts with a wry smile, thinking how little anything changes.

"Well today is come to nothing, for we were so near your namesake and her mistress (Ly Susan Stewart and Princess Augusta) that nothing could be said, and they wacht us as a cat does a mouse, but looks and smiles very very gracious; however I go with the Duchess Thursday, I'll put a post-script in this of it. I beg you won't shew this to anybody, so pray burn it, for I can tell you things that I can't other people you know. Adieu, Dear Suke. Yrs, S. Lennox.

P.S. My love (if I may say so) to Ld and Ly Ilchester, and compliments to the rest. Pray desire Lord Ilchester to send my mare immediately, if he don't want it, for I must ride once at least immediately in Richmond Park. Much depends on it.

P.S. I went Thursday but nothing was said; I won't go jiggitting for ever if I hear nothing, I can tell him."

'Umm,' thought Sidonie, laying the book of letters down. 'Now why did she want her horse returned so urgently? And what, I wonder, did she mean by *much depends on it?*'

And thinking that nobody would ever know the answer to that, she started to read on.

# Thirteen

It was a blazing summer, fine and gold, a summer during which a King fell in love with another King's descendant, and neither of them was ever to be quite the same again because of it. The richness of these halcyon days was particularly noticeable in the morning when the sun, escaping the drenching pink lake in which it had been born, swiftly ascended the heavens, transforming everything it touched. Flowers smiled and opened beneath its rays, trees cast bowers of emerald shade and every bird in the forest swelled its breast in rapturous song.

On this particular morning a mischievous shower was chasing the sun, occasionally tipping down delicate veils of lawn, so that particles of sky, bright as cornflowers, appeared, then vanished, then appeared once more in a gleam of brilliance. Earlier, there had been a haze which had hung over the hills, hiding them in shrouds of mother-of-pearl. And later, when the sun finally gave way and evening came, the rivers and streams would turn to glass, disturbed only by the leap of a silver-scaled fish or a moorhen's sudden plunge.

Riders were out in this sharp bright time, pounding through the rain, lifting their faces to it and laughing, glad of the cold fine drops, hurrying through the cavernous forest, afraid of being late, of missing a lover, of ruining a life. The colour of both of them was up, healthily so, and when they arrived together beneath a great oak tree standing where the tracks crossed and recrossed, they flung out of their saddles and embraced, warm cheek on warm cheek, firm lips desperately seeking those of the other.

"The last two weeks have been a nightmare," said the King.

"Indeed they have," answered Sarah with much feeling, and

clung to him as if at any moment someone would appear to separate them.

"I thought that I would never be alone with you again."

"It was clever of you to pass me that note."

He had done it at the last Drawing Room, a Drawing Room at which the young Princess Augusta had stared rudely at Sarah, and the girl had found herself surrounded by a circle of beady-eyed women whose one purpose it had been to prevent her and the King from talking to one another. But he had been prepared for something of this nature and had come forearmed. Momentarily brushing against Lady Sarah Lennox, His Majesty had covertly slipped a piece of paper within her glove. Reading it later in Holland House, her eyes had shone; the lovers were to meet secretly in Richmond Park. She had immediately added a postscript to her letter to Susan requesting the return of her fast mare, though Sarah had concealed the fact of His Majesty's note by stating truthfully that he had still said nothing to her and she would not go jiggitting for ever if she heard no more.

But now they were alone and the King of England stood gazing at her, smiling and besotted, his expression so loving that Sarah could have wept.

"My sweetheart," he said, and caught her to him, kissing her as if there wasn't a moment to lose. Tight in his arms, Sarah sensed his pleasure and strength, his warmth, his pure and unashamed happiness in the love that only she could give him.

"Speak to me simply," she said.

He stared, holding her at arm's length. "What do you mean?"

"No, Sir, what did *you* mean when you told me to remember what you said to Susan? What is it you want of me?"

"Marriage," he answered quietly. "I want nothing more in life than to marry you."

"Then I accept. Spoken to in straight language like that, I shall deal with you likewise. I agree to your offer. I will indeed become your wife."

The china-blue eyes stared into Sarah's incredulously. "Did you say yes?"

She hugged him, forgetting who he was and thinking only of how much she loved him. "Of course I did, ninny. I've been waiting for you to put it in plain English, that is all."

"Then the matter is settled. When I return to Court this very night, I shall instruct Lord Bute to make the announcement to the Council."

Sarah suddenly looked serious. "But what of the Princess of Wales, Sir? Everyone knows she will object to the match."

The King frowned gloomily. "It is going to be very hard to persuade her. Both she and the Earl are set on me marrying Charlotte of Mecklenburg. But I have no wish to. I don't know the damned girl and besides I am in love with you."

"But how can you get out of it?"

"I don't know," George answered honestly. "I simply don't know. But somehow it must be done. I shall be lost without you, Sarah. I must marry you. You hold my future happiness in your hands."

The day seemed suddenly cold as the shower caught up with them and crossed the sun, soaking the two young people through their riding coats.

"Here," said George, and led Sarah into the shelter of the trees where they sat down side by side on the damp ferns.

Close to her as he was, the King could see every line of Sarah's beauty. He studied her intently like a painter, starting with her eyes, a delicate deep sea shade, both blue and green, full of flickering lights and shadows reflecting all her girlish emotions. Around those eyes he saw the thickness of her lashes, night dark, long as the stamens of a flower. Every aspect of her face was perfect and lovely, the good bones, the creamy Irish skin, the sweeping eyebrows. In a moment of intense melancholy, the sweet and kindly young man absorbed every detail as if he would never be alone with their owner again.

Sarah, undaunted by his staring, returned George's scrutiny, admiring the healthiness of his skin, his beautiful teeth, the sensual mouth created for love, the piercing blue eyes the colour of flowers.

"Is this real?" she said eventually.

"What do you mean?"

"Am I really sitting like this with the King of all Britain, and has he truly just asked me to be his wife?"

"He has. And you are his wife already because of what has taken place between us. In the sight of God we have been joined together."

He took her left hand in his and mimed putting on a wedding ring. Sarah leant forward and kissed him on the lips. "I love you," she said.

"And I love you and always will."

"Do you promise me?"

"I give you my word."

"And I give mine."

And the two lovers clung together as if they knew that no matter how truly they pledged, insurmountable forces were already massing against them.

As dawn broke Finnan lay close to Sidonie and studied her like a painter in that soft light. She was a combination of gems, he thought, the amber hair spreading over the pillow, gold at the ends where the sun had bleached it, ruby red at the roots. Her eyelids were closed, serene, half-moon-shaped, the skin as fine and delicate as pearl and, even while she slept, Finnan saw that Sidonie's lips curled into her lovely humorous smile. In a wondering kind of way he put out a gentle finger and lifted a lock of hair which, as he put it back again, spread itself web-like where he had laid it. She was the most stunning woman he had ever met or, indeed, was likely to, he knew that. Yet because of her enormous talent the doctor felt inhibited, wary of the future, unable to proceed as he would have done with a less exceptional woman.

Finnan had by now come to accept the fact that his love for Sidonie was frighteningly different from that which he had felt for Rosie. His wife had been an uncomplicated Irish girl, a nurse into whose company he had been constantly thrown as a medical student. That they would eventually get married had more or less been taken for granted by both of them, and visions of a comfortable family life had opened up when they had come over to England to further the doctor's career. For a while Rosie had done some part-time nursing with a London agency but had longed for a child and been bitterly disappointed when she had found it hard to conceive.

Something Finnan had told no one, not even Sidonie, had been the fact that his wife was finally pregnant when she died. In that one grim and ghastly accident he had lost everything. For even though the child had been unborn and unknown, he had mourned its loss as deeply as that of his poor little partner who had never known the happiness of holding her baby in her arms.

And now, lying beside this spectacular girl, loving her for her talent, for the pleasure she gave to audiences all over the world as well as for everything else about her, Finnan faced the fact that Sidonie's musical career was hardly compatible with motherhood. Nor, knowing the pressures that Nigel had put on her to give up all that she had worked hard for, would he consider asking her to do so. In the Irishman's mind the position was clear; he could either have a relationship with a woman whose career must come before everything else or settle for family life with someone less ambitious. And yet he loved Sidonie so much that he found it almost impossible to imagine meeting anybody else.

"Why does it have to be like this?" he whispered, and she woke and smiled at him.

"Am I dreaming or is this real?"

"It's real and I'm suffused with guilt."

"Why?"

"I used the key you gave me and came in late while you were asleep."

"Did you take advantage of me, as they say?"

"For shame! I have one or two gentlemanly characteristics left. Anyway I was too tired."

Sidonie propped herself up on one elbow. "What a pity."

He tweaked her nose. "Now who's being naughty?" and Finnan kissed her, wondering how he could live without her when he was in Canada, wondering how he could face any kind of future which didn't include Sidonie.

"I shall miss you when I'm in Montreal," he said quietly.

"So it's definite? It's been confirmed?"

"Yesterday morning. And just as if it happened to show me

I had to go, one of my leukaemia patients died last night. He was fourteen and I thought he was the best lad in the world."

"God, how terrible." Sidonie looked away. "So it's marvellous really that you've got this chance. How long did you say you'd be gone?"

"At least six months."

"I see. What will you do with your flat?"

"I don't think I'll let it. I never quite trust that kind of arrangement. I'll probably just write to my friends and relations and tell them to use it when they're in London. Don't worry, you'll love them, particularly my brothers."

"I'm sure."

Finnan smiled. "I hope my mother comes over so that you can meet her. She's formidable but I think you'll get on."

"How old is she?"

"Seventy-three, though you'd never think it. She still helps to run the stud farm she owned with my father. My elder brother is a partner now."

"Did she take that up when you'd all left home?"

"God, no. She organised the whole house with only a couple of servants, worked alongside Father with the horses, and still had time to give individual attention to five children. She was quite amazing."

"I envy women like that," answered Sidonie. "I just wouldn't know where to begin."

"You have a much more demanding career than she had," Finnan answered lightly, but he wished that Sidonie had said something else, something that could have been interpreted as meaning she would at least have been prepared to try.

"Yes, I suppose so," the musician answered, and once again didn't look at him.

For Sidonie could not trust herself to speak, wanting to be with him always, dreading the thought of his going away. To cover her feelings, she kissed Finnan, snuggling close to him. At that he kissed her in return and the inevitable explosion of passion took place between them. Yet even when their lovemaking was over, Finnan continued to hold Sidonie tightly against him, as if in some way he could prevent the fact that very soon now they must part for a considerable length of time.

The sun was high over Richmond Park, so high that shortly it must begin its journey towards evening, and still the King held Sarah close to him, clinging to her as if they were the sole survivors of a shipwreck and only had each other left in the whole wide world.

"I must be resolute," George said eventually. "I must inform my mother that I wish to marry you so that the news of our betrothal can soon be publicly announced."

Sarah pulled a face. "I think such an announcement will cause a complete sensation."

The King shook his head. "There are many who already expect it."

"Well, Lady Barrington does for sure. Do you know what she said to me when last I met her?"

His Majesty grinned, looking young and relaxed. "No, what?"

"You have heard have you not, my dear, that she is famous for having a beautifully shaped back of which she is intensely proud?"

"I have seen it. It is the second best in London."

Sarah attempted to look demure. "Oh really? Then who owns the best, pray?"

"I have forgot," answered the King, smiling.

"Well, sweet tease, when entering the Drawing Room on my last visit, she met me in the doorway and said, 'Do, my dear Lady Sarah, let me take the lead and go in before you this once, for you will never have another opportunity of seeing my beautiful back'."

His Majesty laughed. "There you are! What did I tell you? There will be little surprise."

"But a great deal of opposition."

"Which I shall overcome."

And with that he got up, pulling his beloved to her feet, and lifted her onto the fast dark mare which Lord Ilchester had recently returned to Holland House. Sarah Lennox leaned down in the saddle and kissed George, where he stood tall by the horse's flank, then watched him mount his own beast and canter away into the deepening day, the shadows of which were just beginning to grow longer. She shivered as a cold breeze blew from nowhere at all and was glad to turn her horse and head for home and safety.

The King went at speed, longing to get the most difficult interview of his life over and done. As he galloped, phrases ran through his thoughts, answers to his mentor's arguments which the young man started to practise out loud as he rode. Yet deep within himself, ruled by the sign of Gemini as he was, His Majesty was capable of separating his mind from his emotions and knew that there would be much in what the Earl of Bute would have to say. Behind Sarah there indeed stood a political activist in Henry Fox and this fact could not be discounted.

"But I love her," said one of the twins that dwelled in His Majesty's soul. "Think of the nation," replied the other.

Thus, by the time he arrived at Kensington Palace, the King of England felt himself to be in a state dissociated from reason, not knowing which way to turn. It was the legacy of his birth sign, and he could have broken down and wept because of it.

"There he is," said Princess Augusta of Wales, standing close to the shutters and peeping down through a window that overlooked the stable courtyard. "He's been out nearly all day, obviously with that slut. This must stop tonight, my Lord Bute. I cannot countenance such reckless behaviour one day more."

"Madam," the Earl replied gravely, "there is just the possibility – and I must earnestly enjoin you to consider it – that His Majesty will not be moved. I have no doubt at all that he sincerely loves the wretched girl. There is a chance that your son might yet dig in his heels."

Augusta groaned. "Since when has England had an English Queen? Whatever next! I have decided on Charlotte of Mecklenburg, who is as docile as a mouse and will do as she is told, and there's an end to it. If George will not be moved then neither will I."

If it hadn't been for the fact that without her he would still be a nobody, a penniless Scottish nobleman scrabbling to make his way, Bute would have exploded, asking his long-nosed mistress if her son's wishes meant nothing to her, stating that England might do very well with a queen born on English soil. But he was not his own man and enjoyed his position and all that it brought him far too much to jeopardise it by speaking his mind.

"I will do all that I can," he answered, bowing and contriving to look both handsome and noble as he did so.

"You must," replied Augusta, sounding Germanic, "Bute, you must. The future of the realm depends upon it."

As the Earl braced himself for the enormous task ahead with a good-sized brandy, the door to his suite was thrown open and to his amazement he saw that the King stood there, unannounced and with the dust of travel still upon him.

"My Lord, I must speak to you," he said, without pre-amble.

"But of course, Sir. I am at your command."

His Majesty strode into the room, closing the door behind him. "Be seated, please," he said, and himself took a chair near the fire which the Earl always had lit in the evenings whatever the temperature outside.

"I presume, Sir," said Bute, deciding to seize the initiative, "that the subject you wish to discuss is Lady Sarah Lennox."

George went bright red, then completely white. "Yes," he said hoarsely.

"How may I help you in this matter?"

Recriminations and threats were obviously now of no avail. The time had come for the Earl of Bute to assume one of his many roles, the paterfamilias and benign confidant, the friend whose wisdom was almost divine.

"I have asked her to marry me," said the King shortly, "and I intend to do so."

His tutor sat dumbstruck, his jaw sagging, giving him a very slightly stupid air.

"You've done *what*?" he said.

Observing him, George knew a moment of pure rebellious delight. For year upon countless year, he had regarded the Earl as being *sans reproche*, god-like in his stature, a beloved guardian to be set on a pedestal and adored. Now for the first time the King saw that the idol had feet of clay, that Bute with his mouth open looked just as silly as anyone else. Somewhere, in one of the chill currents in the King's mind, there was a drowning.

Bute, to his credit, recovered himself quickly. "I wish you every felicitation, Sir, and pray both for you and your country."

George looked at him sharply. "You are implying that it needs prayer?"

"Sir, at the risk of covering old ground, I warned you eighteen months ago that a marriage with Lady Sarah is an impossibility. It places Henry Fox in an inviolable position. You must know this yourself. I am afraid that in this matter there is a straight choice between your happiness and that of the nation."

There was a long silence and the Earl knew that his pupil was weighing his words carefully.

"Is there no way that the two cannot be combined? I love her so much, you see. She means more to me than life itself," George said finally.

"Kings are born not for happiness but for duty," the Earl intoned grandly. "They marry for alliance, for strengthening the position of the throne. Of course it is acceptable, Sir – " Bute coughed delicately. " – for ladies who delight them greatly to become royal favourites."

"I could not ask that of Sarah," His Majesty replied indignantly. "She is too fine a person, too noble a character."

"Then, Sir, we are at impasse."

There was another long silence, broken eventually by the King saying sadly, "Then what am I to do?"

The Earl paused, knowing that the end was in sight, that his pupil's sense of duty to his subjects, so very lively and so easily aroused, was beginning to gain the upper hand.

"My very dear Sir," Bute said finally, "you must allow the Princess Charlotte to become your bride with all due speed and put an end immediately to your liaison with Lady Sarah. Remember that you agreed to the Princess in May. I have a copy of your letter still."

George did not sigh so much as give a terrible shudder, one

which started at his feet and shook the whole of the rest of his body. Bute, in a rare moment of pity, thought he had never seen the young man at a lower ebb.

"But how can I do that to the woman I love?"

"You must tell her that though you love her above all other women, it is your sacred duty to put your country first."

The King got to his feet blindly, heading for the door without looking round. The Earl, guessing that His Majesty was on the point of tears, did nothing to stop him going.

"This day my heart breaks," George said chokingly. "Why was I not born to lesser station?"

And he stumbled out of the room, closing the door quietly behind him. Bute stared after him, wondering if victory was his or whether his pupil might yet change his mind, and thinking, as the shadows of that summer evening darkened, that if the King did indeed decide to cast off Lady Sarah he would be casting away with her his youth and joy.

The Earl shook his head and went off to report all that had happened to the Princess of Wales.

Sunday service was divine, thought Sarah, and smiled at her own small joke. Heaven alone knew how, but after the Drawing Room on the previous Thursday when the King had slipped a note into her glove, an act which nobody could possibly have seen, the gossip was all round London that His Majesty was about to announce his betrothal to Lady Sarah Lennox. As a consequence of this, the Chapel Royal at St James's was packed to overflowing on the following Sunday. Spectacles flashed on noses, quizzing glasses were rife, several people who did not normally carry ear trumpets now appeared with them, and there was an air of barely controlled excitement.

As Sarah entered the Chapel accompanied by her sisters Lady Caroline and Lady Emily, the people divided into two lines so that she passed through them as if she were already a queen. Fox, bringing up the rear, grinned mightily, and twirled his new cane crowned with an ebony negro's head.

"What a beauty! Young Georgie's done very well for himself," bellowed deaf old Lady Granby, and there was a roar of laughter and applause more suitable for the playhouse than a place of worship.

Sarah went in head high, the secret of the royal betrothal clutched tight to her heart, and took her place amongst the other ladies in the gallery, the peers and gentlemen sitting below. The royal pew, however, was situated across the west end of the Chapel on the same level as the gallery and as the King came in from his private staircase, his sister behind him, everyone stood and gazed almost as if they expected him to wink an eye at them. But though he did not do that, George most certainly did not disappoint the onlookers. Having taken his seat he looked round to see if Sarah was there and then, having located her, stared at her with such a look of pure devotion that the congregation seethed with speculation.

"Odds on Sarah as royal bride," was being whispered from person to person. It was generally believed that an announcement would be made by the end of that week.

Very touchingly, the young couple, though they did not speak to one another, made their love apparent for all the world to see. The King quite literally did not take his eyes from Sarah's beautiful face throughout the entire proceedings while she, though attempting not to look in his direction, frequently caught his glance and blushed. Not one soul followed the service and the sermon was delivered to a crowd of craning necks.

Yet there was a general feeling of disappointment when Lady Sarah Lennox did not attend the Drawing Room that afternoon and many people wondered why she had stayed at home. The truth was very simple. The girl was indisposed, or rather had such an extraordinary feeling that all was not well with her royal lover that she claimed to have a headache and begged to stay behind in her bedroom.

But the minute the carriage bearing her sisters and brother-in-law could be heard rattling down the drive, Sarah rose from her bed and went to the window where she stared pensively out on the beautiful summer parkland.

'What can it be?' she thought. 'Why am I ill at ease?'

For certain, the King had looked at her with so much love, so much blatant adoration, that it made Sarah's heart ache just to think about it. And yet there had been a shadow in those blue eyes, a look of wretchedness that could not be overlooked or explained. Yesterday they had plighted their troth, had given each other a promise to be faithful for ever. Today the King was noticeably saddened, at least to her perceptive gaze.

"The Princess and Bute again," sighed Sarah aloud and went downstairs that she might think the better now the house was empty.

It was a glorious day, the sun as hot as ever, the weather just as fine as when she had surrendered her innocence to the King. Moodily, Sarah paced the Saloon, played two pieces by Handel on her harpsichord and then, tiring of being inside, left the house by the door in the east wing and made her way to the Green Walk that ran parallel with the drive on the other edge of the fields. Here it was fresh and pleasant, the row of trees planted on the eastern side throwing a cool shadow at this hour of the day. Thinking about the King, wishing she knew exactly what it was that bothered him, Sarah made her way towards the Great Road humming the tune played by the gypsy fiddler when the haymakers had stopped for their noontime break.

And then, to her utter astonishment, Sarah heard the same tune played on the harpsichord, floating towards her on the summer breeze. Puzzled, she looked all around, then back over her shoulder, thinking the sound must have come from Holland House. But the mansion was no longer there, only a ruinous shell with part of the east wing still standing in its place. The elm drive, too, had vanished and the soft grass of the Green Walk had changed into a hard substance which was not pleasant to the feet.

Without warning, the light of that beautiful summer's day suddenly started to fade and Sarah stood in the gloaming, frightened and confused, certain that she must be dreaming yet feeling terribly alert and awake. The sound of the music continued and looking to her left the girl saw that the long line of shady trees had gone, in their place a high brick wall in which, spaced at intervals, was a series of wooden doors. And it was from behind the door beside which Sarah now stood that the sound of the harpsichord was coming. In the darkness, for it had changed from dusk to night almost in a matter of seconds, she pushed the door open and went in.

She was in a small well-kept garden, a neat terrace with stone flower-filled pots at the far end. Above this terrace loomed a tall thin house, a house which Sarah knew perfectly well could not be there, for the land beyond the Green Walk belonged to Mr Seymour and had no buildings upon it. Yet, illusion though this must be, Sarah could still hear the sound of the harpsichord coming from yet another door, a door with a panel of glass in it, which led off the terrace and into the house. Terrified, trembling, she felt herself drawn irresistibly towards the music. Very slowly, Sarah walked through the garden, ascended the terrace and peered within.

She was looking into a music room of sorts, though furnished most oddly. A great many people, dressed outlandishly and in fashions she simply could not comprehend, lounged on low sofas, some even sitting on the floor, listening to the harpsichordist. Peering sideways to see the player more clearly, Sarah recognised the fall of autumnal hair, the wide smiling mouth, and knew that it was the woman who haunted her, the woman whom the King himself had glimpsed on two separate occasions, the woman who was neither ghost nor yet real, and whose presence in Sarah's life was utterly inexplicable.

And then her attention was drawn to the harpsichord. It was so like her own that Sarah could hardly believe her eyes. Yet there, plain to see, was the mahogany and walnut case, the two manuals, the name board bearing the words, Thomas Blasser, London, 1745. Without thinking what she was doing, Sarah opened the door and stepped inside to examine it more closely.

Feeling that he was in a draught, Rod Rees looked up and saw that the garden door had blown open. Quietly, so as not to disturb Sidonie's playing, he got to his feet thinking to close it, utterly entranced as he was with his client's latest composition, a strange haunting air which she claimed was based on an eighteenth-century folk tune, though Rod could not say that he had ever heard the original.

As he approached the door the agent saw Sarah standing in the entrance and felt every particle of colour drain from his face. Involuntarily, he exclaimed, "My God," though the last thing he had wanted was to make any kind of scene.

"What is it?" asked Sidonie, looking up.

Rod heard his own voice answer her and realised that it had become thin with fear.

"There," he said, "in the doorway. There was something standing there, I could have sworn it."

"It was only the moonlight," Finnan put in reassuringly. "Just a patch of moonlight."

"I thought it was a woman."

"No," answered the Irishman, "there really is nothing there."

And Finnan looked straight at Sarah as if he could not see her. Yet though she could have sworn he smiled just for a moment as their eyes met Sarah, in total confusion, backed away into the darkness, leaving behind the bizarre concert into which she had so frighteningly stumbled.

# Fourteen

"Honour is dead!" said Henry Fox dramatically. "My God, Caro, honour is dead."

"And so will you be," answered his wife tartly, "if you drink another drop tonight. You have consumed a great deal too much brandy, Henry, and are becoming maudlin. I must bid you stop."

"But how could he do it, answer me that? And to someone as beautiful and fine as Sarah? Is this decency? Is this honesty? What manner of man do we have as King of this realm?" answered her husband, ignoring Caroline's instruction and pouring another glassful down his throat in a single draught.

"We have a weak man and that's the truth of it. He's no monster, just clay in the hands of others. It's as well Sarah did not marry him. He would have been on her nerves in no time at all."

"Who knows, who knows?" Fox answered gloomily, and there was silence for a few minutes as the couple watched the sun setting over the parkland.

It was the 7th July, 1761, and the rumour was all over London that at the Council meeting to be held next day the King was to announce his marriage to Princess Charlotte of Mecklenburg and that Sarah Lennox would be out in the cold. And yet Fox still found it hard to believe what the fashionable world was saying. For at the Drawing Room on 2nd July, though the King had been hounded by his sister Augusta, who had openly laughed in Sarah's face, he had looked at the girl with what could only be described as a tender lovelight in his eye. And now it had most astonishingly come to this. The Paymaster felt that he was on nodding acquaintance with public humiliation.

Upstairs, in the privacy of her bedroom, the object of all

the speculation sat writing to Susan, pouring out something of what she felt, telling some of the truth if not the whole of it. For Sarah was too deeply hurt to admit even to her best friend that her heart had been broken by the King's wretched behaviour.

All in all, it had been a very strange few days. Looking back, Sarah could only think that the hallucination had been a presage of doom; the hallucination in which she imagined her own precious harpsichord was being played by the mysterious woman in a house that did not even exist. She had woken to find that she had fainted in the Green Walk, that it was late afternoon, that there were no houses in sight and that the dew of evening was just beginning to dampen her clothes. Shaking and nauseous, Sarah had stumbled home and gone straight to bed, comforted by a nervous Lucy. And from that moment on, or so it seemed to her now, things had started to go wrong.

Four days later she had gone to the Drawing Room to find her royal lover tense and nervous, while Sarah herself had been openly mocked by Princess Augusta and her lady attendants. And then had come the fatal rumour; George was to marry the German princess after all.

"But he is betrothed to me!" Sarah had exclaimed, though only to herself, and had gone into The Wilderness to sit on the stone seat and sob uncontrollably, her world in ruins, all her youthful hopes trampled under foot, utterly disillusioned that the man to whom she had surrendered her virtue could have cast her aside so callously. To make matters worse – or was it perhaps better – Ste and Charles James were both home; the elder boy, taller and thinner, from the Grand Tour, the younger back from Eton. And it was this middle son of Henry Fox and Caroline who came across his youthful aunt in great distress, sitting alone and looking so abject that the boy, now aged twelve, also burst into tears. Rushing to Sarah, Charles put his arms round her and they wept silently together. Eventually though, he asked the obvious question.

"Dearest Sarah, what has upset you? Please tell me."

She looked at him red-eyed and white-faced with no trace of her great beauty at this moment. "I can't. It is a secret never to be spoken."

"Are you with child?" asked Charles practically.

Sarah looked slightly annoyed. "No, that is a naughty thing to say."

"Then what is it? Is the King going to marry somebody else?"

"How do you know all this?"

"It is the talk of Eton. I have been taking wagers that my aunt will soon be Queen of England."

Sarah's chin quivered. "Then you're going to lose them. His Majesty is to marry a German princess."

"Then more fool him." The acuteness that was one day going to make Charles James Fox the rogue politician he was destined to become, gleamed momentarily on his face. "It is he who will lose, Sarah, mark my words. And for making you suffer I shall hound him, I promise you that."

"But I don't hate him. I love him still."

The boy looked wise. "That will pass in time. But now, swear that you won't show anyone else how much he has hurt you. Please."

"But how can I explain my face, Charles? I am as blotchy as an old sow."

"I saw a poor squirrel lying injured beneath a tree. Let us take it back home and say you weep for that."

Sarah looked at her nephew in some amazement. "I do declare you're as wily as your father. It's not natural in a child so young, indeed it isn't."

"Blood will out," Charles had answered, and had led his aunt home by the hand, holding the damaged squirrel carefully in the other, and swearing to all the people he met that day that Lady Sarah Lennox was more concerned for the creature's health than ever she was for the latest whim of His Majesty.

But now Sarah sat at her writing desk, honour bound to tell sweet Susan something of what had transpired.

"I have been very often since I last wrote," she put, "but tho' nothing was said, he always took pains to shew me some preference by talking twice, and mighty kind speeches and looks; even last Thursday, the day after the orders were come out, the hipocrite had the face to come up and speak to me with all the good humour in the world, and seemed to want to speak to me but was afraid."

And indeed how wretched her lover had looked, Sarah thought, and what a desperate situation it was for both of them. And then her natural anger exploded and she wrote, "He must have sent to this woman before you went out of town; then what business had he to begin again? In short, his behaviour is that of a man who has neither *sense*, *good nature*, nor *honesty*. I shall go Thursday sennight; I shall take care to shew that I am not mortified to anybody, but if it is true that one can vex anybody with a reserved, cold manner, he shall have it I promise him."

"Good for you," said Sidonie, and read on a little further.

This said, Sarah jumped to her feet, stormed down the stairs and into the music room. The beautiful wood of the harpsichord gleamed in that light and lovely place, but she, failing to be calmed by the harmonious atmosphere in which she had spent so many happy hours playing on the love gift of her royal sweetheart, banged on the manuals producing a series of discordant sounds.

"I shall never, never, never touch you again," she shouted at it ferociously and then ran outside, deep into the parkland, to scream out her fury where she could not be overheard.

Sidonie, absorbed in the story of Sarah's life, read on to the end of the letter, knowing nothing of the pitiful outburst that had taken place during its composition.

"Now as to what I think about it to myself, excepting this little revenge, I have almost forgiven him;" Sarah had continued. "Luckily for me I did not love him, and only liked him, nor did the title weigh anything with me – "

"I believe *that* though not the first part," Sidonie said aloud, remembering the scene in the haystack.

" – so little at least that my disappointment did not affect my spirits above one hour or two I believe.

I did not cry I assure you, which I believe you will, as I know you were more set upon it than I was. The thing I am most angry at, is looking so like a fool, as I shall for having gone so often for nothing, but I don't much care; if he were to change his mind again (which can't be tho'), and not give me a *very* good reason for his conduct, I would not have him, for if he is so weak as to be govern'd by everybody I shall have but a bad time of it."

Smiling to herself at the simplicity, the duplicity, and the general charm of this original letter, Sidonie put *The Life and Letters of Lady Sarah Lennox* into her suitcase. She closed the lid, thinking that since the strange night when Rod Rees had taken fright at something he saw in her music room, everything seemed to have gone wrong.

Originally, Sidonie had planned a farewell party for Finnan O'Neill, had counted on inviting her parents so that they could finally meet him, and had nurtured a vague notion of saying something about their relationship and whether he wanted her to wait for him, whatever that might mean. And then one phone call had put paid to all her schemes. Rod, who was now telling everyone that he had achieved his life's ambition by seeing a ghost in Sidonie Brooks's flat and was dining out on the tale, had offered her a tour of Russia.

"It's really exciting, Sid bach. Jeremy Nicholas has broken his arm and has had to cancel but the Ruskies want *you* instead. You're to play in the Kremlin on Catherine the Great's harpsichord – "

Sidonie had shrieked with joy.

"And in St Petersburg in the Winter Palace. It's the opportunity of a lifetime."

"When do I leave?"

"In ten days' time. Come to lunch tomorrow and we'll discuss the programme."

Filled with apprehension, Sidonie had asked, "How long am I to be out there?"

"Three weeks in all, Sid bach. You'll love it."

213

Normally she would have been thrilled at such an exciting chance but this particular timing was disastrous. Finnan was due to go on his research trip in a fortnight and that would be while she was still away.

With the assistance of Jannie and Max a party had been hastily arranged but it was to be very different from the one Sidonie had envisaged. Many people were unable to come at such short notice and that included Jane and George Brooks. Nothing was going as planned. She could feel her last chances with Finnan slipping away and she gloomily wondered if this was an omen, an indication of the end of everything she had hoped for.

Carefully stowing away her music with her luggage, Sidonie went to change, angry with herself for being so nervous, wishing that on this last evening of all in Finnan's company she could feel genuinely light-hearted. But just as she got out of the bath the telephone rang and when she heard the doctor's voice on the other end she knew something was wrong.

"May I give your telephone number to the hospital?"

Those words certainly did not augur well and Sidonie felt a plunge of the heart as she answered, "Of course. Are you on duty then?"

"No, it's not that. Actually one of my patients is critically ill and I want to keep in touch."

'Why tonight of all nights?' thought Sidonie, and then felt mean-spirited.

"Anyway, I'll be with you in half an hour," Finnan went on. "I'm really looking forward to it."

"So am I," she replied, and didn't mean a word.

Sidonie dressed carefully in black chiffon evening trousers and a matching top. It was a dashing outfit, more seductive than beautiful, and at the very last second she wondered if she had put on the right thing. But the front doorbell was ringing and it was too late to do anything about it. Feeling unsure, dejected and in a most unsociable mood, Sidonie went to answer it.

Finnan was amongst the first to arrive and it struck her at once that he seemed under some sort of strain.

"Are you very worried about your patient?" she asked immediately.

"I'm afraid so. But I don't want it to spoil our last evening together. Just let's hope the telephone doesn't go."

And with those not very reassuring words he kissed her on the cheek and went to get himself a drink. There was such an atmosphere, such a feeling in the air, that Sidonie was convinced something would go wrong and, sure enough, at about eleven o'clock the phone did ring. Rod Rees, who was standing nearest to it, telling everyone how Sidonie was going to be featured on Russian television playing Catherine the Great's harpsichord and how he was hoping to buy the footage and interest the BBC in making a documentary, picked up the receiver.

"Dr O'Neill? Yes, he's here. Hold the line a moment."

"Take it in my bedroom," said Sidonie, then followed Finnan, hovering in the doorway.

She heard him say, "O'Neill speaking. I see. Right, I'll come straight over," and knew that the worst had happened.

He put the receiver down and turned to where Sidonie was standing. "Darling girl, I can't bear this but I must go. This patient is eighteen and looks like a·little doll, or did once. I've got to see if I can help her."

"Is she dying?"

"Yes. She's just come back to us from the hospice. She's asking for me."

Sidonie threw herself into his arms on the breath of a sob. "Oh Finnan, try to come back. I did want to say goodbye to you properly."

"It's not goodbye," he answered. "I won't let it be."

"No, please don't."

"Listen," said Finnan, "I don't think you realise how much I'm going to miss you."

And with that he kissed her, holding her so close to him that she felt he would never let her go.

But yet again fate seemed to be against them as Jannie walked into the room, exclaimed, "Whoops! Oh dear, I'm sorry," and the lovely moment of intimacy was over.

"I'm off," Finnan said. "If the party's still going when I get back I'll rejoin it. If it isn't, may I use the key?"

"Of course you can. But I've got to be up at five. The Heathrow check-in is at seven."

"I'll drive you there as promised. Tonight won't make any difference."

"Then I'll see you in the morning," Sidonie answered.

"See you in the morning," he repeated, and was gone.

Sidonie stood in the little hallway, looking to where the front door had just closed behind him, wondering how long it would be before he walked back through it again.

"Don't worry, bach, he loves you," said Rod, coming up the stairs from the music room and throwing his arm round Sidonie's shoulders.

"I wonder," she answered.

"Of course he does. It's just that he's scared stiff of you."

"What do you mean?"

"You're hot stuff to handle, Sid. Beautiful, talented, famous. It's enough to make any man run a mile."

"Oh bloody hell," she exclaimed. "Why should it? Why do men have to be such wimps?"

"He isn't, now be fair. It's just that he probably thinks you're not marriage material. He probably doesn't want to stand in the way of your career," Rod added hastily as Sidonie turned a mutinous face in his direction.

"But that's ridiculous. Why can't one have both?"

"You did and it failed and he knows. Think about it."

"Should I propose to *him*?"

"Yes, why don't you. Go on, be a devil."

"But I thought you told me to love 'em and leave 'em."

"Finnan's different," answered Rod, and his Italian face suddenly looked very slightly cunning. "He could be good for you. If you've got to get involved I would rather it was with him than any other bugger."

But even as they talked about it, half-jokingly, Sidonie knew that she would never do any such thing, that Finnan would have to make the running, as her mother would have phrased it.

Fortunately nobody asked her to play the harpsichord that

evening and in view of the fact that the hostess had to get up early to catch a plane, people started to drift off shortly after midnight. With a sigh of relief Sidonie got into bed, hoping to snatch a few hours' sleep, hoping above all that Finnan would come back before she had to leave the house. But when she woke she was alone, the flat silent. Dejectedly, she rose and got dressed, then rang the hospital.

"Dr O'Neill has just left," said an austere female voice.

Thirty minutes later, though, Sidonie was panicking and hurriedly booked a minicab to take her to the airport. And then came the irony to end them all. As the cab pulled out of Phillimore Gardens, loaded with her luggage, she saw Finnan's car turning in.

"Stop!" she shrieked to the driver. "I must at least wave."

But it was too late. The doctor had vanished from sight and Sidonie knew that she must go on, that she could not risk missing the plane for which she was by now already behind schedule.

"Oh, God!" she said aloud. "Can't anything ever go right?"

"Not in my experience, dear," answered the driver lugubriously. "You're lucky to be getting out of it. Where you off to then?"

"Russia," she answered, "and not with love either!"

"That was a good film," he answered. "I always liked Sean Connery best. How about you?"

"I prefer Timothy Thing," she answered. "The new one."

"Timothy Thing, Timothy Thing," the cab driver repeated reflectively. "Can't say that I've heard of him."

And it was in this state, not knowing whether to laugh or cry, that Sidonie headed through the dawn towards life without Finnan O'Neill.


It had been very difficult for Sarah to accept that from now on life would never be the same again. Three weeks ago, albeit secretly, she had been betrothed to the King of England – his affianced bride. Now he was to marry a German princess and she was that figure of pathos, the jilted sweetheart. Yet as far as the rest of the world was concerned she must put on a brave face, pretend that she had only regarded George as a friend, that the plight of her pet animals meant more to her than that of the King. With only her twelve-year-old nephew to confide in, Sarah faced the future with trepidation.

Henry Fox, to show the *beau monde* that the residents of Holland House were in fine fettle come what may, arranged that the young people should act a play and that Caroline would give a little ball. But his sister-in-law knew that these diversions were only delaying the evil hour. Sooner or later she would have to go to Court and face not only her ex-lover but Society, intent on seeing some sign of weakness in her and relishing the smallest piece of tittle-tattle.

His Majesty had, as rumoured, made a declaration to the Council that he intended to marry Charlotte of Mecklenburg but had seemed confused when he did so, a fact noted by many. As luck would have it the King had also passed right by Henry Fox on his way out and had blushed with embarrassment, a fact which had delighted the Paymaster but done little good for Sarah. So, with the royal betrothal now public knowledge, the girl had finally gone to a Drawing Room, determined to cut George to the quick.

The Princess had not yet arrived in England, her mother having died in the interim, of the surprise, Fox declared, so it was still a single man who greeted his courtiers that July morning. Giving the King one quick glance as she went in, Sarah saw to her immense satisfaction that he seemed frightened to death. None the less, His Majesty still advanced towards her as if he could not keep away. Defiantly putting her chin high, Sarah gazed into the middle distance, determined to conceal her pain from all the curious eyes that observed her.

Beside her, the King coughed nervously. She still did not look at him. "I see riding is begun again; it's glorious weather for it now," he said.

Sarah stared into space but contorted her face as furiously as she could. "Yes, it is very fine," she replied.

Just for a second His Majesty gazed at her beautiful, angrily averted profile, and then he turned abruptly away. In the hearts of both of them all that had passed would never, indeed could never, be forgotten. But now the pressures that had been upon him since childhood had culminated in this most cruel of denials and the King knew that his one chance to see the raw sweetness of true love mature into the comfortable harmony of happy married life was lost for ever.

"How brutal is fortune," whispered George to himself when he was finally in his bed alone and, grown man that he was, cried himself to sleep.

In the silence of her room, Sarah Lennox also wept on that hot July night. If she had pushed harder, played the little bitch, nagged and bullied her weak young lover, she might have lived a fulfilled, passionate and fascinating life, ascending the British throne as George's consort. As it was, another woman, the King's own mother, had had the final word, and Sarah's life from that day on was destined to take a very different course.

# Fifteen

To say that Russia was a revelation was to understate the truth. Even in the plane, flying low over dark forests and the first white gleam of autumn snow, Sidonie felt caught up in its brooding atmosphere. The very sights and smells of the place had a strange and splendid air, and as the coach ferried her from the airport to the centre of Moscow, Sidonie stared out of the window through the darkness of sudden night.

The contradictions of the city were instantly apparent, ancient gilded domes and Imperial architecture nestling beside ugly modern buildings, self-consciously aggressive in their stark unattractiveness. Sidonie was still peering out, trying to absorb it all, when the coach finally pulled up in Gorky Street and she and her luggage were deposited at the Hotel Intourist.

Her room was comfortable, modern, and could have been anywhere in the world. And then Sidonie drew the curtains back and saw Red Square by night and knew that she could only be in Russia. For there was St Basil's Cathedral, all different coloured domes, its quaint and whimsical nine churches in one, each with a tower of varying height, looking utterly ravishing in sensational and theatrical floodlighting.

"An artistic and romantic nation," Rod had said to her before she left. "They will welcome you."

"Isn't it strange. One would have thought they had turned their national back on the past."

"Don't you believe it. They guard it jealously. You wait till you see the Kremlin, Sid bach. It's a knockout. All the old things loved and cherished and revered."

Until that moment Sidonie hadn't quite believed her agent but seeing that fairy-tale cathedral so stunningly lit, sensing the atmosphere of that huge exciting square, she knew that it was going to be a most enthralling three weeks. And then her thoughts turned to Finnan and Sidonie wondered what he was doing, reckoning that it was three o'clock in the afternoon in England and he was probably at the hospital.

'I'll phone him the night before he leaves,' she thought, and hoped it wouldn't be too difficult.

Basil Kuzma, Rod Rees's Moscow contact, was waiting for her in the bar wearing a very Russian-looking blue suit. He was not as old as his white hair might suggest, Sidonie thought, regarding him closely, in fact probably about fifty at the most. He had nice blue eyes, quite pale but bright, and raising a glass of vodka to clink his, she found herself warming to him.

"Your room is comfortable? You have everything you need?"

"Oh yes, thank you."

"That is good. This hotel is one of the best. The Cosmos is big, built for the Olympic Games. The Rossiya is enormous, very dark and Stalinist. It can house five thousand guests. I once lost an entire chamber orchestra in there. They were not seen for a whole day."

Not sure whether he was serious or not, Sidonie gazed at him in astonishment.

"This one is good, though. A little modern, a little brash, but good. There are English MPs staying here at the moment. They are fact-finding." Basil sighed. "They often are."

Deciding she liked him, Sidonie nodded sympathetically. "I know what you mean. Now what about the concerts, how many have been planned? Rod wasn't absolutely sure."

"Several. But let us concentrate first on those in Moscow. You are to perform in the Kremlin itself in one of the great reception rooms in the palace. This will be mainly for VIPs, government ministers, that kind of thing. Then you will play at the Tchaikovsky Concert Hall, here in Gorky Street, and again at the Conservatoire Grand Hall. Ordinary people, students and tourists will come to these."

"They do know it's me? They aren't expecting Jeremy Nicholas?"

"Indeed not, the posters have been changed." Basil smiled, displaying a gold tooth, and drained another glass of vodka.

"Besides Sidonie – I may call you this? – you are much more beautiful than he is which the Russian people will appreciate."

"I'm worried about the programme. It's mainly Georgian music. Will it really be suitable, do you think?"

Basil leant across the bar towards her, wagging a playful finger. "I believe you do not know your Russian history. Catherine the Great was on the throne of Russia at the same time as your George III. You are to play her harpsichord which has been brought out of the Armoury Museum and restored. Georgian music is perfect for such an occasion."

But Sidonie wasn't listening, a strange feeling coming over her at the mention of the King's name. On the night of her summer dinner party, when Rod had sworn he'd seen a ghost, she had wondered afterwards if it had been Sarah Lennox, if the sound of the gypsy fiddler's song had attracted the girl who had lived at Holland House two hundred years earlier. Yet Sidonie herself had seen nothing, too absorbed in her playing, and it had been left to Finnan to say that for a moment, and just for a moment, he had glimpsed what he described as a Blue Lady standing in the garden doorway, listening to the harpsichord, an expression of bewilderment upon her face. But now all that was past. She was in an old country, a country in many ways still a mystery to the Western world, while Finnan was soon off to new lands to investigate amongst other things a disease also described as new.

Without thinking, Sidonie sighed and Basil gazed at her sharply. "Are you sad? You leave a husband behind perhaps?"

She shook her head. "No, just a friend. I'm not married any more, though I was once."

"Everyone was once," Basil answered philosophically.

"Yes," answered Sidonie, and looked towards the door, situated at right angles to the bar, half-curious about the group of people who were just walking in.

She would not have believed it possible but the fact was that as she spoke about her ex-husband he had actually come through the door. Nigel Beltram was not only in Moscow but apparently staying in the same hotel.

"Good God!" said Sidonie, thunderstruck and gaping.

"What is it?" Basil asked anxiously.

It suddenly seemed too difficult and, moreover, too tedious to explain the situation, particularly the unbelievable coincidence.

"I've just seen someone I know from England. It's a small world as they say."

"Those are the fact-finding MPs," Basil informed her morosely. "Do you wish to join them?"

"No, thank you. Let's just go on talking. He's bound to see us in a minute. There's going to be no escape."

"You do not like this man?"

"No, I don't. But I'll have to be polite. He'll probably come over here. You don't mind?"

Basil's tooth glinted. "We shall go into dinner shortly and not sit with him. The Russian bear will tell the English bulldog that business is to be discussed between a great musician and her Muscovite agent. He will go away then."

Sidonie yelped with laughter. Nigel, who seemed to have recently acquired yet another chin, certainly looked like a bulldog, his pompous old school tie not improving matters, while Basil had such a beautiful, simplistic turn of phrase that it made her smile, though not unkindly, just to listen to him.

"Thank you, Mr Bear," she said.

"My pleasure, Madame. Now, where would you like to eat? This hotel has three restaurants, the one up here, the Zolotoy Zal, which means Golden Hall and serves traditional food – "

"There please," said Sidonie. "It sounds fun."

"Then let us go. If you walk to the right of me and quickly, the bulldog may not see you. He is at the bar with his back turned."

They made their escape, though Sidonie realised it was only a matter of time before Nigel ran into her, and went down several floors to one of the most delightful restaurants she had ever been in. Tables by the window looked down over bustling Gorky Street, and a dance floor and a group of musicians in traditional dress, playing balalaikas, were placed at the other end. The atmosphere was so much of another culture, of a romantic and extraordinary civilisation, that Sidonie could hardly take it in.

"I thought Russia would be grey and suffering. Not like this."

"It does suffer, it is often grey," Basil answered, "but it is too old, too mysterious a society ever to vanish. Think of our ancient monasteries, our onion-domed cathedrals, our icons and snow-covered palaces. Nothing will ever shift them, be it war or revolution."

Sidonie wept and didn't know why. "How wonderfully said! I shall do my best to play well for Russian audiences."

"Tomorrow you shall see the harpsichord. But now you must regain your strength, for loving and leaving can make one sad."

"And who," said Sidonie, smiling through her tears, "knows that better than a Russian, if Chekhov is anything to go by?"

"A great man," answered Basil nodding his head. "Let us drink to him."

And they raised their glasses and swallowed the vodka contents at a single draught in true Muscovite style.

It was round London in a trice; the royal bride was not so much plain as plain ugly; furthermore she drank coffee not tea, took no wine, had been horribly seasick on the crossing from Cuxhaven to Harwich and had appeared on deck very ill-dressed and wearing neither rouge nor powder! Horace Walpole, waspish and wonderful, had commented that the Princess had fine hair and a "pleasing" countenance, and then had burst out laughing, while the Duchess of Hamilton, travelling with the future Queen, passed on the gossip that Charlotte had grown frightened and turned pale at her first glimpse of St James's Palace.

Standing ready to receive her as the coach finally drew to a halt were all the courtiers and beauties of England, including Lady Sarah Lennox. And some of the King's attendants, watching his face narrowly as he first set eyes on his future bride, thought they discovered a struggle to conceal the disagreeable surprise he felt on seeing a female so plain and awkward.

"The great difference between the Queen and Lady Sarah forms a very striking contrast," whispered Lord Glenbervie to his wife, and the two of them had smiled in pure malice.

Fox, for himself, could hardly credit Charlotte of Mecklenburg's looks – or rather lack of them. She was very pale indeed yet, oddly, her features were almost simian. Her nose was broad and tipped at the end, her mouth was large, while her eyes looked like boot buttons in her colourless face. As to her figure, it was thin and insignificant with mean and minute breasts. The only thing of beauty about the poor girl was her hair, which was very soft and of a fine dark shade. By contrast, Fox's sister-in-law, dressed in her bridesmaid's clothes, glistened like a silver moon.

The question as to whether or not Sarah would stand as bride's attendant had brought the family almost to a state of civil war. The girl herself had wanted to accept the invitation, believing that there would be "great talk" if she did not do so and determined to defy the *beau monde* to the end. For, as daughter of the late Duke of Richmond, her role would be that of chief bridesmaid and there would indeed be gossip if she refused. Caroline, on the other hand, was all for turning the offer down with dignity and Lady Susan Fox-Strangeways agreed with that. The Earl of Kildare, Sarah's brother-in-law, said she would lay herself open to rumour if she did not go, and his wife Emily, who had given birth to a boy at the end of July, was more in favour than against. It was Fox who had the final word, as was to be expected.

"Well, Sal, you are the first *vargin* – ", he had rolled the word round his tongue, " – in England, and you shall take your place in spite of them all as chief bridesmaid, and the King shall behold your pretty face and repent."

Leaning forward on his desk and speaking in a whisper, Sarah had answered, "Secretly, Sir, I thought to thumb my nose at him, if you will forgive the phrase."

"Thumb and be damned. Ignore your sister. You must do it, girl."

And so it had been agreed between them that August evening. But now it was September and the royal wedding day and Sarah, her agony turned to anger, her love to loathing, was dressed in a gleaming robe of white lute string with

226

silver trimmings, the entire gown bedecked with a thousand pearls. She stood deliberately close to the Queen who paled into an insignificant shadow by contrast. Revenge had been taken, Sarah's blazing contempt was seen on all sides for the triumph it was.

For reasons best known to herself the Princess of Wales was not present to receive her new daughter-in-law, who had gone through a form of proxy marriage in Germany and so could already be considered the Queen. Instead it was the young King who told his seventeen-year-old bride what she must wear for her wedding and, with a great deal of obvious trembling, Charlotte retired with her ladies to get dressed.

The ceremony was due to take place at eight o'clock and at a few minutes to the hour, His Majesty and his attendants left for the Chapel Royal while the bride emerged from her quarters as the royal wedding procession, led by a fanfare of trumpets and drums, formed up.

"God's life," exclaimed Walpole to his nearest companion, "I've seen better in Billingsgate!"

For the Queen had practically vanished in a gown of white and silver and an endless mantle of violet-coloured velvet, lined with ermine, which was fastened to her shoulders by a large bunch of pearls. All this could have looked well had the mantle remained in place, but the weight of the thing dragged itself and almost the rest of her clothes halfway down the unhappy girl's waist. It was almost impossible to move in such a garment and had it not been for the assistance of the Duke of York and Prince William, supporting the bride on either side, Charlotte would have been hardly able to drag herself forward. Coming to the rescue with the sweetest of smiles, Lady Sarah Lennox bade the other nine bridesmaids pick up the train and so they proceeded, Sarah directly behind the bride as principal attendant, Susan Fox-Strangeways walking last.

Fox was vividly reminded of another occasion in the same Chapel Royal when the King had stared at Sarah throughout the service and the *beau monde* buzzed with gossip. Now the very same feeling was in the air as the wedding party approached the altar, the chief bridesmaid a mere pace or two behind the place where the bridegroom stood. The King, however, conducted himself well until the Archbishop of Canterbury said the words, "And as Thou didst send Thy blessing upon Abraham and Sarah to their great comfort."

"He can't conceal his confusion," whispered Walpole delightedly. "His face is flushed as a fruit."

Fox, too, noticed with malice how ill at ease His Majesty seemed and so apparently did everybody else, for there was an audible murmur in the congregation. And when the King and his bride took their seats on the state chairs situated at one side of the altar, the Princess of Wales facing them on the other, it was noted by all present that His Majesty could hardly keep his eyes from the lovely bridesmaid who, according to Walpole, had all the glow of beauty peculiar to her family about her that day.

By now it was half past ten at night and there was a general longing to get to the reception and have something to eat and drink. But it seemed as if the dullness of the bride was already beginning to affect the former gaiety of the bachelor King's court. For when the multitude trooped back from the Chapel Royal to the Drawing Room they found that supper was not ready and that there must, of necessity, be yet another boring delay.

"I could play the harpsichord while you wait," suggested the new Queen in French.

Walpole rolled his eyes. "God in His mercy grant me patience. One could almost be moved to pity."

"Shush," said Fox.

Horace lowered his voice. "But look at her, dear fellow, draped in finery yet half undressed." Out loud he shouted, "Bravo, Madam. Do play please," and clapped his hands. "God be praised, but I hope she don't sing," he went on again. "Oh 'Zounds, she's going to!"

And there the entire wedding party sat while the small, whey-faced figure, freed at last by her ladies from the all-consuming train, took her place at the harpsichord and began to play, accompanying herself as in a thin reedy voice she attempted to sing a melody written by the Neapolitan, Pietro Paradies.

Horace Walpole closed his eyes, pretending to concentrate. From where he sat Fox could hear him muttering, "No looks, no style, no hope. Lud, Sir, you've made the wrong choice, so you have," and prayed that nobody else had caught the wit's words.

Watching her, watching the man who once had loved her, Sarah felt as if her heart would burst. She wanted to laugh, she wanted to cry. They were both so utterly pathetic, the poor plain Queen in particular. And, though she hated her above all others, Sarah longed to tell Charlotte to stop, to say she was making a fool of herself, that she had no talent and the *beau monde* would already be sharpening its claws. Beautiful and poised, the sixteen-year-old girl gazed at her rival with something so close to compassion that she wondered at her own generosity of spirit, and could not explain it even to herself.

The travelling alarm had gone off at eight o'clock Russian time and Sidonie had rolled over in bed, desperately trying to switch it off. By any standard, even Muscovite, she had a monumental hangover, and the very thought of having to get up and be bright daunted her. Yet outside lay Moscow in the daylight, Red Square, St Basil's and the Kremlin. Feeling like a horrid old drunk in a Western, Sidonie plunged her head under the cold shower. However, the horse trough treatment worked and an hour later, having breakfasted on coffee and some extremely strange things to eat, she was down in reception as arranged the previous night with Basil Kuzma.

This morning, however, the impresario was not alone, a young Russian man who audibly whistled as Sidonie approached, standing beside him. Ignoring the unorthodox greeting she sailed up to them and said, "Hello, I hope I'm not late. I think I had rather too much vodka last night."

"No such thing," put in the stranger, smiling broadly.

"Be quiet," said Basil. "Sidonie, may I introduce to you Alexei Orlov? I wonder if he could accompany you to the Kremlin today as I have some urgent work to do and he is also trying to improve his English."

"Are you the violinist?" Sidonie asked the newcomer, sure that she had heard the name.

"Yes. Soon I come on tour to Europe. Basil is my manager. How do you do, Miss Brooks. I have a tape of yours. A friend of mine brought it back for me from France." Alexei said all this without pausing for breath and then added, "I am a great admirer of your work. An honour," and with that he kissed Sidonie's hand and bowed.

"Well, I hope you'll return the compliment and let me hear you play. I read about you in the *Independent*. They say you're quite something."

"Quite something?" Alexei looked puzzled.

"It's colloquial speech. It means very good indeed."

"What's colloquial?" said Alexei, and shrugged a pair of the most expressive shoulders that Sidonie had ever seen.

He was good-looking in that slightly Tartar way that some Russians have, for he had a faun-like cast of feature and almond-shaped eyes. In build, the violinist resembled that famous dancing defector, Baryshnikov, being small, tough and wiry. Though not a great deal taller than Sidonie herself, Alexei's few extra inches none the less gave an impression of strength and agility.

"I'll tell you later," she answered him, then looked at Basil. "When shall I see you?"

"This evening. I want to take you to the TV centre. They would like to televise a little of the concert in the Kremlin."

"Shall we meet in the bar at six?"

"Make it downstairs. There is less likelihood of running into the bulldog."

"You bring a dog too?" said Alexei, thoroughly mystified.

"I'll explain that as well," said Sidonie, and with that they set off for Red Square.

She had never really understood exactly what the Kremlin was. Stalinist regimes and the ensuing propaganda had left Sidonie with the impression that it was some grim grey building from which officials of the KGB sent coded messages and spied on the rest of the world. But now the extraordinary beauty of the place was revealed as she stepped with her violinist escort into one of the largest squares she had ever seen. One side of it was completely taken up by a massive towered wall behind which could be glimpsed a green-roofed palace and the golden onion domes of at least two cathedrals. Immediately opposite stood the amazing St Basil's, to the right the only eyesore in Sidonie's opinion, the red granite tomb of Lenin.

"Where's the Kremlin?" she said, gazing round.

"There, behind the wall."

"But that's a palace."

"The Kremlin is a city," said Alexei, obviously stunned by her ignorance. "It is medieval, fortified, very beautiful. Come, Englishwoman, I show you." And with that he took her by the hand and led her, without protest, through the entire square and down to the Moskva River where the wall continued along the riverbank to the place where once there had been the drawbridge.

"Now do you understand?" he asked impatiently.

"Yes. I'm sorry. I just had no idea."

"You wait till we get inside. It will blow your mind."

"I thought you didn't know what colloquial meant," said Sidonie accusingly.

"Sometimes I surprise me," answered Alexei, and winked a topaz eye.

"When am I going to hear you play?"

"Later. Now look and learn."

They walked up a steep ramp and passed within the walls of a citadel. Inside stood a collection of buildings so fine that Sidonie did not know where to look first, the exquisite Kremlin Palace which, so Alexei told her, had over seven hundred rooms and halls, being only a part of the hidden complex. Beyond the Palace lay Cathedral Square, round it clustered three cathedrals and two churches, all glistening white in the sun, the golden domes reflecting every ray and throwing patches of gilt onto the pale paving stones below.

Above these reared Ivan the Terrible's Bell Tower, the tallest building in the citadel, its dome as golden as the rest, its shadow falling over the tree-filled garden beneath it. But despite all this splendour, the overpowering atmosphere created by early Russian art, the lingering smell of incense, the icons covered in jewels, it was the exhibition of Russia's mighty past that caught Sidonie's imagination.

Housed in a building that had once occupied the place of the Palace Armoury was an exhibition like none she had ever seen. Here, in huge glass cases, were lovingly preserved the personal possessions of the Tsars. She saw the enormous riding boots hand-made by Peter the Great and the dual throne he had occupied with his idiot brother, a small opening behind it through which their sister used to whisper instructions. She saw Ivan the Terrible's throne of ivory, his fur-trimmed crown, the glistening jewels and regalia, a robe worn by the last Tsar of all, the murdered Nicholas II.

"And now the dresses," said Alexei. "You will like these."

And there they were, the Coronation and wedding gowns of the Empresses and Tsarinas, all so small Sidonie wondered what size they could possibly have been, made from sumptuous fabrics and mounted on dummies so that they looked incredibly lifelike.

"Here," called Alexei, beckoning. "Catherine the Great's things. What a woman, no?"

"Did she really have hundreds of lovers?"

"Thousands. I would like to have lived then."

Sidonie laughed. "Why? Do you think you would have been one of them?"

"I would have done my best. It's a family tradition."

"What do you mean?"

"My great something uncles, Gregory and Alexei, both enjoyed her favours. I am named for one of them."

"Well, well," said Sidonie, most amused by this extraordinary young man.

"In the end, when she was sixty, Catherine fell in love with a twenty-two-year-old, Plato Zubov, a lieutenant in the Horse Guards. He was made for life!"

"My God, that was going some. A toyboy if ever there was one."

"Toyboy?" enquired Alexei, looking puzzled.

"The young lover, usually kept, of a much older woman."

"Oh, I see." The violinist looked her up and down thoughtfully. "How old are you, Miss Brooks?"

"Thirty-four and don't be naughty. How old are you?"

"Eleven years less." He shrugged his beautiful shoulders. "Who cares? Now, concentrate."

A silver tissue gown of great delicacy was the most splendid piece in the Empress's collection but it was the smaller things belonging to the lovely lecherous Catherine which impressed Sidonie more. She stared at earrings and bracelets, brushes and combs, but best of all liked the Empress's snuff and make-up boxes. There was something intensely human about them, as there was about a pair of spectacles lying on a desk which also housed Catherine's quill pens and inkwell.

"Now we see the carriages," said Alexei. "Come!"

They left the wondrous glass cases and walked into an enormous room containing the conveyances of the Russian royal family. Coaches decorated by François Boucher and which had carried Peter the Great, Catherine, and Elizabeth Petrovna vied with one another as to which was the most beautiful. But it was two rather off-beat items which particularly appealed to Sidonie; a huge sleigh, mounted on runners, the compartment on top the size of a garden shed, and a child's dogcart.

"What are these?" she asked Alexei, tilting her head back to see the full extent of the sleigh.

"It belonged to Elizabeth Petrovna, Peter the Great's bastard girl. He married her mother later on. Anyway, she travelled from St Petersburg to Moscow in three days in that to seize the crown."

"She must have gone like the wind."

"Sixteen horses pulled it and they did not stop day or night. Can you see the stove inside to keep her warm?"

"Yes."

"Well she slept, ate, did everything in there. Let's hope she emptied the chamber pot when she wasn't in a village."

"That's rude! Tell me about the dogcart."

"That was Peter the Great's when he was a little boy. I like it. It makes him real."

"So do his boots. But where's the harpsichord?"

"In the Palace. Come on."

Wondering whether Alexei's bossiness was partly an affectation, Sidonie followed him through a white tunnel which brought them out in the Palace.

"It's been taken into the ballroom for the concert. That's up on the first floor."

And the violinist hurried up an ornate staircase and down a chandeliered corridor to a pair of magnificent doors, the Russian eagle carved over the top of them.

"Are we allowed in?"

"Of course. This is where you are to rehearse."

The room was immense, its balcony overlooking the river, Carrara marble pillars decorating the white and gold-leafed, crimson-draped walls. At the far end of the ballroom, opposite the balcony, was a raised dais on which the orchestra had once sat. On this, right in the middle, stood a splendid harpsichord which, as Sidonie drew nearer, she recognised as a Jacob Kirkman of about 1750.

"It's wonderful," she called to Alexei. "A Kirkman in what looks like good condition."

"It was tuned again this morning."

Taking off her coat, Sidonie sat down, feeling the keys quiver beneath her touch, then suddenly elated by all the amazing sights she had looked at that day, launched into a fiendish Scarlatti sonata unaware that Alexei was gazing at her as if until that moment, despite all his brash behaviour towards her, he had not really seen Sidonie properly at all.

The triumph was complete. It was Sarah Lennox and not the Queen who was the toast of London and any doubts that had lingered about her acting as bridesmaid had now been laid finally to rest.

On the morning after His Majesty's marriage a grand Drawing Room had been held following the King's Levée. Dressed in her bridesmaid's gown it had been Sarah's duty to stand beside the Queen with the other bridal attendants, all of them, including Her Majesty, in a line, while her loyal subjects were presented to the bride. The Duchess of Hamilton was to introduce the women, while the Duke of Manchester performed the same task for the men.

In the midst of this ceremony Lord Westmorland, a very old Jacobite, a loyal supporter of the Bonny Prince himself, had come somewhat grudgingly to pay his respects. Moving down the line of ladies the old man, whose sight was sadly failing, had fallen on his knees before the most beautiful of them and raised her pretty hand to his lips, exclaiming, "Now there's a bonny lass!"

The colour of a rose but laughing for all that, Sarah had said, "But I am not the Queen, Sir," and passed him on in the right direction. The entire court had noticed that, for all his short sight, the old man had been thoroughly disappointed by the real thing.

The story had swept London and George Selwyn, famed wit and conversationalist, when he heard of it had given his seal of approval by raising his glass to Sarah and Lord Westmorland, saying, "Oh he always loved Pretenders, you know!" The nickname Beautiful Pretender had been born and Sarah had been cheered in the theatre and toasted at balls and parties, while the handsome Earl of Erroll, whom Horace Walpole had considered the most conspicuous figure at the Coronation, where Erroll had acted as High Constable of Scotland, had asked, nay begged, for Sarah's hand in marriage. The season which had begun so disastrously, so horribly, had ended in glory, only marred by the fact that Ste was departing once more and Charles James was in the sullens because his cousin Susan Fox-Strangeways, with whom he fancied himself in love despite the fact he was only twelve years old, had returned to the country.

Ste's advice on saying farewell to Sarah had been, "Don't refuse a good match when you can get it, and don't go to plays and operas too often."

Yet it was at the playhouse, which she had no intention of giving up, that Sarah's life had changed completely. Remembering the time when the King had sat in the box opposite and stared across at her throughout the performance, Sarah had glanced over to see who was there this night and been intrigued to note it was a stranger to her. A truly elegant figure sat in the place once occupied by George, a slim handsome languid creature with all the style and beauty of a French marquis.

"Who's the dandy?" she whispered to Lady Harriet Bentinck who sat beside her.

"I've no idea. What a very pretty fellow!"

"La, but he is. I shall make it my business to discover his name."

Lady Harriet had laughed. "Smitten, Lady Sarah? I would have thought you were being more careful about men these days. Once bitten, twice shy, and all that."

"You refer to His Majesty? A mere *divertissement* on my part."

"Really?" Harriet was obviously not convinced.

Sarah thought it wiser to remain silent and took to studying the gentleman opposite with rather more interest than she actually felt. It was at that moment, however, that he looked up, saw her staring at him, and gave a bow.

"I really feel I should like to make his acquaintance," Sarah murmured to her companion.

"Then let us hope you can do so before Christmas is upon us."

"It certainly would make a good ending to the season to be seen on the arm of a charming fellow such as that. In fact it would be a triumph," answered Sarah, graciously inclining her head to the stranger as into her mind's eye came a vision of the King's face if such a desirable outcome were indeed to take place.

The recital was, in Sidonie's opinion, the most exhilarating experience she had ever had. The Russian hierarchy, including one of the old Romanovs, by a miracle welcomed in Russia these days, stood to applaud. And the greatest applause of all had come for an item that she had added at the very last minute, an adaptation by Sidonie of a Handel piece in which the violin and harpsichord played together. The combined sound had been overwhelming. Alexei was without any doubt at all a genius of a very special kind. In his hands the violin sobbed and sighed and sang, and he had the great gift of empathy for music from any period, seeming as much at home with Renaissance, Baroque, Classical or Jazz.

The only blight on the evening had been the presence of the

British MPs among the audience, though Sidonie realised that by now Nigel must be aware she was in Moscow as posters with her photograph were spread about quite prominently. But as soon as she started to play she forgot him and the moment when Alexei, in rather ill-fitting evening clothes, got up, his violin in his hand, was one which she would never forget. The magnificent ballroom thundered with applause as a Muscovite and an Englishwoman made magnificent music together.

The reception afterwards was held in the Tsar's state dining room, an honour indeed, and Alexei whispered, "They love you, Miss Sidonie. Not all foreign guest artists get this."

"But it isn't just for me. There are lots of other dignitaries here."

"Yes, ambassadors and MPs, that sort of thing. But you and I are the only people from the arts."

"Isn't that the director of the Bolshoi Ballet over there?"

"Well, other than him." Alexei squeezed her waist. "You play real good. It was a great honour when you accompanied me."

"I think that's the bit they'll show on television."

"They'll show as much as they can. It was a triumphant concert, little darling."

"Do you *really* need English lessons?" asked Sidonie, smiling but narrowing her eyes at him.

"If you will be my teacher. But now I must ask you a question."

"What?"

"Why does that fat dark English guy keep staring at you?"

"Guy is an American word so doesn't really apply to him. And he does it because he and I used to be married."

Alexei's jaw dropped most satisfyingly and he said something in his own language which Sidonie took to be enormously rude.

"You are his wife?"

"I was, in the past tense. We were divorced several years ago."

"But he loves you still. I, Alexei Orlov, can tell this. But we will defy him. Come." And tucking her arm through his the young man, who in Sidonie's eyes was growing more talented and more eccentric by the minute, whisked her away to greet some of his compatriots.

It was inevitable that Nigel would speak, though, and shortly before the buffet was served her ex-husband, a glass of champagne in hand, came purposefully towards her.

"We escape?" asked Alexei.

"No. I'll have to say hello."

"Brilliant, darling," said Nigel coming up to Sidonie, and had kissed her on the cheek before she could move away.

"I'm glad you thought so," she answered coolly. "This is Alexei Orlov, the violinist."

"Well played," said Nigel heartily, and Sidonie saw that he was doing his all-boys-together act.

"I'm glad you liked it. Do you play an instrument, Mr Brooks?"

"Beltram actually. Nigel Beltram. No, I don't have much time for that sort of thing. Too busy in the House."

Alexei looked bemused. "But housework is so dull. You should try to play piano at least. It lifts the soul."

He bowed and walked away, leaving Sidonie and Nigel to stare at one another.

"Thank God that little jerk's gone. Now how about dinner? The food here is bound to be ghastly. I've found a super restaurant in the Swedish hotel. Do say you'll come. It's high time we resumed diplomatic relations."

Sidonie hesitated. "Look, Nigel, it would be extremely rude to leave when I'm one of the guests of honour. But I have this fated feeling you're going to go on and on if I don't. So I'll make a bargain. If I have dinner with you tomorrow night will you promise to leave me alone after that?"

Some awful mental process took place behind Nigel's eyes, she could see, and whatever he concluded obviously satisfied him for he smiled broadly and said, "Meet you in the roof bar at the hotel tomorrow at seven sharp. Don't be late now," then he blew her a kiss and walked away.

"Has he gone?" said Alexei, rejoining her apparently from nowhere.

"Yes, but not for long."

"No, not for long. He wants you back."

"Well, he ain't getting me and that's that," Sidonie replied firmly. "Now let's go and circulate. You can be my translator."

"OK. It's a deal."

And with that she and the Russian prodigy plunged into the crowd.

# Sixteen

Midnight, thought Lady Sarah Lennox, is a damnably lonely time when one is awake and the rest of the house sleeps. Yet the important, the vital, letter to Susan must be finished to catch the morning's post. For now a pretty coil had come about. In endeavouring to find out the identity of the French Marquis, as Sarah had nicknamed the elegant stranger, she had not only caught his eye but his attention and Mr Thomas Charles Bunbury, dandy of Barton Hall in the parish of Barton and Mildenhall in Suffolk, had been in hot pursuit of her ever since.

"He has (what is call'd) followed me constantly whenever I have been in town, I have not put myself in his way (do ye take me), for at Leicester House (*en presence de ma soeur*) we changed places 3 times and he followed us; at night I went with my sister to the Play, there he was in the front boxes and came in a minute to my *house and corner*; this you will allow is *particular*. My sister, who is quick at those sort of things, has settled it that he will make his declaration immediately, but I think not; and why? Because that, talking of people that married for money and rank and so forth, he said he had the comfort to think, that if he married a *fine* lady, she would love him vastly, for that he was so poor that she must live upon love and bread and butter with him. This I took as a hint he did not intend to marry, and so told him, "I thought he had much better not marry in a hurry, as he would not find it easy to meet with such a person," and I believe I looked a little angry, for he ask'd me what was the matter, but I did not tell him, as you may imagine, but said it was nothing; he looked either angry or blank, I don't know which, but said very little and handed me out. I have

241

not seen him since. You will say I might find out what he thought by his conversation, but it's generally loud and of indifferent subjects, only broad hints now and then that he likes me, asking me constantly where I am to go, and when I shall be in town, and that he only comes to see me and so forth . . . He has got a *free access* into this house, by coming to see Ste and talking politicks to Mr Fox. He is worse than Lord Shelburne I think. I have not seen him since the Play. I have worried you with a tiresome letter about myself, but as it is a *case* (and that they generally are long) which you are to decide upon, I shall make no excuse but go on."

But Sarah did not in fact, laying down her pen and putting her arms above her head as she stretched and yawned. It was late and she was tired and yet it had been essential that she write to Susan telling her all she felt about Charles Bunbury, as the Marquis styled himself.

The two girls had decided some while ago that Susan should help Sarah when it came to the choice of husband. Stunned as both of them had been by His Majesty's behaviour, they had regarded the Earl of Erroll's proposal as something of a joke, but the beautiful Bunbury was different. Terrified of losing yet another suitor and, even worse, her dignity in the eyes of the ever-watchful *beau monde*, Sarah had decided to accept Susan's advice in the matter. So far, not a single person in London had been able to detect the smallest sign of the inner conflict and torment which Sarah had endured secretly ever since the King had passed her by for another. No longer caring what happened to her so long as she maintained her apparently carefree character, she had now reached the stage where marriage to anyone, provided he was both pretty and eligible, seemed the most desirable thing in the world. Delighting herself with the thought of George's face on the morning her betrothal would be publicly announced, Sarah held her letter up to the light.

Because so much of what she truly thought had to be written down, she and Susan used code names for the three men who so far had or seemed likely to seek Sarah's hand. George was Prince Prettyman, the Earl was Ajax, and Charles the

Marquis. It was as good a cover as any and having reread her letter to make certain she had used pseudonyms throughout, Sarah finally got into bed. Yet sleep would not come and in the darkness she saw a mental picture of the Marquis's stony face when he had handed her out of her carriage.

Both Lady Caroline and Mr Fox insisted that his remarks about marrying a fine lady were a kind of proposal and that she ought to think seriously about it, but Sarah was not sure. There was something about Charles Bunbury, some intangible thing, that puzzled her. Deep in her mind was the suspicion that he suffered from innate vanity, that he loved everything about himself, his clothes, his exquisite hair, worn to below his ears, his handsome features, and that she, once so hotly pursued by the King himself, represented an ideal person to be seen with round the town. Yet Charles had not liked it when she told him not to marry in a hurry. Did he perhaps think that was her way of refusing him and had he taken offence?

Sighing deeply, Sarah turned over and tried hard to sleep but again unwanted images came into her mind. Why was it that she still thought of the man who had robbed her of her virginity, to this day torn between love and hate by her tumultuous memories of him? If Court gossip could be relied upon, His Majesty was very contented with Charlotte and it was rumoured that the mousy Queen was already pregnant. It would seem that the couple had settled down completely to married life, dull though it was. Sarah supposed, without bitterness, that a boring routine must suit the man she had once held so dear.

"It wouldn't have been like that with me," she murmured into her pillow. "I would have kept Prince Prettyman on his toes."

And then Sarah wondered if that was what was wrong with her, if men found her too challenging, other than Ajax of course, who was all brawn and no brain and simply couldn't be taken seriously. With these none too comforting ideas she finally fell asleep, only to dream that everything was nightmare and in truth she had married the King, that St James's Palace had become a great court, a centre for men of wit and learning where scholarship and gaiety walked hand in hand, all overseen by a beautiful Queen whose ease and graciousness were the envy of everyone who knew her.

By the time she got back from Heathrow it was midnight and the Garden Flat seemed the most desolate and lonely place on earth. Standing in her bedroom, her suitcases dumped on the floor around her, Sidonie could have wept. Never since she moved in had the flat felt quite so empty nor so devoid of the happiness she had come to associate with it.

Lack of sleep wasn't helping, Sidonie knew that. She had left Pulkovo, St Petersburg's airport, at seven o'clock in the evening, seen off by a waving Basil and an Alexei who had brushed his eyes with his sleeve and called her "a great and true artist", before kissing her on both cheeks. Then, nonsensically, she had arrived at Heathrow at ten, having lost two hours on the flight. Though it was midnight in London her body was telling her that it was two o'clock in the morning and all Sidonie wanted to do was go to bed. But her mind was still in overdrive and she knew she would have to stay up at least another hour, a trick she had long ago learned after giving a concert, in order to get any rest at all. Sitting in the kitchen, sipping tea, Sidonie thought back over her Russian tour.

For a great many reasons it had·been one of the most successful she had ever undertaken. The powerful combination of the vast empire of the Tsars, its warm-hearted people, ever willing to show her by their applause in what high esteem they held her and, of course, the exuberant personality of the multitalented Alexei, had created a never-to-be-forgotten impression.

The one bad memory had come from Nigel, as was probably to be expected. After the evening she had spent with him, at which he had eaten little while consuming a great deal too much vodka, he had wanted to go to bed with her. Forcing his way into her room in the hotel he had pinioned her against the wall and smothered her mouth with foul-breathed kisses. Releasing her hands as he undid his trousers, he had given Sidonie the opportunity to struggle free, push him hard, drunkenly swaying as he was, and bolt out. Looking back over her shoulder, her final view of Nigel had been one of him lying flat on his back on the floor his trousers round his ankles, a terrible pair of white Y-fronts well in evidence.

The only address Sidonie had had on her was Alexei's and she had made her way to his flat by taxi and there spent the night giggling with relief, drinking domestic champagne and eating black market caviar. As soon as dawn had come up and Russia had risen to go to work, they had started an impromptu concert, she on the piano and he on the violin. Eventually he had seen her back to the hotel, accompanying her to her room where Nigel still snored in his horrible knickers. Going back down to reception, Alexei had telephoned in-house while she just laughed helplessly.

"Hello. Mr Beltram MP? This is the KGB. We have been watching you. You are in a woman's room wearing large loose pants. For this crime you are banished to Siberia for eighty-two years. Now move your arse, you fat old fairy."

High on champagne, on giggling, on their shared talent, they had breakfasted together then Sidonie had gone on to do a four-hour rehearsal. It had been marvellous, vividly reminding her of her student days in Paris where life had been hard work combined with great and glorious fun.

When the time to go to St Petersburg had eventually come, Sidonie had felt sad to leave the delights of Moscow, though the breathtaking sight of the Winter Palace, fabulous as a dream, and the Hermitage, built by Catherine the Great of the funny little spectacles and snuff box, to house her art collection, had in some measure compensated. But then Sidonie's phone had rung on the very night of her concert in the legendary Malachite Drawing Room of the Empresses, where the last Tsarina of Russia, she who was doomed to be shot in a squalid cellar, had been dressed for her wedding.

"This is the KGB," a voice had said. "Are you wearing knickers? If not you are sentenced to forty-nine years in Siberia without any."

"Such rudery can only be Alexei," she had answered. "Where are you?"

"Downstairs in reception. I'm hoping to do an encore with you."

Such lovely silliness, such frivolity, had put Finnan to the back of her mind and it had been almost with a sense of guilt that Sidonie had gone to ring him on the night before he was due to fly to Canada. But there she had reckoned without the Russian telephone system. Lines out from the hotel were limited and there were large queues at the phone boxes and notices warning of six-hour delays. If she had been in Moscow Sidonie could have gone to Basil's office and asked him to get her through but in St Petersburg she knew no one and had been forced to wait. By the time she got a line it was eleven o'clock at night in London and only the answerphone spoke at the other end.

"If you hear this I want you to know I'm missing you very much indeed. The tour is a great success and I will write as soon as I get back. I love you, Finnan. I really do," Sidonie had said breathlessly, wondering which was giving her the courage – being in a country still relatively savage, so used to hardship and drama that pretence seemed ridiculous, or Alexei's refreshing influence. But whatever the reason she had done it and the message was there on Finnan's machine.

During the last ten days of the tour, Sidonie had been certain that the violinist was developing a youthful passion for her. She had looked up sometimes, even when playing, to see those Slavonic eyes staring·at her with such brilliance she had been left in little doubt as to what he was thinking. Despite her feelings for Finnan, Sidonie had been immensely flattered, drawn to Alexei's youth and vitality, which affected everyone with whom he came in contact.

He had taken her out to dinner on her last night, joined by Basil who had travelled from Moscow on the Trans-Siberian Express.

"How romantic that sounds. I'd love to go on it," she had said to the two Russians.

"Next time you come – and there will be a next time," Basil had answered. "I mean it, Sidonie. I am writing to Rod tomorrow to invite you back."

"Next time," Alexei had added softly, "we will perhaps be on our honeymoon, and we will take that train of snows and vanish for a whole month."

She had laughed but something about the way the violinist

had said the words sounded as if they were not meant to be funny. And now he was gone and Finnan was gone and even the cat was still in the cattery.

"Alone again," said Sidonie aloud, and unpacking her sponge bag made her way to the bathroom and prepared to forget everything in sleep.

The engagement notice had gone out in early February. "The Duke and Duchess of Richmond have pleasure in announcing that a marriage has been arranged and will shortly take place between their sister, Lady Sarah Lennox of Holland House, Kensington, and Thomas Charles Bunbury Esq., MP, of Barton Hall, Barton and Mildenhall, Suffolk."

It had caused a stir because the young couple were both so beautiful and rich, or rather would be one day. For though Charles Bunbury had little money at present, he was in fact heir to a baronetcy which included very large estates and a substantial fortune. It was a marriage made in heaven, some thought, though others speculated that Sarah had gone for the prettiest beau she could find just to spite the King, while Horace Walpole cruelly declared that Bunbury was taking a wife to "show himself more a man". However nobody dared ask him to explain the implications·of that remark.

A constituency had been found for Mr Bunbury that he might fit in more easily with the highly political family into which he was marrying, and Charles also joined Johnson's famous Literary Club. But neither politics nor learning were his true loves, for the French Marquis had a passion for the turf, and was never happier than when surrounded by the racing fraternity. Horses were his entire life and it was as well for Sarah that she could be enthusiastic about them. Indeed it struck her as admirable that such a pretty fop as her future husband was so clever, indeed downright inspired, when it came to buying and matching horseflesh. Charles might be described as a chicken orator, an infant Hercules, by his political detractors, but when it came to racing matters he was considered by many to be a considerable authority.

"Do you love him?" whispered Charles James to his aunt.

"Of course, I do," she answered a shade too vehemently.

"So, he's going to make you happy?"

"Why shouldn't he, he's the most elegant fellow in town."

"Elegance ain't all," the boy answered succinctly, then he paused and added, "Charles ain't *too* elegant, is he Sal?"

"What do you mean by that?"

"Nothing," answered her nephew airily, and refused to be drawn further.

The weather changed and grew warm, the Queen grew swollen as a grape, Sarah was fitted for her wedding gown, and the King suddenly and coincidentally fell ill. Out of the blue he was attacked by a feverish cold which failed to clear up normally. This caused him to cough violently, the coughing accompanied by an "oppression on his breast", which His Majesty described as being like a stitch. He was blooded seven times and three blisters were applied to try and cure him.

There was something about this cold that worried everyone. Yet nobody, not even the royal physicians, could say exactly why. It seemed to have a mysterious severity to it and one or two of the older and more superstitious wondered if, coming when it did, it was a judgement on the King for having trifled so shockingly with Lady Sarah's affections. Thus May passed and the bride, gazing fondly on her fashionable fop, stopped counting the days and prepared to go to the altar, not in a grand royal ceremony but at a simple affair in the chapel of Holland House.

She woke with a pricking of her thumbs, with a certain hollowness in the pit of her stomach which convinced Sidonie strange forces were at work again, that the day would not pass without some sight of Sarah. Yet, fascinated as she was by this other life, this other time that ran parallel with her own, today the musician felt frightened and uneasy. She realised now how much Finnan's acceptance of the paranormal had meant to her, how reassuring his Irish ease of manner had been. Suddenly she was nervous at the idea of six months during which odd or alarming experiences could occur without having anyone to confide in. Finnan would not only be missed for his kindness and companionship, his lovemaking and passion, but for his sound common sense as well.

It was Sunday, though without the comfortable things Sidonie connected with that day. There was no music coming from any of the other flats and Jannie was either away or not baking, for there was no smell of bread either. Suddenly the first chill of winter was in the air and, getting out of bed with a slow reluctance, Sidonie went to put on the central heating and tidy her neglected home.

There was a pile of correspondence waiting for her, but one letter with a Canadian stamp she tore open immediately. It was what she had hoped it would be, a letter from Finnan albeit a brief one.

"Darling girl, As you will see from the address I have arrived safely and am now starting to settle in. The hospital is marvellous, very modern and with all the up-to-date equipment one could ever wish to see. The natives are friendly and the house which is being rented for me is charming and spacious though nothing like the old flat and my beautiful crazy neighbours. (I mean you are the former and Jannie the latter, of course!)

Heading the research team is Professor Joe Teck (quite a character I can assure you, he looks like an American footballer!) assisted by a cracking lady called Dr Jeannie O'Rourke. This would appear to denote both Scots and Irish ancestry but so far I haven't found out about this. She is an extraordinary combination of things, having thick blonde hair which appears to be natural and enormous blue eyes, yet is formidably clever and well-qualified for all that. I am terrified of her.

It broke my heart that I missed you on that last morning. Binkie, my poor little patient, left her troubles behind her at about five a.m. and that is why I was so late. I know I needn't have stayed with her but somehow I wanted to, knowing that you would understand.

I miss you already, miss the music you made in every aspect of my life, but I am sure time will fly and it will soon be spring. Take care, Sidonie. Regards to Jannie and Max. Also do give my best wishes to Sarah Lennox and company!! Please write to me soon. Fondest love, Finnan."

Sidonie took the letter into the bathroom and sat reading it,
several times in fact, while she relaxed in the foam. There was
a PS which pleased her. "I will try and ring on the Sunday you
return, in the evening. It will be about six o'clock your time
(about two p.m. here). I hope to catch you in."

Several things struck her about the letter, one being
that Dr Jeannie O'Rourke sounded far too glamorous for
comfort, though Sidonie consoled herself with the fact that
the woman was probably married, the other that Finnan had
not mentioned her breathless message on his answerphone,
given under the influence of Mother Russia and the impish
genius Alexei. It occurred to her that perhaps the Irishman
might not have heard it, and this idea appealed to her more
than the thought that he might be deliberately ignoring it.
Very cheered by the news that she would actually speak to
him today, Sidonie, having telephoned her parents to say she
was safe and well, set out to collect the cat ignoring a great
compulsion to go to Holland House.

The wedding day was very bright and fair, golden sun illuminating the park, while the private chapel, situated in the west
wing beneath the library, once a long gallery, was packed with
flowers. Elegant people crowded the pews, several Macaronis
amongst them. The Duchess of Richmond, the Lovely, lit the
front stall with her dazzling looks, though not managing to
put Emily Kildare, her sister-in-law in the shade. The Duke,
dressed superbly, was to give the bride away, while Mr Fox,
not chosen to do so, contented himself with thinking it was
a fine turn-out and everyone who was politically important to
him was present in the chapel.

Dr Francis, a former chaplain at Holland House, had been
asked to conduct the ceremony, and this was considered very
suitable as he had in the past taught all the young people,
including lessons on how to act in amateur plays. And now he
stood waiting, gowned and ready, Bible in hand, for the bride
to make her appearance.

It had been arranged that Sarah should walk the short
distance to the chapel, taking the outside path and only coming
through the house if the weather were inclement. Accordingly

the servants, every one of them, had lined up in the entrance hall and as the bride came down the stairs in her silver gown, a white petticoat trimmed with silver beneath, they cheered and opened the front door for the wedding party to step through.

There were two attendants, Lady Susan Fox-Strangeways and Sarah's younger sister, Lady Cecilia Lennox, now aged nearly twelve. Both of these were dressed in lavender blue which complemented the bride's beauty, which this day Mr Fox thought transcendent. Yet it was with a strange sense of alarm that Sarah took her brother Richmond's arm and stepped out onto the curving steps leading into the courtyard. It seemed to her that there was an odd feeling in the air, a feeling she associated with the ghostly woman. And as she walked towards the chapel, Sarah glanced back over her shoulder uneasily.

"The King's not here, if that's who you're looking for," drawled her brother. "He's sick as a dog and like as not thinking about funerals not weddings."

"That is a terrible thing to say."

"But yet 'tis rumoured."

The sound of the organ was drowning conversation and the bride thought it best not to answer. Raising her chin she walked proudly into the chapel and straight up the aisle to where her bridegroom, dressed in purple satin like the dandy he was, awaited her. Smiling, Sarah turned to hand her bouquet of summer flowers to Susan, and it was then that she saw her, the unmistakable hair catching her eye immediately.

The woman stood at the back of the chapel, behind the pews, wearing that usual half-frightened, half-entranced expression of hers. It occurred to Sarah to call out that there was a stranger in their midsts, that an uninvited guest had come who now stood watching the ceremony without permission. But it was too late; Dr Francis had begun to speak. Deliberately catching the stranger's eye to show that she was aware of her presence, Sarah turned away and concentrated on the important task of getting married.

As soon as she had brought Catty Scarlatti back and settled

him in with a tin of sardines, Sidonie had gone out again, drawn compulsively to Holland House.

On that cold September day, with the leaves crunching beneath her feet and the sky the cool bright blue of irises, Sidonie made her way up Holland Walk and then turned left, entering the park by the path that ran beside the youth hostel. There were people everywhere, looking at the flowers, taking the air, making a noise, and Sidonie wished that she could be alone to appreciate the place, to imagine its former splendour in peace.

It was perhaps this need to escape that turned her feet towards the courtyard, towards the fire exit of the youth hostel, the door that she had gone through on the very first occasion she had seen Sarah Lennox. And now, it seemed, that by this very simple means Sidonie had yet again entered a time fault, for a servant in clothes of the eighteenth century ran down the corridor just in front of her.

There were lovely sounds in the air, of music and laughter, and the high bright shrillness of excitement, and everywhere an almost tangible gaiety. Unseen by a crowd of revellers in whose midst she found herself, Sidonie was swept along and it was no surprise to end up in a flower-filled chapel, the organ booming, a minister in vestments standing before the altar, the bridegroom sitting in the front, his back towards the congregation.

It was an eloquent back, slim and shapely, clad in purple satin lavishly trimmed with lilac lace. Sidonie was just appreciating the extreme elegance of its owner when he turned and looked straight at her. Certain that he could not see her, she continued to stare at him, guessing that this must be the exquisite Charles Bunbury himself, the man whom Sarah was destined to marry.

He was unbelievably good-looking, there was no denying that. A thin aristocratic nose dominated Bunbury's features but his glittering dark blue eyes were also fine and his mouth beautifully shaped. He had interesting hands which were quite square and practical in comparison with the rest of him. Sidonie could imagine him handling horses with the greatest of ease.

Suddenly, a wild sharp smell of lilac blossom filled the air and Sarah entered the chapel, exquisite as ever, her midnight hair threaded with flowers, a choker of white pearls nestling against her creamy skin. The bride was seventeen years old and looked disturbingly lovely.

She walked up the aisle without seeing Sidonie, the musician knew that. But when the girl turned to hand her bouquet to a small sweet thing who could only be Susan, Sarah's marvellous eyes picked out the intruder. The bride stood staring for a second or two, uncertainty struggling in her face and then, almost with a shrug, she turned away and put her hand into that of the exquisite bridegroom whose languid manner did not change at Sarah's delightful touch.

Remembering how the King had thrilled beneath it, Sidonie could only feel despair that the two young lovers, Sarah and George, were now irrevocably parted, each one of them gone to a partner not only incapable of fully appreciating their splendid sensual worth but also unable to give them the passionate love they craved.

She turned at that, leaving the wedding behind her, anxious to get back into her own century and the familiarity of the flat. But this time it was hard to do and Sidonie wandered about in the park, hearing the sounds of the wedding feast floating down from the big house, until it became dark and she was suddenly aware of the distant noise of traffic from Kensington High Street.

Somewhat shaken by the difficulty in coming back, the sound of Finnan's voice speaking inside the Garden Flat was so eerie and unexpected that Sidonie positively fell through the front door, tripping over a large bouquet of red roses which stood propped against it. It was the answerphone, of course, and too late to pick up the receiver she stood helplessly listening to the doctor's voice say, "I'll try again another time. Hope to hear from you," before the line cleared. Horrified, Sidonie gazed at her watch and saw that it was six o'clock. The experience in another dimension had lasted roughly four hours. Then she remembered the flowers and went to get them, hoping desperately that they had come from Finnan.

The card attached read, "Sorry I behaved so badly. Forgive me? I still love you, Nigel."

"That's all I bloody well need," Sidonie shouted.

Just then the phone rang again and switching off the answering machine she leapt to lift the receiver, wondering whether Finnan had decided to take a chance and ring back.

"Hello," she said, panting slightly.

"Sidonie?" answered Nigel's glutinous voice. "Is that you?"

"Yes, of course," she snapped back. "Who did you think it was?"

"I didn't recognise you. You sounded out of breath. I just want to know if the flowers arrived."

"Yes, thank you, they did." Sidonie tried to control her voice. "Look, Nigel, you shouldn't have sent them."

"I had to, I behaved appallingly. But I need you back. I'm still in love with you. Let's start seeing each other again."

"I hate that euphemism and the answer is no. Our relationship ended in court, Nigel."

And with that she hung up. The phone went again instantly and Sidonie switched the answerphone back on.

"I'm not giving up so easily," said Nigel's voice. "I'm still in love with you and I can't help it. I'm getting you back, Sidonie, if it's the last thing I do."

There was a click and the dialling tone as he hung up. Running back the tape Sidonie realised in horror that Nigel's call had wiped off Finnan's. And though she played it back several times all she could hear were the doctor's last few words.

". . . Hope to hear from you."

Damn you, Nigel, she thought, and went to her desk to write to Finnan.

But the day's strange experience had tired her more than she thought and Sidonie just sat there, staring at the blank sheet of paper. Somewhere, at another level of time, Sarah Lennox was probably leaving for her honeymoon with the beautiful Bunbury. Somewhere, a girl would be spending her wedding night with the man she had chosen to replace the King in her affections. And knowing the outcome as she did, Sidonie sighed for her.

"What was that?" said Sarah.

"What?" repeated Charles, his face pale against the pillows, his lawn nightshirt making him look even whiter.

"Somebody sighed in this very room. I heard it."

"Nonsense, come to bed."

They were still at Holland House, the wedding feast having gone on far too late into the evening to contemplate setting forth for Suffolk. But to compensate for this disappointment, the young couple had been put in a very grand room, usually reserved for the Duke of Richmond, the great draped bed hurriedly decked with flowers for the wedding night.

"Are you sure it was not you who sighed?"

"There was no sigh, Sarah, just the murmur of the wind."

"How prettily you said that," she answered, and with those words the bride got into bed, her dark hair loose and brushed out, and snuggled against her husband's chest.

He pulled her into his arms, kissed her a few times, and then performed his matrimonial duty without love, without passion, without anything resembling what had passed between her and His Majesty, virgins though both of them had been at the time.

Sarah lay in the candlelight staring at her new husband, his face in repose more exquisite than ever. She had never felt so disappointed in her entire·life. Her French Marquis was, after all, nothing but a cold fish, unaroused even by her extraordinary beauty. The perfunctory intercourse she had just endured filled her with feelings of dislike and, with a sinking heart, Sarah thought of all the years that lay ahead of her tied to a man behind whose handsome appearance lay a soul devoid of inner fire.

# Seventeen

It was a revelation, like a dream come true; the city of Paris in springtime was without doubt the most beautiful on earth. To Sarah, who had never visited the capital before, the very smell in the air was enough to give pleasure. The flowers clustering in the markets, the bakers' shops, the watered dust from the streets, all combined in a unique odour which seemed to her to be the very essence of the French metropolis. And this family visit – for Bunbury's wife was in Paris with her sisters Caroline and Louisa, her two elder nephews Ste and Charles James, and an irrepressible friend who delighted in the name of Clotworthy Upton – could not help but be both pleasurable and amusing. No pastime being more stimulating than to sit in the Tivoli Gardens, smaller than Vaux Hall but somehow more interesting, and watch the world passing by; pretty men, fine ladies, whores and washerwomen, scoundrels and scandalmongers, uneasily rubbing shoulders as they thronged past in the daily parade.

"Is it not *fine*?" Sarah said to Ste, and he nodded with enthusiastic agreement.

He was twenty now, exactly five days older than Sarah, but alas had inherited none of the beauty of his aunt's side of the family. For the fact was that Ste looked remarkably like Mr Fox, being both portly and heavily jowled. Unlike his father, however, he was also rather deaf which made the young man difficult in strange company, while his character was reputed to suffer from certain other weaknesses.

The truth was that he had been born a compulsive gambler and by the age of fifteen had already become massively in debt. And even when after a great deal of effort Ste had cured himself and given up the tables, his passion for clothes and horses undid him once more and he had again plunged towards ruin. If it had not been for his indulgent father, who constantly settled his bills, Sarah paled to think what would have happened to her eldest nephew. But for all that there was nothing cruel about Ste. He was merely weak. He found temptation impossible to resist, and as a result was adored by his contemporaries who could see his faults only as a mirror of their own.

Charles James, on the other hand, was growing up precocious yet amusingly so. At fourteen he was a slave to fashion, on one occasion arriving at the Playhouse with his hair powdered and *coiffé en aile de pigeon*. He was now fully in charge of dramatic performances at Holland House in which he both starred and directed the other actors. Currently he was feigning jealousy because Sarah spent more time talking to Ste than she did to him, and demonstrated this by going into a fit of the sulks, which he was doing as the family party sat in the Tivoli Gardens waiting for the firework display to begin. Knowing her nephew was glowering, Sarah ignored him and instead turned deliberately towards her sisters.

"I realise one should not say this but I do miss Susan."

Caroline's face grew angular, an art she had unconsciously mastered as she grew older. "Truth to tell, so do I, though I would never dream of saying so in front of her father."

"Would Lord Ilchester be horrified, do you believe?"

"I think he would."

There had been a great change of circumstances in the lives of the Foxes. Just before Sarah's marriage to Charles Bunbury, Caroline had been created a peeress of the realm in her own right, being elevated to the rank of Baroness Holland in April, 1762. A year later Henry Fox had followed her into the peerage. On 16th April, 1763, he had received the title of Baron Holland of Foxley, Wiltshire, his life's ambition at last fulfilled. Looking back to how he had once eloped with Lady Caroline Lennox and created a scandal, the new Baron felt that Society had finally forgiven him. But history has a naughty way of repeating itself and no sooner had the old fox become complacent than things started to go wrong for his niece.

During the Christmas celebrations of 1763 there had been a great family gathering. Sarah and Charles Bunbury had come from Suffolk and Susan from Somersetshire to join in the festivities. The theatricals were organised by Charles James who, that year, had hired a professional actor to take the leading man's part. Sarah, who had learned to make the very best of her marriage, allowing her husband freedom to go off with his friends while she enjoyed her own social life, flirting a little with some of the better looking men, found it so wonderful to be back at Holland House that she noticed nothing at first. In fact it had been her husband, aged twenty-three by then and more dandified than ever, who had first pointed it out to her.

"He's an attractive fellow, that Irish actor."

"William O'Brien? He certainly has melting eyes and a glorious smile."

Charles had nodded. "Your friend Susan seems to think so."

"*Does* she?"

"Indeed. And he's equally smitten with her, poor fool."

"Why do you say that? Why do you call him fool for liking her? Just because you prefer men's company to that of your wife it does not follow that everyone is the same."

Charles had stood up, very slim and tall. "What are you implying, Sarah?"

"Nothing," she had answered, "nothing at all."

For though it was true she was left to her own devices while Charles hung about with his racing cronies, what wife so comfortably situated could grumble at it? Marriage had turned out to be a loveless experience, nothing like Sarah had expected, but for all that life was enjoyable enough.

Yet Charles Bunbury had been right. Observing Susan and William O'Brien together nobody could deny that they were deeply attracted one to the other. Caroline and Henry Fox had seen their niece's obvious infatuation and Mr O'Brien's equally obvious reciprocation, and were quite relieved when, Twelfth Night over, the handsome Irishman departed. But they, who had once deceived Caroline's parents so cleverly, did not think hard enough. With the coming of the new year, 1764, the lovers continued to meet, very secretly and very discreetly.

In the spring, Susan had been having her portrait painted by the well-known artist, Catherine Reed, and William had been in the habit of meeting her occasionally at the sittings. Whether Miss Reed was responsible or whether it was servants' gossip, the fact remained that the matter had been reported to Susan's parents, Lord and Lady Ilchester. Anger had not described their reaction. Mr O'Brien had been pronounced penniless, worthless and Irish to boot. Susan had been ordered to give him up and, amidst an ocean of tears, agreed on condition that she could see her lover alone to take her final leave.

The couple had met on 1st April to say farewell. Four days later Susan Fox-Strangeways had celebrated her twenty-first birthday and had come of legal age. The very next morning she had set out early for the artist's studio declaring that she was going to have breakfast with Lady Sarah Bunbury, currently staying in her town house, on the way. But Susan had only been gone a few moments when she discovered, to her apparent consternation, that she had left behind a particular cap in which she was being painted. Turning to the footman who accompanied her everywhere, Susan had asked him to return home to fetch it.

The watchdog out of sight, Susan had literally run to where William O'Brien awaited her in a carriage. The couple had hastened to Covent Garden Church and had been married then and there, afterwards going to Mr O'Brien's villa in Dunstable whence the news of the elopement had reached the ears of the bride's furious family. Only Mr Fox, now Lord Holland, had stood by the girl, remembering his own far from saintly past. He had given Susan an allowance of £400 per year for three years, and had worked tirelessly to get William a job abroad, at a safe distance from the fulminating Lord Ilchester. So it had been that in September, 1764, Lady Susan and Mr William O'Brien had sailed for New York to become flax farmers.

"How strange it is without her," Sarah said to Caroline now.

Caroline turned to look her sister fully in the face. "But are you missing your husband as well, my dearest?"

"Of course I am," Sarah answered, just a trifle too emphatically. "But he did not want to come and that's an end to it. There is much to do with the horses at present."

"I wonder you do not have a child to keep you company."

"I am doing what I can," Sarah answered, looking away, only for Louisa, now aged twenty-one and married for six years without a baby, to join in the conversation.

"There are some particular saint's relics at St Cyr which, if you pray to them, give one a child. Apparently the Dauphine went and became pregnant."

"Are you going?"

"Yes, I am. I think you should come with me, Sarah. After all, you have been married almost three years now."

"Very well, I'll accompany you if it would please you," her younger sister answered carelessly.

"They say the Queen is about to produce again."

"When *isn't* she producing? Married not quite four years and two and a half children already."

"Sarah!" said Louisa, pretending to be shocked. But she was smiling, wondering what would have happened if her sister had become Queen.

Looking at Sarah now, Louisa remembered a story Caroline had repeated. Apparently their sister had gone to the Palace to see the newborn Prince of Wales, lying in his bassinet, gurgling prettily. Sarah had robustly kissed the little creature, declaring it a fine young animal, a beautiful, strong, handsome child, and been reprimanded by the nurse for not calling the boy a prince. At that very moment the King had come along, visibly trembling, and enquired whether Sarah had had fine weather all summer. She had apparently answered, "Yes", and that had been the sum total of the conversation. That he was still attracted to her had been the consensus of the fashionable world.

'And now,' thought Louisa, 'here she is without her husband and without a child. I do hope all is well and that she is not still attracted to *him*.'

But Sarah's sister said nothing of her fears and let the sound of the orchestra fill her mind, relaxing as she sat back on her little chair and watched the dancers.

Ste, presently in favour with Sarah, stood up and made her a bow and they danced off together, laughing a good deal when Charles James looked sullen.

"Will you step out with me?" Louisa said to him kindly, for she *was* that, and generous and good-hearted into the bargain.

"My pleasure, my Lady," her nephew answered gallantly, and in a moment they were all on their feet, Clotworthy Upton, nicknamed Tatty, taking Caroline by the hand.

Changing partners, the family party continued to laugh and enjoy themselves until finally, rather warm from their exertions, they sat down again to watch the fireworks, Ste gasping formidably.

It was a fine night, the pretty twinkling candle lights strung from tree to tree round the circular wooden dance floor illuminating not only the faces of those below but also the leaves and the sky, which was a soft lavender shade, full of dusk. With a sudden spluttering sound followed by a burst of colour, the fireworks began, roaring magnificently into the gentle evening as Sarah shivered with a sudden inexplicable presentiment.

Paris was the only bright spot on a particularly grey horizon. Much as Sidonie despised herself for allowing it to happen, she had been plunged into gloom ever since Finnan's Christmas phone call, the whole idea of which had been to exchange greetings verbally rather than by letter.

The first mistake, as she realised now, had been to cut short her visit to her parents and drive home on Boxing Day in order to speak to him privately. Finnan had written in his Christmas card that he would telephone at two p.m. British time and, accordingly, Sidonie had got home by twelve and then hung about watching television, generally wasting what should have been a jolly day. But when the phone hadn't rung by four she had started to panic and two more wretched hours had followed during which she simply hadn't known what to do. Then, at six, Sidonie had finally dialled Finnan's number, having written to ask for it immediately after his message had been wiped from her answerphone.

A woman had spoken at the other end and Sidonie had stood, receiver in hand, too stunned to say a word. Finally, she had pulled herself together.

"May I talk to Dr O'Neill, please."

"Sure," answered the husky assured Canadian voice. "Hey, Finnan honey, there's a call for you."

There had been a slight delay and then he had spoken, and Sidonie had known at once that Finnan had been imbibing the Christmas spirit fairly liberally.

"Hello, darling girl, how are you?"

"Hello, Happy Christmas. You sound as if you're enjoying yourself."

The words had come out more sarcastically than Sidonie had intended.

"Yes, I've a few friends round for drinks," he had answered somewhat defensively. "What are you up to?"

A mad fit had come over her. "I'm off to Rod's this evening. He's entertaining at home. He's got some Russian musicians over."

"Anyone you know?"

"Yes, Alexei Orlov. He's great fun and a brilliant violinist. We really hit it off in Moscow."

"Good. Did you have a pleasant Christmas Day?"

"Very quiet but very nice. What did you do?"

"One of the medical team has got a log cabin on the lake. A whole crowd of us were invited there for lunch."

"It sounds blissful."

For no reason other than her own sense of insecurity, Sidonie could feel herself getting irritated.

"I hope you didn't come back home just to phone me," she said sharply. "And by the way, what happened?"

There was a pause. "I'm sorry. The truth is I forgot the time delay. Please forgive me. I just wasn't thinking."

There was a faint noise as if someone had just walked past the doctor and Sidonie felt that they might as well have walked on her grave.

"Of course I forgive you. Don't give it another thought. Happy New Year, Finnan, I've got to go. You get back to your friend."

He didn't correct her use of the singular. "Happy New Year, darling. Write soon please."

"I'm off to Paris on the 30th. I'm playing on New Year's Eve at a private party. I'll send you a postcard. 'Bye."

And with that Sidonie put down the receiver, wanting to cry but furiously determined not to be a wimp. Instead she immediately dialled her parents' number.

"Hello," Jane's voice answered.

"Mummy, it's Sidonie. There's been a change in my arrangements. I'd like to come back home for a couple of days."

"Oh, how wonderful, that will be a treat."

"The only thing is, I daren't miss practice with a concert so near. Can you phone Silbury Abbas and ask if I can play there?"

"Of course. I'm sure they'll be delighted."

"Then I'll just pop up and beg Jannie to do the cat for a little bit longer."

And that had been that. She had returned home like a sad child, certain that Finnan had found himself a sleeping partner, convinced that she herself had been little more.

"Put it behind you," said Jane, seeing her daughter's face.

"What?"

"You know perfectly well what I mean. You must forget all about your Irishman for the time being. It's no good conducting a long-distance affair. Lines of communication sometimes get confused."

Sidonie stared at her mother with narrowed eyes. "Are you suddenly psychic?"

"No, just good at guesswork. The Christmas call went wrong, didn't it?"

"He had a woman there. She answered the phone."

"That doesn't prove a thing. Suppose your young Russian friend had picked up your hotel extension? Finnan could just as easily have jumped to the wrong conclusion."

Sidonie shrugged her shoulders. "I suppose you're right. But . . ."

"My darling, even if I'm wrong there is nothing you can do about it. All I beg is that you don't take the situation to heart like you did your divorce. You wore yourself to a shadow over that."

"That was because I was anxious to get it over. I just wanted to be shot of Nigel. This is a bit different," Sidonie answered defensively.

"Maybe, but take my advice all the same. Wait till the man comes back. You'll be able to gauge the position as soon as you see him. Then you'll know what to do about it, won't you?"

Sidonie smiled at her. "You're very wise today."

"Does that irritate you?"

"Only a little. And that's probably because you can see right through me."

"Oh no, I can't," Jane answered instantly. "You're too talented for anyone ever to be able to do that. It's just that I understand certain things. Put Finnan on ice, darling. Concentrate on having some fun. Have a fling with a Frenchman; that would do you good."

"Are those your instructions, Mother?" asked Sidonie primly.

"You're too old to order about but I know what I should do."

"Ought I to tell Father of your terrible ways?"

Jane laughed. "You may if you wish, but it was he who taught me them in the first place, child bride that I was."

And her mother certainly still looked remarkably young, Sidonie thought, her short dark hair stylish and fashionable, the fight for her figure bravely holding out.

"I'm thirty-four. You were twenty-one when I was born. Not much hope for me then, is there?" Sidonie suddenly felt enormously depressed, full of an urgent nagging need to have a child. "I wish I'd got pregnant by Finnan," she added, morosely.

Jane looked at her, her expression acute. "Did you tell him that?"

"Of course not."

"Perhaps you should have done."

"What makes you say so?"

"He might well regard you as an icon. Someone to be put on a pedestal."

Sidonie shook her head vigorously. "I had a similar conversation with Rod and the whole thing makes me furious. What am I supposed to do? Wear a label saying, 'I may be a musician but you strike a chord with me'? Men are utterly pathetic. Bugger the lot of 'em."

"Even the infant prodigy?"

"Alexei? No, he's different. He doesn't give a monkey's as they say."

"Then it's a pity he won't be in Paris," her mother answered crisply.

"What do you mean? He's a child, an infant, hardly out of his Babygro."

"So what?" said Jane unconventionally, and smiled a rather knowing smile.

Even in the biting wind the city was beautiful, Sidonie thought. She stood in the Place de la Concorde, her Russian hat pulled down over her ears, considering the fate of Marie Antoinette who had met her death in this huge and desolate place. The story Sidonie had heard, the story which had brought the Queen's tragedy home to her more clearly than anything else, was that of the wretched woman being forced to relieve herself publicly in the courtyard of her prison in the Conciergerie when the sight of the awaiting tumbril had moved her to fear. Just like Catherine the Great's funny little spectacles it was this account of human weakness that had made the French Queen suddenly seem real to the woman from another age.

It was the morning of New Year's Eve, a hint of snow in the air, yet despite the cold weather Sidonie had arrived in the French capital the day before in order to sightsee on foot. Of all the cities in the world, Paris was her favourite for walking in, and knowing the place as well as she did, Sidonie now strode through the great square just as if she were still a student and headed up the Champs Elysées, stopping for a coffee in a little café held dear in memory.

She had risen at six that morning and had already done three hours' practice which would be followed by another session later on. But now she was free to explore and without hesitation the musician made her way beyond the Arc de Triomphe and along the Avenue Foch towards the Porte Dauphine. It was through this city gate that Marie Antoinette had arrived in Paris in 1770, a fifteen-year-old bride come to marry the Dauphin. Sarah Lennox would have been twenty-five by then, Sidonie thought, and already disillusioned, a broken marriage behind her. How times appeared to change and yet did they, did anything ever really alter?

Going through the Porte, Sidonie made her way along the Rue de Suresnes into the Bois de Boulogne, singing as she went.

"As I stroll along the Bois Boulong with an independent air, you can hear the girls declare, 'He must be a millionaire.' Then I hear them sigh and wish to die, and see them wink the other eye, at the man who broke the bank at Monte Carlo."

But the words were already dying on her lips as she came round the corner by the lake and saw that a festival was in progress, a pretty pageant with everybody in fancy dress. Smiling at the charm of this delightful crowd, every man, woman and child dressed in period costume, and all from the mid-eighteenth century at that, Sidonie hurried forward to join them.

She saw storybook children running and bowling hoops, saw ladies of high fashion studiously ignoring military men who ogled and smiled and elegantly bowed. The sparkle of candle lamps hung from trees, boats on the lake were lit by lanterns. Dandies and fops jostled both each other and the flower-sellers who wandered amongst them clutching baskets full of their delicate wares. In the air was an indefinable perfume; the combined essence of opulent scent, unwashed skin, carnations, horse chestnut trees and dust. In the distance, fireworks cracked and banged, their luminescence cascading through a sky the colour of lilac. It was a scene of unbelievable gaiety and splendour enhanced by the presence of one particular jewel-bright girl. For sitting in the shadow of the trees and regarding Sidonie with a gravely sweet smile was Sarah Bunbury, born Lennox.

She should have expected it, the musician realised that. Yet the sight and smell of the crowd had seemed so real she had really thought herself to be witnessing some sort of carnival or, perhaps, the making of a historical film. Yet here was Sarah, in Paris, saying "Good evening," and holding out her hand, recognising at last that Sidonie posed no threat, that be she ghost or living creature she certainly meant no harm. The modern woman would have spoken then, would have gone to cross the barrier of centuries and touch Sarah's arm, but without warning the vision blurred and faded like a mirage in a desert, then was gone.

It was daytime and it was cold and snow had begun to fall in the Bois de Boulogne. With a shiver deep to her bones, Sidonie snuggled into her coat and went to hail a taxi to take her back to her hotel in the Rue Saint Hyacinthe. Yet even in the comfort of her room it seemed that memories of the past were everywhere. The hotel was a converted eighteenth-century mansion which had belonged to one of Marie Antoinette's principal ladies-in-waiting. Indeed the Queen and Louis XVI were supposed to have stayed there, rather in the manner of Queen Elizabeth I who had bedded down practically everywhere, Sidonie presumed.

Suddenly feeling lonely and wondering quite how to fill in the next few hours before she was due to practise, Sidonie decided to go down to the bar. But even as she neared reception a familiar voice reached her and she began to hurry, eager with anticipation.

"Madame Brooks, she is here?"

"Oui, Monsieur."

"Please tell her I await her. Orlov. Alexei Orlov."

"Without knickers," shrieked Sidonie, and flew to meet the violinist who stood in the small hallway dressed for the cold, his head encased in an enormous fur hat on which he had pinned a badge with the word "Artificiel".

"You cheat," she said, pointing to it.

The expressive shoulders rose. "My French is not good enough to give a lecture to protesters on the needs of the Russian economy."

"What do you mean?"

"I love animals but I love people too. We need to sell hats, we need to sell everything."

"Enough!" said Sidonie. "I can't bear to see you serious. It doesn't suit you."

Alexei embraced her, kissing her smackingly on both cheeks before brushing her lips with his. "I am always serious. Now, have you eaten? We have lunch, no?"

"Just a snack. I'm playing tonight."

"Then you should eat plenty. Me, I am a glutton before a concert."

"When there's something to glut on."

"A pun," answered Alexei. "This I recognise." He held Sidonie at arm's length. "I have missed you, Tovarish. I was so happy when Basil told me you would be in Paris at the same time as me. How long can you stay?"

"I'm engaged to play at a charity performance in the Château de Chambord on Twelfth Night. Renault cars are sponsoring it. I'll be leaving on the 3rd of January."

"Me too," said Alexei and grinned. "Rod fixed it."

"Is this the start of your European tour?"

"You bet. All the big cities of France, then Italy, then Britain. I shall be successful, I think. Rod has got me a Wigmore Hall date by pulling much string."

"You'll be a wow," Sidonie answered and impulsively took his hand. "Are you coming to hear me tonight?"

"Where are you playing?"

"In a private house in the Marais. It's rather a prestigious party for New Year's Eve."

"Can you get me in?"

"I'll do my best."

"Then what shall we do afterwards?"

"I've been invited to stay on but I suppose I could slip away."

"It doesn't matter. As long as we see the New Year in together."

"I'd like that."

It was just as if they had only been apart for a few hours. Their bantering line in chat resumed where they had left off and it was with a light heart that Sidonie went off to practise, having first made sure that it would be possible for Alexei to have a seat at the back of the room.

"The performance begins at nine and the party at eight. It will be dinner jackets, by the way."

"But, of course."

"Do you still have the same one?"

"Naturally. I am very fond of that suit."

"Well, that's just as well," said Sidonie and went off laughing into the bitter afternoon.

She dressed extra carefully for this concert, fully aware that the chic of Parisiennes was something to be reckoned with. Layers of chiffon were Sidonie's choice and scarlet the colour. An expensive French *coiffeur* worked a miracle with her head so that a style of tousled elegance emerged, one or two curls appearing to escape from a Grecian knot which it had taken him an hour to create. Round her neck Sidonie put a Bedazzle choker of Venetian beads with clustered earrings that would not fly about as she played.

"Not bad," she said, looking at herself in the hotel mirror, and then ruined the effect by putting on woollen mittens to keep her hands warm until the very last moment before she went to the keyboard.

Tonight Sidonie was to play a François Blanchet harpsichord made in Paris in 1756. It had been taken to the house in the Marais that afternoon and tuned, while Sidonie had practised in her old workshop in the Rue de Richelieu not far from the apartment of her teacher Monique Amboise. Dauntingly, Madame Amboise, now in her late sixties, was to attend tonight's performance.

The Marais had once been an aristocratic district of Paris and still contained stylish mansion houses built in the six-teenth, seventeenth and eighteenth centuries. And it was at one of these in the Rue St Antoine, currently owned by Pierre Sévigné of the French banking family, that Sidonie's taxi dropped her at exactly seven o'clock that evening. Swishing into the enormous entrance hall from which rose a glorious double staircase, the musician tried not to stare too obviously at all the signs of opulence and high living.

Hovering behind the English butler who had let her in was Sidonie's host, his idea of a charming New Year's Eve for his friends obviously being to secure the services of a famed

English harpsichord player and pay her agent a great deal of money to do so.

"My dear Madame Brooks," the Frenchman said now, kissing her mittened hand without any visible sign of surprise. "I am charmed to meet you. The harpsichord is ready in the *grand salon* but first perhaps you would like to make yourself comfortable."

And with that Sidonie was whisked into an adjoining reception room, complete with its own bathroom, where a maid waited to take her evening cloak and hang it up, attempting to get at the mittens as she did so.

"I'll keep those on," said Sidonie in French. "It's important to have my hands warm when I play."

"Certainly, Madame," said the girl, and curtsied.

'This is the life,' thought Sidonie as she made use of the facilities, checked her make-up and hair, and then regally ascended the right hand staircase to the landing where her host awaited her.

Sévigné gave a little bow. *"Très belle, Madame.* Now, may I offer you a drink?"

"After the concert I'd love one. I simply daren't beforehand."

"I quite understand. But I have ordered a bottle of champagne to be put on ice for you. It is from my own vineyards and I am rather proud of it."

"That sounds wonderful, Monsieur Sévigné. As is your house."

Pierre smiled. "I love it, of course. It has been in our family for the last hundred years but before that it belonged to the Princes de Conti. One of their many residences."

"Do you live here all the time?"

"During the week, yes. But at weekends I go out of town."

Sidonie was dying to ask if he was married but thought it might be misconstrued if she did. Instead she said, "You must have a marvellous life."

"Yes and no. It can be boring. I am really most happy when I am either travelling or entertaining. And tonight I entertain in style. My party is geared to the eighteenth century. It is to be entirely in costume."

"You should have told me. I would have hired something."

"Not at all. You look absolutely charming. You and I alone will remain in modern dress."

"I'm afraid my guest, the one I telephoned you about, doesn't know it's costume either."

"Ah yes, Alexei Orlov. I can't wait to meet him. According to the newspapers he is a young man likely to take Paris by storm."

Sidonie grinned. "He plays superbly and he's also quite a character, it's true."

"Like Nigel Kennedy?"

"No, not like that at all."

"Ah ha," answered her host enigmatically. "Now, Madame Brooks, let me show you where you are to play. I am sure you would like to warm up."

"Yes, please."

"Follow me."

He turned and led the way, throwing open two massive white doors, encrusted with gilt embellishments, which led into an enormous salon. It was one of the most elegant rooms that Sidonie had ever seen in a private residence. Completely decorated in white and gold, its chandeliers reflected in many mirrors, it had rich burgundy velvet curtains sweeping to the floor drawn across three huge pairs of French windows to keep out the night. In front of them a small platform had been erected on which stood the Blanchet harpsichord.

"Marvellous," said Sidonie, playing a chord and admiring the classical scene painted inside the lid. "I'll practise for a quarter of an hour before your guests arrive."

"I'll leave you in peace then," answered Pierre and went out.

It was a very strange feeling, being left alone in that room which but for the subdued electric lighting looked just as it must have done two hundred years earlier. Suddenly consumed by the past, the atmosphere of this morning's experience still clinging to her, Sidonie bent over the keyboard and started to play a Scarlatti sonata, the execution of which left no room in the performer's mind for anything else at all.

Known as Sonata 264, it followed such a tortuous line

that it was enough to throw the listener into a state of total bewilderment, let alone the player. Gasping almost, Sidonie came to the end only to hear the sound of applause. Startled, she looked up and saw that the audience had come in while she was playing, that she had spoilt all the evening's arrangements by practising far too long. Nervous of her host's reaction, Sidonie searched the crowd for him.

He wasn't there, neither was Alexei. Only the guests, powdered and patched, terribly authentic looking with their air of dissolute revelry, sat and watched, their eyes fixed on her, every one. And it was then that Sidonie thought she was going to faint, for it was happening again. For the second time in twelve hours she was looking at Sarah Bunbury.

Thoughts flew like birds: that the ease with which she was slipping from present to past was now something to be dreaded, that Sarah was growing older, that time must be passing more quickly for her than it was for Sidonie. For it was a beautiful young woman in her twenties, her figure rounded and voluptuous, who sat surrounded by French gallants. Sarah had aged by several years even since that morning.

Bunbury, as elegant as ever, sat at a distance from his wife and it was another man, his head bent towards Sarah, who had the place beside her. But as Sidonie stared at them he looked up, straight into her eyes, and the musician shuddered deep within her soul.

Eyes dark as stone stared at her, eyes set beneath brows which were crooked, turning up in slants at the corners. His mouth was harsh, thin as the slash of a sword, yet with the curved lips of a sensualist. The man's hair was black, even more so than Sarah's, but while her skin was fresh, the colour of roses, his was sallow. His body, though small, was compact, suggesting that he might be well-endowed in matters pleasing to a lady, and the very way he sat seemed arrogantly to confirm this.

How she was aware of it, Sidonie did not know, but somehow she realised that he could not only see her but knew what she was, a ghost from the future, a creature of no substance or reality. With her gaze locked into his, Sidonie watched as he slowly smiled, then his eyes became molten in appreciation of her. Then she knew nothing more as the harpsichord came up to meet her and she slumped forward over it, a trickle of bright red blood tainting one of the exquisite keyboards.

# Eighteen

An appreciation of style and beauty being an innate part of the French character, the arrival of any newcomer endowed with those qualities always caused a stir of interest, and nowhere more so than in the capital. The *beau monde* having signalled that a new and exciting personality had come into their midst, everyone desired to meet the stranger, and so it was that Lady Sarah Bunbury, on her second visit to Paris in the winter of 1766, eighteen months after her first, suddenly found herself the focus of attention and gossip.

Looking back, she assumed that the presence of her family during her first stay had precluded her from such giddy triumphs as she was experiencing now, though admittedly she had at the time been kissed on both cheeks by the King, old Louis XV, who had declared aloud that doing so gave him pleasure.

All the Foxes, including the two boys, had been invited during that visit to the Prince de Conti's country seat, L'Isle d'Adam, a beautiful château built on an island in the middle of the River Oise. Sarah had been much flattered there by the musicians and scientists, artists and intellectuals, who thronged the place. Going home had not been easy and Sarah had returned to London to find life in turmoil.

Due to political skulduggery and a general shifting of sides, her brother-in-law Lord Holland, the erstwhile Henry Fox, had been dismissed from the post of Paymaster. To make matters worse Sarah's husband, Charles, was amongst the group who had thrust Henry out, namely the faction headed by the Duke of Bedford. It had been embarrassing to say the least but Sarah, who did not discuss such matters with her husband, her first concern being to keep her marriage on an even keel, had not broached the topic with him. Matters had come to a head when Lord Kildare, Sarah's brother-in-law, in whose house she had been brought up, told her that he did not approve at all of Charles Bunbury's reward, an appointment as Secretary to the new Lord Lieutenant of Ireland, the thoroughly unpopular Lord Weymouth.

But Bedford's plotters had fallen again and Sir Charles, who had succeeded to his father's title and estates in June, 1764, had consequently lost the Secretaryship. It had been something of a relief even though it meant a drop in income of £4,000 a year. Yet Sarah had had little time to think about such matters when in the summer of 1765, Madame de Boufflers, the mistress of the Prince de Conti, arrived at Barton to go to the races. Together the two women had attended the midsummer meet and seen Gimcrack win at Newmarket.

"Is he not the sweetest little horse that ever was?" Sarah had asked the Frenchwoman.

"Almost as sweet as you, *chérie*. Everyone in Paris asks after you, especially the Prince. He wants to know when you will be returning to us."

"Now that the Duke of Richmond, my brother, has been appointed Ambassador, I suppose I have every excuse."

"You do not need an excuse. Come and see us. Even the King has enquired about you."

"How is His Majesty?"

Madame de Boufflers had pulled a face. "He is a worried man. The Dauphin has recently been suffering high fevers and indisposition."

"And the King has no other son?"

"No. But let us not speak of such sad things. When are you coming to Paris? I would like a firm date."

"I shall ask my husband to settle it."

"He intends to accompany you?"

"Of course."

"Ah! That will be a blow to the *gallantes*."

"Will it? Oh dear."

Intrigued, Sarah determined to push Charles for an answer at the first opportunity.

Generally speaking she had had a horrid time ever since she left Paris in the spring of 1765. What with the sacking of Lord Holland, a fact which had thrown him into poor health and low spirits, and the death of her beloved nephew, child of Emily and Lord Kildare, at whose deathbed Sarah had faithfully remained for three terrible weeks, the long months had been an ordeal. Furthermore, her visit to the shrine at St Cyr had done no good. Sarah still had no baby to play with, no one to fill her many lonely hours.

'But what saint could compete with my husband?' she had thought to herself.

Not once with him, not even once, had she felt that magnificent explosion of fire which coupling with the King had brought about in her. On the infrequent occasions when Charles did make love to her, though she considered that a misnomer, she remained cold as a fish.

'Perhaps it is my fault,' Sarah wondered sadly. 'Perhaps you can only conceive a baby when you are mad with passion.'

The one bright spot during these dismal eighteen months had been the marriage of Ste, still very fat and deafer than ever, to a dear sweet girl who loved him. In April, 1766, Lady Mary Fitzpatrick, daughter of the Earl of Upper Ossory, had become his bride and the young couple had set up home at Winterslow, near Salisbury. Here they lived happily but to a level of extravagance that knew no bounds. There was hunting, shooting and private theatricals for the unlimited numbers of house guests, Ste having built a little theatre especially for that purpose. He had also started gambling again and his debts were once more beginning to mount, though he kept very quiet about that fact.

The other joy to Sarah at this period of her life was the revival of her correspondence with Susan, now settled in New York where the handsome Mr O'Brien was trying his hand at various occupations and finding none to his liking. To make her friend's life more bearable, Sarah had started to send gifts of clothes, together with a chaise and harness, and other smaller luxuries.

Yet nothing could compensate the girl who had been taught love by a king for the emptiness of her marriage. She, who had always been so fit, was taken ill twice during the six months leading up to the long-awaited second Paris trip, unaware that stress was at the root of all her problems. Eventually, however, her husband was ready to travel and it was arranged that she, Sir Charles and Frederick Howard, the fifth Earl of Carlisle, should set sail at the end of November, 1766.

Carlisle had come into the lives of the Bunburys in 1764 when he had been sixteen years old. A schoolfriend of Charles James Fox, Sarah had known him as a boy at Holland House. But now the youth had grown tall, slim and remarkably handsome. Three years his senior and heavily married, Sarah had flirted with Frederick and soon he had fallen hopelessly in love with her. It was an exquisite sensation for both of them, deliciously frustrating. He longed for her body, she constantly refused it, declaring she was a faithful wife and a true and loyal heart. But recently, though she would not have admitted it to anyone, not even to Susan, the meagre comforts of her marriage bed had sent her thoughts, though so far only her thoughts, down many a wayward path.

Strangely, her arrival in Paris at the centre of what appeared to be a *ménage à trois* had, contrary to Madame de Boufflers's fears, seemed to attract the gallants rather than put them off. In the few days since Sarah had appeared in the capital, it was obvious that she was already a success. Fops and dandies bowed to her in the street, she was cheered at the Palais Royal where she, Charles and Carlisle had gone to gamble. To add to this triumph, Sarah had already acquired a coterie of followers. At least ten young men made it their business to be everywhere she was, following her from place to place. Nobody bothered in the least about her husband, who was generally considered a good fellow, obviously up to games of his own as he allowed his wife's sweetheart to escort her to the balls and soirées that he, Bunbury, considered might well be boring. Of these possible lovers the Duc de Chartres had been the first openly to declare himself, formally asking Sarah to become his mistress.

"You may keep your young Lord as well," he had added nonchalantly.

Sarah had reacted furiously. "My young Lord, as you call him, is not my lover. I am the wife of Sir Charles Bunbury and aware of my duty."

"How boring for you," de Chartres had replied with equanimity. "Let us hope that Paris will soon teach you the ways of the world. Remember, when it does, that I shall be waiting."

But despite her frosty reply, Sarah loved the flattery and the flirting. She considered herself an English fortress under attack from the wily French, having absolutely no idea how long she could hold out under their barrage an utterly intriguing and delightful prospect. With a contented sigh, Lady Sarah applied paint to a face which, though thinner through illness, now had a special glow to it.

Tonight was particularly exciting for there was to be a ball and concert at the Temple, the Prince de Conti's Parisian home. The Temple had once been the dwelling place of the Knights Templar and consisted of a gaunt medieval tower, originally built as a donjon, a beautiful palace which had belonged to the Grand Prior, and an extensive garden. The whole lay within a walled enclave and was reached by passing through an ancient gateway.

After the dissolution of the order of warrior monks, the King of France had appointed the place for the private usage of the royal family but it was the present Prince de Conti who had converted the palace to suit his tastes. It was now light, airy and elegantly appointed, and it was here that the nobleman did most of his entertaining. Full of excitement at being invited to such an historic place, Sarah and her husband, their doting companion one step behind them, entered their chaise and drove through the darkened streets.

Yet, even at first sight, there was something about the Temple which frightened Sarah. Though the ancient palace was exquisite, lit by a thousand candles, it seemed to her that the shadow of the donjon loomed over all and she was seized by a strange presentiment that it had been – and indeed would be – the scene of much agony and despair. But with the music playing, with people dancing, with a huge room laid out for supper while another was given over entirely to cards, how could she be sad? Determined to enjoy herself, Sarah allowed the Duc de Chartres to lead her out for a minuet as Charles left for the gaming tables and young Carlisle looked on miserably.

"Just witness that poor fellow," said de Chartres laconically. "He watches every move you make. You are cruel, Milady."

"If that is so why do you pursue me?" Sarah answered swiftly.

"Because you are beautiful and I desire you. I will not rest until I possess every inch of you." Sarah opened her mouth but de Chartres cut in on her. "And if you are about to tell me yet again of your virtue I would answer you thus. Why is it that you and your husband live such separate lives if all is well with you?"

"We do *not*," Sarah replied indignantly. "We are always together."

"That is a patent falsehood. But enough of your husband, he bores me. Let me tell you instead about some of the fascinating people here tonight. You see that woman over there, so ravaged yet so beautiful, wearing purple."

"Yes."

"She is the Duchesse de Gramont who has for her lover her own brother. They have been practising incest together for years. He is the Duc de Choiseul, that decadent bull mastiff in silver."

Sarah could not answer, too horrified by what she was hearing, simply staring at the Duc round-eyed.

"However, recently, the Duchesse has been falling in love with her nephew the Duc de Lauzun. But Lauzun's attentions have wandered elsewhere and she is furious. Intriguing is it not?" de Chartres went on.

"I think it sounds sordid and revolting."

The Duc shrugged. "It would not appeal to me certainly. By the way I had better warn you. Lauzun eats women for breakfast and has already pledged to be the first into your bedchamber."

"But he doesn't even know me."

"That would not deter Lauzun. Seriously, *chérie*, you must watch yourself with that one. He believes it his right to try out all the new beauties that come to the Temple. They say no woman in Paris has truly arrived until Lauzun gives his *approval* and that the Prince encourages him in this."

"The Prince de Conti? But he is such a nice man."

The Duc shrieked with laughter. "A great man, yes. Nice, no. Lauzun is his favourite. Just you wait and see."

With a certain trepidation Sarah curtsied as the music came to an end, then glanced round surreptitiously.

"He's not here yet," whispered de Chartres. "He will make a point of being presented, rest assured."

And with that he left her, going off to speak to the incestuous Duchesse whose lovely face bore all the signs of depravity, like a perfect flower that secretly devours flies. Within seconds of the Duc's departure, Carlisle was at Sarah's side.

"I claim this dance, my Lady," he said, with a terrible attempt at joviality.

Just for a split of a second Sarah looked at him closely and instantly despised herself for leading him on. He was so autumnally handsome, crisp and brown as fallen leaves, that she felt cruel for keeping him attached to her by such tenuous threads as unspoken promises. If all had been right and proper she would have released him to go courting, as did his schoolfriend Charles James, incessantly so. Yet her fear of being spurned kept her holding on to him. She had lost a lover and, as far as passion was concerned, she had lost a husband too, and Sarah's nature, descendant of that lustiest of monarchs Charles II and his French mistress as she was, demanded love.

"You shall have it, Sir," she answered coquettishly, and placed her hand in that of the eager young nobleman, ignoring the fact that poor Frederick's palm was very slightly moist.

An appreciation of style and beauty being an innate part of the French character, the arrival of any newcomer endowed with not only those qualities but also talent caused an obvious sensation. Added to this was the fact that the English musician had fainted in the most spectacular manner in the house of Pierre Sévigné. All at once the name of Sidonie Brooks was on the lips of the entire Parisian jet set.

She had been picked up from where she lay slumped over the keyboard of the Blanchet harpsichord and carried away as if she were a broken doll.

"Careful with her," she had heard a familiar voice call out as she was moved.

But when Sidonie finally opened her eyes it had been to see she was in a palatial bedroom, lying on a bed, the crimson drapery and golden crested eagle of which denoted that it had once belonged to Napoleon.

A man dressed as an eighteenth-century nobleman was taking her blood pressure, while Marie Antoinette was cleaning up Sidonie's forehead.

"Oh dear," she said, then added predictably, "Where am I?"

Pierre Sévigné came into her line of vision. "My dear Madame Brooks, you are still in my house. You fainted while you were practising and we brought you in here to recover."

Sidonie struggled to sit up. "But what about the concert?"

"You won't be able to play, I'm afraid," said the nobleman. He shook Sidonie's hand formally. "I am Dr Laurent, one of Monsieur Sévigné's guests. This lady is my wife and is also a doctor. I'm afraid that you have received a bad cut to your forehead and require a couple of stitches. I have already rung the hospital. My junior is on duty and expecting you. I would do the suturing myself but – " He spread his hands and gave a charming Gallic smile, " – it took me hours to get into this costume and it would take another hour to get out of it. But, you can believe me, Dr Vallier is an excellent young man. His stitching will not mar your beauty in any way."

"You're very kind," Sidonie answered, "but I can't let everyone down like this." She turned to Pierre. "Not after all the trouble you've taken."

He raised a soothing hand. "Your friend Alexei has stepped into the breach. He had his violin with him by a lucky chance."

Sidonie smiled faintly. "He takes it everywhere, I don't think he trusts it out of his sight."

Pierre nodded. "So all is well. Monique Amboise is here, by the way. She hopes to see you before you go."

Madame Laurent spoke for the first time. "If you will take my advice, Miss Brooks, you should return to your hotel when you have been sutured and have a good rest. You've suffered a nasty crack and, besides, fainting itself can be caused by stress. You professional musicians push yourselves far too hard."

Sidonie nodded. "I'll certainly do as you say but may I just have a quick word with Alexei. I've got to tell him what's going on."

"Of course you may. We'll leave you alone."

With everyone gone, Sidonie felt free to give the Russian a hug, for he came through the door looking wretched with worry, his terrible black tie halfway round his neck where he had tugged at it nervously.

"I've got to go to hospital," she said, as he laid her gently back on the pillows.

"I know. I am devastated that I cannot attend with you. But I told them I would play. Do you mind?"

"How could I mind? You've helped me out of a terrible situation."

"I meant, do you mind that I can't be there to hold your hand?"

"No to that too. It's only a couple of stitches. But the woman doctor told me to go back to the hotel afterwards. I won't be able to see the New Year in with you after all."

"There you are wrong. As soon as I have finished here I will join you. It will be about eleven. We shall drink champagne."

"I'll probably be in bed."

"Is that an invitation because, if so, I accept with pleasure."

"You're not to tease an injured woman."

Alexei's expression suddenly became serious. "Why did you faint, Tovarish? What happened?"

"I saw a ghost," she answered, testing him, wondering how he would react.

He nodded seriously. "I had that experience when I was a child."

"What did you see?"

"I think one of the murdered Grand Duchesses. I was visiting the Winter Palace with my parents and I saw this girl on the stairs. She was not in modern dress and she was running down, oh so swiftly, with such a joyful expression on her face."

"What did she look like?"

"She was pale with wide dark eyes. I think it was Tatiana."

"Then you believe they were assassinated?"

"Yes, all of them. But tell me what *you* saw."

"Later, in the hotel. I daren't keep them waiting. Thank you for taking over the concert."

"I would do anything for you," Alexei answered, "even and including making myself an overnight sensation."

Sidonie shook her head. "You are just so naughty. Now go away."

She was back in her room shortly after ten; stitches in, forehead frozen, clutching some sleeping pills to take later. Pierre's housekeeper, a gorgeously thin Frenchwoman called Amélie, had insisted on seeing her safely into bed, and Sidonie had thought how nice it was, like a return to childhood.

"You are sure you will be all right, Madame?"

"Positive, thanks. You've been so good to me. I *am* grateful."

"I will telephone in the morning to see how you are." Amélie paused in the doorway. "Did something frighten you in the *salon*?"

"Why?" asked Sidonie, hedging.

"Because the house has many memories," the older woman answered simply. "Not all of them can be good."

"Who was the Prince de Conti?"

"It is a title reserved for one of the king's sons. Not the eldest, you understand."

"So Sarah continued to mix with top people."

"Sarah?" repeated the housekeeper.

"One of the ghosts."

"So you saw them," said Amélie, and, nodding, turned to leave.

At exactly quarter past eleven Alexei walked through the door of the hotel room with an expression on his face that could only mean one thing. He had been given a tumultuous reception and was already being hailed as an *enfant terrible*.

"I don't think they missed me," said Sidonie wryly, smiling at him.

"They did miss you, particularly the men. It is because I am Russian that they loved me. Everyone thought I was a poor starving youth. There is something very romantic about people from a country that few have visited. One rich American lady has already offered to sponsor me."

"Toyboy?"

"You bet." Alexei grinned. "She's taking me out to dinner and coming to Chambord."

"You really are unbelievable!"

"An opportunist maybe. But, sweetest Sidonie, I have champagne. Pierre sent it for us."

And with that the violinist opened his case to reveal several bottles.

"I don't know that I ought to drink."

He turned to her, instantly contrite. "I have not asked how you got on. I am so selfish."

"Well, I've been stitched up, the anaesthetic is wearing off, and my head hurts. Other than that I'm fine."

Almost in one move Alexei threw off his dinner jacket and got down on the bed beside her, cradling her in his arms so kindly that Sidonie suddenly wanted to cry.

"Forgive me. I think only of myself. From now on I am your nurse. Order me."

"Then pour some champagne. If I blow up, I blow up." Sidonie hesitated. "Alexei, there is something I feel I ought to tell you."

"And what is that?"

"I have a sort of boyfriend, someone I'm very fond of. He's in Canada at the moment on a research project."

The Russian turned to look at her from where he stood opening the bottle.

"I did not think that someone as beautiful as you would be without admirers. It was to be expected. Are you going to marry this person?"

"I don't know. He hasn't asked me."

"Then he is a fool. I would be your husband and not hesitate."

"I'm not sure I want to get married again. Nigel put me off."

"That is not surprising. Now, Sidonie, stop talking and listen. I shall spend the night here, on the floor if you insist, in order to look after you. And I will not force my attentions, that is the right phrase, isn't it?"

"It is."

"Then may I?"

"Yes."

And with that they clinked glasses and prepared to see in the New Year.

The eagerly anticipated arrival of the Duc de Lauzun was almost an anticlimax. Sarah saw a small, neat, dapper young man come into the reception room and bow to the Prince, and thought that the best thing about him was his suit of expensive brocade.

'So you're the one set to seduce me!' she thought, and arranged her features into a glacial smile as the Prince and the Duc advanced towards her.

De Conti nodded indulgently as Sarah curtsied. "I beg your kindness, Milady, for my Lauzun. He is very wild, very extravagant, very pleasant. He will do you the honours of Paris better than anyone. Permit me to pay you his respects. I stand surety for his desire to win your favour."

Very much to her surprise, Lauzun bowed as if bored to sobs at this introduction and Sarah, in response, dropped one of her impeccable curtseys and said, "How dee do?" between gritted teeth.

"Well, thank you," he replied, dabbed at his upper lip with a lace handkerchief, and sauntered off to where an elegantly aristocratic slut sat in a chair consuming the Duc with her hot blue eyes. If he had announced it at the top of his voice, Lauzun could not have made his lack of interest in Sarah more obvious. But there was worse yet to come. The slut, who was the type to whisper loudly in public, thrust her head to within an inch of Lauzun's and muttered something into his ear. He shrugged eloquently.

"She's not bad," he said in a loud and carrying voice, "but for the life of me I do not see anything in her to turn a man's head. If she spoke good French and came from Limoges, no one would give her a second thought."

There was a shrill burst of laughter and Sarah wished that the floor would open and swallow her up.

"Who is that woman?" she said to Carlisle who was, as always, hovering close at hand.

"Madame de Cambis, Lauzun's mistress. Apparently she is mad for love of him but he is profoundly bored with her."

"Why?" asked Sarah crossly. "She looks willing enough."

"That's just the point. She fell into his arms without a struggle, whereas the Duc loves a conquest."

"Oh, does he?"

"What man does not? Yet I have pursued a lady till I could drop with fatigue and still have no smile from my sweetheart."

"Are you referring to me?" said Sarah, venting her spleen on the hapless youth.

Carlisle looked nervous. "There is no one else to whom I would give that name."

"Then I believe you to be indiscreet, Sir. I am a married woman as well you know."

"But yet I felt I had cause for hope."

"Hope? For what? That I would become your cheap whore. Marry, come up, Lord Carlisle, I thought you just to be a friend."

How cruel she was, Sarah thought, as she saw the boy's face go a deep and raw-looking red. She had given him enough reason to be encouraged, God only knew, and now here she was chastising the poor wretch because Lauzun had upset her.

"I would never betray Sir Charles," she added for good measure. "Never!"

"Even though he does it to you?" Frederick muttered.

"I beg your pardon?"

But before Sarah could ask the lordling to repeat what he had just said, indeed before either of them had time to get more heated, a call for supper was made by the Prince's major-domo, and there was a general exit in the direction of the dining hall where once the Grand Prior of the Knights Templar had sat down to dine.

Within the hall several dozen small tables had been prepared and it was to one of these that the Prince de Conti now ushered Sarah, only for her to find that the hot-eyed slut, Madame de Cambis, was sitting one place away from her, an empty chair between them.

'No doubt,' thought Sarah as the Duc de Lauzun came to claim it, 'this is the Prince's idea of a joke.'

Across the space, Lauzun's mistress preened herself for battle and Sarah, impulsively accepting the challenge, did likewise. Sparkling, her smile full of mischief, she turned to the Duc with a tiny yawn.

"La, Sir, I must apologise for the paucity of my French. I never could concentrate on my lessons for I found the language to be the idiom of leisure, and preferred to go riding with my brothers than bother learning it."

Lauzun twitched his lips, his eyes insolent. "You do not like our native tongue, Milady?"

"It is not so much that, Monsieur, as trying to master the nuances of dialect. For example, I have been told that a Parisian accent is not to be emulated whereas that of Limoges is the one the *beau monde* strives for."

This said, Sarah gave the Duc a saucy grin and turned her attention to the foie gras which had just been set before her. Lauzun stared at her hard-eyed before he raised his crooked brows and murmured, "Touché," which caused Madame de Cambis to curl her sultry lips into a pout. From where he sat, the Prince de Conti smiled to himself that his stratagem was working so well, convinced that his favourite might just have met his match.

To say that Armand de Gontaut, Duc de Lauzun, was world weary was to give a mere hint of his outlook on life. By the time he was a boy he had seen it all. His father, Louis Antoine, Duc de Gontaut, the Maréchal of France, and that extraordinary nobleman, the Duc de Choiseul, who looked so like a bull mastiff that he was known as *le dogue* had married sisters. Originally, while Choiseul was still a bachelor, Gontaut's wife had been his mistress and in fact it was generally accepted that Lauzun was *le dogue*'s son. Whatever the case, Lauzun's mother had died giving birth to her child and had, on her deathbed, commanded her twelve-year-old sister to marry Choiseul in order to take care of him. Thus Lauzun's nominal father and his actual became brothers-in-law. But this was not to be the end of the complications.

Choiseul's sister, retired early to a convent because she could not find a husband, eventually consented to marry the ghastly Duc de Gramont. Having done so, she separated from him at once going to live with *le dogue* and his young wife, and sharing her brother's bed according to common gossip. Within this nest of vipers and whispers young Lauzun had been brought up.

The close friendship between the Duc de Gontaut and Madame de Pompadour, Louis XV's mistress, meant that Lauzun had spent his childhood with her, sitting on her lap, playing with her jewels, reading out loud to her as soon as he had learned his letters. But it was not only the art of reading in which Armand had been instructed at the court of Versailles. His "delicious lessons" began the moment he was in his teens. He took them with servants, ladies, actresses and even a cousin of Madame de Pompadour herself, and the fact that he had entered into an arranged marriage with Amélie de Boufflers did nothing to stop this rake's progress. He enjoyed sexual liaisons to the·full and as a married man continued to sleep with the wife of Choiseul's younger brother. But in this adulterous adventure, Lauzun met opposition from an unexpected source.

The incestuous Duchesse de Gramont, regardless of the fact that Armand was her brother's nephew, decided to fall in love with him. Spurned, she then accused him of corrupting the morals of the Duchesse de Stainville, his uncle's sister-in-law, causing such a furore that the lovers took fright and parted. Very angry with this interference in his private affairs, Lauzun had reacted by pointedly ignoring the Duchesse de Gramont, setting up a pretty little actress in her own apartments, and sending for Madame de Cambis to come and sleep with him at Versailles. His boredom with his current mistress had begun then and there, when she responded to this summons within four hours. And now he sat at table, his back slightly turned to her, thinking that the next person into his bed would be the beautiful English Milady and that the slut-faced de Cambis had to go.

"Armand," said his lover with a petulant sigh.

"What?" He hardly bothered to do more than turn his shoulder.

"I want to talk to you."

"You are doing so."

"I meant privately."

"Not now," Lauzun answered angrily. He leaned towards Sarah. "How long are you staying in Paris, Milady?"

"Another few weeks, though I fear my husband is already bored with it. He misses his exercise you know. At home he is a great man for the sporting life."

"Really?" The Duc attempted to sound interested. "And which is your husband, Madame?"

"He is sitting over there. The handsome one wearing claret velvet."

"Handsome indeed. *Un beau garçon.*"

"I am very fortunate."

"Oh yes," answered Lauzun, and looked deeply into her eyes.

Sarah returned his glance, thinking how hard his pupils were, like pebbles, dark stone, two points of flame. Staring at him in this way she felt her senses dance as though she were in a wonderful dream and could think of nothing nicer than to lie in the Duc's arms with not a stitch of clothing on her body.

"Have you heard of Madame de Montespan?" whispered Armand.

"Was she not a mistress of Louis XIV and accused of being a witch?" Sarah answered softly.

"Not so much of being one as resorting to spells to gain the King's love. Well you, Milady, have something of her sorcery about you."

"What do you mean, Monsieur?"

"That you only have to look at a man and he is completely captivated."

"I was thinking the same about you," answered Sarah, then wondered how she had dared to say it.

"Were you?" said Armand, and smiled with amusement. The little flames in the pupils of his eyes flickered, died and suddenly he looked quite normal again.

"I shall call on you and Sir Charles Bunbury tomorrow." He stood up and kissed her hand. "Adieu till then."

"Adieu," Sarah replied, once more her usual self and wondering what had come over her.

Madame de Cambis stood up and linked her arm through her lover's. "I think it is time I went home to bed," she said, her lovely mouth only an inch from the Duc's.

"Then I'll see you to your carriage," he said, and turned to give one last look at Lady Sarah Bunbury.

# Nineteen

She was in a state of utter confusion, her thoughts and emotions hovering between a delicious sensation of excitement and a nasty feeling of guilt. She was on the brink of a love affair, she knew it, yet much as she wanted it, much as she longed simply to fall into bed with him and let the inevitable happen, the very idea of infidelity struck her to the heart.

He had not made love to her on New Year's Eve nor the following morning either. Alexei had simply nestled in beside her, drowsy with sleeping pills as she was, and gone straight to sleep himself. And the next day he was up and in the shower, singing loudly in Russian, when Sidonie had woken up.

"Remind you of anything?" he had said, sticking his head round the bathroom door.

"What?"

"The night we spent together in Moscow when you were escaping from Nigel."

"Oh yes."

"Did you sleep well? Are you feeling better?"

Alexei had walked into the bedroom dressed in a towel and Sidonie had thought what a nice body he had, strong and compact, his arms muscular with so many years spent handling a violin.

"Much. I'll get up in a minute."

"No hurry. I'll go and fetch you some breakfast."

"I'd rather come with you. I'll turn funny if I stay here much longer."

They had gone out to a little restaurant together and had stayed there all morning, drinking coffee, sipping brandies. And then they had gone to Alexei's rehearsal room and Sidonie, sitting comfortably in a chair and feeling very spoiled, had listened to him practise. Afterwards they had lunched with

Monique Amboise, volubly worried about Sidonie's accident, and by the time they had come out it had grown dusk and everything had changed. For there on the front page of the evening papers was a rather juvenile looking photograph of Alexei and a story headlined, "Russian sensation comes to the rescue."

Sidonie thought quizzically as Alexei sat down to read that the saying about an ill wind was absolutely true. However wicked a charmer Sarah's friend had been in his own time, however much his hypnotic eyes had affected Sidonie in this century, he had done Alexei Orlov an enormous favour.

The cream of Paris society had been at Pierre Sévigné's party, including the director of a French television network, the editor of a large circulation popular daily newspaper, who obviously had contacts, to say nothing of two extremely influential music critics. Alexei had stormed into all their lives like a revelation. The fact that he was attractive, a gifted musician and came from a mysterious nation whose internal affairs were chaotic was enough. The Russian violinist was suddenly the man that all Paris wanted to know.

The next few days had been extremely odd, yet elating. The morning papers had carried news items about Alexei and as a result his concert on the 3rd January at the Palais de Chaillot was a complete sell-out, with students standing at the back. On the morning after that, alongside the reviews, all of which raved about him, appeared a photograph of Sidonie, complete with the full details of her fainting and subsequent head injury. After that, very much as if they were the flavour not only of the month but of the New Year as well, both of them were besieged by requests for interviews and, for the first time in their lives, paparazzi followed them in the street while an evening paper reproduced a photograph of them walking hand-in-hand. This last gave Sidonie a certain disquiet in case French newspapers were on sale in Canada.

By now she had begun to suspect that the sponsors of the charity concert at Chambord had something to do with all the sudden interest, because tickets for that were already on the black market. The popular papers had concluded that she and Alexei were on the point of becoming lovers and this, added to their much spoken of genius, had made anybody who was anybody want to hear them play.

Though Alexei was obviously their favourite, Sidonie had several attributes which the French adored. She had been educated in Paris by a Frenchwoman, she was a declared Francophile, was beautiful, talented and had fainted into the arms of a mercurial Russian prodigy, or at least that was the way the story was being told. In a way it was like a dream come true, a taste of true celebrity status.

"I think we should make it all real," said Alexei as they drove out of Paris in their hired car on the way to the Loire Valley.

"What do you mean?"

"The papers say we are lovers – or about to be – so why don't we prove them right?"

"I'm years older than you are and besides there is that man in Canada I told you about."

"He is an idiot. A Russian would not muck about. He would say 'Sidonie, I love you and that's it.'"

"How unromantic."

Alexei shrugged his beautiful shoulders. "Possibly, but it is direct. I do not do this pussfoot. I speak my mind."

"Good for you. And the word's pussyfoot."

"Who cares? Sidonie, I adore you. I have done ever since you came to Russia. Please, just once, let me make love to you. The man in Canada will never know. Besides, he has probably got someone to keep him company, don't you think?"

Sidonie heard again that husky Canadian voice at the other end of the telephone.

"I've no idea what I think. To be honest, he doesn't seem quite the type to me," she said thoughtfully.

"All men are the type."

"But some more so than others. Oh, Alexei, the older I get the less I know. Experience counts for nothing. I just have an incredible knack of messing up my life completely."

The Russian looked at her wryly. "Nigel was certainly a mistake. Does he still pester you?"

"Not really. He seems to have phases."

"Like the moon."

"Probably. He's a Cancer after all and they're lunar subjects."

"Me, I am a Leo. A big pussy cat."

"And a show-off."

Sidonie smiled at Alexei indulgently, full of feelings for this extraordinary creature who appeared to alter the lives of everyone who knew him.

"Maybe I am, but so what? Sidonie, what is going to happen with us?"

"I don't know," she answered.

And she didn't, too mixed up, too emotionally confused for any sensible thought.

Originally the two musicians had been booked into an hotel not far from the château but in view of their overnight celebrity they had been invited to stay with one of the sponsors. Judging by the distant glimpse of his magnificent home as the car turned into the acres of parkland which surrounded it, Monsieur de Chenerilles must be very wealthy indeed.

"All this expensive living is getting too much," said Sidonie. "I don't know how I'll settle down to normal life. My flat's a hovel in comparison with what I'm becoming used to."

"What about mine?" exclaimed Alexei. "You try living in a Moscow tenement."

Yet despite their joking mood both of them were silenced as the car made its way up the long and winding drive.

There had been a fall of snow in the night and as far as the eye could see there were glistenings and gleamings of white diamonds. Great trees that in their time had seen the cavalcade of all the nobility of France pass beneath their branches stood silent, aloof almost, the survivors of the babel, wearing their frosty crowns with dignity.

Beneath the white-laced cedars the lawns glittered shades of sugar plum while the château itself looked like something from legend, drenched in milk, fine and fabulous, a pearl in a shell of sea spray.

"How wonderful," said Sidonie.

"I've never seen anything quite like it," Alexei answered, and she knew he meant it literally, that never in his total experience had the Russian been to a more beautiful place still remaining in private ownership.

Their host turned out to be a woman, a chic intelligent creature of indefinable years and immense sophistication.

"Chantal de Chenerilles," she said, holding out a long lean hand with surprisingly short fingernails, varnished red, her fingers covered with expensive rings. "I asked you both here most selfishly," she went on in a voice that had a delicious crack in it. "I am an amateur pianist and adore musicians."

Alexei kissed the extended hand. "And I adore you for inviting us to stay in your beautiful home."

*"Charmant,"* said Chantal, *"charmant."*

'Born to be a toyboy,' thought Sidonie uncharitably and then, remembering her own recent thoughts, felt ashamed.

"I will show you to your rooms," their hostess was saying. "I do hope you'll find them to your liking. By the way, I have taken the liberty of getting my music room ready for your practice sessions. It seemed to me to be more convenient for you."

"That sounds terrific," said Alexei enthusiastically.

"Do you have a harpsichord, Madame?" asked Sidonie more cautiously.

"But certainly. It goes with the château and I believe has been here for at least two hundred years. I recently had it restored in order to preserve it."

"Is it a Blanchet?"

"No, it is English. A Blasser."

"Good gracious, so is mine. At home I mean. It's dated London, 1745."

Chantal looked delighted. "Mine is London, 1753. Let me get you settled in and then you shall have a look."

Sidonie had a sudden presentiment that fate was about to overwhelm her in every possible way and felt she knew the answer as she asked Madame de Chenerilles, "Has your family always lived here?"

"No, far from it. It was originally built in the fifteenth century for one of the King's loyal men but, in the seventeenth, was given to the Duc de Gontaut by the Marquise and Duchesse d'Étoiles, otherwise known as Madame de

Pompadour, of course. He was a firm favourite of hers though I do not believe they were ever lovers, as sexually she was cold."

"I didn't know that."

"It is a fact, odd though it seems for Louis XV's favourite mistress. However, Gontaut, in his turn, gave it to his son Armand, the Duc de Lauzun."

"De Lauzun, de Lauzun?" repeated Sidonie. "Why do I know that name?"

"You have probably read about him. He was a great womaniser and was said to have practised magic and hypnosis and God knows what else in order to make his conquests." Chantal smiled, her lovely face quite lined but wonderfully lived in and lively. "Quite a man, eh? I expect these bedrooms could tell a tale or two."

And with that she threw open the door of a vast room, a log fire burning in the grate, made rich by the warmth of its deep peony pink drapery, a similarly curtained four-poster bed opposite the long windows.

"It is as comfortable and cosy as I could make a fifteenth-century building," remarked Chantal, almost carelessly. "There is a bathroom en suite where once there used to be a cupboard. And you, young man, are opposite – in the Prince de Conti's bedroom."

"I shall never recover from this," said Alexei.

Chantal smiled enigmatically. "Perhaps not. Now, when you have made yourselves at home come downstairs to the *salon*. My maid will unpack for you. You can concentrate on having a drink and seeing the rest of the house."

It was an extension of Paris, another flight into a dream world, for the château, though built in the fifteenth century, was on a much older site. Down in the cellars, now covered by a piece of sheer but toughened glass, were the remains of a mosaic floor.

"There was a Roman villa here?" said Sidonie in awe.

"Indeed, and in the grounds are the ruins of a temple from the same period."

"So there has been a dwelling here almost since time began?"

298

"Not quite that long but a good while anyway."

"Is the place haunted?" asked Sidonie as they made their way up the cellar stairs.

"Oh yes. There is a Roman soldier who walks in the grounds and I often hear noises coming from the music room."

"Tell me," said Alexei, agog, both with his hostess and the château, Sidonie thought.

Chantal turned to Sidonie. "Someone plays the harpsichord."

"How very creepy. I wonder who it is?"

"I think perhaps the wicked Duc himself. I believe that he was quite a good musician, though how he found time to practise with all his womanising and other hobbies I shall never know."

Going in, a glass of superb claret in her hand, Sidonie could well imagine that the great room contained memories of the past. Hung with paintings and portraits, all with a musical theme, joined together by exquisitely carved garlands of wood, it seemed almost as if it were full of people. And the instruments standing within were wonderful, beautiful and rare, the only comparatively modern piece a Steinway grand piano.

"I studied at the Conservatoire," Chantal said simply, "but gave up my ambitions to be a concert pianist when I married. My husband was an industrialist, fifteen years older than I was. He was killed in a helicopter crash some time ago."

"How terrible."

Chantal moved her hands expressively. "He left me all this and more money than I know what to do with. But, alas, I never had a child to share it with."

A tangible sadness hung in the air and Sidonie reflected that material possessions can never compensate for certain lacks.

"Shall I play for you?" she said to lighten the atmosphere.

"I would be thrilled."

"Do you like this?"

And Sidonie played "The Duchess of Richmond", a jolly minuet composed by that talented aristocrat the Earl of Kelly.

"How odd!" said Chantal when she had finished.

"In what way?"

"A little while ago you asked about the ghost and now you're playing its song!"

"*This* is what you hear?"

"I'm certain of it."

"What a strange coincidence," Sidonie replied automatically. But she no longer believed that, certain now that she had come to the Château des Cèdres for a reason, that something of great importance was about to take place.

"Adultery," mouthed Lady Sarah Bunbury to her own reflection, which frowned at her severely from the looking glass, "is not only a disgusting word but a disgusting act. I shrink from it, so I do."

Her reflection raised its eyebrows and smiled somewhat cynically, for truth to tell the thought of infidelity was a constant but delicious tease. Never had she been so courted – for what price poor Carlisle's efforts compared with that of the wordly Frenchman? – and never had Sarah felt herself to be so enmeshed in a web of such lustful intrigue.

Confusion was everywhere, pulling her in several directions at once. Excited by the Duc de Lauzun's obvious admiration, drawn like a butterfly into his compelling eyes, Sarah was riven with shame at the thought of her beautiful Bunbury, as pretty and good-natured a husband as ever woman could wish, being betrayed. Yet, in honesty, their intimate life left much to be desired. After every coupling, Sarah was left with the depressing impression that Charles felt such things to be his marital duty rather than a pleasure. Furthermore, she still had not experienced with her husband, not even once, that thrilling explosion of ecstasy which the King's lovemaking had aroused in her.

"La, it's a terrible coil," she sighed, and wished that guilt had never been invented.

Since that night in the Temple, Lauzun had pursued her with both relentlessness and skill. Ingratiating himself with her husband, the Duc had introduced the bored baronet to the *jeu de paume* and then, with Sir Charles safely out of the way, had whispered a declaration of undying love in Sarah's ear. She had pretended not to hear what he said, but when a letter expressing the same sentiments had arrived she had had little choice but to read it. Of course, she had returned it, and shortly afterwards had told him she did not want a French lover, that lovers caused scandals, and if he spoke of love again she would have no choice but to bar the door to him. But for some terrible reason all these protestations had the opposite effect on the Duc, who continued to visit her with every sign of affection.

Meanwhile, the sluttish Madame de Cambis had demanded that Lauzun choose between herself and Sarah. Without hesitation, the Duc had bundled up his mistress's letters and returned them to her in a bulging packet. That very night she had gone to bed with the Chevalier de Coigny, but the Duc had merely laughed and raised two fingers in the air. It was heady stuff, the essence of high seduction, and Sarah stood poised, almost ready to give in, waiting for some signal from fate which would tell her what her next move ought to be.

They had been in Paris a month now and had kept Christmas there, Sarah enjoying the experience enormously. But now it was the eve of New Year, the new year 1767, and Madame de Boufflers, the Prince de Conti's amusing mistress, was giving a grand supper in her house in the Marais. There was to be dancing, a concert, and all kinds of jollification and Sarah, knowing that the Duc would be there and certain that he had fallen genuinely in love with her despite his *vast* reputation, dressed herself with care, her maid pulling her stays tighter than ever, the *friseur* weaving an entire flower garden – or so it seemed – into her hair.

"Will you be wearing your diamonds, Milady?"

"Most certainly, tonight I intend to sparkle."

She smiled at her own feeble joke but was glad, when the chaise bearing herself, Charles and the inevitable Carlisle, drew up in the Rue St Antoine, that she had dressed to kill. Exquisite women and elegant men were alighting from their carriages and moving inside to ascend slowly the double staircase and be received by Madame de Boufflers, who stood at the top. The quality of the clothes beggared description. Brocades, velvets and silks were everywhere, all so profusely trimmed with bows and flowers, jewels and gemstones that one could hardly see the material beneath. Most relieved that her dress was strewn with a thousand glittering brilliants which enhanced the diamonds at her throat, ears and wrists, Sarah proudly climbed the stairs, head high, aware that she was in every way one of the most dazzling women present.

Lauzun, of course, was waiting for her, a vision himself in dark green satin. But even as he kissed her hand, running his tongue surreptitiously over her fingers, Sarah exclaimed in surprise.

"What is it?"

"I do believe I see a familiar face."

"Where?"

"Over there, the man in the blue velvet suit. Surely he is the Earl of Kelly."

The Duc followed Sarah's eyes. "That's the musician giving the concert."

"Then we are in luck. The Earl is one of the finest harpsichord players in the country, trained by Johann Stamitz in Mannheim. He is a director of the Edinburgh Musical Society, you know."

"Really? I must invite him to play for me. I enjoy the harpsichord and consider myself to be reasonably accomplished."

"And in the art of love?" asked Sarah pertly.

"Hopefully you will soon find that out for yourself."

And with those words the Duc drifted away as Charles and Carlisle came to stand at Sarah's side.

The evening had been arranged with great care by their hostess. After an hour for refreshment the concert was scheduled to take place in the *grand salon*, this followed by a buffet supper for which three separate rooms had been set aside. There would then be dancing and cards until the New Year when everybody would be expected to join a chain dance led by Madame de Boufflers herself. It was all very amusing and light-hearted and yet Sarah felt slightly ill at ease. There was an atmosphere in the house she could not pinpoint and she found her thoughts, rather reluctantly, turning towards the ghost.

She had not seen the woman for months, over eighteen in

fact, and had begun to think the haunting was over, that the vision standing beneath the trees in the Tivoli Gardens, the vision which had faded before Sarah's eyes, had been the last. Yet tonight there was a feel of the creature, as if she might appear at any second. Thrusting such thoughts away, Sarah, Lord Carlisle tagging a pace behind, went to the refreshment room, surrounded by her usual admiring troupe of dandies, determined to put such dismal thoughts from her mind.

Yet even the gossip, the witty speeches and risqué anecdotes could not enliven her. Relieved that she could finally sit quietly, Sarah was one of the first to go into the concert, taking her place beside that of Lauzun in the front row. A dais had been raised in front of the curtains and on to this some ten minutes later strode Thomas Erskine, sixth Earl of Kelly, one of the most gifted musicians of his day.

"Bravo," called Sarah and, looking over, the Earl acknowledged her with a bow of his head.

He was a handsome man, prematurely grey at thirty-four years old but with a clear young skin and dashing dark brows above bright bluebell-coloured eyes.

"Oh là là!" chorused several of the ladies but the Earl ignored them and with much flurrying of coat tails sat down at the harpsichord, launching into his programme with two of his own compositions, both minuets, one entitled "The Duchess of Richmond", the other, "Lord Fothergill". As a socialite, Lord Kelly often wrote music for aristocratic gatherings and Sarah had little doubt that a minuet entitled "Madame de Boufflers" would be played before the night was out.

His own work getting him off to a good start, the Earl played the Sonata VI by Paradies, went on to a flowing composition by Arne, then let fly on a fiendishly difficult piece by Scarlatti, the Sonata 264. Enraptured with every note, her senses swimming, Sarah watched the long strong fingers scurrying over the two manuals, going so fast they almost turned into a blur.

'How small they are for a man,' she thought, 'they seem almost like a woman's hands,' and the very idea terrified her.

Half realising what she was going to see, Sarah raised her eyes to find that the Earl was no longer sitting at the harpsichord. In his place, in exactly the same position as he had been, was the girl with the fox-coloured hair. Sarah knew a moment's madness, for how could a ghost play an instrument, how could a phantom make a living man vanish and take his place? Frightened out of her wits, Sarah felt herself sink into a kind of catalepsy.

Something about her stillness must have alerted Lauzun because at that moment he tore his eyes from his beloved and looked at the harpsichord player. She saw him gasp and then freeze, almost as if he were carved from stone, and watched his eyes become still and dark as he stared straight ahead.

'He's seen her,' she thought, and for no reason the idea of this made Sarah panic, almost as if she wanted to protect that red-haired apparition who came into her life without warning yet whose actions never proved harmful.

In consternation, Sarah looked at the dais and knew then that she had indeed gone mad. For the Earl was sitting there again, tackling the keyboards with *élan*, while very quietly, under his breath, the Duc de Lauzun was chuckling, a sound so extraordinary that it sent a frisson of fear through Sarah's heart.

"Oh, God," she murmured, "oh, my dear God."

And the last thing she saw as she slipped almost elegantly downward, was a row of surprised faces and the floor coming up to meet her.


Dinner over and coffee and brandy taken in that most majestic of drawing rooms, Sidonie was ready for sleep. And the thought of lying in the imposing four-poster was so delectable that she was finally forced to say to her hostess, "If you'll forgive me, I'd rather like to go to bed. I had my stitches out yesterday and it seems to have made me tired."

Chantal was on her feet at once. "But of course, my dear. I'll come up with you to see that you have everything."

"There's really no need."

"But I'd like to."

As they climbed the gracious staircase leading to the château's upper floors, her hostess smiled. "I can't wait to hear you both practising tomorrow. It will make the house seem so alive."

"Have you decided which of us should have first turn?"

"Alexei suggested that you went second so that you could have some extra time in bed. He is very concerned for you. I think he loves you very much."

Chantal said this with a great simplicity which was typically French. Where an Englishwoman would have apologised for interfering, for not minding her business, she spoke with refreshing frankness.

Sidonie decided to adopt the same tactic. "I love him too, in a way. But he's very young and there's somebody else."

"Who loves you as much?"

"That I don't know. I thought so at one time but he hasn't declared himself, to use an old-fashioned phrase."

"Men like that are so irritating. I think in these enlightened times one ought to be able to ask *them*."

"I was afraid of frightening him off."

"Complications! If I were you I would have an *affaire* with the young man. Maybe it will help you to see things more clearly."

"What do you mean?" said Sidonie, turning to look at the Frenchwoman, her hand on the bedroom door.

"All the while you are together and you have not slept with him you will be in doubt. Once you have, you will know which one to choose."

"I'd never thought of it like that," answered Sidonie, smiling despite everything. "Thank you, I'll probably take your advice."

'How wonderfully amoral,' she thought as the door closed behind Chantal.

The room rushed to meet her, absorbing her into its very fabric. "Bed, here I come," said Sidonie in response, and rapidly undressing and having the quickest of washes, snuggled into the four-poster's historic depths. She was asleep at once, deeply but not peacefully, for Sidonie, exhausted as she was, was none the less subjected to one of the most vivid dreams she had ever had in her life.

It seemed to her that she was standing at the top of

the beautiful curved staircase, head on one side, listening intently. From a room on the floor below came the sound of a harpsichord and she clearly identified the music as the Scarlatti Sonata 27. Drawn against her will yet longing to see who was playing, Sidonie, very conscious of the fact that she was only wearing black satin pyjamas and that it was a bitterly cold night, started to descend.

The door of the music room was slightly open and through it she could glimpse the player, his profile turned towards her. He was not old, despite the fact he had white hair, for it was a young face with dark brows that Sidonie could see. Very quietly she crept forward so that she could have a better look. And then she stopped, riveted by the explosion of sound, for here was Scarlatti interpreted as she had never heard him before. Every note, every nuance, every descent and leap of the left hand, every repeated chord, was different. Stunned, Sidonie stood in the doorway and absorbed the music as the man played on, apparently unaware that she was observing him. And then another sound penetrated that unorthodox display of brilliance. Somebody was coming up the stairs.

From where she stood, shivering in her thin nightclothes, Sidonie wheeled and saw Sarah Bunbury walking hand-in-hand with that naughty creature who·had caused her to faint. Suddenly terrified, not knowing whether this was dream or reality, Sidonie sank back into the shadows, as still as her racing heart would allow.

They passed right by her, exchanging a kiss before they went into the music room, and Sidonie heard Sarah call out, "Oh well played, my Lord," as the sonata came to an end.

"Gracious, you startled me," answered the musician in English, his voice cultured but decidedly Scottish. "Have you been there long?"

"No," answered Sarah's escort, his accent French. "We've only just come up the stairs. Why?"

"Somebody was watching me from the doorway, or at least I thought so."

"Who?"

"It was a woman, I believe, but to be honest I didn't look at her properly."

"It was probably one of the servants," Sarah answered carelessly.

"I expect so."

"Anyway she's gone now. Oh please, Lord Kelly, play my minuet."

"Very well, here it is, 'Lady Sarah Bunbury'," and he launched into a bubbling piece that utterly captured the girl's irrepressible personality.

Dream though this must be, Sidonie's emotions changed from fear back to enchantment. Here was an unknown work by the Earl of Kelly dedicated to one of history's most delightful characters and she was being privileged enough to hear it. Very carefully she edged forward once more and again peeped inside.

Sarah and the Frenchman were dancing while Thomas Erskine, Lord Kelly, one of the most celebrated musicians of his time, played with such skill that Sidonie was left breathless.

"Oh, God, don't let this dream end," prayed Sidonie. "Listen to the man! He's simply magnificent. I just want to eavesdrop as long as I can."

"What was that?" said the Frenchman, surely Lauzun himself.

"What? I heard nothing."

"That woman's in the doorway again," said the Earl. "I can see her out of the corner of my eye."

"I'll teach her to spy on her betters," said Sarah's suitor with force, and crossed the room in what seemed to be a single stride.

Sidonie fled, up the stairs in her bare feet, her heart pounding, engulfed by a feeling of total terror. And it was in this awful state that she leapt down the corridor, flew inside her bedroom, into the depths of the four-poster bed and huddled beneath the covers.

There was absolute silence, not a mouse breathed, and she knew then that it had been an illusion, a creation of her own mind. For what were Sarah and the Earl of Kelly doing in a remote château in the Loire Valley? Unless, of course, the Duc de Lauzun was the link. Had it happened again, had she travelled in time and space, or was it a dream? Suddenly, Sidonie felt she could stand no more strain and burst into tears.

"No, no, Monsieur," called Sarah. "Let me take care of it."

"Why? She's *my* servant."

"Yes, I know. But she may be frightened. I'll see to her."

And with that Sarah neatly sidestepped the Duc and rushed up the stairs in hot pursuit of the black-clad figure whose mane of hair revealed her true identity.

"What are you doing here?" Sarah called softly. "What is it you want with me?"

But there was no reply and turning into the corridor she just had time to see her quarry rush into Sarah's own bedroom and close the door. Curious rather than angry, Sarah hurried after her, pushed the door open again and stood in the entrance staring inside.

Just for a second she thought the room was not the same, the furniture changed. The great blue bed was different, draped now in rosy red, the polished dressing table that carried Sarah's horde of pots, powders and pomades, unguents and oils, was gone, in its place one with many more mirrors and different things upon it, bottles and outlandish utensils she could not recognise. Clothes were lying on a chair, clothes that resembled no apparel Sarah had ever seen. And then she blinked and everything was restored to normal. The room as she knew it had returned and Sarah was left with a strange feeling of disappointment that once again the phantom had slipped from her grasp.

"Well?" said Lauzun, coming up behind her.

"I could not find her. She must have run away and hidden."

"Did she come in here?"

"No," lied Sarah.

The Duc looked at her with narrowed eyes. "Do you dabble, Milady?"

"In what?"

"The pursuit of knowledge."

"I'm afraid I don't understand you."

"Do you not?"

He was looking at her cynically now, his curved brows rising at the ends.

"No, I don't," declared Sarah hotly. "What are you implying?"

"You have heard of the Hell Fire Club?"

"Oh yes," said Sarah, "I most certainly have."

For who had not? Started by Sir Francis Dashwood, the Earl of Bute's Chancellor of the Exchequer, the Order had become notorious, succeeding the Mohock Club but far worse in its practices. In the rudely shaped groves of Medmenham Abbey and in the High Wycombe Caves, rakes, dandies and politicians practised a form of devil worship, replacing Christ with Satan and the Virgin Mary with Venus. But this was not all. Sarah had heard terrible stories of initiation ceremonies that parodied religious worship, of Black Masses involving naked females, of orgies in a Roman Room where the participants were whores from London. It was said venereal disease was so prevalent amongst the Club's members that they called one another *Signor Gonorrhoea* and *Monsieur de Croix de Venus*.

"You have never been there have you, Armand?"

"No, I have not. But some years ago one of its brethren came to stay with me; John Wilkes."

"Oh, him."

"You do not like him?"

"He publishes terrible things in *The North Briton*. Cruel satires that offend the King."

"The King?" repeated de Lauzun, raising his brows. "Are you then such a loyal subject that this worries you?"

Sarah flushed uncomfortably. "I think downright viciousness is unforgivable."

"I see that we might argue," answered the Duc soothingly. "So let us talk instead of other things, of magic and alchemy and turning lead to gold."

"I believe you think I practise it, or something of that nature," she answered defensively. "But truly that isn't so. What is it about me that gives you such an impression?"

"You have a familiar, a woman. I saw her on New Year's Eve, playing the harpsichord in place of the Earl of Kelly, and I saw her again just now."

309

"Then it is not all my imagination," Sarah said under her breath.

"Far from it."

She turned to look at him, liking Lauzun still despite this slightly sinister conversation. "Then if you saw her too, what is she?"

"A ghost perhaps, or maybe something a little more subtle."

"What do you mean by that?"

"Perhaps she comes from another age entirely. Perhaps she has not yet been born but has somehow managed to walk through time."

"But that's not possible."

"It is, very very possible. Have you never had a dream of some coming event and then it transpires as you dreamt it?"

"Not really."

"Well, a great many do, and that is an example of time going out of rhythm."

"I can believe that, in premonitions, but I cannot credit the rest of the things you are saying."

"Ah," said Armand, and put his fingers together.

"But if she *is* so special, if she is a being from a different century, why did you laugh when you saw her?"

"I was laughing not at her but with amusement, because I thought, wrongly, that there was another side to you, a hidden aspect. I believed we shared something more than just great attraction."

"Don't say any more, Monsieur. If I think you are a warlock I will hate you."

"No, that is where you are wrong, my dear. You will never, never be able to hate me for the rest of your days on earth."

"I could try," said Sarah, and turning on her heel walked away from him.

# Twenty

Afterwards, in the years that followed, when she was looking for explanations, Sidonie thought of her visit to the Château des Cèdres as one of the major turning points in her life. For it was while she was there that, in her opinion, she finally learned to play the harpsichord, and it was during those same few days of her stay that she also learned the art of self-deception. But whether the good of one outweighed the evil of the other could never truthfully be judged. Though, as Sidonie supposed later, she would have sacrificed almost anything, including her peace of mind, to have improved her musical skill in the sudden and extraordinary way she did.

She had woken from the dream, her mind teeming with sound, the notes of the Earl of Kelly's playing still echoing in her brain. Unable to sleep, yet unable to go to the harpsichord for fear of disturbing the rest of the household, Sidonie had dressed warmly and gone into the grounds for a walk. Trudging through the snow, still not certain what had happened to her during the night, whether it had been a dream or her own kind of reality, the feeling that destiny was about to lay its hand on her was inescapable. Sidonie experienced a sense of the inevitable as the sound of a violin broke the silence of that ice-sharp morning. Going towards it as if she were pulled, she made her way to one of the château's outbuildings.

Alexei was standing inside, his back turned to her, zooming through a work by Paganini with such virtuosity that Sidonie could only watch in rapt admiration that at this early hour of the morning anyone could play so well. Totally unaware of her presence, the Russian finished with a triumphant sweep of his bow across the strings, and Sidonie burst into applause.

"Bravo, well done."

He turned rapidly. "Sidonie? You scared me stiff! What are you doing here? I thought you were asleep."

"I woke early and wanted some air."

"What time is it?"

"About seven I think."

"Good. I can get in another hour's practice."

She looked at him curiously. "I didn't realise you were such an early riser. Didn't you sleep well?"

Alexei grinned sheepishly. "No, I was awake most of the night. I kept thinking about the ghost in the music room. Do you know I could have sworn I heard it."

"What do you mean?"

"I thought I heard the harpsichord play in the middle of the night. It was eerie. It's amazing what imagination can do when everything's dark."

Sidonie said slowly, "I thought I heard it too but I wasn't sure whether I'd dreamt it or not."

Alexei put his violin down on a bale of hay and came towards her. "You looked pathetic when you said that."

"In what way?"

"Young and vulnerable, like a little girl. Come on, let me cuddle you."

He put his arms round her and drew her tight to his chest, folding her into the depths of his coat, pressing his body against hers. Somewhere, in a part of her brain untouched by emotion, she knew that the struggle with her conscience was over, that she was about to have sex with Alexei Orlov, that it would be ridiculous and uncomfortable but that here, in the place which had once stabled the château's horses, she was going to become his lover.

Alexei bent his head and kissed her, not giving her one of the friendly jolly kisses they had exchanged in the past but a deep and passionate embrace. Her lips parted beneath his and a strange excitement was born between them. Putting his hands on either side of her hips, Alexei pulled her closer to him.

"I want you," he said, his voice sounding strained.

"Here? Like this?"

"Why not? Are you cold?"

"No."

And then frenzy broke over them like a wave and, not waiting to undress, Alexei lifted Sidonie backwards onto a bale of hay then, still standing, leaned forward over her. She gasped as her clothing was pushed to one side and he entered, brutally almost, as though he had been waiting all his life for this moment and now could hardly contain himself. But the rhythm he set up within her was wonderful, exotic and powerful, as if he were a Tsar and she some little concubine slave girl.

Shame and guilt were gone and Sidonie threw herself into the flood of this vigorous young man's physical urgency. They thrust hard, like two healthy creatures in love with the sensations they aroused in one another, and then Alexei suddenly stopped.

"I don't want it to end too soon."

She smiled up at him. "You've still got your coat on."

"I've got everything on but it doesn't matter. It's good like this."

"I know."

He began to move again, slowly at first, but then faster and faster. Deep within, Sidonie felt an intense sensual pleasure begin to build and head towards its inevitable climax.

"No going back," she called, as an explosion of sheer erotic bliss filled her entire body. But Alexei was unable to answer as he flowed into her, every second one of immense sensation.

"My God," he gasped as he dropped onto the straw beside her. "That was the best I've ever had. You're terrific."

"So are you," she answered, snuggling against him, still in the relaxed stage before memories of Finnan came back to torment her.

"Can we do it again?"

"What now?"

"No, tonight in bed. Properly, like grown-ups."

"Wasn't this grown up?"

"It was heaven," answered Alexei, and closed his eyes.

Half an hour later they walked back to the château hand-in-hand only to find Chantal was up and that breakfast was being served in one of the morning rooms.

"You have been for a walk?" said their hostess, her knowing glance taking in the expression on their faces.

"Neither of us slept very well," Sidonie replied quickly. "Alexei thought he heard your musical ghost, and I did too, strangely enough."

"Perhaps so," answered Chantal, "though I must confess I slept soundly. Now, would you like some hot coffee?"

Having eaten a croissant, Sidonie went for a bath and then, dressed in trousers and a warm sweater, made her way to the music room. Walking in she half expected to see the harpsichord player, his young face with its white hair turned towards her, but the place was quite empty, not a sign of any psychic phenomena disturbing the calm. Opening the lid Sidonie sat down at the instrument and tried to remember the dream.

It came to her at once, like a revelation, and, putting her hands on the keys, she started to play as she had heard the Earl of Kelly do so. Down hurtled her left hand in that same unorthodox sweep while the right played a series of rapid repeated notes each with a different texture.

"*Mon Dieu*," said Chantal from the door. "I have never heard Scarlatti interpreted like that. Oh, forgive me, I did not mean to interrupt."

But Sidonie did not answer as the spirit of the dream possessed her totally and she began to reproduce all that she had heard. Yet, irritatingly, one thing eluded her. The tune of "Lady Sarah Bunbury" would not come back and the more she tried to recapture it the less Sidonie could find it. But it did not matter, nothing mattered, compared with the wealth, the tumult of music that was pouring out of her. The Earl of Kelly was in the room, she was aware of his presence, and almost felt him touch her wrist when she played a note incorrectly.

"*Incroyable!*" whispered Chantal to Alexei, both of them standing in the doorway, not daring to move. "This is surely how these pieces were played in the eighteenth century. What has happened to her?"

The young Russian smiled, full of age-old smugness, believing with masculine vanity that his lovemaking had opened the

314

floodgates for his woman's talent. And Chantal, being French and worldly, saw his look, interpreted it correctly and did not believe it. There was an almost spiritual depth to what was happening in her music room and she guessed at something beyond earthly explanation.

Sidonie started into the "Duchess of Richmond" with a look of pure delight on her face. "Listen," she said, "the Earl is using her nickname. Can't you hear the music saying 'The Lovely, The Lovely'?"

"I would never have thought of it," answered Chantal. "How did you?"

"Perhaps it was the ghost," Sidonie replied, and just for a second the two women exchanged a glance.

"Then it has done you a great service," answered her hostess. "Lauzun is a better man than I thought him."

"I think perhaps you are haunted not by the Duc but the composer himself, the Earl of Kelly."

"If that is so then I am privileged," answered Chantal seriously, and went downstairs looking thoughtful, leaving the two musicians on their own.

The January forest was bitter, a cold sheet over the ground, the trees harsh with glittering ice, a shower of quicksilver falling from the heavens to blot out the dark earth with its crunching cloak. Nothing moved in the stillness, even the sheep bells were silenced, the forest creatures quivering noiselessly, the proud deer merely breathing vapour as they huddled together for comfort. Only the two people sheltering in the stable made any sound but even that was only of low, urgent conversation.

"Oh please," begged the Duc de Lauzun softly, "oh please, Sarah, let me have that which I desire most in life."

"You know I can't, Monsieur. I am a married woman. I took a vow to honour my husband and this I intend to do for the rest of my days on earth," his companion answered him forcefully.

"But he's a bum fiddler."

"I *beg* your pardon?"

"Never mind," Armand answered wearily. "Sarah, I have

fallen in love with you. I shall not rest until we have experienced together the sweet pleasure of the flesh."

"Then you will have a weary life, Monsieur, for I do not intend to give in."

"Just once, just once," breathed Lauzun, and he pressed his body close to hers, certain that he would get a response, which after a moment he did, as Sarah relaxed slightly and the Duc felt the heave of her breasts against his chest. This was obviously the moment to force home his advantage and Armand did so, lowering his lips to hers and drawing out Sarah's tongue with his own.

To say that he desired her would have been to express the matter in cool terms. Lauzun longed for Sarah with an intensity that frightened even himself. He truly felt that he would never be able to live quietly again unless he knew her carnally and yet, though he had ruthlessly laced her wine on numerous occasions with an aphrodisiac potion, she seemed impervious to it and Sarah Bunbury retained her honour.

And yet the mystery was, and it *was* a mystery to him, despite everything, she found him physically attractive, Lauzun knew it. But still she resisted and not with cloying coyness but apparent sincerity. It seemed that Sir Charles Bunbury whom Lauzun felt positive was a sodomite, though a subtle one indeed, held the keys to her heart and nobody else would ever get inside. But alone with her in the dimness of the stables with only the occasional stamp of a horse to disturb them, the Duc was overcome with the notion that it was now or never, that if he could only get her to agree to intercourse, their relationship would change for ever more.

"Oh Sarah, Sarah," he whispered, and very gently eased her back onto a bale of hay that stood waist high behind them.

Pinioned like this she allowed him to kiss her and even sighed and groaned a little as his lips slid beneath her fur mantle and onto her breasts. With his tongue flying, Lauzun caressed her nipples and was satisfied with the response. Then, slowly and easily, staying in control as much as he could, Lauzun began to lift her long flowing skirts, their hems wet with snow, to the level of Sarah's thighs.

Glimpsing them, seeing their white beauty above her dark stockings, the Duc became crazed and his hand flew to his own clothing to release the painful pressure building within. Now he was only seconds away from achieving the desire of his heart. Anticipating the sheer raw joy of entry, Lauzun thrust forward.

With an exclamation of horror, Sarah wriggled out from beneath his grasp and ran to the other end of the stable, pulling at her dishevelled apparel.

"How dare you!" she said in a low, menacing voice.

"Oh God," said the Duc, almost in tears, "I thought you wanted it."

"Well, I didn't and I believed you to be above rape, Monsieur."

Suddenly ashamed, Armand turned away from her, hiding his body from her furious gaze, angry that part of him still bore signs of wanting her so desperately.

"Forgive me, please. I made a genuine mistake." He turned back to look at her, once more fully in control of himself. "But one thing I will not do is apologise for being in love with you. I have more genuine feelings for you than I have ever had for any woman."

"In that case," said Sarah coldly, "I think Sir Charles and I should leave for Paris immediately. We will depart early tomorrow morning."

"Your youthful admirer as well?" asked the Duc spiritedly. "Small wonder I thought you game for a romp, Sarah, when that boy trails after you everywhere you go. Why, in the capital you are known as a shameless coquette thanks to your flagrant behaviour with him."

"But my husband accompanies us everywhere."

"Then more fool him."

She swept out into the snow at that, her hem sending up a plume of white feathers, her hood obscuring all but her furious profile.

"Go then," Lauzun shouted after her. "Good riddance to you; you're nothing but a teasing bitch."

Sarah did not answer, stalking off into the snowflakes with that quick lively step the Duc loved so well.

"One day I'll have you," he muttered under his breath. "One day you'll be willing. One day, and I shall not scruple if I must summon up a dark power to achieve it, it is *you* who will ask *me* to love you. And then let us see what the answer will be."

The concert at the Château de Chambord marked a turning point in the careers of both Sidonie Brooks and Alexei Orlov. She, already a celebrated musician, now passed into the ranks of the distinguished, and was described as such by a weighty French newspaper.

The playing of Madame Brooks has now grown in such stature that she must surely be ranked as one of the most distinguished harpsichordists in the world. Her interpretation of eighteenth-century music, particularly of the works of Scarlatti, is unique in its experimental nature. For here, surely, is the genuine sound of those times or as near to it as any twentieth-century musician can achieve. Sidonie Brooks has moved into the celebrated ranks of those rare beings, a performer of majesty, commanding respect with every note she plays.

The same newspaper wrote about Alexei.

Here is genius; young, raw and sweet. This unknown Russian violinist, still only twenty-four years of age, has erupted onto the musical scene with all the vivacity and temperament of his mother country. Youthful impetuosity still hallmarks his playing but yet with what skill does this *enfant terrible* tackle the great classical works. When maturity comes to this performer he will set the world alight, that fact is beyond dispute.

"There you are," said Sidonie, "you're a genius."
"What do they mean *will* set the world alight? I thought I already had."
"You've certainly sent mine up in flames," Sidonie answered

truthfully. "I don't think anything will ever be quite the same again."

"That's because I make you feel good in bed."

"Not only that. Just having known you has been enough."

"You sound as if it's all over. It isn't, is it?"

"No, of course not. Why should it be?"

"I thought maybe that man in Canada had been in touch."

"How could he have been?" asked Sidonie crossly. "He doesn't even know where I am."

Alexei stared into her face. "I upset you by saying that, didn't I? I'm sorry, I didn't mean to."

"It's not you."

"Then what?"

"I'm upset with myself."

"Whatever for?"

"For having betrayed him with you."

"For Christ's sake," said Alexei, looking genuinely angry, "he's got crumpet in Canada, you told me so yourself. You said a woman answered his phone."

"Maybe it was just a friend, and why is it that foreigners always have to pick up the worst of our expressions?"

"Is saying crumpet rude then?"

"In a way. It means a woman regarded as an object of sexual pleasure."

"Does it?" Alexei started to grin. "Then, Sidonie, you are crumpet. Gorgeous, glorious crumpet."

"Oh, shut up."

"No, I won't. Here, come and kiss me."

And he leant over her and drew her mouth under his.

They were back in Paris, both staying in the same hotel, and it was the morning of Sidonie's departure for England which would have made them sad had it not been for the fact that Alexei was going with her, though only for the weekend, before he flew to his next engagement in Berlin.

Their relationship, or so Sidonie kept trying to tell herself, was one based on friendship. But knocking this theory on the head was the fierce power of their lovemaking. Perhaps it was because Alexei was younger than Finnan, perhaps it was because he hadn't an inhibition in the world, that he raised her to heights of sensation she had not known existed. And yet how cheap she felt comparing the two men who had recently taken her to bed. Raddled old strumpets probably did that, she told herself, and felt the pang of betrayal that always accompanied thoughts of the Irish doctor she had believed she loved so much.

"Oy," said Alexei, "you're getting serious. Now stop it."

"Sorry."

"Is anything really the matter?"

"No. I'm just lamenting the fact that the party's over – France I mean – and now I've got to go back and face reality."

"But you'll be inundated with engagements. You see."

"I expect so." Sidonie smiled at Alexei. "I'll miss you."

"I'm only touring for six months, then I'm going to have a holiday in Britain. I have decided this."

"And I have decided I'll go with you."

"That," said the Russian, kissing her nose, "is part of my plan."

They flew from Paris in the late afternoon and arrived at Heathrow at dusk; clambering aboard the little bus that took them to the long-stay carparks, Alexei guarding his violin which had gone with him on the plane.

"I hope to God I can remember where I left the car," Sidonie remarked, peering through the twilight.

"Haven't you got a ticket?"

"Yes, somewhere or other. But it doesn't give the location."

"Oh dear."

But with the help of the bus driver they sorted themselves out and set off through the raw January night towards London, Alexei staring at the lights of the motorway and saying, "So this is England."

"A scar on its face more like. But there are beautiful parts. You'll love them."

"I'd love anywhere if you were there," Alexei answered gallantly, and Sidonie smiled at his sweetness, only one of the Russian's many endearing qualities.

The Garden Flat in Phillimore Gardens was quiet as the

grave and its owner shivered as she crossed the threshold, Alexei close behind her. Memories of Finnan came rushing back again and the musician felt like a cheap drab as she showed Alexei the bedroom and told him where to hang his things. But he noticed nothing, was not aware of her sudden silence as he rushed round examining the place, dashing down the stairs to the music room and giving a great shout of delight.

Sidonie stood on the top step listening to him, trying to come to terms with the situation, trying to find a recipe for peace of mind. But there was none other than to live only for the moment, to pretend that Finnan was as faithless as she, to put into practice the self-deception she had started to learn in the Château des Cèdres.

"What a harpsichord!" Alexei was saying. "Where did you get it?"

"At an auction in Ireland. It's got the owner's initials carved underneath the name board. Do you want to see?"

"Yes, please."

Sidonie unscrewed the board. "There, look at that. S.L."

"Who was she?"

"She? I always thought it was a he."

"That's because you're prejudiced. This harpsichord was definitely owned by a woman."

"Good God!" exclaimed Sidonie.

"What?"

"I've just guessed who it might well have been. Sarah Lennox. It would make sense. And Ireland would fit in with her life after Bunbury."

"Bunbury who?"

"Sarah's first husband. He was a great man of the turf, a horse breeder, a racing buff."

"When was all this?"

"In the eighteenth century, when Catherine the Great ruled Russia and slept with Alexei Orlov."

"Why do you think it belonged to Sarah?"

"Because she used to live in Holland House which is just over there." She pointed towards the door leading to the garden. "And because, my darling Russian toyboy,

321

she is my own private, personal and very very special ghost."

It was indeed the way of the world. When Sarah had arrived in Paris during the month of November she had been the darling of Society. By the time she was due to leave in February of the following year she had been castigated as a little whore, a coquette, a bitch who held men off in order to lead them on. She who had been so sought after, so copied and admired, had fallen from grace with a vengeance.

Horace Walpole's great friend Madame de Deffand was speaking for the rest of Society when she wrote to him, "She is all off with the Duc de Chartres. He made the running for a while, but then so did twenty others. Lauzun holds the field, and I don't think she minds that much one way or the other. He seems rather a blind and shield for her affair with Lord Carlisle, so that she sees him only to put the world off the scent. Her good Baronet seems to think that both look alike to him."

But though she was shrewd enough, the old French lady was wrong in her written opinion. Quite the reverse had happened. Though Sarah hardly knew how to face it herself, could hardly bear to admit the truth, she had undergone a sea change when Lauzun had tried to make love to her. Some terrible lusty thing had been awoken in her, some inherited longing for sexual adventure. She could not forget the sight of him, ready for coupling and spurned at the last second. In a part of her that she did not admire nor even fully understand, Sarah suddenly became obsessed with the thought of Armand de Gontaut, Duc de Lauzun.

She, Sir Charles and Carlisle had left the Château des Cèdres on the morning after the incident and returned to Paris, where Sarah had appeared to embark on an affair with the Chevalier de Coigny, currently sleeping with Lauzun's ex-mistress. Just as she had intended, news of this latest scandal soon reached the Duc's ears and he had hurried to the capital to find out the truth.

Sarah would have given herself to him there and then, so delighted was she to see him again, but there was no opportunity. It was February and the end of the French visit. A few days after Armand's return, the Bunbury coach bowled out of Paris with that of the Duc de Lauzun close behind it. He had got leave of absence from his guard duties at Versailles and was accompanying his sweetheart as far as he could on her journey to Calais.

'And I had no need even to cast a spell,' he thought to himself in wonderment, and then suspected, shrewdly, that it had been his rough state in the stable, his momentary vulnerability, that had both excited and caught her attention.

He wondered if there was any chance of consummation during the journey but Lauzun's hopes were dashed on this score when, on the party's first stop at a dark and dirty inn at Pont St Maxence near Chantilly, he was forced to share a room with Lord Carlisle, who promptly challenged him to a duel.

"For the love of God," Armand answered languidly, "can't we do it in Paris? It'll upset the lady if we set to here."

"Don't sully her name with your lips," hissed Frederick, puce pink with agitation. "Have you seduced her, vile man?"

"Unfortunately, no," answered Lauzun, yawning. "Have you?"

"Of course not. I respect Lady·Sarah."

The Duc laughed derisively. "You tragic little tripehound, don't add hypocrisy to all your other failings. Why, the lady would only have to lift a finger and you'd be in her bed arse-naked."

"How dare you!" shrieked Carlisle, and slapped Armand round the face.

"You're as big a fool as ever pissed," the Duc snapped angrily and, taking poor Carlisle by the collar, threw him halfway down the flight of stairs.

"Come outside," gasped Frederick, flat on his back and glaring malevolently.

"Cock brain," Lauzun responded and, shutting the bedroom door, turned the key in the lock.

Hearing all from where she lay beside a peacefully slumbering Sir Charles, Sarah giggled beneath the sheets and then took herself to task for being so irresponsible. She

was married to a good man whose only fault lay in his lack
of passion. She had no cause to be delighted that two men
were fighting over her.

'If only I were frigid,' she thought and then, remembering
her ancestry, that her grandfather had been the love child
of Charles II and a French slut, albeit a high-born one, that
her brother the Duke of Richmond had been in and out of
women's boudoirs since he had barely arrived in his teens, she
was hardly surprised that the passion the King had aroused in
her had finally been rekindled.

"Oh, Charles," she said, and laid her hand on his chest.

"Good night, my dear," he answered sleepily, and gave her
a chaste kiss on the cheek.

It was in this state of hostile neutrality that the Bunbury
party finally arrived at Arras, a day's journey away from
Calais. And it was here that the Duc de Lauzun regretfully
decided that he must return to Paris and his duties at
Versailles. And it was also in Arras that Frederick Howard,
Earl of Carlisle, played his trump card.

He had stated all along that when the Bunburys left France
he would continue on alone, touring Europe and seeing the
great sights, joining his schoolfriend Charles James Fox in
Italy. But now he announced, with one triumphantly beady
eye on Armand, that he had changed his mind, that he was,
after all, going to return to England with Sir Charles and Lady
Sarah. Sick with jealousy, Lauzun ground his teeth but had
had no option other than to get into his carriage, wave the
trio goodbye, and head back to Paris.

"Oh God," groaned the Duc as he finally lost sight of his
Lady, still waving hard, "if only I'd been able to have a good
sturdy roger with her just once." Then he took himself to
task for using this word which had originated in the American
colony of Virginia and became universally popular rather than a
decent, or indecent?, French expression. But language aside,
his longing for Sarah was becoming unbearable and tears had
been in his eyes when he had said farewell.

"I'll come to England soon," he had whispered under his
breath.

"Oh please, please," she'd answered, and Armand had

thought he had seen a gleam of moisture on her lashes too.

The time had come to say goodbye, and in the unappetising surroundings of a Heathrow airport coffee bar at that. It had always struck Sidonie as amazing how scruffy international travellers seemed to be and now, glancing round, her thoughts were reindorsed. Everywhere was a welter of blue jeans, while earrings, tattoos, beer guts and aggressive boots abounded.

"And that's only the women!" she said aloud.

"You make a joke?" asked Alexei.

"I do but it's boring if I repeat it."

"O.K."

Neither of them was feeling particularly talkative, both aware that after this parting nothing would ever be quite the same again between them, that Alexei would be lionised as a prodigy throughout Europe, that Sidonie would be sought after as a truly great interpreter of eighteenth-century music.

"It's been great fun," said Sidonie as they walked towards passport control.

"Don't say it as if we'll never meet again. You're coming to the concert in Venice, remember?"

"I will if I can. But Rod was hinting at busy times ahead after my Purcell Room concert."

"Well, try." Alexei took hold of Sidonie's hands. "Whatever happens I'll see you when I get back. Don't forget our holiday together."

"Of course I won't. Have a good time."

"I will."

He kissed her and walked away, his violin case firmly in his hand. Sidonie gave a little wave but Alexei didn't see it, already showing his passport, on the way to the next part of his life.

The rider caught up with Lauzun at the inn in Boyelles where he had stopped to refresh himself at midday.

"Monsieur le Duc de Lauzun?" asked the messenger

breathlessly, gazing at the gleaming equipage outside the inn, the horses loosened from the traces and being watered.

"Yes, what is it?"

"I have a letter for you, Monsieur, from the inn at Calais."

Lauzun was so pleased he could have kissed the man but instead gave him a very good *douceur*.

"It is from the lady I presume?"

"Indeed it is, Monsieur."

Breaking the seal, the Duc read the contents and felt that, at last, he had truly won Sarah's love.

"My dear Armand, You have utterly changed my heart, my friend. It is sad and broken, and although you hurt me so, I can have no thought save for my love. I had no idea such a thing could happen, and I imagined myself too proud, too virtuous, for my happiness ever to depend on a French lover.

The wind is against us, and I am not sorry. It is better to be in the same country. I shed copious tears. I told Sir Charles that I had a headache, and he was satisfied with that. Lord Carlisle did not believe it, for he gazed at me very seriously. Heavens! All this that I am doing must be very wicked, since I try to conceal it, and I, the most truthful woman living, am obliged to lie and deceive two people whom I esteem so highly!

They are both out, and I have chosen to stay indoors to write to him who is dearer to me than the repose which I have lost for his sake. I dare not send my letter to the post by one of our servants so I have appealed to the waiter in this inn. He has an honest kindly face."

Lauzun sipped his wine and sighed. Victory was his, it was only a matter of time now before Sarah became his lover. He read the rest of the letter swiftly but let his eyes linger on the ending.

"Come, so as by your presence to fill your mistress with the greatest joy to which she can look forward. I have no fear of your not understanding my ridiculous French. Your heart and mine will always understand each other. Adieu, for I am afraid of being taken by surprise. Remember that it is for you alone that there exists your Sarah."

"Oh, my darling," said Lauzun, kissing the paper passionately. "Two weeks at the most and I will be at your side."

# Twenty-one

The Duc de Lauzun was as good as his word. Organising his Court duties, leaving behind his young amiable chit of a wife, he sailed for England in the middle of February and, arriving in London, deposited himself on the French Ambassador, the Comte de Guerchy. However, the *beau monde* was not deceived. The formidable combination of Madame de Deffand and Horace Walpole, who kept up a continuous correspondence one with the other, had already alerted everyone in town that the Duc had come to England for love of Lady Sarah Bunbury and that the Ambassador's receptions and ceremonies of presentation were merely a blind for Lauzun's true purpose. And, sure enough, when the official part of the Duc's visit was finally over, he vanished into the Suffolk countryside as a guest of Sir Charles Bunbury and his wife.

"What the devil does her husband think he's playing at?" said Lady Diana Spencer, who had married Viscount Bolingbroke in 1757 and was now, ten years later, in the process of getting a divorce from him.

"God knows," answered Lady Mary Coke, as big a wasp as ever buzzed round Society.

"There's something rum about that feller. He don't seem to realise how a pretty woman like Sarah attracts admirers."

"Don't or won't! It's my belief he actively encourages the situation."

"But why?"

"Perhaps Milady's flirtations distract attention from his own activities," said Lady Mary, fluttering an eyelid.

"Oh, so *that's* it."

"Who knows? There is no proof. But if not, then he's either an innocent fool or else gets a vicarious thrill from contemplating his wife's amorous intrigues."

"A pretty coil indeed."

But while tongues wagged and eyebrows were raised, Sir Charles Bunbury continued on his enigmatical way, announcing after a few days at his country seat, Barton that he was bored and would be returning to London. Staring at him in amazement, Sarah could believe neither his indifference nor her luck.

"But I shall be left alone with the Duc," she said protestingly, half hoping Charles would at long last notice that Lauzun admired her and do something about it.

"I'm sure you'll be able to entertain him, my dear," her husband answered absently.

"But for how long will you be gone?"

"I don't know yet, possibly two weeks, maybe three. It all depends."

"On what?"

"On whom I meet," Charles replied vaguely, and with that Sarah had to be content.

However, managing an adulterous affair in an establishment full of servants loyal to their master was not as easy as might be imagined. For several nights the prospect of how to avoid being caught daunted both the lady of the house and her would-be lover.

"Might I not creep into your room when everyone is asleep?" he said finally, lowering his voice even though they were in the garden.

"Yes, you could try. But you must be quiet. If we are discovered we are undone."

"Are we?" asked the Duc cynically. "Surely your husband must be aware of the fact that I long for you. Does he truly believe either of us could resist such a temptation?"

"I don't know, I don't know," answered Sarah in confusion. "I must confess it does seem very odd."

"It's inexplicable. But whatever Bunbury's motives, I can wait no longer. Tonight I am coming to you."

How strange it was, thought Sarah, lying in bed in the moonlight, that though she was on fire for Armand she still hesitated about committing the carnal act with him. Why was it that her passionate nature did not simply allow her to fall into his arms and be done with it? But something, somewhere, held her back from the final commitment.

'Oh, my God,' she thought, as she heard his delicate step on the landing and her door swung slowly open. 'Tonight let me be wicked, let me just this once have no scruples whatsoever.'

But that, in fact, was not to be.

Sitting in her garden in the weak February sunshine, Sidonie read Lauzun's published account of his life and couldn't help but smile at the episode dealing with Sarah Bunbury's doomed attempt to stay out of trouble.

> At length, one evening, she told me that I might come down to her chamber when the household were gone to bed. I awaited this longed-for moment with the utmost impatience. I found her in bed, and supposed that I might take a few liberties. She appeared so offended and distressed by them that I did not persist. She allowed me, however, to lie down beside her, but she required of me a moderation and reserve of which I thought I should die. This charming torment continued for several nights. I had ceased to hope for consummation, when, clasping me on one occasion with the liveliest ardour, she gratified all my desires.

"Poor old Lauzun," Sidonie said to the cat, which was watching a bird and hoping for the best. "She did lead him a dance. Mind you, he gave me such a fright in Paris that I can't really feel sorry for him."

The marks on her forehead where she had been cut and stitched were fading now but the memory of her spectacular faint in that equally spectacular house had hardly diminished. Nothing about that trip, about the strange events in the Château des Cèdres, of the exotic love affair that had started on a bitter January morning, had grown less clear with the passing of time.

Yet Sidonie had had to discipline her thoughts away from all that as a burst of interest in her playing, resulting from the French newspaper reviews, became apparent. Rod had left exactly sixteen messages on the answerphone while she had been abroad, all of which were volatile and enthusiastic.

"Come to lunch, now," he ordered on several of them.

Sidonie had rung him on the Monday after Alexei had gone. "I've only just got back," she lied. "When do you want to see me?"

"Now, this minute. Congratulations, Sid bach. You've really done it this time. What came over you?"

"I'll tell you when we meet. How about tomorrow?"

"Done. Come to the office·at twelve o'clock. I'll put some champagne on ice."

"Steady on, you'll turn a girl's head," she had answered, and put the receiver down.

There was a heap of mail waiting and, riffling through the pile, Sidonie saw two envelopes which bore a Canadian stamp. Her heart sank and she almost did not open them, then felt furious with herself. Not only had she had an affair with another man but she was actually being so unkind as to ignore letters written to her in friendship. Fighting off tears, Sidonie unsealed the letters and took them into the garden with her book, *Memoirs of the Duc de Lauzun*.

Finnan's correspondence was fairly general in tone, commenting on the hospital, discussing life in Canada, talking about his colleagues. Only in the last paragraph had he said he missed her and couldn't wait to see her again. Sidonie read the words as if they were addressed to someone else, as though it had been another person who had loved the Irish doctor and gone to bed with him. Was this then, she thought, the secret of infidelity? Was a divine schizophrenia the answer to it all?

Grey in mood, she shivered in the sudden cold wind and went inside, automatically taking her place at the harpsichord. And it was then that a small miracle happened. Out of nowhere the tune of the Earl of Kelly's composition, "Lady Sarah Bunbury", came back into Sidonie's head. Her fingers leaping onto the keyboards, she started to play.

When she looked up again it was dark and the lights of the youth hostel were on in Holland House. Going to the upstairs window, Sidonie looked across at the shell of the building which had known so much in the way of love and

332

passion, drama and despair, and wondered when and how she would see it again as it had originally stood in the greatest of its days.

She had given in to him at last and was thoroughly enjoying every moment of it. After several nights when she had forced poor Lauzun to lie still beside her, Sarah had overcome the dictates of her conscience and, flinging her arms round him, had covered him with kisses. A second later they had both been stark naked, her breasts firmly cupped by Armand's hands. But that had been only the beginning.

Granted what he had for so long craved, the Duc de Lauzun had taken no chances that she might refuse him again. In one swift move he had taken possession of Sarah, filling her with a vast unrelenting part of himself, and waiting only one second for her to protest. But Sarah had merely gasped and Lauzun had proceeded to build on his advantage, gliding in and out with a steady thrust which in the past had made his conquests beg for more. And this latest one was no exception, pulling him closer so that he was able to penetrate her secrets even more deeply.

"This is incredible," she whispered.

"New to you?"

She murmured something that sounded like, "Once before", but Armand ignored that and concentrated only on giving both of them pleasure, plunging and driving mercilessly, creating within himself and the girl he rode a great sea of intense sensation.

And then, in the midst of this magnificent rhythm, the Duc paused and Sarah cried out, terrified that he might be about to stop completely. Hearing her, Lauzun knew she was finally his and the small restraint that had been holding him back from his usual ardour was gone.

He dug fiercely and strongly, twice as fast and twice as hard as before. And now the magic began. In the dim distance, Sarah sensed the start of an incredible pulse, and recognised it as that wonderful explosion which she and the King had shared together. Building in strength and intensity it swept over her, suffusing her body with a superb sensual shock. Spasms of rapture engulfed her and she shivered and shook, calling out her pleasure.

Lauzun, hearing Sarah's cries thrust wildly, to the very hilt, then flowed into her, dropping down beside his new mistress in a final exhaustion before he closed his eyes and slept. But that night had been a revelation to them both. Twice more they tasted the forbidden bliss of lovemaking, each time unbelievably improving upon the last. And then, in the hour before dawn, Lauzun eventually tiptoed back to his own room.

After he had gone, Sarah lay quietly, watching the sky lighten, aware that a new appetite had been born in her. The experienced Frenchman, his knowledge of love and lust obvious from his accomplished performance, had brought her into a state of awareness that might yet prove dangerous. For, having tasted the fruit, Sarah knew she could not live without it. Somehow, she thought, she must extricate herself from her cold unyielding marriage and spend the rest of her days joyously with the man she had come to adore.

"All for love," she murmured. "As long as everything is done for love then it must be good and true."

And there lay the panacea for Sarah's conscience. Love excused her transgression, love was her guiding star.

"Armand and I will be together for ever," she murmured into her pillow before she fell asleep.

The next few days crackled with passion. Like two starving beggars set before a feast, Sarah and Lauzun coupled at every opportunity. The weather suddenly improving, they rode out a good deal and were for ever tethering their horses and walking into the sheltering woods. Sarah had never experienced such intense physical delight and knew quite certainly that she and Armand must live together or even marry if Sir Charles Bunbury could be persuaded to embark on that most hazardous of paths leading to divorce.

Yet even in the height of this glorious delirium the situation began, very subtly, to change. It occurred to Sarah that Armand had said nothing about the future, that he was perfectly content to wander in a sexual paradise without any kind of commitment. Awful warnings about women who gave

their all eventually losing everything began to go through her
mind. The seeds of uncertainty were sown.

"The trouble with women," her naughty nephew, Charles
James Fox, had once said, "is that when you start with 'em
they always want to know how you'll finish."

Sarah thought of those words now and had to agree with
her precocious young relative who had first gone a'raking, as
he called it, at the tender age of fourteen. She had become
obsessed with sharing Lauzun's life completely, for only that
could justify her fall from grace, her flagrant adultery. She,
in common with all of her sex, wanted to know how the
relationship would end.

She broached the subject one bright March day with the
hearty wind coming in off the sea, booming its cheerful voice
round the flat lands of Suffolk, teasing the heads of the fine
pale daffodils, ruffling the fur of the hares that danced in the
fields till dusk.

She and Lauzun had ridden out early, glorying in the
morning, heading off in the direction of Thetford where they
stopped, taking their picnic into a meadow beside the river.

"How beautiful you are," said Lauzun, propping his chin on
his hand, as he lay on a rug and stared at Sarah's cloud of hair,
dark as pitch and flying out in the breeze.

"Am I?" she answered, her profile turned to him, her clear
green eyes gazing into the distance.

"The most beautiful woman I ever served."

"And there have been many?"

Lauzun smiled reminiscently. "A few, but all leading to you.
Everything I learned at the hands of others was in preparation
for the day you came to me."

"I see." Still Sarah did not look at him. "Then I take it I give
you greater pleasure than any woman previously."

"Indeed you do. A million times."

Her eyes flicked in his direction. "Should I read into that
statement that you love me more than anyone else in the
world?"

Armand spread his hands in a grand gesture. "But of
course."

Now the great eyes were looking intently into his, their

expression earnest and imploring. "And I love you, my darling. So much so I can no longer endure living this shabby lie."

"What do you mean?"

"That our love has made a future with Sir Charles impossible to contemplate. It would be a torment beyond belief. Therefore, Monsieur, I am asking you to prove your words. For the love of Sarah Bunbury I want you to forsake everything and everyone and elope with me to Jamaica."

Lauzun stared at her blankly. "Jamaica?" he repeated unbelievingly. "Why there?"

"Because I have a wealthy kinsman who lives on the island. He has no children to consider and I know will give us refuge with delight. I can be sure of his friendship and indulgence even in the face of the greatest scandal."

The Duc shook his head very very slightly. "Jamaica," he murmured again.

Sarah stood up. "Don't try to answer now, my heart's sweet love. Think about it and give me your reply in a week's time."

And with that she climbed onto her horse, gathered up the reins, and went off at full gallop before the Duc de Lauzun could utter another word.

The lunch with Rod was both hilarious and rewarding. They dined at Rules in Maiden Lane, which Sidonie's agent adored because of the traditional English food.

"Much better than all that Italian stuff," he said, looking at the menu, rolling his olive eyes and raising his shoulders in a way that only someone whose forebears came from the land of grand opera could possibly do. "Now tell me, Sid bach, what's all this I keep hearing about you playing as they did in the eighteenth century? A musician transformed is what the French papers said."

Sidonie looked at him shrewdly, wondering just how much her agent would believe.

"I had a psychic experience if you really want to know. I stayed in a château near Chambord supposed to have a haunted music room and had a peculiar dream about it."

"Which was?"

"That I actually heard the Earl of Kelly playing his own compositions."

"Blimey!"

"His entire method was different, a completely new – or old – approach. It was quite extraordinary. Anyway, to cut a long story short, when I played at the charity concert I copied what I dreamt I'd heard. Then came those reviews."

"Well, there's certainly been some interest since they appeared. Mind you, it's cautious. You know what the English are like."

"Talking of that, how are the tickets going for the Purcell Room?"

"Not bad, not bad at all." Rod looked reflective. "A haunted music room, eh? Do you remember the Blue Lady in yours?"

"Well, I didn't see her, though Finnan said he did."

"There was definitely a woman standing there. I'll never forget it as long as I live. Scared the pee right out of me."

"Don't be vulgar."

Her agent flashed his eyes at her. "How is our Irish friend, now that you come to mention him? He must be due back soon."

"Yes, next month, I believe."

"You *believe*, you *believe*? Don't you bloody well know?" Rod's face took on a highly suspicious expression. "Here, there's something going on, isn't there? Sidonie, have you been having fun and games with Sexy Alexei?"

She frowned at him reprovingly. "Not everyone's like you, you know."

"Oh yes they are, given half a bloody chance. Come off it, Sid. I know that look."

"Oh, all right then. Yes, I am having a bit of a fling with him."

"Talk about while the cat's away the mice go out to lunch!"

"There's no need to be like that. Anyway, Finnan's got someone else in Canada."

"I doubt that, Sid, I doubt it very much indeed. Anyway, too late now, as the nun said to the sea cadet. So you'll be going to see the Boy Wonder in Venice, I presume."

"Yes."

"Then I'll be joining you. Thought it was time I met the little bleeder. I'm bringing Dalo by the way."

"Who's Dalo?"

"My new tart. She dances in *Cats*. She's the one with the wiggly bottom."

"They've all got wiggly bottoms. Why do you call Alexei a little bleeder? You sound as if you've taken a dislike to him already."

"Because every time I hear the name Alexei Orlov I get a mental picture of Nigel Kennedy in a fur hat."

"Then get rid of it. He's nothing like that at all."

"Then let God be praised for his infinite mercies," said Rod, and tucked into his jugged hare with relish.

Venice in March, finely balanced between the sea mists and fog horns of winter and the first delicate appearance of window boxes, of outdoor canary cages and hungry pregnant cats. By these last signs it was possible to know that spring had arrived, though according to the Venetians themselves this particular season did not start until 15th May. Yet from the hotel-owned gondola taking the English visitors to their destination, Sidonie could see signs of activity denoting that the days of Canaletto skies, luminescent and indescribably blue, and waters glistening serenely in the sunshine, were near at hand.

Decorators were out in force, hanging in precarious cradles outside the great palaces which lined the Grand Canal, giving their majestic facades a restorative coat of paint. These gothic mansions once the homes of merchant aristocrats and old nobles, stood each with its own gondola post, its boatyard and entrance hall beneath, a tribute to the Venetian builders who had conjured up the most beautiful city in the world out of the lagoon. Looking at them in awe and admiration, Sidonie wondered how many of them still survived in private hands and how many had become hotels and apartment houses.

Everywhere the eye could see, landing stages were being swept and cleaned. In front of the hotels, the palaces, the restaurants and cafés, mooring posts reared out of the Canal, bright and cheerful, gleaming gold and indigo, while the great craft attached to them bobbed rhythmically like sleek black swans.

"Super," said Dalo, "really pretty." And Sidonie nodded, thinking it was not the adjective she would have used, but she mustn't be unkind.

Dalo had a girl's head on a boy's body, like many females who danced for a living. She also had a mop of curly suspiciously blonde hair which she tossed about a good deal, simultaneously creasing her face into a million merry smiles. Her favourite expression was "let's face it", and Sidonie found her monumentally irritating, particularly when Dalo adopted what she considered to be a serious expression and rearranged her mouth before launching into a conversation about something fractionally intellectual. Dressed for Venice, she wore leggings which showed every curve of her tight behind and a clinging jacket. Sidonie wondered how the bottom would fare when let loose in the Piazza.

"It's a bit tatty though, isn't it?"

Sidonie looked at her in astonishment, then said, "Well, let's face it, it's very old."

They had booked to stay in the Gritti Palace, expensive but wonderful, and as the hotel gondola drew up alongside the landing stage, Dalo gave one of her many grins.

"Oh goodness! I bet they used to get up to some things in there."

"They still do," answered Rod, and fondled her buttocks.

Escape was all and as soon as Sidonie had checked in and rapidly hung up her clothes she made her way by water taxi, this particular one so old and ornately decorated that it resembled a miniature floating Orient Express, to the rehearsal rooms near the Teatro Fenice where she had been reliably informed the violinist was practising.

Climbing up some stairs in a rickety building which had seen better days, Sidonie quietly entered the studio at the top where Alexei was working with a pianist and, aware that neither of them had noticed her, she sat down near the door to listen.

To say that his playing had improved enormously would have been a gross exaggeration, but there *was* a change in it, albeit a subtle one. Somehow, Sidonie thought, the Russian's technique had sharpened, while the emotion he put behind every movement of the bow seemed to have grown deeper. There was a darkening to the sound he made and it sent a frisson down the length of her spine.

She must have made a little noise for he turned and looked at her, his face momentarily blank with surprise before it widened into a delighted smile. Observing him like that, just for a second while he was off his guard, Sidonie saw that Alexei, too, had undergone a sea change, though this one far more elusive.

It could possibly have been the fact of his suddenly growing up, for the look in the eyes was more confident, the smile more certain, the general bearing somehow more assertive. Or was it that he had tasted success wherever he had gone and the old Slavonic Alexei had vanished under a veneer of Western sophistication?

"You've changed," said Sidonie.

"And so have you."

"How?"

"You are even more beautiful."

"Flatterer," she answered, and put her arms round him.

Alexei dropped a quick kiss onto her lips. "Listen, I'll do twenty minutes more and then we'll go for a drink. O.K., Maestro?"

"O.K., Signor," the pianist replied, and waved a hand at Sidonie.

She felt good suddenly, conscious that she was in one of the most beautiful cities in the world with one of the most attractive men.

"When did you arrive?" Alexei asked.

"About an hour ago. Listen, Rod's here too – with a bimbo."

"My God, I wasn't expecting him as well."

"He's come to hear you play, and to impress the girl-friend."

"What's she like?"

"Thinks she's the bee's bloody knees."

"Oh dear! Never mind, I will push her in a canal for you."

And with that the Russian picked up his bow and rushed through the last twenty minutes of his practice.

It was high afternoon when they left, the spring sun at its warmest, enabling them to sit outside. They had drinks in a little café overlooking the Palazzo Vendramin where Wagner died. Neither Sidonie nor Alexei spoke, preferring to listen to the sounds of the great water-filled city; the slap of the gondolas as they rode at their moorings, a distant snatch of song, the shrill high cries of the market people. Over all these noises rose the shouts of the gondoliers as they warned fellow oarsmen that they were passing either to the left or right, their calls punctuated with whistles, oaths and the occasional, "Oy oy!"

"Have you been in a gondola yet?" asked Sidonie.

Alexei smiled fondly. "No, I was waiting for you. I want to go in one with a little dark cabin on top where I can make love to you like Casanova used to do."

"You've been seeing too many films and, besides, modern gondolas don't have those," Sidonie answered reprovingly.

The Russian sighed. "Spoilsports! Not even the Italians have any romance left."

Out of courtesy to Rod, and also because Alexei was anxious to meet him, they dined in the hotel, sitting beneath the chandeliers, looking out at tantalising glimpses of the Grand Canal. Dalo wore a tight black dress slit to the thighs, sending the waiters into a controlled frenzy, while the violinist, for reasons best known to himself, had put on a dinner jacket. Sidonie noticed with amusement that it was new and, though admittedly off the peg, came from Paris.

"Russia must be super," Dalo was breathing. "I'd love to go there."

"You should."

"The trouble is I like warm climates. Just lazing on a beach suits me fine."

"We do have a coastline," Alexei answered, but the dancer was no longer listening, giggling at the waiter who was making much of pouring her wine.

"I'm looking forward to the concert," said Rod, determinedly dragging the conversation back to music.

341

"I hope it will be good. I shall try hard," Alexei answered, very much on his best behaviour in front of the great London agent. He turned to Dalo politely. "You will be there, of course?"

"Oh yes, I wouldn't miss it for anything, though I must admit it's not quite my scene, but then, let's face it, it wouldn't do for us all to be the same, now would it?"

"What kind of music do you like?" asked Sidonie, genuinely interested.

"Oh, Queen, Elton John, Lloyd Webber obviously. I'm hoping to transfer to the Broadway *Cats*. New York's my kind of town."

"But it's very violent surely."

"I can take care of myself. I'm totally streetwise," answered Dalo and, looking at her, Sidonie decided that she probably was.

"Then after dinner I suggest we walk through the alleyways to a marvellous café where there's a Venetian fiddle player. I came across it quite by accident," said the Russian innocently.

"I didn't mean that sort of streetwise," Dalo answered, giggling. "But count me in anyway."

And with that she wriggled in her seat and playfully smacked Alexei's wrist before moving her chair fractionally nearer to his.

Nothing, thought Lady Sarah Bunbury wretchedly, was going according to plan. By now, if she had had her way, she would have been on the high seas, with a lusty wind for Jamaica taking her ever further from England and all the complications that lay there. Instead, she stood in the doorway of her London home in Privy Garden, unbelievably waving goodbye to both husband and lover who were off together to take the waters at Bath. If fate had a sense of humour it would most assuredly be roaring with laughter at her predicament.

Lauzun's answer to her proposal of elopement had been far from satisfactory. He did not mind, or so he said, giving up everybody and everything to run off with her, but he feared, and with these words the Duc had put his hand on his heart and

looked most solemn, that Milady would get bored stranded at
the end of the world with no position and no social life. She
would grow wretched, blame him for her troubles, and they
would both end up in hell.

Deep, deep down, just below her level of consciousness,
Sarah knew that he was absolutely right, but she, vainglorious
little thing, would rather die than admit the truth. The refusal
to elope took on the colour of an insult and resentment was
born, a festering resentment that daily grew greater. The era
of disillusionment had begun.

Cleverly, or so Sarah thought, she masked her true feelings
behind a great show of affection. But in that she undees-
timated Lauzun who interpreted her gushing correctly. In
telling the truth he knew he had committed a *faux pas* and
smiled ironically at himself that he should ever have been fool
enough to be honest with a woman.

It was at this point in the proceedings that Charles Bunbury
returned from his mysterious travels in such a terrible state
that he was put to bed immediately and the doctor sent
for. The Duc, observing all, wondered what house of civil
reception, catering for what needs, had recently had him as
a guest.

"Poor fellow," he murmured to Sarah, "perhaps Bumbury
might have been a better name for him." But Sir Charles's wife
only stared at him blankly and Lauzun instantly regretted his
rudery.

It was decided that such a debilitated condition as the invalid
exhibited could only be dealt with by London physicians and
so it was that the three of them, husband, wife and lover, set
off for the capital together. But in town, though Sir Charles's
condition had by now improved, it was perceived that the
waters of Bath would bring about the final cure.

"I shall accompany you, Monsieur," the Duc announced in
a sudden fit of guilt.

"How very noble," his host answered languidly.

"You do not mind?" Lauzun whispered to Sarah when they
were alone.

"I consider it a kindness in you." She had given him a radiant
smile but the Frenchman had seen ice behind the sun.

"I will only stay two or three days and then I will return to you, and to all that we do together." He had raised one of his slanting brows but his mistress had not appeared to notice. "I shall be back on Friday, just before noon. Will you be here?"

"I expect so," Sarah answered.

"Will you close your door to the world so that we can . . ." He coughed delicately.

"Yes, indeed."

But now, as she waved her lover off, Sarah's spleen overflowed. She would teach him to refuse her proposal of marriage, for an elopement was only another form of it to be sure. And what better way to conduct her lesson than to disappear with the man Lauzun disliked most? Lord Carlisle was in London and kicking his heels; it would be only charitable of her to relieve his boredom. With a flurry of skirts, Sarah sat down at her desk and quickly wrote a letter.

"Of course my parents never understood me," Dalo was saying. "They weren't artistic at all. Mum only sent me to ballet because it was the thing to do."

She was drinking sweet wine, giggling nonstop, and was sitting so close to Alexei that had she been one inch nearer she would have been inside his new dinner jacket with him.

Sidonie surveyed her glumly and downed another glass of Soave wondering whether she was going to get drunk and rather hoping that she might. It was impossible at this exact moment to work out whether she was angry or amused. Dalo's intention to seduce Alexei was by now so glaringly obvious that Rod had gone into one of his introspective moods and could not be counted on for pithy comment.

"Tell me more about your family," said the violinist, gazing into the would-be temptress's eyes, and Sidonie's hackles rose that men could be downright stupid enough to fall for such obvious full-frontal attacks.

Dalo's serious mouth appeared. "I never felt part of them. Let's face it, we can't choose our relations, now can we? I say your friends are your friends, and your lovers are your lovers, if you know what I mean."

"Yes," answered Alexei huskily, "friends and lovers are very important indeed."

"Fasten your seat belts," quoted Sidonie, "I think we're in for a bumpy ride."

"You're lucky to have known your parents," Rod put in, breathing steam into his wine glass. "I only ever knew my mother. My father, rot his Italian socks, had skipped home by the time I was born."

"Perhaps he was Venetian," Alexei suggested brightly. "Perhaps he's here in this very café."

The tuning-up of the fiddler who wandered from table to table serenading the ladies became distantly audible.

"Perhaps it's him," said Dalo, and giggled wildly.

"I should hardly think so," Sidonie answered acidly as a young man of about twenty-five, dressed in the full *zingaro* gear, wandered in, violin tucked under chin.

"Well, whoever it is," said Rod, standing up, "I'm going to sing along."

'Oh God, he's pissed,' thought Sidonie, and was glad. Glad that horrid little Dalo was going to have a somnolent and snoring sleeping partner, glad that Rod's behaviour, outrageous or otherwise, was about to detract from anything his girlfriend might do.

The fiddler launched into *"La donna è mobile"* to which Rod gave voice, quite well and lyrically considering his state of inebriation. The other patrons laughed and applauded and a small dog barked.

"I think," remarked Sidonie, "that it might be time to go home."

Alexei caught her eye and for the only time in their relationship she saw that his expression was unreadable. "Not yet," he said, and she knew that something had changed, that the first fine careless rapture was over. Not wanting to look put out, she glanced at her watch, holding it up so that she could see it more distinctly in the candlelight.

"Well, another quarter of an hour then," she answered.

"I could go on all night," said Dalo. "I mean this is the breath of life to me. I just love it; travelling, strange places, flying. It's all magic."

"Fuck off," Rod replied, swaying in the breeze.

"Don't you speak to me like that! Just because you're an agent don't you think you can come it with me all high and mighty."

"Rod, my boy," said Sidonie, linking her arm through his, "I'm tired and I want to go back to the hotel. Will you walk with me?"

"Of course, Sid bach. Let's leave these two on their own. I've a funny feeling they're well suited."

And accompanied by the "Grand March" from *Aida*, to which the fiddler was giving his all, they precariously descended the steps leading down to the alleyway and headed towards the Grand Canal.

"She's a bitch," muttered Rod as they teetered their way through the darkness.

"It's not the bitchiness I mind, it's the stupidity."

"So a clever bitch is acceptable?"

"Probably, yes."

Rod squeezed her arm. "You should be more of a bitch, Sid bach."

"In what way?"

"Use men as your playthings; don't let them use you."

"Meaning Alexei?"

"Not particularly, though you want to watch that one."

"Don't you like him?"

"I imagine he's a genius, though I'll give you a proper opinion on that when I've heard him play. And geniuses – it's probably genii but bugger it – only stay that way by being bloody selfish."

"One of the French papers referred to me as one."

"You, sweet Sid, are the exception. You are the only person amongst my many and varied clients to whom I would apply the word nice."

"How ghastly!"

"Is it? Oh, well. Don't take any notice of me, I'm drunk."

And with that Sidonie Brooks and Rod Rees wove off into the velvet night, making their way over one of the arched bridges that spanned a small canal, laughing at the echoes their voices made as they leant over the parapet and simultaneously, and for no apparent reason at all, sang, "And to *hell* with Bur-gun-dee!"

# Twenty-two

It was over! The love affair that had contained so much heat and passion had turned to ashes. Armand de Gontaut, Duc de Lauzun, had by his own foolishness ended his liaison with Lady Sarah Bunbury. And yet, in retrospect, he could not see that he had done anything wrong, other than to say what was truly in his heart. Once more, the wretched man chided himself for the great mistake of having been honest and open with a member of the opposite sex.

'Games,' thought Lauzun, 'all must be games with women. And in future I shall do nothing but play them.'

He gripped the ship's rail with both hands and stared in a melancholy manner at the receding shoreline of England. Soon the white cliffs would be nothing more than a blob. And soon the memory of Lady Sarah, the woman who had utterly captivated his heart, would begin to fade.

"I shall never roger her again," he sighed, for he was, when all was said and done, a basic creature. "Mon Dieu, if I only had the power to turn back the clock."

But even his magic arts could not bring such a thing about and the Duc masochistically surveyed the events of the last few weeks, seeing at every step where he had made error upon error.

The first mistake had been to say he believed Milady would tire of life in Jamaica, the second, to accompany her husband to the spa town of Bath. Armand had returned to find his mistress gone, on a visit to her brother the Duke of Richmond, so the servants had said, her travelling companion none other than that silly boy, the Earl of Carlisle. In a fit of jealous pique, Lauzun had written her a furious letter.

"If you do not return to London immediately, you leave me

no choice but to regard you as the most wicked, false and perfidious of women."

He had sent it to Richmond's seat at Goodwood and from thence had come the reply.

"The violence of your tone has poisoned all the charms of love. None the less, I cannot find it in my heart to hate you. I shall be returning to London within two days and will send word as soon as I arrive."

He had been all impatience, of course, and on the second day had gone to her house to greet her. There had been no sign of Milady and though he had waited all the afternoon and evening, she still had not put in an appearance. When midnight came, Lauzun had returned to his lodging and paced the floor. Then, after a sleepless night, a messenger had arrived at six o'clock in the morning asking him to call on Lady Sarah immediately.

Lauzun had flown on the wings of love, only to find his mistress tucking into a hearty breakfast. For an hour he had waited in torment while the servants filed in and out with various dishes. Then he had been forced to sit through the reverse process as everything was carried out again in stately procession. By the time Lauzun was finally left alone with the woman he desired most in the world, almost two hours had elapsed.

And then Sarah had turned to him and, instead of whispering words of love, had delivered the death blow. Much, she said, as she cared for him, much as she wanted to remain his friend for the rest of her days, she felt that had he truly loved her he would have been prepared to risk all and escape to a foreign shore in order that they might be together.

"But I only stated what I believed, that you would eventually grow bored and miserable and blame it on me."

Sarah had pouted, looking decidedly petulant, and just for a moment Lauzun had been overcome by a wild desire to wring her neck.

"Don't spoil yourself, Madame, with posturing and poses. You know as well as I do that I spoke the truth. But I can see that you will not be content until you have twisted everything round as a sop to your overweening vanity. Have a care that you do not frighten away those who genuinely love you," he had said bitterly.

"Oh boo!" Sarah had replied, and snapped her fingers in his face.

In the effort not to strike her, the Duc felt suddenly faint and just for a second, had reeled to the floor. It had been at that moment, of all the dire times to pick, that Sir Charles Bunbury's married sister, Mrs Soame, had entered the room. From his sorry state on the ground, Lauzun had seen her eyebrows hit her cap in surprise.

Sarah had acted appallingly. "Come in and look after this poor wretch," she had called out gaily. "He is my lover and I leave him to you."

And with that she had stepped over the Duc's inert frame and taken a post chaise to Bath.

He had followed her, more fool him, only to be rebuffed once more. And that had been the end of it. Hurt, his pride wounded, made to look a fool because of his momentary black-out, Lauzun had settled his bill at his lodging house, packed his things, and in a sorry state, feeling utterly depressed, had headed for Dover.

"Farewell, Sarah," he said now, staring at the receding cliffs of England. "I hope you realise with what dangerous fire you have started to play."

And that stated, the Duc went below to seek solace in a large measure of liquid refreshment.

She hadn't known what game she truly played, that was the hell of it. It was fine to dismiss Lauzun out of hand, fine to adopt airs and graces, but now that he was gone there was such an emptiness in her life that Sarah scarce knew how to contain herself. The Frenchman, so charming and experienced, had introduced her to the delights of a physical liaison, indeed the Duc de Lauzun had taught her how to make love. And now he was gone for good.

In running to get away from the situation, Sarah had cherished the hope that even at this late stage she might be able to mend her marriage, that she could put her new knowledge into practice and at long last arouse the fires of passion that surely must somewhere be hidden in Sir Charles.

The post chaise carrying her to join her husband had made good speed and Sarah arrived in Bath during an afternoon, the entire journey having taken twenty-eight hours, including an overnight stop, during which Lauzun had caught her up and made a thorough nuisance of himself. The stagecoach from Bristol to London via Bath now completed the journey in seventeen hours, less than half the time taken by the Royal Mail, but Sarah considered this kind of travelling too uncomfortable to countenance and preferred a longer trip.

Having gone to the Plume of Feathers in Southgate Street and deposited her maid and luggage, Bunbury's wife took a sedan chair to the Pump Room where, much as she expected, Charles was sitting amongst a bevy of beaux, listening to the harpsichord, passing time before dinner, which was served punctually at four. Looking at him critically, Sarah thought that he was still one of the most handsome creatures alive, his only fault being his slenderness which, on the other hand, set his clothes off to great advantage.

"Sir Charles," she called brightly, and hurried forward to kiss him on the cheek.

There was a flutter amongst his friends who, with a great deal of bowing, took their leave.

Looking at her shrewdly, or so Sarah guiltily thought, her husband raised an eyebrow. "I wasn't expecting you so soon. I thought you would be spending some time in London with Lauzun."

"He has returned to France. Urgent affairs, I believe."

"You'll miss him," Charles answered drily.

"And so will you," she rejoined, and her husband said nothing further.

Returning to the Plume of Feathers, the couple dined together, then strolled forth. As it was a Wednesday there was no ball and as public gaming had been forbidden long ago by an Act passed in 1745, the couple went privately to the Duchess of Marlborough's house to play faro and ombre. And if it had not been for the nagging of her conscience, Sarah would have found the evening most pleasant.

'Yet I must not let guilt ruin everything. If I can only turn it to advantage by teaching Charles to love me,' she thought desperately.

With this uppermost in her mind, she met his eye where he sat at another table, and gave a smile and a tiny little wink, which obviously caught him quite off guard for he flushed and looked down at his cards.

"Damnation," muttered Sarah to herself, and Lord Irvine, her partner, said, "What?"

So it was with a troubled mind that she walked back to their lodging, arm-in-arm with her husband. And it was with certain trepidation that Sarah laid aside her shift and got into bed unclothed. Charles was already within, his lawn nightshirt crisp and beautifully ruffled, but he looked up in surprise from his book at the feel of her warm flesh beside him.

"What's this?"

"An expression of how glad I am to see you."

And with that she removed the book from his hand and, bending over, kissed him on the mouth in the French way. Charles gave a strange sort of moan but did not pull away as Sarah's lips ran down the length of his body. Though he was not truly partial to this kind of sexual activity he knew that he was growing hard and let out a yelp of ecstasy as his wife trailed her mouth all over him. Then, as he lay there, she mounted him and started to ride slowly up and down. Charles Bunbury was in a frenzy, the sensation driving him wild. But though this coupling was the best they had ever shared, Sarah knew no satisfaction. For, as soon as he had climaxed, groaning his pleasure as he did so, Charles closed his eyes and, after swiftly bidding her good night, went to sleep.

Sarah lay awake, staring into the darkness, wondering what it was about her husband that made him so different from the hot-blooded Duc de Lauzun, and slowly, and at long last, it began to dawn on her. Remarks had been made about Charles Bunbury almost from the moment she had met him, remarks which she had never understood and therefore ignored, that is until this moment. But suddenly all was clear. He was, as Charles James Fox would have put it, a rum duke, an odd

353

fellow, who preferred the company of his own sex to that of the ladies.

"Oh, my God," she whispered silently.

Quite clear now were the hastily executed matrimonial duties, duties done at such spasmodic intervals it was small wonder that after five years of marriage she still had not conceived a child. Explained, too, were Charles's mysterious absences, particularly the last which had left him so ill and worn out. Frantically, Sarah wondered what to do and decided that she must not tell a living soul, not even her dear friend, Susan, with whom she still corresponded regularly. The fact that her husband was of a different sexual persuasion to most men must remain a secret never to be revealed.

But what of herself and her needs? The King had taught her passion, Lauzun had not only revived but enhanced that knowledge. After his embraces she could never be content with what little Charles could do for her. Now, in a moment's clarity, Sarah bitterly regretted the games of pride which had lost her the intriguing Frenchman.

Bath, as always, was like a tonic. A city of unparalleled charm, whose extraordinary history was intriguing enough without the added bonus of a beautiful situation, fine air, and the atmosphere of civilised living, Sidonie was uplifted the minute she set foot in it. And, as had become a habit with her these days, she arrived earlier than necessary in order to explore. It was May, the weather gentle and, as soon as she had checked into her hotel, the musician set off to climb Lansdown Hill and walk at Mount Beacon, looking down on that gem of Georgian architecture made unique by the extent of its Roman remains.

She was in a strange mood, desperately needing solitude, which was odd for anyone who worked so many hours on her own. Sidonie had flown back from Venice to prepare for her concert in the Purcell Room, wondering whether perhaps she should have stayed at home after all. Dalo's determined efforts to get Alexei into bed had become boring rather than annoying, but still had cast a blight over what should have been a relaxing few days.

"You don't *like* her, do you?" Sidonie had asked the Russian in astonishment.

"She amuses me," he had answered, which had not been entirely reassuring.

"The price of Alexei's new-found fame, Sid bach," Rod had remarked, watching the couple from a distance.

"Would I sound big-headed if I said I once thought he had a passion for me and wouldn't stray elsewhere?"

"Not big-headed, just naive. Men are always straying."

"Don't be sexist, so are women."

"Well, then."

"Do you think he'll go to bed with her?"

Rod shrugged. "Possibly, I don't know. I've chucked the old boot out in any case."

It hadn't been the most satisfactory of conversations and an uneasy feeling had come over Sidonie. Determined not to let anything ruin the all-important concert, she had taken the time-honoured cure, throwing herself into work like a lunatic, adding to every piece in her repertoire the sound she had learned from the Earl of Kelly.

As always, music had cured her and she was just beginning to feel in really good spirits again when another letter from Canada had arrived.

"Dearest Sidonie, The months have gone by so quickly that I can hardly believe it is spring already. It seems no time at all since Christmas and our last phone conversation. I did try you a couple of times after that but the answerphone was on and I didn't leave a message as I thought you were probably away.

Things are going particularly well here, so much so that I am staying on another few months in order to get as far ahead with the research as I possibly can. St Mary's were a little lukewarm about extending my leave but things have been finally sorted out. I won't bore you with the details. I now hope to be home either in late summer or early autumn, I'm not sure which as yet. I can't wait to see you. There will be so much to catch up on!

My brother and his wife came to stay in the flat for a few

days in January but said you weren't around. I expect you were in France where, or so I hear on the grapevine – yes we even have one in Canada – you got brilliant reviews. I couldn't help wondering if Lady Sarah had anything to do with your transformation. Perhaps you will tell me when you see me.

Take care of yourself and do try to write if you have a spare moment. My fondest love, Finnan."

She wished, foolishly, that he'd said, "I miss you like hell because I'm madly in love with you and can't think about anything else," but then remembered Alexei. Suddenly the reason why Finnan was not returning took on a more sinister note. Looking back over the letter, Sidonie became convinced that despite its friendly tone, the doctor had not only read her reviews in the French papers, but also the story of her relationship with the Russian violinist. Sickened, she wondered how she was going to get through the forthcoming recital.

Sidonie had been booked to play in the Guildhall in Bath where, according to Rod, tickets for the concert had been sold out for some time following the reviews for her Purcell Room recital. The consensus among British music critics had been very much in accord with their French counterparts. Ms Brooks, it was generally agreed, had gone through some sort of metamorphosis and had emerged as "one of the most important harpsichord players alive today. Sidonie Brooks's mastery of eighteenth-century music is almost without equal."

"Home and dry, Sid. Home and dry," Rod had said, but now there was another audience to face, another challenge to her skill. Sighing a little, the musician got to her feet and made her way back down the hill and into the city.

It was easier, Sarah thought, to let Charles spend the evening with his friends and for her to mingle amongst the other guests at the Thursday ball in the Upper Rooms. Richard Nash, the famous Beau of Bath and Tunbridge Wells, had stated that the balls should begin at six o'clock sharp, and this custom still prevailed, despite the fact that the poor old wretch had died five years earlier, in 1762, in shabby poverty. Watched now by the new master of ceremonies, Sarah curtsied to Lord Frobisher and was led out for a minuet.

But though she appeared to concentrate entirely on her partner, Bunbury's wife was, in fact, alert to every newcomer who entered the room. She was waiting for Lord Carlisle to whom she had secretly written asking him join her.

Frederick Howard was nineteen years old by now and still a virgin, for his devotion to Sarah would never have let him betray her with another woman. His failure to join Charles James Fox on the Grand Tour had caused disappointment and annoyance to his old friend. Henry Fox, Lord Holland, who was recuperating from illness in Italy and staying with his son, had composed an ode in imitation of Horace about the wretched young man's infatuation. Secretly delighted to be the cause of so much flattering gossip, Sarah was determined at long last to show Carlisle the real meaning of love.

The object of her schemes arrived at the ball at eight o'clock, beautifully attired but looking somewhat weary.

"My my, dear Frederick, you seem done up," said Sarah pointedly as they danced together for the first time. "I hope you are not too tired to please a lady."

"What do you mean?" he asked, gasping slightly at her strange remark.

"I'll answer that later," was the provocative reply. "Now tell me, where are you staying?"

"At the Katherine Wheel."

"In the High Street?"

"Yes."

"Well, tomorrow you are to move into the Plume of Feathers with me. It will be much more *convenient*."

The poor Earl blushed, wondering if it was only in his fevered mind that his beloved's words held so many innuendoes.

"Very well, I will."

"Good. I am sure, dearest Frederick, that you will not regret it."

He simply couldn't be mistaking her meaning, the wretched young man thought. Perhaps, at long last, his most cherished wish was to be granted. With this in mind, he pulled Sarah close to him during the country dance and felt her deliberately press even nearer. Then a horrible idea struck him.

"Where's Lauzun?" he asked abruptly.

"Gone back to France – for good!"

"Thank God for that."

He was all for slipping out of the ballroom then and there, to see how far Lady Sarah intended to go. But she would not agree to this and, as it transpired, Frederick had to wait until next day for his introduction to the delights of intercourse. Sarah, her brain cool, very much she imagined as a courtesan must feel, seduced him in the same way she had done her husband only a few nights before. It was wonderful, she thought, to be in control, to watch Carlisle's face as she mounted him. Lacking experience, he climaxed fast but it was not long before he was ready again and, this time, Sarah showed him how to take the lead.

"Oh, how glorious," he gasped, as once more he soared into ecstasy.

"No," answered his mistress, "you are merely beginning. One day you will find out what the word passion really means."

"I think," answered Frederick, truly happy for the first time since he had met Sarah Bunbury, "that then I might well die of joy."

Sidonie's first evening in Bath was delightful. She had dined alone in a small wine bar and then gone to the Theatre Royal thinking, as she looked round its superbly restored Georgian interior, that Lady Sarah Bunbury must have sat as she was doing now, gazing at the building's elegance before concentrating on the play.

There had been no sighting of the girl, no experience of time turning in on itself since the dream. Yet, Sidonie wondered again, had that really happened? Had she been privileged enough to set eyes on the great Earl of Kelly and actually hear him play?

How strange that she should have seen Sarah so frequently in France and not at all since she came back to England. And, odder still, though these glimpses into another century had taken place within a matter of days in Sidonie's world, time was obviously passing at a different rate for Sarah. The woman outside the music room had been an experienced beauty far removed from the innocent young girl whom Sidonie had first seen as a reflection in a mirror at Holland House. In short, Sarah was obviously growing older at a far quicker rate than Sidonie.

These thoughts were uppermost in her mind as the musician walked back to her hotel near the Abbey, and got her key from reception. Irritatingly, as she went through the bedroom door, the phone by the bed was ringing and it seemed almost an intrusion, a rude awakening to the demands of the present century when she had been so happily lost in another.

"Hello," said a vaguely familiar voice as she picked up the receiver.

"Hello, who is it?"

"Me."

"Who's me?"

"Nigel."

Sidonie's heart sank and she sat down heavily on the bed. "What do you want?"

"To see you. I'm in Bath as it happens, and I thought it would be rather nice if we could meet up."

"Look, I thought I made it perfectly clear that our association is finished," she answered harshly. "We both have different lives now. There's nothing left to say to one another."

"I'm trying to be supportive," Nigel answered sadly. "I've bought a ticket for your concert. You see, I'm so proud of you."

"That's very kind but it still doesn't alter the case. We were married once, we aren't any more. We must get on with our own affairs."

"Please," said Nigel, "please darling. Let me just see you this evening and I promise I won't bother you again."

It was to that kind of emotional blackmail she should have shown most resistance, Sidonie knew it. She should have told her ex-husband to leave her alone for good and all, then banged down the telephone. But some reprehensible streak of weakness simply wouldn't allow her to do so.

"It's late and I'm going to bed. I'll meet you for coffee tomorrow morning," she answered reluctantly.

Nigel paused, as if he were going to argue, then said, "I look forward to it. I'll meet you in the foyer at eleven o'clock."

"How did you find out where I was staying?" Sidonie asked suspiciously.

"I'm booked into the same hotel actually. I saw your name in the register. I'm in Bath for the weekend."

"Oh, God," she said silently, and replaced the receiver.

She was dreaming again, this time that she wandered in the streets of Bath as once they must have looked. Sidonie saw people in sedan chairs being carried to the bath house and, wandering inside, glimpsed through the steam which perpetually hung on the surface of the water, men and women bathing together, all of them attired from head to foot in the most extraordinary bathing clothes. The women were clad in stiff canvas gowns, ridiculously wearing hats and carrying before them a small tray on which stood the essential snuff and powder boxes. The men wore drawers, shaped like large modern-day directoire knickers, and waistcoats which, like the women's gear, turned yellow in the hot and sulphurous water. Watching a nubile female being helped out, Sidonie saw that it was Sarah and followed like a ghost as the girl was stripped naked, put into a flannel nightgown and carried back to her lodgings. Dodging through the crowds, Sidonie pursued the sedan chair to an inn called the Plume of Feathers.

She was invisible, she was positive of it, because she entered Sarah's room and stood watching as Milady was put to bed to sweat. But no sooner had the attendants gone than there was a gentle knock at the door and Sidonie saw a handsome youth come in, also dressed in night attire. Shocked but fascinated, she watched him climb in beside Sarah. Then both nightgowns were thrown out and left to lie on the floor and she fled as the couple started to move in a way that left no doubt as to what they were doing.

'And under her husband's very nose,' Sidonie thought as she mingled with the patched and powdered populace, wandering into the Pump Room where crowds of people buzzed like humming birds, ate Sally Lunn cakes oozing with butter, undoing all the good of the rigorous bathing, listened to music, laughed, flirted, played cards.

The sheer vitality of the second half of the eighteenth century consumed Sidonie Brooks as it never had before and she was sorry when she woke alone and silent, to see it was four o'clock in the morning. But yet it was not altogether peaceful in her world. Very gently but very persistently there was a knocking at Sidonie's door.

"Who is it?" she called, but there was no reply.

Still under the influence of the dream, her head spinning slightly, the musician got out of bed.

"Who is it?" she called again.

"It's Nigel," his voice answered from the other side of the door. "Can I come in a minute?"

"No, you can't. Please go away. Do you realise what the time is?"

"No, I'm not sure. The fact is I'm feeling terrible. I've got a splitting headache and wondered if you'd got any painkillers."

"No, I haven't. Go and ask the night porter."

"I've been looking for him but there isn't anyone around. Oh, please help me, Sidonie. I really do feel ghastly."

Very much against her better judgement, his ex-wife opened the door a crack and peered out, only to see him leaning heavily against the wall, sweating profusely and looking exceedingly pale. Momentarily, Sidonie wondered if this could be some kind of trick, part of a plan to get into her bedroom, then decided that nobody was that good an actor, particularly Nigel Brooks, MP.

"You'd better come in," she said.

Her ex-husband lurched past her and crashed on to the bed with a groan. Putting his hand to his forehead, he whispered hoarsely, "I'm very ill."

"Have you been drinking?" Sidonie asked suspiciously.

"No, of course not."

But the smell of whisky on his breath told her all she needed to know.

"I think you'd better leave immediately. You've obviously

got a hangover and there really is very little I can do about that."

He opened his eyes. "Why are you always so bloody unkind? In all honesty, what have I done to you? My only crime has been loving you too much. That was why I wanted you to give up your career and be a full-time wife all those years ago. I can see now that I was utterly in the wrong, the last of the dinosaurs, but I meant well, believe me."

Put like that, said with just the right note of pathos in the voice, it was very hard indeed to argue, and Sidonie for no good reason found herself apologising.

"We were both very young at the time. It wasn't anybody's fault really –"

"Yes, it was mine," Nigel interrupted, his voice cracking. "I struck you and that was utterly unforgivable. I behaved like a brute and a bastard and you were quite right to leave me." He heaved a sob. "Oh, Sidonie, just say you forgive me for that unspeakable act and I will leave you alone for ever more."

'How pompous he is,' she found herself thinking. 'Every word he says sounds like a political speech. Forgive me, Tory lady, for the unspeakable act of knocking your hat over your eye.'

"Well?"

"Well what?"

"Am I forgiven?"

'Can I die a happy man?' Sidonie's irreverent thoughts ran on.

Composing her features sternly, she said, "It was all so long ago. Can't it be forgotten?"

"*Do* you forgive me?"

"Yes, of course. Now, don't you think you ought to be getting back to your own room?"

"Yes, I suppose so," Nigel answered in an Eeyore voice, and heaved himself to his feet.

Sidonie stood staring at him, wishing that her brain would stop this nasty habit of going outside itself, regarding situations analytically. How fat he looks, she thought, how unwholesome, unappetising really.

"Well, good night then," he sighed, and went to kiss her on the cheek.

Afterwards, Sidonie thought her great mistake had been flinching away, because Nigel pulled her close to him almost spitefully, pressing against her body in a way that she found both disgusting and suggestive.

"I'm still in love with you," he said hoarsely.

She pushed him to arm's length. "This is turning into a repetition of Moscow. I think it best for both of us if you leave at once."

For answer, Nigel sank his lips on to hers and gave her a long sucking kiss which had the blood turning to forks of ice in her veins.

"I'm ready for you," he muttered thickly, and his hand began to fiddle inside his dressing gown.

"Get out!" Sidonie shrieked. "Just get bloody well out. We are divorced, you have no rights over me at all."

But it was too late, Nigel had flung her back on the bed and was pulling up her nightdress. Against her thigh, Sidonie felt the knock of his penis.

"If you dare," she hissed in a voice so menacing that even she didn't recognise it, "if you dare rape me I will have you through every court in the land. Don't think I'll be afraid. I'll ruin you, you bastard."

He ignored her, trying to insert, panting and frantic.

A grim thought went through Sidonie's mind, that the more one fought the more bestial the rapist became. Was her best tactic, knowing he was quite capable of hitting her, to offer no resistance? But she needn't have worried. Gasping for breath, Nigel attempted penetration, thrust in once, and was finished.

Sarcasm became Sidonie's new and obvious weapon.

"Hardly worth it, was it?" she said, shoving his inert body to one side. "Well, I'm not going to spend the rest of the night listening to your snores. Goodbye."

And with that she snatched the key from Nigel's dressing-gown pocket and crept off down the corridor to his room where she wept bitter tears like drops of blood at the enormity of what had just been done to her. But in the cool clear light

363

of day, Sidonie knew perfectly well that she could take no action against him. Her ex-husband's attempt at rape had been ludicrous, pathetic really.

Yet the thought of doing nothing in retaliation was nauseating. In a moment of pure malice she took his fashionable grey suits and silk ties to the balcony and tied them to the balustrade, where they fluttered like pennants in the fresh morning breeze.

# Twenty-three

She had by now become somewhat deranged. Sarah was aware of that, aware that in her frenzied quest for love she was actually allowing herself to do nothing more than indulge in sordid liaisons and shabby affairs. Yet she could not stop herself, even though at times she felt like a Roman empress of long ago, wallowing in an orgy of sexual adventure and experiment. Even worse, she enjoyed it, addicted to lechery as she had become. Lady Sarah Bunbury was as callous as a whore, as cheap as a hired slut, but excused herself her depraved actions with the thought that it was all part of her search for the right man, the lover with whom she could spend the rest of her days on earth.

The descent had begun, the abandonment of her principles had commenced when her adventure with Carlisle, whom she felt she had initiated so well into the art of love, had proved to be short-lived. Sir Charles had no sooner returned from Bath, pronouncing himself recovered, than he had gone down with a stomach complaint. Temporarily in funds, thanks to his horses consistently winning at Newmarket, he had decided on the strength of it to spend some time in Spa in France, informed by his physicians that a second cure was indeed advisable.

So, in the summer of 1767, the new lovers had parted, Sarah instructing Carlisle that he was not to correspond with her directly but only through the offices of George Selwyn, a mutual friend. The Earl, much saddened, had joined Charles James Fox in Italy at long last, while Sarah had gone meekly to France, trying to look like a dutiful wife.

Spa, truly little more than a village, had proved to be an amiable, idle, somewhat boring place, and Sarah had been able to indulge only in the mildest of flirtations with a certain young Count Ravinski, a mere eighteen-year-old yet recovering from wounds received in a duel over his mistress's honour. Charles, however, was restored to his old self. Sparkling-eyed and fit, he became once more a divine elegant, gaming from morn till night, hosting lavish breakfasts and balls for his new-found friends.

But the idyll had finally come to an end and the Bunburys had returned home in late summer to find themselves involved in family matters. Ste's wife had given birth to her first child, Sarah being present to hold her hand, while Sir Charles sought re-election to Parliament.

And then had come the autumn with its usual round of pleasure, George Selwyn often visiting Privy Garden at this time to give Sarah news of Carlisle and, whilst doing so, escorting her to the playhouse and the opera, dining and dancing with her in the blue room at Almack's, while Sir Charles just looked on and smiled at his wife's latest little intrigue.

It was this, Sarah thought afterwards, that was the final trigger. If he had raised his voice about her seeing so much of Selwyn, if he had been angry that they whispered in corners about young Frederick, she could have tolerated the situation. But her husband's indifference, rum duke that he might be, was finally too much to stomach. She began to invite gentlemen of rank to dine with her alone in Privy Garden and afterwards, if not on that night, very soon, into her boudoir.

It was during these encounters with all the eager rakes of London, that Sarah felt she simultaneously plumbed the depths and soared to unknown heights. The titillation of a new man every few weeks, a new body to be discovered, strong and virile, was the most enthralling of experiences. Yet the feeling of cheapness when the affair was over and she was on the lookout for another, the shame that welled up from time to time, was indescribably awful. Sarah had never been so excited nor so miserable in all her life.

Naturally, gossip was round town in a matter of days. Her lovers, full of wonder at Sarah's performance, thrilled beyond measure that she could make them groan in ecstasy with her tricks, boasted volubly when they had slept with her.

It became a matter of pride to have had carnal knowledge of Lady Sarah, then talk about it. It was considered a social stigma for a man not to receive an invitation; those too old were sneered at, those too young encouraged to try their luck. The name of Sarah Bunbury became a byword for all that was decadent, all that was debauched and forbidden.

It wasn't long, of course, before someone whispered the truth in Sir Charles's ear and he, at long last, stirred himself from his usual apathy.

"I hear my home's become a whorehouse," he said bluntly as he and Sarah sat alone, the servants dismissed.

"I don't understand you."

"Really? Well, at my club it's all the talk. They say you're little better than a doll common – and twice as enthusiastic. I'm surprised at you, Sarah."

She was so upset, so sick with herself, that she used fury for her weapon. "And what am I supposed to do when you show no interest in me? Why, you have not served me for a month."

"Couldn't get a place in the queue," Charles retorted laconically.

"You have brought this upon yourself," Sarah stormed in reply, stung to the quick by her husband's sarcasm. "You are not man enough to make love to me. Small wonder I am seeking someone who is."

Charles Bunbury went very white, his suave features suddenly pinched and thin. "I have given you a home and everything you wish," he snarled. "I have given you a comfortable life and turned a blind eye to your lewd habit of engaging in pointless flirtations, yet you accuse me of lacking manhood. It is true that I do not have your obscene and insatiable desires but I have never failed in my duty to you."

"Duty, duty," Sarah sobbed. "It should have been done for love."

Her husband ignored her. "You have gone too far with me this time. As far as I am concerned our marriage is over and done. Oh, don't worry, I will continue to feed and clothe you. But you'll bring no further disgrace on my house. In future you can do your whoring elsewhere. And if you should meet this paragon you seek, then begone, and good riddance to you, you evil little slut."

And with that he turned and slammed from the room, more dignified and more authoritative than Sarah could ever remember him.

She cried all night and most of the next day and then, so low had she sunk, looked round for a place of assignation where she could continue her love games unhindered. It was at that moment, as she searched the streets of London, discreetly gazing out from her carriage window, she finally realised she was crazed, that the lusty behaviour of her royal great-grandfather, nicknamed Old Rowley after a particularly rampant ram, had been echoed in her. But she could no longer help herself.

"I'll do as I please," Sarah said defiantly. "I'll make love as often as I wish. Why, it's prejudice against women that men are considered amusing for raking, but we are called harlots for the very same act."

The poor unhappy girl found exactly the place she was seeking in Long Acre. It was a series of elegant apartments reached by a staircase which opened onto a little courtyard with only a passage wide enough for a carriage as entry. Below was a dining house of sorts, though the waiters served food and drink solely to the occupants of the rooms above. A private key gave access to the staircase and another to the apartment chosen, over the door of which an iron bar could be put down when it was occupied.

"I'll take a room for tonight," she said airily to the sleazy, faceless woman who managed the place.

And now there was the additional thrill of clandestine meeting and intrigue. Heavily veiled, hiring a closed carriage, Sarah made her way through the darkness only to find that her latest choice, the actor William Powell, whom Sarah had seen six years earlier standing in for David Garrick and had admired ever since, had arrived before her. Masked and cloaked, dramatically she thought, he was standing downstairs making much of ordering the finest food and wines.

"My dear," he said, as Sarah stepped from her coach, "I never thought such happiness as this could be mine."

She thought then that this could be her great love, handsome and fascinating as he was, and that maybe her search was over. And, indeed, Will proved well-made and lusty, performing as well in the bedchamber as ever he did on stage.

"Tell me something," he said as they sat afterwards in front of the fire, eating the delicacies brought up for them and put in the dining room, the waiters never being allowed to enter the room beyond.

"What is that?"

"Does it not bother you that you have a reputation, that you are considered fast, notorious even?"

"Not a whit," Sarah answered carelessly. "I do not see why women should not enjoy the same pastimes as men."

"Perhaps it is their fear of motherhood," Will said thoughtfully. "Are you not terrified you might conceive?"

"I can't," she replied with the same nonchalance. "I was married for years and nothing ever happened. It is obvious there is something wrong with me. One of my sisters is the same."

"That's as well for you, then, if you want to play in a man's world."

Sarah smiled lazily. "Yes, isn't it? By the way, I'm enjoying this wine – are you, Mr Powell?"

"I'm enjoying you even more," he answered, and with that they hastened from the table and returned once more to the bedchamber.

Their affair lasted several weeks, during which they visited the Long Acre house as often as Mr Powell's stage engagements would allow. Sarah, with some idea of fidelity, went to see every performance and sat applauding with the rest, smiling secretly at what she knew about the man bowing so solemnly. She had convinced herself that she was truly in love with him, that, like her friend Susan, she was about to run off with an actor. And then everything came to a head one wicked night.

They had both drunk far too much wine and had, most

indiscreetly, carved a message in the wood surrounding the window. "Mr P——, the actor, and Lady S—— B——, have more than once made offerings to Venus at this altar."

Afterwards they had made love vigorously and then, when both were finally replete, talked before they slept.

"I'm worried about the situation," Will said, propping himself up on his elbow and looking down at Sarah's beautiful face, just beginning to show its first signs of dissipation.

"In what way?" she asked, gazing fondly back.

"I can't go on like this."

"What do you mean?"

"If I dance all my jigs with you, Sarah, how will I ever meet anyone else?"

She bristled angrily, pulling the sheets to her chin to hide her nudity. "Why should you want to? Aren't I enough for you?"

"More than enough. You can please a man more cleverly than any woman I have ever met."

"Well, then?"

"The point is that one day soon I shall want marriage. An actor cannot go on for ever. I will need a companion for the years ahead."

Poor little Sarah, senseless fool that she had become, entirely mistook his meaning.

"Oh Will," she cried joyfully, "if only you knew how much I want just such a friend. Oh thank you, thank you."

"For what?" he said, frowning at her in surprise.

"For asking me to be your wife," she answered, a smile of pure gratitude transforming her features.

He moved away from her. "You mistake me, my dear. You are the type men roger, not wed."

She stared at him in silence, unable to comprehend what he was saying.

"Frankly, Sarah, you are governed by your senses. In truth, I pity Charles Bunbury, not envy him."

Clutching at the rags of her dignity, Sarah stood up and wrapped herself in her cloak. Every muscle in her body was shaking. She could no longer avoid the reality of cruel truth but with a pathetic attempt at some semblance of honour, she left the room and did not look back.

The closed carriage waited in the courtyard. But once returned to her matrimonial home, respite did not come. Sarah lay awake knowing that her reckless behaviour must stop, that her descent into hell must end. Weeping bitterly, she lit a candle and made an entry in her journal.

"I can no longer go on like This. I am drifting like a Rudderless Ship. I must somehow salvage my Soul."

The letter had arrived unexpectedly.

Tearing it open, Sarah read: "My dear Madam, I have heard your name most highly spoken of. I commend myself to you. I shall call next Thursday with your friend Miss Kitty. Ever your faithful servant, Captain Roderick Shaw."

For two weeks, she had led a blameless life, and now felt her heart fall at this new temptation. She did not know the identity of either the writer or her purported friend, until Sarah remembered a small, rather gnome-like woman on the fringes of good company, admitted despite the slight breath of scandal which attached itself to her, tolerated only because it was amusing to make fun of her. Remembering this, Sarah allowed the couple in when they were announced on the day arranged.

One look was enough to confirm her worst recollections of Kitty – and to see that the gallant Captain had risen through the ranks. His florid complexion, bulging blue eye and too-ready, loud laugh were enough to reveal all.

"Ha, ha, ha," he chortled, "a pleasure, Ma'am. I hope you'll pay me the honour of accompanying the good lady and m'self to Vaux Hall Gardens. Booked a box in the hope of your esteemed company."

Disliking the pair on sight, Sarah answered, "Thank you, Sir, but I would rather not. Let you and Kitty proceed together."

"Nonsense," Roderick replied heartily. "We wouldn't hear of such a thing. Come, Lady Sarah, I won't take no for an answer."

Suddenly seeing the loneliness of her situation, Sarah

changed her mind. After all, what harm could come of it when the eager Miss Kitty could scarcely keep her hands off the repellent fellow?

The box the Captain had secured was well placed and Sarah saw several people she knew, all of whom ostentatiously cut her dead. Cowed, she bent her head, her eyes filling with tears and wished herself far away.

"Now, now," said the Captain jovially, "can't have any of that. It don't do for a lovely woman to be sad." And he filled her glass with a bumper of champagne.

Sarah drank deeply and felt some of her good spirits return. Looking up once more, she saw Kitty waving frantically at Lord Cavendish who, with less fervour, was returning her greeting.

"La, the dear soul," the foolish woman was gushing, "I've sore neglected him recently." She gave the Captain a coy glance. "I'm duty bound to join Milord for a while. Pray excuse me."

She rose to leave the box, then turned back, wagging a finger archly. "Now you're not to be jealous, Roderick. I'll not be long. Lady Sarah, I deliver my sweetheart into your good hands."

"Well," said the Captain as she disappeared, "alone at last, eh?"

"Yes, it would appear so."

"Then would you care to stroll? The walkways here are the finest there are, at least in my view."

Thinking that to admire the greenery would at least give them something to talk about, Sarah got to her feet. "Indeed yes, some fresh air would be pleasant."

It was cold outside the box and she shivered. Bowing, the Captain offered his arm which, with certain trepidation, Sarah took, thinking it impolite to do otherwise. Thus, proceeding close together, he steered her in the direction of the Walks.

The gardens at Vaux Hall were indeed both spacious and beautiful, covering several acres and, charging only one shilling entry fee as they did, were more popular than the exclusive Ranelagh which demanded two shillings and sixpence, though that sum included tea and coffee. Another attraction of Vaux Hall was that together with the green walks, lit by lamps hung in the trees, it also had dark walks without illumination. Here lovers hastened. Sarah's brother, the Duke of Richmond, had once diverted himself in these very walks with Miss Patty Rigby. And now, to her dismay, Sarah found that she was being firmly propelled in that direction, the Captain having one hand gripped hard beneath her elbow.

"Where are we going?" she said.

"Where I've wanted to be with you ever since I saw the inscription."

"What inscription?"

Roderick winked an eye at her in the gloom. "You saucy girl, you."

"What *are* you talking about?"

"Mr P., the actor, and Lady S.B., have more than once made offerings to Venus at this altar. 'Zounds, when I read that I fair burst into a sweat. I cast round for someone who knew you but the only one was the damnable Miss Kitty."

"Oh, be off with you, you're nothing but a bag of wind, Sir," Sarah answered, instantly turning on her heel and marching away.

"I'll give you wind!" the Captain answered, chasing after her heavy-footedly.

For answer, Sarah stuck out a pointed slipper and was rewarded by the sight of the military man crashing to the ground like a badly made skittle. Stunned, he lay still for a moment flat on his face then hauled himself up onto all fours puffing noisily as he did so. Unable to resist the temptation, Sarah delivered him a hearty kick.

With a roar, the Captain staggered to his feet and swung round to glare at Sarah, his hands grabbing for her. Alarmed by the menace in his bulging eyes, she let out a shriek, but the next second a black-cloaked figure appeared at a run from behind the hedge, taking them both by surprise.

"You blackguard," yelled the stranger. "Take that, Sir, on your lousy pate, Sir," and there was a thwack as an ebony cane descended hard on Roderick Shaw's thinning ginger curls.

"Eh?" cried the Captain in surprise and then, soundlessly, descended in a heap at Sarah's feet. Stepping over a long leg which extended across the pathway she shook her head, all the breath out of her, and turned to look at her rescuer, her eyes growing wide at the sight of him. Tall, slim, extremely pale, with an aquiline nose and dark red hair worn very straight, the man could have come straight from a canvas by Titian. There was also something vaguely familiar about his face.

"Do I know you, Sir?" Sarah asked, taking his offered arm as together they swung off back down the pathway leaving the Captain sprawled on the ground, groaning slightly.

"Gordon," said Sarah's rescuer, with a bow, "William Gordon, at your service."

"*Lord* William Gordon?"

"The same."

"Then I believe we are related, remote cousins in fact. I am Sarah Bunbury."

If he had heard of her naughty reputation, Lord William gave no sign of it, merely kissing her proffered hand.

"Well, well, in what strange circumstances does one catch up with one's family!"

Sarah glanced back over her shoulder. "Should we send someone to his assistance."

The lordling let out a howl of laughter. "Why? Let him rot, filthy old fart catcher."

He was obviously a highly unorthodox young man for all his classical looks.

"Very well," said Sarah, amused.

"Good. Now, may I take you home? I'm sure you've had enough of Vaux Hall Gardens for one evening."

"It would be a pleasure," she answered, and meant it in every way. A pleasure to be in his company, to be looked after, to be treated like a respectable woman.

"I think you should know," she said, as the carriage door closed behind them and they headed for Privy Garden, "that I have a *fierce* reputation."

Lord William smiled in the darkness. "I'm not altogether surprised, my dear."

Suddenly, the funny side of the situation, of life, of everything, struck Sarah so forcibly that she cracked with laughter. With tears streaming down her face she turned to her cousin.

"I'm full of 'em you know. Surprises I mean."

"I can't wait to find out," answered William and in the faint light drooped an elegant eyelid.

She had kept a journal ever since she was a girl and now Sarah poured out her thoughts into it.

> What hand of Fate brought me to the pleasure gardens on the very night Lord William Gordon should be there? The Moment we met we were drawn together like two Magnets. Already I feel that I have encountered the other Half of my Soul. I have put the past Behind Me and started a new life devoted entirely to Him who is already Dearer to Me than that Life itself.

The language was flowery, she realised it, but Sarah in writing such things had spoken from the heart. In the moodily romantic person of her distant cousin she felt certain she had, at last, met the man destiny had intended for her.

He had seen her back to her home that night, bowed and taken his leave, but the very next day Lord William had called.

For neither of them had ever known anything quite like it. To Lord William, Sarah was the most lovely woman on whom he had ever set his eyes. At twenty-three, a year younger than he was, he thought her figure perfect, her face and colouring divine. Added to this was her unique ability to make love. Deciding, very sensibly, that her previous experience had only served to make her better for him, William forgot all about Sarah's past and merely concentrated on the entrancing present.

She thought him divine, with the looks and beauty of a Venetian, for the first time here was a man who truly loved her and whom she could love in return without constraint.

Briefly parted at Christmas, when she and Sir Charles had

visited Barton together for the sake of convention, the lovers renewed their affair in January. Yet, though their trysts were kept secret, behind the closed doors of the Long Acre house, tongues were already beginning to wag.

"I see Lady Sarah's at it again," said Lady Mary Coke to George Selwyn.

"At what?"

"You know very well what. Bawdy behaviour I believe it's called. What a slut that woman is."

The old hypocrite sighed heavily. "Yes, indeed. I fear it will be my sad duty to write to poor Carlisle informing him of the worst."

"You can tell him from me he's better off without her. Of all the randy women I've ever met, Sarah Bunbury leads the field."

"Should I tell him that too?"

"Pray do so."

However, when it came to it, George Selwyn could not bring himself to be quite so unkind, and in his letter of 26th February, 1768, merely said it was the consensus of opinion that Lord William Gordon had better leave town.

"And what's Bunbury doing about it all?" asked Lady Mary, voicing what everyone else was thinking.

"He's washed his hands of her, or so it's said."

"I think the man is damnable decent to have put up with all he has."

"Hear, hear."

And so the spring went on, full of cruelty and gossip, Sarah's husband throwing himself into life with his racing cronies while she and William, more passionately devoted than ever, passed each day with lovemaking and laughter. Yet of all that halcyon period, that season of showers and champagne, there was one day in particular that for many many reasons, some of them with hindsight, remained in Sarah's mind for all time to come.

It being an unseasonably warm March, the lovers had taken a picnic into the countryside round Chelsea village. Lying on rugs, drinking half pint bumpers as was the fashion, they had stared at one another without speaking.

"I wonder what the future will bring," she said finally, thinking aloud.

William had turned his handsome eyes on her. "As long as it contains you I frankly don't care. All I want is that we should stay together."

Sarah had become serious. "But, sweetheart, how can it? I am married to Sir Charles Bunbury. In the end I have to answer as his wife."

"There is such a thing as divorce, you know."

"Oh, but what agony to achieve." A new idea had occurred to Sarah. "I suppose we could always elope," she'd said, and then remembering Lauzun, wished she had not spoken.

But unlike the Frenchman, William's features had brightened. "What a splendid plan, such a heroic concept. Two lovers together against the world, united in the eyes of God but sinners for all that."

"So you would give up everything for me?"

"Willingly," William answered, composing his somewhat sombre features into a steadfast look. "Name the place, name the hour, and I am your servant."

It was everything that Sarah could have wished to hear and she later made love to him with enormous fervour, savouring the feel of him as if she were the violin and he the bow sweeping strongly in and out of her, a maestro indeed. Looking up at him, his brow bedewed with the sweat of lovemaking, his straight hair ruffled by his ruthless movements, Sarah believed she had never felt any sensation so intensely and, when she reached the climax, thought that never again could such a feeling be repeated. There seemed something very special about it, as if some shattering event had taken place, and she thought about it for the rest of that golden day and deep into the night.

"Today," she wrote in her secret journal, "I surely achieved the height of Human experience. When Lord W.G. was within – " Sarah had blushed as she wrote such a deliciously daring thing " – I felt that I was joined to him completely; with Body, Soul and Mind. Yet all had an air of innocence, as if he were Adam and I Eve, robustly Together before the appearance of Satan's serpent."

Yet even those words could not adequately express what she had felt. There had been something so very special about that particular congress that she knew no way in which to describe so fine and so sublime a sensation. Yet it was as well, perhaps, that she did not. The writings in her diary were the most daring and quite the most dangerous statements Sarah had ever written. Nervous, almost, that such a thing should ever be discovered, she placed her journal under lock and key before retiring to bed to dream of her lover.

# Twenty-four

Avebury, as always, proved to be a safe harbour, a source of healing, and Sidonie was only too glad that she had taken a few days off from her schedule to spend time with her parents. She hadn't been home since Christmas, nor seen them since the Purcell Room concert, and her feelings of pleasure to be back in their wonderful old house were acute. Using her own key, bowling through the front door, Sidonie called out, "Hello. Where are you?"

As always, she was immediately swept up into their lives. George Brooks, now retired, gave up a great deal of time to the Citizens Advice Bureau, while Jane continued with her painting, though with very little sign of improvement, Sidonie thought wryly. It was as if they lived in another world, another time almost, hardly touched by depression or upheaval, or the fact that beyond their beloved home and garden lay an ugly place obsessed with drugs, crime and general beastliness. But Sidonie dwelt on none of those aspects, just glad to be with them, away from the ever increasing pressures of her professional life.

"There's an auction in Marlborough that might interest you," said Jane on their first evening together.

"Oh really? Why's that?"

"The catalogue advertised some papers connected with Holland House, Kensington. Part of a private collection."

Sidonie felt an instant excitement. "I wonder what they are. Can we go to it?"

"I was hoping you'd say that. There's a mirror I want to bid for."

"Oh, good."

Marlborough on a Friday morning was bustling with shoppers and tourists, and the auction rooms, despite the ongoing recession, were thronged with dealers, as well as the usual collection of people who went to sales just to watch, mixed amongst those genuinely interested in bidding. The Holland House Papers turned out to be Lot 216 and, highly intrigued, Sidonie went to look at them.

There was a collection of letters, all carefully preserved in plastic sheets, some of which bore the signature of Henry Fox. Two were signed "Caroline" and there was one each from Emily and Louisa. But the thing that caught Sidonie's eye and to which she felt herself irresistibly drawn was what appeared to be a diary. Opening it at the first page, she read, "Sarah Lennox – Her Journal, February 25th, 1755, Kildare House, Dublin. Her tenth Birthday." Sidonie banged it shut, holding the leather-bound book tight to her chest, realising that she was gasping.

"What is it?" asked Jane curiously. "You look as if you've seen a ghost."

"I have in a way. You know I told you I've made a study of the people who used to live in Holland House, particularly Sarah Lennox."

"Yes?"

"I can't believe my eyes, but this is her diary. My God, I've simply got to have it."

Her mother reacted superbly, just as if she were in a film, and Sidonie could have kissed her. Sliding her eyes round the room, Jane said, "Don't look excited. There are dealers everywhere. Act nonchalantly."

Her daughter burst out laughing. "I'll do my best, but this is a find in a million. Thank goodness you spotted it."

"Walk away," answered Jane from the corner of her mouth. "There's a Lovejoy staring at us."

"Oh, Lord!" said Sidonie, and got the giggles.

As it transpired there were only two other people bidding against her; the Lovejoy figure, his attention obviously aroused by Sidonie's, and a dry-as-dust bald-headed man with no sense of humour, whom the musician guessed came from a museum. An American woman in check trousers and a plastic rain hat entered the bidding earlier on, obviously wanting to buy a piece of English history, but dropped out at £100. The museum man went to £500 and stopped, by which time the dealer had lost interest. Sidonie, raising her hand and winking at the auctioneer, this last done to amuse her mother, became the owner of the Holland House papers at £505.

Longing though she was to read Sarah's journal from cover to cover, Sidonie resisted. Avebury was home, and home meant eating and drinking and gossip, and she had come to see her parents not stick her nose in a book. Very conscious of the fact she hadn't visited them for a long time, Sidonie charmed the guests at a dinner party Jane gave that evening, consciously acting the part of a celebrity which she felt sure her mother wanted, then playing the piano afterwards. So it was late when she finally got into bed.

Intending to read only a few pages, Sidonie began, finding it difficult at first to decipher the eighteenth-century script. But as soon as she had mastered it she was hooked. Vividly, from the thoughts of an inquisitive child through to the observations of a teenage girl, Sarah's life was conjured up by the vibrant words.

'Lovejoy didn't know what he was missing,' she thought. 'This is the past as it really was lived.'

I am quite determined I shall write to Lady Susan I did not Love H.M. but merely liked him, despite the Fact it is not true. Though he is a Man of neither Sense, Good Nature, nor Honesty, I was quite set to love him.

"My God," said Sidonie softly, "the real story at last." And then her blood ran cold.

Such a thing happened that I scare know how to explain it. It had snowed heavily for some time but Today, the Weather being not so fierce, we went into the Grounds. There, whilst sitting in The Wildernesse, Charles James being tamed sufficient long to stare as well, I beheld a Creature that up until that moment I had regarded as a Servant or Wench, having seen her before about the House and Gardens and though, remarking on her Strangeness, had thought little more of it. But today, having perceived the Creature gazing rudely, I gave chase. My Quarry escaped within the whirl of Flakes but yet I remarked there was something uncanny in her Demeanour, as if she be Spirit or Phantom and not formed of Mortal Flesh.

To read about herself in words written two hundred years before she had been born gave Sidonie the most extraordinary feeling of fear and yet there was a fascination to it. Shivering, she read on.

Holland House, 11th June, 1768. I today wrote to Lady Susan but told her nothing of it, nor have I said a word of my Shame to a living Being, other than to *Him* whose very existence is my sole purpose in staying alive. I am with Child by him and soon the World shall know of it, for how can such a Thing be hid? And those who have mocked all these Years and said my Husband had no good stuff in him to make a Child, will chatter and tear my Character, with no need to lie, for there will be the Truth for All to see. The consensus will be that Lady Sarah Bunbury is *enceinte* with a Bastard, as so deserves such an out and out Whore.

Sidonie found herself wishing the most ridiculous thing; that she could see Sarah and somehow cheer her up, explain that her predicament would not have been considered quite so outrageous in modern terms, though to be married and expecting a child by another man was not the most desirable of situations in any century.

'I'll go to Holland House when I get back to London,' she thought, then realised that her relationship with the dead girl had taken on a new dimension, that she was now deliberately seeking to conjure Sarah up, and would not feel truly content until she had encountered her at least once more.

She wept as she wrote the words, so frightened and so worried that for some days now her lips had felt frozen, to the point that she could not smile and even found difficulty in speaking.

Sarah had first suspected the worst in early April when the monthly flux from her body had failed to appear. At the same time her breasts had enlarged and felt tender and, inexperienced though she might be about pregnancy, she had guessed at once that she was with child. When the May flux did not appear either there could be no denying the awful truth.

She had been utterly shocked, truly believing what she had told William Powell, that barrenness ran in her family and that both she and her sister, Louisa Conolly, were its victims. It had never occurred to her in all this time that it could have been Sir Charles's fault, that his seed was useless, and the fact that they rarely had intercourse had nothing whatever to do with the case. But now the glaring truth was out. A liaison with a potent fellow had produced the inevitable result and Sarah thanked God that her child's father was someone she adored with all her heart, not one of the cheapjack rake hells she had allowed to be free with her body.

At first she had written William that she did not want to see him. But the strain of bearing the burden alone had been too much, and she had called on him unexpectedly and unannounced, her tear-stained face revealing more about her condition than any words could say.

"You're with child," he had said, guessing instantly, and had gone to kiss her.

Sarah had not answered, merely nodding her head dumbly, then bursting into a million tears, soaking William's shirt and the front of her dress.

"What am I going to do? Oh, God, help me, what am I going to do?" the unhappy girl had sobbed.

"Several things," William had replied cheerfully. "For a start you can congratulate me on fathering a child, my first, I'll have you know. Secondly, decide when and to where we shall elope. Thirdly, give me a proper kiss, not that silly snivelling thing."

He was like sunshine, clearly delighted with the news, his pale features animated and his deep eyes calm and cheerful.

"I cannot decide anything," Sarah had said dolefully. "I simply don't know what to do for the best."

Her cousin looked thoughtful. "It might be a good idea if we didn't elope but let the child be born in wedlock. At least in that way it can avoid the stigma of bastardy."

"But what shall I say to Sir Charles?"

"You could not – ?"

"No, I could not. The meagre sexual relationship we once shared is over for good and all. Besides, he calls me whore and can hardly countenance to look at me."

"Then you'll have to use your powers of persuasion," William had said firmly, and with that Sarah had to be content.

But writing in her journal, seeing the words "*enceinte* with a Bastard" in black and white, was more than she could stomach and now she wept afresh, wondering how long it would be before the whole world heard of her shame.

The journal ended abruptly and with the most extraordinary entry.

> Goodwood, 25th August, 1781. With him to Holland House and what a strange Event. We could Both have Sworn we saw something, felt the Impact, indeed so. But Nothing there at all. I cannot Write of it More. In two Days time my new Life begins. Sarah Lennox.

It was past one o'clock in the morning but Sidonie sat staring at the words, puzzling over their obscure meaning. Nothing she had read before cast any light on the "strange Event", whatever it was, and it was obvious that from this point onwards Sarah had started a new journal.

"My God, I'd like to get my hands on that one as well," Sidonie muttered, and then realised that her parents must by now be fast asleep and, somewhat contritely, put her bedside light out.

She lay in the dark thinking extraordinary thoughts. She was going to see Sarah again, on three more occasions in fact, the last to be very special. Somehow, it was reassuring to know, not terrifying as her trips into the past once had been. Sidonie remembered the sickness she had felt when she had gone back to the great hayfield, the sheer fright of running down the corridor in the Château des Cèdres, and was glad that those traumas were over for good.

'Unless, of course,' she considered, with that lovely first haze of dreaminess, the hypnotic state before sleep, 'there are references to me in her other journal. But that I'll never know.'

And with that she fell asleep and dreamed once more of the Earl of Kelly, though this was just a dream and not a visit to the past as she was positive the other had been.

When she woke next morning, it occurred to Sidonie that in some way she had been destined to go to Holland House all along, for it was only through the means of Sarah she had heard the eighteenth-century master play. She knew then that this whole episode in her life, extraordinary though it was, had been one of total enrichment. That Holland House and its occupants had led her to a major turning point, both in her career and outlook.

"Can you play at Silbury Abbas on behalf of cancer research?" called her father up the stairs.

"You bet," Sidonie called back and, unbidden but lovely, memories of Finnan came rushing and she wondered how long it would be before he returned from Canada.

"I love it here," she shouted impulsively.

"We love having you," Jane answered. "Do you have to go back on Monday?"

"I'm afraid so."

"What are you going to play for them?" her father asked, still on the telephone.

"Tell them a selection of eighteenth-century music concentrating mainly on the works of the Earl of Kelly, including a piece I recently discovered called 'Lady Sarah Bunbury'."

"Bunbury? Anything to do with the chap who owned the first Derby winner?" George Brooks asked, covering the mouthpiece with his hand.

"The very same one," answered Sidonie, and smiled to herself at all the odd coincidences.

# Twenty-five

It had been hanging over him like a small yet ever-present cloud since the time of Sarah Lennox's wedding to Charles Bunbury. Then, he had thought nothing of it, an illness which had started as what appeared to be a common cold, though with incredibly severe symptoms and aftereffects. The doctors had bled him seven times, applied three blisters and purged him till he hardly dared be more than a few feet from the water closet. But this rough treatment for what was little more than a bronchial infection had, harsh though it was, finally cured him. The King had been pronounced fit and well and ready to continue with his daily life.

But then, in 1765, it had happened again. The illness, as before, had started as a cold and got worse, the same stitch in the chest, as he thought of it, coming back. From January until March he had been cupped for his fever and kept very quiet. The doctors, or so it seemed to George, had taken his pulse every few minutes, had bled him white, and purged him so violently that he had lived on the pan, hewn from solid marble, of his privy. The condition was obviously serious enough for a Regency Act to be considered, and by mid-May this had been passed.

He would have recovered sooner, the King was aware of that, if his ministers, pressing home the advantage of his temporary weakness, had not tormented him with their wiles and cunning. In a fury, George had dismissed the whole lot of them but, having made no arrangements as to who should succeed, had finally been forced to crawl, begging them to return to office. It was on this occasion that the name of Bunbury had again come to the King's attention, Sarah's husband being suggested as Secretary to the new Lord Lieutenant of Ireland, a posting that had, thankfully, not come off.

It was only now that George had realised for the first time how much his physical condition affected his emotions. A tendency to get flustered had developed in him and he had fallen prey to agitation. His sleep pattern had entirely changed as a result, and he had got into the loathsome habit of sleeping for little more than two or three hours a night. Not only was this tiring but extremely debilitating, making it small wonder that he became easily irritable and subject to fits of gloom.

Yet, though the illnesses and high dramas of 1765 had passed in God's own good time, they had left a permanent mark on him. In the words of his doctors, King George had now become prone to "periods of flurry". And there was nothing more guaranteed to bring about such an attack of extreme distress than the mention of the name John Wilkes.

A pornographer, a Satanist, a member of the Hell Fire Club, a duellist, a strident critic of the Royal Family through his newspaper *The North Briton*, John Wilkes, Member of Parliament for Aylesbury, a living thorn in the King's side, had finally been exiled from the British Isles when he had fled to France in order to avoid standing trial for libel.

But now, in the summer of 1768, not only was the devil's man back but raising the rabble, making trouble, a true "chieftain of riot and disturbance". Having had the audacity to put up for Parliament for the county of Middlesex – and to be elected! – the new MP's supporters had marched from Brentford to London shouting Wilkite slogans, smashing windows, doing great damage to the Mansion House where it was known that the Lord Mayor was violently opposed to the people's hero and all that he stood for.

The situation had worsened. Wilkes, determined to fight his outlawry, to appeal against it, had finally offered himself for arrest. But, on his way to the King's Bench prison, the rabble had unshafted the horses and pulled his coach themselves, going along the Strand and finally putting Wilkes down at the Three Tuns Tavern in Spitalfields.

Yet, though rioters demonstrated outside the prison in St George's Fields, Southwark, when Wilkes was finally sentenced to a term of twenty-two months, never had any incarceration been more pleasant. Lodged in a first-floor apartment with a fine view over the Fields, Wilkes had held court. Every day scores of gifts arrived from his admirers, including those in far-away America. Superb delicacies were sent: salmon, pheasant and other game birds, hams, turtles, cases of wine and brimming casks of ale. From Maryland came forty-five hogsheads of tobacco, while money and other donations poured in.

Allowed visitors of either gender, Wilkes's sexual needs were catered for by a string of willing young women, including the wife of a City alderman whose idol the rabble rouser was. Yet all the while the Satanist lived a life of luxury, unrest was rife in every other quarter, and it was with little joy that the King retired to his favourite hide-out, Richmond Lodge, in the Old Deer Park, for the warmer months.

Earlier that summer of 1768, the mob, led by striking Thames seamen, had marched in the direction of George's retreat and had got as far as Kew Bridge, where the gates had been shut in their faces. The King had been forced to return to London in view of the worsening situation, the Riot Act had been read, the militia called out, and several people outside Wilkes's prison had lost their lives in what became known as the St George's Fields Massacre.

By 15th May, though, the riots had been quelled, yet the situation left the King only too well aware that somehow or other the prime instigator, that lewd libertine responsible for it all, must be disposed of. It was in this frame of mind that George once again left London for his hideaway, wishing that he could remain there permanently, removed from the strife of duty, the noise and turbulence of the uneasy and festering city.

Rather against his better judgement he had asked Princess Augusta, his mother, to accompany him, thinking London to be unsafe for her, particularly in view of the general contempt and loathing in which the Dowager Princess was held. During the May riots a Boot and a Petticoat, a none too subtle reference to the Princess and her lover Bute, had been paraded on a gibbet through Cornhill, and with law and order barely restored it hardly seemed safe to leave the ailing woman behind. For though she was only forty-nine years old, the Dowager Princess's health now showed definite signs of deterioration. Nevertheless, it was with a sigh of relief that her son deposited his mother at the White House at Kew, and made his way on through the park to Richmond Lodge.

"I shall call on you tomorrow," he had promised dutifully as they parted.

"Do not forget," Augusta had responded in that tone of voice which turned every request into a command.

"No, Madam," George had answered, and given the instruction to drive on.

All the children were with the King and Queen on this trip; six-year-old George the Prince of Wales, five-year-old Frederick, three-year-old William, two-year-old Charlotte, Edward, aged one and the baby Augusta. The Queen, at that moment, was not pregnant. Yet, much as he loved his family, George found a strong need within himself to be solitary, to go out of doors and leave behind the sound of their small shrill voices. So it was with pleasure that he set off to ride through the forest on the following afternoon, keeping his appointment with his mother, looking forward most of all to the journey itself.

The White House at Kew had been leased by the Capel family to the King's father, Frederick, and had only recently become one of His Majesty's residences, Augusta having used it up until now. Adjoining Kew Village and Green, the most pleasant way to approach the house was by way of the long stretch of riverbank, and this route the King presently took, enjoying the fresh breeze that blew across the reach of water, a sharp clean smell in its essence.

It was a beautiful June day, near midsummer, and the sun, still high, shimmered on the rippling sheet of the Thames. Overhead, the sky was china-blue, the colour of the King's eyes, small white clouds, delicate as blossom, sailing slowly over its broad expanse uncluttered by buildings or spires in this rural setting. The afternoon, or so it seemed to George, drinking everything in with much gratification to his spirit, was the colour of sweet peas, all pinks, whites and blues. The fields and woods on the far bank were rosy and fresh, the water clear and cool, and there was a smell of flowers in the heady, languorous air as he turned away from the river and its salty zephyrs.

Entranced with the glory of the day, the King of England was calm and at peace, more so than he had been for months. And when he dismounted outside the White House, handing the reins to a bowing ostler, and went in search of his mother, he half hoped that she would be out and he could spend the time until her return in solitary contemplation of nature's loveliness. But this was not to be.

He found Augusta in the garden, sitting beneath an elm tree, a large muslin cap upon her head. She had grown no more beautiful with the passing years and now her look of natural severity did not lessen as she motioned her royal son to come and sit with her.

"A lovely day, Madam," he said, planting a kiss on her uncompromising cheek.

"Indeed yes, though too hot for my tastes."

"But so much better here than in London."

"That is true certainly. Effie, that is Lady Effingham, who has just come from town, tells me there is a stench in the streets, caused by the recent riots she believes, fit to rob a man of his wits."

"Really?" George was not listening, staring out at the charming vistas all around him, wishing he had been born a farmer not a king and could stay here dreaming on the riverbank for the rest of his mortal span.

"Yes. The *beau monde* are leaving in droves. The capital is not the place for civilised folk this summer." The Princess droned on and George allowed himself to drift into a brown study until a certain name caught his attention. ". . . even that rascally boy Fox is against him."

"What did you say?"

Augusta snorted. "I do believe you were not listening. I may as well not waste my breath."

"I'm sorry. My attention was momentarily distracted by those beautiful butterflies in the flowerbed. What about Charles James?"

"Effie says that the precocious brat has declared against Wilkes and the mob."

"Gracious me. I would have thought him a mite too rebellious for that."

"So would I. Certainly."

Mother and son sat in momentary silence thinking about Lord Holland's middle son who, along with his brother Ste, had been returned to Parliament in the recent general election, the elder of the two representing Salisbury, Charles James, though still only nineteen years of age, becoming the member for Midhurst in Sussex.

"A precocious family altogether if you ask me," the Princess said cruelly.

Lulled by the day, the King stepped into her trap and asked, "Why do you say that?"

"The old man, Holland, creamed off all the profits of the Paymastership, the sons are inveterate gamblers and owe a fortune, and as for the sister-in-law, your precious Lady Sarah – "

"What about her?"

"She is pregnant by another man," announced Augusta triumphantly. "She has betrayed Sir Charles Bunbury and is carrying a love child."

George's heart quickened its beat and he turned on his mother almost angrily. "And how is this known? Were there witnesses in the bedchamber for God's sake?"

"Sir, you forget yourself. It is your mother to whom you speak."

He jumped to his feet. "I don't care who I say it to. What I want to know is how such a thing is common knowledge. Poor Lady Sarah! What has she done to deserve this?"

"She's sinned, that's what. It's known on both sides of the Channel. She's just a common harlot."

It was upon him! In the middle of that lovely afternoon, with the sun lowering gently over the crystal river, a feeling of such emotional imbalance, such fierce frenzy, that the King could have cried out his anguish aloud.

"She is *not*," he rejoindered. "She is a good woman and if aught is amiss with her then it is through no fault of her own. Cruel circumstances, Madam, can force people willynilly into acts that they would not otherwise countenance. It is the filthy minds of others, the thoughts of loathsome gossipmongers, that spread the poison, not the actions of the pure in heart."

He had risen to his feet, his face flushed and florid, his hands in two tight fists. "I'll have no more of this talk, d'you hear?"

"How dare you," said Augusta furiously, but the look on her son's face stopped her in her tracks.

"No more, no more, no more," the King shouted in great agitation. "Oh God, that I were a private man and could defend Lady Sarah with my own strong arm."

And with that the King of England plunged the length of the garden in a storm of tears that was pitiful to behold.

The axe had fallen. Sarah had been sent for to come from Barton Hall to Holland House for a family conference and knew, even as her carriage went briskly up the great elm drive, that terrible trouble now lay in store. It was July, she was four months pregnant and starting to swell, and somehow, cruelly, the news was out. Horace Walpole writing to Madame de Deffand in Paris had remarked on Lady Sarah's being with child and she had replied, "Truly, truly, I knew the condition of Milady S." But as to quite *how* everyone had found out, Sarah was at a loss.

Yet the answer was simple enough. Her flagrant affair with William Gordon, let alone her scandalous behaviour during the previous winter, had been enough to alert one and all. And this, coupled with the fact that so many years of marriage to Charles Bunbury had not produced a baby, was enough to confirm their worst suspicions. Sarah Bunbury was expecting a bastard and had clearly retired from London to hide her shame. And now the gossip had filtered through to Kensington and Sarah had been called upon by Lord and Lady Holland to account for herself. With a feeling of sheer dread, she alighted at the lower steps, crossed the courtyard preceded by a footman and entered her girlhood home.

Stepping through that vast front door and into the entrance hall, Bunbury's wife believed she would almost prefer death to this ordeal, for the place seemed to be entirely populated by servants, the family obviously keeping well out of sight in order to avoid confrontation too soon.

Aware that the silence of the house was practically audible, Sarah slowly followed a sharp-facèd maid to her old room in the east wing, taking one despairing look at the summer parkland before allowing the girl to help her change from her travelling clothes to pre-dinner undress, a flowing white gown prettily threaded with a scarlet ribbon. Knowing that garbed like this her shame was hidden, Sarah surveyed herself critically in the glass.

"Lady Holland awaits you in her sitting room, my Lady," announced the girl slyly, her reflection grinning.

"Then I will attend her," answered Sarah with dignity and made her way majestically down the Great Staircase.

She had never seen her sister so drained of colour nor so arresting. Against her pallor, Caroline's dark hair fell like a mourning veil, while her eyes were sombre, as though they contained a veritable well of tears.

"So," said Lady Holland, without preamble, "all London says that your child is not your husband's. Are they right?"

"Yes," answered her sister, chin trembling but raised, "it is the truth. I have endured a loveless marriage, Caro. Charles has given me all creature comforts with the exception of one, the warmth of his heart. You, who married for love in the face of your family's wrath, must surely know what this means. I do not criticise my husband, believe me. All I say is that it is not in his nature to be a married man. He prefers a life of freedom, where he may be with his horses, his racing friends, then all's well for him. Our physical bond grew less and less strong and I eventually sought love elsewhere. To my shame I have recently indulged in an adulterous affair, the result of which is growing within me. I carry the child of Lord William Gordon, and though I am deeply ashamed of any hurt I might have brought to you and Lord Holland, I am not ashamed of the fact that he and I love one another."

There was a considerable silence, then Caroline turned to look out of the window. "We come of tainted stock," she said eventually in a soft, bitter voice. "Even in my boys I see the family weaknesses. How can I blame you for something that is in our blood?"

"If it is in my blood to seek love, then I am guilty," Sarah answered. "But I cannot see, in all humanity, wherein lies the crime."

There was another long pause and when Sarah looked closely at Caroline's averted back she saw that her sister was crying.

"Oh, please, sweetheart," she said, hurrying towards her, "don't upset yourself. I am a slut, when all's said and done, but I so desperately needed a man to love me."

Within a second the sisters were in each other's arms and Lady Holland was holding Sarah tightly, just as she used to when she was a child.

"Everything will be all right," Caroline soothed, "somehow we will make it so."

"But what of Lord Holland?"

"Leave him to me," answered his wife firmly.

And it was into this scene of sisterly affection that Henry Fox walked some ten minutes later, and was glad to see it. He was old now and felt even more so due to his poor health. Convinced that his sons' enormous debts were the only problems he could further cope with, Henry said, "What's to do, eh?"

"Sarah is carrying Lord William Gordon's child," Caroline replied forthrightly.

"And what of Bunbury?"

"He has not spoke to me since Christmas," his sister-in-law answered, on the brink of tears.

"Has he thrown you out?"

"No, I stay at Barton; he lodges with friends in Newmarket."

"Then will he let the child bear his name?"

"That I don't know."

"I believe I must see to it that he does," said Lord Holland grimly.

"But how?"

"I will find a way, rest assured."

And somehow this was comforting and the two women felt confident that Henry Fox would sort the situation out, and a calm came over what could have been a horribly ugly scene.

"The baby will be born here, in Holland House," Caroline

said firmly. "I want you to collect your things then move in straightaway."

"But what if Sir Charles should not approve?"

Lady Holland shook her head. "Poor man, I hardly think he will care as long as he does not have to be involved."

"You can leave Sir Charles," Henry Fox repeated with certainty, "entirely to me."

Summer was just on the turn, the great days of open windows and chairs in the garden absolutely at their peak, when the telephone rang, shattering the golden peace of an afternoon devoted to laziness. Yawning, thankful that she had practised for four hours that morning and therefore did not feel guilty that she had slept in the sun, Sidonie struggled off her lounger and went to answer it.

"This is you?" said a voice at the other end.

"Alexei! Where are you?"

"At Gatwick. I am getting into a taxi now. Goodbye."

And with that he had put the receiver down before she could say another word and Sidonie had been left for one entirely blank moment staring at the clock, wondering if she had time to get organised. Cooking at home was out, she decided, which relieved the pressure somewhat. Humming a tune at the very thought of being in the Russian's erratic presence again, she had a bath to remove the sun-tan oil and put on a pair of silk trousers with a beautifully draped matching top purchased in Paris.

"And all for Dalo's lover," she muttered as she applied make-up.

But she didn't believe that, not really, and was glad the British part of Alexei's tour had begun.

She was just getting the ice out of the freezer when the buzzer rang and a voice announced, "I am arrived." Going to the front door she saw the Russian struggling in with a mountain of baggage, the precious violin case on top of the lot.

"You've bought clothes in every country," she said accusingly, and he laughed and answered, "Nowadays I dress very sharp. It is my new image."

He was as volatile as ever and twice as attractive now that the rough edges had been knocked off and he wore French suits, Italian shoes and a watch made in Switzerland. Yet with his new persona, the silk-shirted prodigy, the best dressed Russian of them all, the age gap between them seemed somehow to have widened. Or was it merely that she was seeing him in a different light? Or even, perhaps, that she herself had changed?

They dined in La Parapluie where Jannie and her Pack were having a meeting, the woman with the pink hair, Max and all. To a man they recognised Alexei from recent newspaper coverage, then spent the rest of the evening talking in falsely loud voices to cover the fact they were attempting to eavesdrop on the two musicians. Eventually, though, the strain became too great and Sidonie asked if they might join their table.

Any doubts she might have had about Alexei's sexual chemistry were promptly put to an end for once and for all. The women gushed unceasingly and Sidonie heard the violinist being issued with so many invitations to drinks, meals and God alone knew what else, she could scarely credit it.

"Where are you staying?" asked the pink-haired woman.

"Tonight, with Sidonie – "

"Lucky her," somebody interrupted.

"After that in an hotel."

"How long will you be in London?"

"A week at first. I am playing at the Wigmore Hall on Tuesday. Then I go to Birmingham, Manchester and Leeds. Then I come back to London for another concert, on to Cardiff, ending up in Edinburgh."

"I hope you'll have an opportunity to see something of the countryside."

"I intend to make time for a holiday," Alexei answered, and gave Sidonie a very obvious wink which sent a frisson through every female present.

"I adore your toyboy," said a loud voice.

"Hot stuff," Sidonie replied with vigour, and there was another small shock wave.

It was all good clean fun and afterwards as they walked back down Kensington High Street, the others trailing round them in twos and threes, Sidonie and Alexei deliberately held hands. Jannie, more than somewhat tipsy, took the Russian's other hand and insisted on skipping up Phillimore Gardens.

"Good thing Finnan's still away," she said tactlessly, as they took leave of one another in the communal hall.

"Finnan? Is that the guy in Canada?" asked Alexei, once they were inside the Garden Flat.

"It is."

"Do you still hear from him?"

"Of course. We haven't fallen out; it's just that it's been a long time and my affair with you didn't help me to see things too clearly," Sidonie admitted with just a slight tinge of bitterness.

"Do you regret sleeping with me?"

"No, of course not. It's just that I'm not very good at the infidelity game."

"You were looking for love," Alexei answered acutely. "Most human beings do that."

"Did you, with Dalo?"

"She looked, I watched," Alexei answered. "Would it have made any difference if I had?"

"Yes, I suppose it would," Sidonie said slowly.

"A matter of pride? Or because you're in love with me?"

"Listen, Alexei, I haven't got permanent designs on you, if that's what you're thinking. I adore your friendship, you're one of the most fascinating people I have ever met or am likely to. But I'm not looking for anything long-term between us. I really could see a conflict of careers let alone anything else."

Did he look very slightly relieved, she wondered, as he answered, "You spoila da fun," in a phoney Italian accent.

But Sidonie was never to know, for a second later Alexei had taken her in his arms, passionately kissing her and she, yet again, succumbed to the strong physical bond that lay between them and let all thoughts of other things flow out of her mind.

She was never to see her lover again, that was final, so stipulated Sir Charles Bunbury when Lord Holland finally caught up with him at Newmarket. In return for this condition it was agreed that Sarah's husband would resume the appearances of normal married life, allow the child to be born in his London home and give the infant his name.

"But what about Sarah?" Henry Fox had asked tentatively.

"What do you mean, my Lord?"

"Will you take her back as your wife, in every sense of the word?"

"No, that I can never do," Bunbury had replied, and Henry had thought to himself that Sir Charles was deeply saddened by whatever it was that had caused the rift in the first place.

"Then why go through with such a farce? Either you forgive her or you don't."

"Then I don't. Lord Holland, I realise that I leave a lot to be desired as a husband, that the antics of the marriage bed do not greatly interest me, but I gave Sarah a comfortable home and a good life. She rewarded me for this with a string of reckless affairs. I cannot find it in my heart to forgive."

"Then what will become of the pair of you?"

"That I cannot say," Bunbury had answered, slowly shaking his head, and it had seemed to Henry Fox that a reconciliation based on such flimsy foundations could bring no happiness to anyone concerned. But he had done his duty and secured a future for Sarah's child, and there was an end to it. With a heavy heart, Lord Holland had returned to London.

A few days later, Sir Charles and Sarah had followed him, publicly reunited for the first time since New Year. They had returned to London ostensibly for the season, though it was only Bunbury who went out and about, Sarah preferring to remain in the house in Privy Garden, away from the eyes of the curious and the catty. At length, though, feeling she would die of boredom, she had gone to Holland House to while away the last few weeks of waiting.

It was an extremely cold winter, a bitter frost lying over the home park and farmlands. But, despite the freezing temperatures, Sarah made it a rule to take a daily walk, as brisk a one as she could manage, for the sake of her health. She would set off either down the elm drive, or along Green Walk, or towards The Wilderness, where she would sit on the stone seat and write her journal.

Yet, on the 18th day of December, 1768, heavy with child and peering out at the first few sporadic flakes that heralded a snowstorm, she did not feel inclined to go. But what else was there for her to do other than sit by the fire and make desultory conversation, or work on her embroidery? Wrapping herself up warmly, Sarah decided that it would be better to go out.

As she stepped into the cold crisp air she was vividly reminded of that time long ago when she, Susan, and the two boys, had played in The Wilderness. She had chased the ghost that day, the ghost she had not seen since the carefree hours with Lauzun in the Château des Cèdres. How odd, she thought now, that the Duc had also observed the apparition. But then he was one who practised black arts as did that monster Wilkes. Sarah felt quite certain that, if that man had his way, he would start a revolution in Britain which would end with the overthrow of the monarchy. Poor George, how sad it would be if he were ever to go down.

Just for a moment Sarah stood still in that bitter day, remembering the feel of his body so close to hers when they had both been young and headstrong, and found that she was weeping cold tears. A terrible premonition shook her from head to toe and she had a vision of the King, agonised and suffering, bound in a grim constraining chair.

"No, no," she screamed aloud, "that must never be."

"Sarah," called a distant voice in answer to her cry, seeming to come from out of the desolate and icy landscape.

"Who's there?" she shouted back, suddenly alarmed.

There was no reply but the snowflakes began to fall as thickly and swiftly as if they were being tipped down from out the sky. Deciding to abandon her walk, Sarah turned on her heel and headed towards Holland House – and it was then that she saw them! As though she had conjured her up just by remembering, Sarah beheld the phantom woman standing motionless in the snowflakes, an unidentifiable figure at her side, somehow an incredibly sinister sight.

"No," Sarah shrieked again, suddenly too cold, too tired, too heavy with child to cope.

"Sarah, Sarah," the answering voice came once more.

But nothing could help her now. The white earth, the grey

sky, tipped crazily and became one and Sarah was falling down and down into a whirlpool of pain which sucked her into its freezing heart as the colourless day faded and everything went black.

# Twenty-six

It was as well that one of the gardeners had seen her lying in the snow, as well for the sake of both herself and her child that he immediately called for help. They had carried her, half-conscious, into Holland House and there Caroline, seeing at a glance what was happening, had ordered that her sister be put in a coach and taken at once to her home in Privy Garden. In normal circumstances she would never have inflicted such an ordeal on a living soul, but with all the world waiting to see if the child was to be born beneath Bunbury's roof, Lady Holland had had no choice. With Sarah slumped against the padded interior, every jolt an agony for her, Caroline had only prayed as they journeyed through the snow that they would get there in time.

As it happened, her hopes had been fulfilled. Sarah, well into labour, had been hurriedly put to bed and the eminent obstetrician, William Hunter, his fee secretly paid for by Lord William Gordon, had arrived to bring the baby into the world. The age of the untrained old midwife, going to maternity cases carrying the stool which was a symbol of her trade, was now, mercifully, coming to an end. For these days ladies of quality were either attended by William Hunter or one of his many students, "men midwives" as they were known.

With Hunter's help, Sarah gave birth at dawn on 19th December, just as Sir Charles was returning from an all-night session at his club. Hearing the thin cries of the newborn coming from the room above, he had shrugged an elegant shoulder and turned to Lady Holland.

"So it's done then?"

"Yes." She had put her hand on his arm. "It is good of you, Sir Charles, to do what you are doing. I, for one, will be grateful to you for the rest of my life."

He had looked at Caroline sombrely, and she had seen how hollow were Bunbury's cheeks. "I still love her in my way, that's the damnable part of it."

"Oh, how sad that the marriage should have come to this."

"It is a living torment," said Charles, and Caroline wept openly that her sister should have caused so much pain to this creature who, for all the rumours about him, had behaved as a man of honour.

"Will you go up and see her?" she asked through her tears.

"I think not. I need to prepare myself, for to do so will be something of an ordeal."

Realising that he did not even know the sex of the child, Caroline said, "Sarah has a daughter, a little scrap of a thing. Oh, Sir Charles, please do go, say you will. She has not had the easiest of deliveries."

He stood there wavering and Caroline, seizing the chance, took his arm and led him up the stairs to the bedroom on the first floor where the mother and child were housed, then hovered in the doorway. He could not look at his wife, this fact distressing Lady Holland enormously, but bent over the cradle with all his smiles reserved for the innocent child. She knew then, as Sir Charles put down a gentle finger to stroke its swansdown hair, that he would love the little girl come what may.

"What are you to call her?" he said, his back still averted.

"I thought perhaps Louisa, that is, if you approve."

Bunbury turned to look at Sarah for the first time and the contempt in his face withered her heart. "It really has nothing to do with me," he answered coldly. And Caroline, overhearing all, sighed and wondered how long this couple, so out of love and so tormented in their separate ways, could go on existing together in such circumstances.

"Come Sir," she said tactfully. "Let us leave them to their rest. May I order you some breakfast? I personally am famished."

He nodded wearily. "I'll join you. Good day to you, Madam," this last thrown over his shoulder. And with

that the nominal father of the newborn child swept from
the room.

Having read the journal from cover to cover, Sidonie knew
that sometime in the future she was destined to glimpse a
pregnant Sarah in blinding snow. Yet what had distressed
her when she had read the entry was the fact that, on this
particular occasion, she, Sidonie was unwittingly to act as bird
of ill omen, that the sight of her would alarm Sarah so greatly
that she would fall and go into labour, that the journey of sad
little Louisa Bunbury into the world would be brought on by
the eerie sight of herself. Knowing all this, yet determined
that somehow or other she must try not to terrify the girl,
Sidonie in fact was quite unprepared for what happened when
the incident finally took place.

It had been a hot day when Alexei arrived and it was even
hotter the next. As it was Sunday, they stayed in bed for a
while, then got up to go into the garden.

"Today, I practise for one hour only I think," said the
Russian, yawning lazily. "And I give your neighbour a thrill.
I ask her to listen. That is if it's O.K. with you."

"Has anyone ever told you," answered Sidonie, shaking
her head but smiling at the same time, "that you are the
most unmitigated show-off ever known to God or man?"

"Yes, you, always, all the time. That is why I am in love
with you."

"You shouldn't say that sort of thing. One day somebody
will believe you."

"But I *do* love you."

"What," said Sidonie, only half joking, "would you do if
I asked you to marry me or live with me or something on
those lines?"

"I would say not yet. I am but a boy – "

Sidonie snorted audibly.

" – and have my way to make in the world. If you can wait
ten years, Tovarish, then I accept."

She chucked a cushion at him. "Listen, mate, I'll be over
the hill and down the other side by then. For what it's worth
I'd like to have a family before I seize up entirely."

"I, too, but I am not ready for this yet." In that disconcerting way he had of suddenly being enormously wise, Alexei added, "The Canada man is your age, isn't he?"

"A year or so older."

"Then he is the one. It will break my heart but I think you should settle for him."

"You are an absolute bastard, *premier cru*," she shouted in response, and threw everything that was to hand.

Yet though she was laughing, inside Sidonie felt torn to shreds that what she had really known all along, that Alexei was not only too young for her but had too big a career ahead, was obviously true. And in his Slavonic intuitive way he sensed something of this, for the violinist suddenly became very gentle with her.

"I take you to dinner tonight, somewhere really special," he said. "You name it; the Ritz, the Savoy Grill."

"For an ex-Communist you've got some mighty capitalist ideas."

"That is why I am ex," Alexei replied, and there was no answer to that.

They decided on somewhere less formal, a restaurant in Knightsbridge that Sidonie liked, and it would have been an enjoyable and relaxed evening if it hadn't been for the fact that Nigel, in one of his moon phases Sidonie presumed, decided to phone. Alexei picked up the receiver before she could get at it and with her heart in her mouth in case it was Finnan, Sidonie listened to the conversation.

"'ello. Miss Sidonie Brooks? Yes, she is here. Me? I am a friend of hers." There was a pause. "I said friend, not boyfriend. Anyway, what is it to you? Don't shout. I believe you are Fatty Beltram MP, the one with the big white knickers. If so, leave Miss Brooks alone or I thump you."

"Here, give it to me," Sidonie said, with a note of desperation. "Nigel? For God's sake! If you continue to ring here I shall have the number changed. Now, once and for all, leave me alone."

"What is the matter with that jerk?" asked Alexei as she crashed the receiver down and pulled the jack out of the wall.

"I think he's developed a drink problem. Every time I see or speak to him he's absolutely legless."

"Dalo calls it squiffy."

"She would."

"Perhaps we should introduce them," Alexei said solemnly. His voice changed. "Is there nothing you can do to get rid of him? You can't let him go on pestering you like this."

"I could take out an injunction I suppose."

"You must do it, Sidonie. I do not like the thought of you alone here with that lunatic wandering around."

"I promise I will if it happens again. Now don't let's talk about him any more or it will ruin the evening."

But despite the fact they laughed a lot, Nigel's phone call cast its shadow and Sidonie was glad to head for home once more, suddenly ill at ease and inexplicably tired.

It was one of those long evenings of summer, just newly dark by the time they got back to Phillimore Gardens. On an impulse, Sidonie decided to go to the flat via Holland Walk and the door that led into her garden, and, leading Alexei by the arm, turned into the walkway leading off Kensington High Street. In the distance she could see the lights of the theatre and youth hostel and the great slumbering shape of the ruined house. And then, indefinably, there came a change. The air grew cooler, swiftly and sharply, and a cold wind suddenly blew down the length of Holland Walk.

"Brr," said Alexei, shivering, "it feels like Moscow."

But his voice was fading, growing distant, and there was a falling sensation upon Sidonie as if she were going under an anaesthetic. Then she stepped into a white tunnel and saw at the far end a snow-drenched park and a girl, swollen and misshapen but for all that recognisable as Bunbury's wife, standing amongst the swirling flakes and staring blindly in Sidonie's direction.

"Sarah," she called, not wanting the poor pregnant thing to be afraid.

Over the centuries came the reply, "Who's there?"

"Sarah, Sarah," she shouted again, but Sidonie had done more harm than good, as it was inevitable she must. There was a cry like that of an animal in agony, and the girl, one arm flying involuntarily aloft, fell down onto the bitter white ground. The walls of the tunnel closed in and Sidonie was in darkness, the only recognisable thing the essence of Alexei, the unique smell of him which told her he was somewhere nearby.

"Oh, God," she said, and flung herself towards him.

She saw in the sudden light of the street lamps that his face was white. "What was that, for Christ's sake?" he said.

"Did you see something?"

"I had an hallucination. There was snow, blinding snow, and the shape of a woman."

"Anything else?"

"Nothing, except for a terrible scream." He began to run, pulling her along with him. "Let's get inside. I think this place is haunted. God, it frightened me. When I saw the Grand Duchess it was gentle, lovely almost. But this was horrible."

"She was going into labour, that's why she cried out like that."

He turned to look at her, giving Sidonie a most curious glance. "How do you know?"

"Because I recognised who it was. I know her story, everything about her. I'm sorry, Alexei. Just for a moment you glimpsed someone who lived two hundred years ago, though to her it was the present day."

"Are you talking about time warps, the quantum theory?"

"Yes," said Sidonie, praying that this great and wonderful friend would not make fun of her, "I sincerely believe that I am."

What was destroying Lady Sarah, eating away at her like a canker, was Sir Charles Bunbury's aching misery. She had been proof against his fury, his scorn, his enmity, but to watch him day by day, so unhappy that he could no longer eat properly, was more than she could stand. She had felt cheapened and degraded by her adventures as a drab, as something only just removed from a common harlot, but now she felt despicable. She was slowly killing a man who, when all was said, had done her absolutely no harm whatsoever.

To make matters worse was her knowledge that William hovered in the background, only kept from coming to her with enormous difficulty. He had threatened by letter to attend Louisa's christening at Holland House where Lord Holland himself had stood godfather, and only by begging him not to agonise her, had Sarah persuaded him to remain at home.

"But she is my child," he had written back.

Her grief had overflowed into her journal.

How I detest Myself for all the arrant Misery I, and I alone, have Caused to Innocents. Lord William Agonises to see his Child, while Sir Charles doats upon Louisa as if She were his Flesh and Blood, rather than his Contemptible Wife's love Bratt.

And it was all perfectly true. Charles loved the baby as if it were his own, showering the little scrappy creature with gifts, spending time in the nursery with her whenever he was home. Sarah had once come upon him rocking the cradle, singing a lullaby, and the sight of it had been like the lash of a whip. She felt less than the dust for, even now, she could not stop thinking of William Gordon and how much she still adored him.

After the birth she had lain on her couch for some weeks, receiving family and what few friends she had left. Then, with the coming of the new year, her strength had returned and Sarah, unable to face Charles's wretchedness a moment longer, had packed up and gone to Suffolk with Louisa, leaving him behind in Privy Garden. But of course her husband was only part of the reason for her going. At Barton, away from the eyes of the world, she was free to see William without hindrance. The love affair that had never really ended was rekindled with more ardour than ever before, and, meeting secretly, Sarah and William began to make plans for the future.

"Just walk out," he said. "Do it simply. We'll go to the Duke of Dorset's country seat, Knole, near Sevenoaks. He's my boon companion and will shelter us for as long as we like."

"But I can't leave in that way."

"Why not?"

Stated in those terms it was hard to find an answer and, besides, with the birth two months behind her, the old magic between them had started again. They were sleeping together in William's lodgings for they could not bear to be apart.

"You can't turn your back on a love like ours," he had pleaded, his pale romantic face even whiter. "My God, Sarah, I shall soon go mad. We are destined to spend the rest of our lives together yet still you remain with your husband."

Her body ached for his. Her soul seemed shared with William's, but it was her conviction that only by removing herself could she put Sir Charles out of his living agony, that finally made up Sarah's mind for her. So it was that on 19th February, 1769, she told the servants she was going for a walk, a walk from which she never returned.

It was the last time she was ever to see her matrimonial home. Lord William Gordon was waiting at the crossroads in a closed carriage. With not even a change of clothes, her baby left behind with its nurse, Sarah stepped inside and into the arms of her lover, and the long drive to Kent, to a new life as an adulterous but happy woman, living in carnal sin, began.

If she had thought it could be that simple, Sarah Bunbury was to be swiftly disillusioned. Within two days of the elopement, her sister, Lady Louisa Conolly, had rushed to Knole, her equipage going up the drive as if the Devil himself were coachman. Sarah was informed that she must return to Holland House immediately for little Louisa was sick and crying for her mother.

It had been the one approach she had feared, for Sarah loved her child, had been intending to send for her when the dust was settled. But now, not certain whether this was merely a ploy or whether her sister was telling the truth, the baby's mother felt she could not take the risk. With Lord William gloomily standing outside, watching until Sarah's conveyance vanished from view, she had returned to Holland House, where a grim-faced Sir Charles had taken little Louisa to be cared for.

The family were foregathered in the Library, all of them,

grouped together, as solemn as Sarah had ever seen them. Lord and Lady Holland were there and backing them up were Thomas Conolly, come especially from Ireland, Ste and his wife Lady Mary and Charles James Fox, trying desperately hard to look serious. The only people missing were the Duke of Richmond and the Lovely, but their absence was immediately explained.

"The Duke has took to his bed with nerves. You have undone us all by your crass behaviour," said Caroline by way of opening gambit.

"How is my baby?" Sarah answered to this, "For her health is of more importance to me than that of anyone else, be he even my brother."

"If that is so then why did you desert her?" answered Thomas Conolly angrily, more upset by his wife's distress than he was by the actual event itself.

"That was only a temporary measure. I fully intended to send for her."

"So say you now, but is that the truth of it I wonder."

"Do you doubt my word?" Sarah asked haughtily.

"Yes," said Thomas, and turned a furious back, staring out of the window and stroking his chin.

"What's done is done," said Lord Holland, speaking for the first time. "What is more to the point is talk of the future. Sarah, what are your intentions?"

"To live with William Gordon, and for the child, *our* child, to be with us."

"You should be ashamed of yourself," boomed Caroline. "Sir Charles has been more than good to you. Whatever his faults he has behaved impeccably throughout this whole sorry affair."

The remark drew a general rumble of agreement, even Charles James murmuring, "It's true, Sarah."

"I know it's true," she answered. "He has been, indeed is, the most indulgent husband alive. But it's for his sake that I must go. To stay with him would be to ruin the rest of his life, let alone my own."

"But what about the rest of Louisa's life?" asked Lady Mary

Fox, curiously and not unkind. "Surely she would be happier brought up within the safety of marriage than by two people living sinfully."

Sarah drew herself up with dignity. "I believe, Lady Mary, that a child reared by its natural parents, two people who love each other and their offspring, would be far better off than a child raised within a marriage wherein the partners hate one another. For, you can believe me, though I do not hate Sir Charles nor he me that emotion would soon come about, forced, as we would be, to act out a false situation day in, day out."

There was silence, then Lord Holland said heavily, "I would not be too sure, Lady Sarah, that that hatred has not already begun. Your husband entrusted me with this letter which he asked me to give you should you refuse to return to his home. But before I do so I will ask for the last time what you intend to do."

"To take my child and live with Lord William Gordon," she repeated bravely.

"Then so be it," and he handed her a document bearing Sir Charles's writing.

"Do you know its contents, my Lord?"

"I most certainly do," replied Henry Fox, and with that he rose to his feet, addressing the others in the room. "We are wasting our time, good people. This foolish intractable woman must now be left to plough her own furrow and face the consequences."

Caroline also got up. "You are no longer welcome here, Madam. I would ask you to take your leave as soon as you can."

It was like a death blow and Sarah, who had up till this point managed to keep calm, wept bitterly. "Don't you see," she sobbed, "that I am doing this because I can no longer bear to inflict either myself or Lord William's child upon my poor husband?"

But they were not listening to her, sweeping out of the huge room without a backward glance, only poor fat Ste turning in the doorway to give Sarah a sad and sorrowful look, shaking his head, before he, too, departed.

Sobbing aloud, Sarah opened the letter which Lord Holland had given her.

"I hereby give you notice, that if you refuse to return yourself and Louisa to my care, you leave me no alternative but to begin the process of divorce. I shall immediately put the matter into the hands of my solicitor, John Swale, who will file suit against Lord William Gordon for his criminal conversation with you, and a second suit relieving me of the obligation to cherish and support you. Do not think I shall hesitate for one moment. You have pushed me to the limit of my endurance – and beyond. Charles Bunbury."

So it was over. She had lost a King and a husband but at least she had gained a true and loyal heart.

"All for love," breathed Sarah, and prayed to herself that she had, at long last, set her foot upon a path that would lead her to the fulfilment and stability she so desperately craved.

She left Holland House at dusk, taking Louisa with her, unable to bear the thought of a night under such an unwelcoming roof. Having no carriage of her own, Sarah instructed Caroline's coachman to deposit her at the Swan with Two Necks in Piccadilly, a hazardous journey in the dark. There, having slept very little, Sarah boarded the public stagecoach at four o'clock the following morning bound for Southampton, her destination the address that William had told her to go to in case of trouble. They breakfasted in Bagshot, Sarah withdrawing to feed her child, then dined four hours later at Arlesford. After that they did not stop until they arrived at Southampton at seven o'clock that evening, Sarah only too glad to take a room for the night at the Dog and Duck. Finally, the next morning, she hired a chaise to take her to Mrs Bissell's lodging house in Redbridge.

Mrs Bissell, unlikely though it seemed, was known to a friend of Lord William's who had stayed with her whilst eloping abroad. Her house had been recommended as remote and peaceful, while the landlady herself was a good-hearted country soul who bustled about trying to make her guests comfortable. As Sarah stepped through the front door she saw a beamed and whitewashed room, heavy oak furniture, rag rugs scattered on the polished floor and patchwork curtains at the windows. There was a smell of baking and beeswax and, miraculously, Louisa, who had not travelled well, stopped crying.

Glad that she had done so much acting in her younger days, Sarah told Mrs Bissell her tale. She had married without the approval of her parents or friends and, as a result, was ostracised in town. Because of this she and her husband were desirous of living together privately in the country and Mrs Bissell's lodging house seemed the very haven of tranquillity they were looking for. If all was in order and the landlady agreed to their lodging with her, Sarah would send for her husband, Mr William Gore, to join her within a few days. It was a convincing act and Mrs Bissell was charmed. Thus, on the following Sunday, his Lordship arrived and the lovers were reunited at last, together with the child they had brought into the world.

It was like paradise, like being in the Garden of Eden. The cold spring days grew warmer, snowdrops and crocuses sprang in the woods where they strolled, Louisa in her bassinet, sometimes pulled by her father, sometimes her mother. This life of rustic domesticity seemed to be all that anyone could ever desire and Sarah began to believe, in that deluded way self-deceivers have, that she and William really were husband and wife, that they had been married for some time and were the most blissfully happy couple in the world. Full of these thoughts, the two of them threw themselves into their roles and went out and about, socialising with the inhabitants of Redbridge, blissfully unaware of the sensation they were causing. William, with his dark red hair and sadly romantic features was every woman's dream. Sarah, with her black tresses and beautiful face, set the men alight.

"Mr and Mrs Gore must be quality folk," Mrs Bissell's closest friend, Mrs Tyler, said to her.

"Oh they are, my dear. So well-mannered and beautifully spoken, the pair of them."

"Did you read in the newspaper about the runaway lovers?"

"What lovers would they be?"

"Apparently, the Duke of Richmond's sister, Lady Sarah Bunbury, has deserted her husband and run off with Lord William Gordon. They have a child with them, so it's said."

"Gracious!" Mrs Bissell's face had clouded. "You don't think it could be . . ." Her voice trailed away.

"It's possible I suppose. But if it is, then it would have been a cruel hard thing to have deceived you so."

"Indeed it would. What do you think I should do?"

"Watch carefully and we'll confer again."

So it had been left. But the landlady was now on her guard and was horrified to learn Lady Sarah Bunbury's child was called Louisa, while Mr and Mrs Gore's daughter bore the same name.

"What do you think about that?" she asked Mrs Tyler.

"I think it's very suspicious, that's what. I think something should be done."

"What sort of something?"

"Leave it to me," Mrs Tyler answered mysteriously, and winked a beady eye.

On 17th March, St Patrick's Day, the lovers toasted Sarah's Irish upbringing with the usual bumpers of champagne. Laughing and jolly, they sat in front of the fire after their morning walk, the baby gurgling happily, a bunch of guinea-bright daffodils on the table. Loving life they felt that this idyllic existence would go on for ever. And it was into this delightful scene that a stranger walked, shown in by a darting-eyed Mrs Bissell who announced him with the words, "There's a visitor for you, Mrs Gore."

Sarah and William glanced at one another in consternation, certain that their whereabouts were a secret known only to them. But the figure who bowed politely before them, grey-haired and serious countenanced, seemed vaguely familiar to Bunbury's wife, and she jumped to her feet in alarm.

"Lady Sarah Bunbury?"

"Yes."

"You will remember me, no doubt. I am John Swale, Sir

Charles's confidential solicitor. And you, Sir, I take it, are Lord William Gordon?"

"Yes, I am. What of it?"

"This, Sir. I have here a writ issued by Sir Charles Bunbury who is suing you for damages on the grounds of your having had criminal conversation with his wife." From behind his back, Mr Swale produced a sheaf of papers which he thrust into William's unsuspecting hand. "And I issue you with it herewith," the solicitor added nastily and allowed himself the pleasure of a small smile.

"How the hell did you find us?" asked William furiously.

"You were informed against, Sir. Your little deception is over. Your romantic adventure is at an end."

"Oh no," said Sarah, the cry torn from her. "How cruel. We have been so very happy, you see."

"Happiness at the expense of others rarely lasts, Madam," the lawyer answered gravely. "I bid you good day."

And with that he turned his back and walked away, his very gait, the dignified disgust of it, saying more than words could ever do.

# Twenty-seven

The tears had sprung into his eyes so fast, so uncontrollably, that he had been forced to leave the Drawing Room and seek solitude in order to indulge in a fury of weeping. The deepest, darkest depression was upon him, his mood so vile, so black, that in its thrall the King could envisage nothing but years of despair stretching away in front of him.

April, 1769, had been a particularly horrible month. The Devil's man Wilkes, freed from prison and standing yet again for Parliament, had got himself elected for a seat in Cornwall. And, as if this were not bad enough, Sir Charles Bunbury had appeared before the Ecclesiastical Court stating that Lady Sarah was of a loose and abandoned disposition, that she had been wholly unmindful of her conjugal vow, and had contracted and carried on a lewd and adulterous conversation with Lord William Gordon. To crown it all George's sister, Princess Augusta, now married to the Duke of Brunswick, had declared loudly that Bunbury's wife was a slut and that he would have been quite justified in putting her under lock and key long ago.

The Drawing Room had buzzed with gossip.

"Who would have believed Sir Charles to have had it in him? I always thought him so languid. Yet he verbally assassinated his wife in the witness box, they say."

"He's a changed man according to all who've seen him."

"Yes, I grant you that. But I still cannot get over the speed with which he has acted. As soon as he discovered where the lovers were hiding, he served a writ on Gordon. And now, a mere five weeks later, he has already appeared in court."

"She has fled to Scotland to avoid the scandal, I hear."

"Silly bitch! It will follow her for the rest of her days. Bunbury has sworn that he has not seen nor cohabited with

417

her since January and that he last had intercourse with her in the winter of '67. Can you imagine it?"

"How will she ever hold up her head again?"

"God knows."

Of course the King had overheard it all, little titbits of tittle tattle coming from every corner of the room. Much as he had tried to keep calm, much as he had wanted to rise above it, he none the less could feel one of his dreaded periods of flurry coming on. For the truth was that he blamed himself for Sarah's misfortunes, believed that he, who had robbed her of her virginity, had started her on the road to hell. George also thought, and this was what made him cry so bitterly now, that had he not jilted Sarah Lennox, had he had the strength to stand up to Bute and marry the girl he wanted, this terrible tragedy would not have befallen her.

And it was true, of course. As his Queen and consort he would have given Sarah all the love she could cope with and the need to beg for it elsewhere would never have arisen. Sobbing uncontrollably, the King let his imagination wander over such a happy prospect, thinking that even his children would have been nicer, better looking, if they had not had ugly Charlotte for a mother. But there he pulled himself up guiltily. The poor thing had been a good wife, devoted and loyal, hanging on his every word. Yet, he wondered, would he have got quite so flustered, quite so damnably depressed, if Sarah had brought her sunshine into his life.

But it was impossible to conjecture thus. He had gone his way, she hers. He had ended up marrying a woman he did not love who obediently produced a child for him every year. Sarah had also entered into a loveless marriage but had had the courage to run away with someone she cared for, and had given birth to her only child as a result. Deeply moved by the thoughts of what might have been, the King sank his head into his hands.

Every word the *beau monde* said was true; Sir Charles Bunbury had undergone a sea change of such magnitude that he was scarcely recognisable as the dandified creature, easy-going almost to the point of stupidity, who had wooed and won the most beautiful girl in town. Now a thin, sardonic, energetic whiplash of a fellow had sworn on oath in court that his wife was unfaithful to him and that it was impossible for him to have fathered her child.

The process of divorce was necessarily complex and somewhat drawn out. Yet Sir Charles had attacked the matter with such vigour that by June he had been granted the preliminary part, a partial divorce and separation freeing him from any obligation to maintain or support his wife. It now rested with the plaintiff as to what should be done next. Only by private Act of Parliament could he obtain the final decree which would allow him and also Sarah, of course, to marry again. But she herself was powerless. The non-guilty party alone could bring such an action.

"Do you think he will do it?" said Sarah, having obtained a copy of a London newspaper in which the matter had been fully reported.

"I don't know," answered William uninterestedly.

"Why do you say it in that voice?"

"Because it doesn't matter. We're perfectly happy as we are, I believe."

John Swale had called on them again in Redbridge, this time serving Sarah with the citation from the Ecclesiastical Court. At that, Mrs Bissell, declaring that she ran a respectable house, had asked them to move on. It had seemed to the lovers then that the only place where tongues would not be wagging, where they would not be recognised instantly, was Scotland. Accordingly, they had made the difficult journey from London to Berwick, catching the stagecoach at Waltham Cross at forty minutes past nine at night, then stopping at Ware for their first halt. The entire trip took four days, the second stop being spent at Barnaby Moor, where they fell into the inn, exhausted, at half past nine and had to rise again to be off at four in the morning, while on the third evening, the coach party were put down at Rushyford, also extremely late. It wasn't until the fourth night that they finally drove into Berwick where Sarah, William and the child had alighted with the other passengers but had said goodbye to them at breakfast, the remainder of the group going on to

Edinburgh. The runaways, at last within striking distance of their destination, had hired a chaise to take them to Earlston where they had been loaned a house by James Hume with whom William had been to school.

"Sanctuary," breathed Sarah, as the square whitewashed building, prettily situated on the banks of the River Leader, at long last came into view from the carriage window.

"What a journey," answered William. "I could sleep for a week."

"Well, now you can," she said, smiling at him lovingly. "Here we'll have all the time in the world."

And with that she had gone inside to set about making a comfortable home for them.


They had arranged to meet in Edinburgh after making their separate ways there. Alexei was playing in Manchester the day before, so it had seemed easier for him to go direct, whereas Sidonie, who hated long journeys, flew from Gatwick. She always claimed that by the time she was finishing her second drink the plane was touching down, and therefore enjoyed this particular flight as much as most. And today was no exception. They flew through a cloudless sky, the hostesses were chatty and friendly, being under no undue pressure, and Edinburgh airport was both slick and smart. As always when she came north of the border, Sidonie got wild ideas of buying a run-down castle, restoring it even beyond its former splendour and turning the place into a concert hall as well as a sumptuous home. A sort of McGlyndebourne was how she pictured it.

A taxi took her to her hotel, an elegant Georgian building in one of the many streets lying behind Princes Street. Sidonie was astonished to see that it bore a plaque stating that it had once been the town house of Thomas Erskine, sixth Earl of Kelly, Director of the Edinburgh Musical Society in 1757 and Deputy Governor in 1767. Shivering at the thought that she seemed in almost an uncanny way to be following in the great man's footsteps, Sidonie set off to find her practice room, lent to her by the Music College, and have a good look round before meeting Alexei's train.

It pulled into Waverley Station almost to the minute and the musician got the usual thrill of introducing someone fresh to a beloved city, seeing it anew through his eyes, glad that it was not quite the end of July and the seething masses who attended the Festival had not yet arrived.

"Guess what!" she said, kissing Alexei joyfully on the cheek. "We're staying in an hotel that was once the Earl of Kelly's town house."

"The man of whose work you are now supposed to be the world's greatest exponent?" he asked in an Arts programme voice.

"Who says so?"

"I read it in the paper so I knew it *must* be true."

"You," said Sidonie, kissing him again, "are starting to crack English jokes. This could be dangerous."

"It's the tour," he answered. "I met so many people and saw so many places and learnt English humour. But isn't Britain *dirty*, apart from the jokes! My God, one of these days your entire country will disappear under a pile of litter."

"You're telling me. I simply loathe it. But enough of that. You've been a smash hit. I read *that* in the papers."

Alexei laughed. "The worst review said I was a cross between Tom Cruise and Paganini. It called me the biggest sex symbol ever to hit the violin."

"Who said it, the *Sun*?"

"No, the *Daily Mirror*."

Sidonie shrieked. "Well, according to the *Express*, you're the boy wonder who made Nigel Kennedy look in the mirror."

"Nigel *who*?" Alexei asked innocently, and she shrieked again.

Aware that the Earl of Kelly's compositions were going to be more than popular in his native city, Sidonie had decided to concentrate on his work for the main part of her recital. And proof of the wisdom of this choice could already be seen by the glimpse of enthusiastic students peering through the window in the door of the rehearsal room. Sidonie ended the session with a firecracker version of the Scarlatti Sonata 27 and heard them applauding her in the corridor outside.

And those same music students were on their feet and cheering when that night Alexei Orlov, more inspired than Sidonie could remember hearing him, played the Mendelssohn Violin Concerto as never before. High and sweet rose those passionate notes, loud, clear as a bell, soft, gentle as the song of wind and sea, lifting the spirits of everyone privileged enough to be in the audience.

After a virtuoso performance of such magnitude, he shouldn't have given an encore. But the students were in full voice so he played silly things for them: Russian songs, Fritz Kreisler jokes, the Beatles. They stood to applaud, every one of them, even the very old, and Sidonie through her tears saw that he had gone from her for good – that Alexei was too special, too extraordinary, ever to belong to one woman, that before him lay the glittering prizes of life and all he had to do was stretch out his talented hands to take them.

"Hail and farewell," she said as she rose with everyone else, a flame of a woman, enormously beautiful at that moment, and let the waters of sadness and joy course down her cheeks.

There was a vast crowd in the·star dressing room in the Usher Hall, fellow musicians, journalists and critics and, surprisingly, Chantal de Chenerilles.

"Good heavens," said Sidonie, struggling to get to her side, "I didn't realise you were going to be here."

The Frenchwoman gave her an elegant kiss. "I am staying with the McDuff of McDuff for six weeks. I intend to tour and see something of the Festival. But, of course, I couldn't resist Alexei."

Sidonie wondered if she ought to read anything into that remark, but simply said, "It's lovely to see you again."

"And you, my dear. I shall be attending your concert, of course."

"It might seem something of an anticlimax after this."

"Your music is different," answered Chantal intelligently. "When you play it is like listening to drops of crystal. When Alexei plays he takes hold of one's soul."

"And one's heart?"

Madame de Chenerilles smiled her enigmatic smile. "No doubt he does that too."

They left Edinburgh three days later, Chantal in her Rolls Royce, Sidonie and Alexei in their hired Volkswagen. The Frenchwoman had pressed them to join her but Sidonie, acutely aware that this was the last time she and Alexei would be alone together, refused.

"We're going to all sorts of places – Loch Ness, the Isle of Mull, even hunting for the love nest of a heroine of mine in Berwickshire. We'll probably go to Glenfinnan, too. Where Bonny Prince Charlie landed," she added as Chantal looked blank.

"At the beginning of the '45?"

"Yes, indeed. God, if only he'd marched on to London instead of listening to his advisers and turning back. We would have had to rewrite the history books."

"It was as close as that?"

"A whisker away," answered Sidonie, and thought how different things would have been for Sarah who, presumably, would never have met George, reigning as Elector of Hanover and exiled from England as he would have been.

As they headed out towards Loch Lomond, the sight of which had Alexei craning out of the car window, she said, "Would you have preferred to go with Chantal?"

He put one hand over hers on the driving wheel. "Sidonie, this is *our* holiday, not hers. She's a marvellous woman, has been very kind to me, but you and I have something very special together. We are the same kind of people."

"Are we?" she asked, in some surprise.

"Yes, most certainly. We have a talent shared by only a few. We are closely linked because of it."

"You wouldn't think so to see the way some of our fellow musicians go on."

"Disregard that, we are loving friends."

"Which is probably better than lovers."

"Probably," Alexei answered, and just for one revealing moment looked enormously sad.

They stayed in a castle converted into an hotel on the bonny, bonny banks of the loch, Alexei absolutely insisting that they did so. And it was there a lovely thing happened. Being so close to Edinburgh, people were staying who had attended his concert and, after dinner, he played for them, other guests crowding in to hear, the staff cramming the doorway. It was a night that Sidonie was never to forget, her last great memory of him, her final realisation that the brashly extrovert young man she had met in Moscow now not only had an international reputation but a following wherever he went.

"I'm proud of you," she said in bed afterwards.

"And I'm proud of you, prouder of you than of anyone I've ever met in my life. Do you remember once when I asked you to go on honeymoon with me on the Trans-Siberian Express?"

"How could I forget?"

"Does it matter to you that it will never happen, that life got in the way?"

"Not at all," answered Sidonie serenely, lying only a tiny bit. "I told you recently that I never expected anything to come of our relationship."

"Then that's all right," said Alexei, and closed his eyes, falling asleep in her arms as softly and as easily as a child.

It was hard to say when Sarah first realised how desperately unhappy William had become. One day, or so it seemed to her looking back, they had been walking on the wooded banks of the river hand-in-hand, his handsome poetic face calm and beautiful, the next a scowl had appeared on those romantic features and he had adopted the distressing habit of sighing.

There had never been a more comfortable little house than Carolside, nor one set in more picturesque surroundings. Built on the very shore of the river, the woods sloping down to the water's edge, it should have been a haven where a lifetime of harmony could be spent. And yet, or so it seemed, no hiding place, not even in Scotland, was remote enough. Somehow or other both families had found out to where Sarah and William had fled, and a bombardment of letters promptly began.

The Gordons wrote to their son that he was a fool to have resigned his commission in the army for the sake of a woman, that he would have to exist on a mere £500 a year without his salary, and that unless he returned home and resumed his military career it was the only sum he could look forward to for the rest of his days. And this above all, romantic though he might be, spelled out to the runaway lordling the dire prospect that stretched ahead.

To Sarah the approach was different. With every letter she received she was informed of yet another illness in the family, all caused by her wicked behaviour. Caroline had taken to her bed, Lord Holland was sinking, Louisa was hysterical, Emily depressed. As for little Louisa, she was condemned to a life of sneering and ostracism even though Sir Charles, who had incarcerated himself in Suffolk in order to avoid the pity of his friends, would gladly take her off his unfaithful wife's hands.

The cracks began to appear in their relationship when a copy of *Town and Country* was sent to them anonymously. In it was contained a vile article in which Sarah was described as Messalina and William as Gordianus, and which also said that when Sir Charles Bunbury had contemplated challenging Lord William Gordon to a duel he was dissuaded by one of his friends who told him that Sarah had had so many lovers if he were to work his way through them alphabetically, Gordianus's name would not appear for ten years.

"They call you whore, Sal," said William, reading it.

"I told you when we first met that I had indulged in some squalid affairs. I have never been anything but honest with you," she had answered, the tears springing in her eyes.

"But this article makes you out a cheap drab."

And with that he had banged out of the house and had not come back until after dark. The poison was in and spreading and the first heady unrepeatable weeks of passion were over and done for ever.

In April the showers came and did not go away so that William, who relied on walking and fishing to keep his spirits up, was kept prisoner in the house. It was at precisely this time that Louisa began to cut teeth and cried morning, noon and night, developing a series of rashes that made the poor child even more miserable.

"Can't you keep her quiet?" William had asked moodily.

"No, I can't," answered Sarah in exasperation. "You try."

"Damned if I will," he had retorted, and slouched off into the downpour.

Finally though, the weather had cleared and the pair of them had taken the opportunity of getting a little air, going along the riverside path which they had named Lovers' Walk when they first arrived in Scotland and all was rosy.

"What did your parents say in their latest letter?" Sarah asked, more by way of conversation than out of curiosity.

"That they have no intention of increasing my allowance and that Sir Charles Bunbury's divorce, if it ever comes off, will take at least another eight years."

Almost as if she were scoring points, Sarah answered, "Well, Lord and Lady Holland are both ill, my sisters have put on mourning, and the Duke of Richmond has boils. And all because of us."

Lord William had stopped walking and turned her to look at him. "It's hardly worth it any more, is it?" he had said softly.

"What do you mean?"

"That if we are causing so much pain to other people, let alone ourselves, it's time one of us saw sense."

And with that he turned on his heel and strode away in the direction of the house.

"William," Sarah had called after him. "William." But there had been no answer.

Not wanting to crawl, to be so lily-livered that she ran begging, she had delayed her return, rocking Louisa in her arms until the baby slept. Then, finally, Sarah had pulled the bassinet home slowly, hoping that she would find William in a better frame of mind.

He was not there. And when she searched through the rooms, Sarah had found that his clothes and toilet items were missing. Panic-stricken, she had run to the stable, only to see that the horse he had bought to convey the two of them around, was gone. With dusk falling she was alone in the house, miles from anywhere or anyone, with nothing but a small and defenceless baby for company.

"Bastard!" she had shrieked to the hills. "Bastard!" But there had been no reply except the sound of the gurgling river.

After two of the most terrifying days and nights of her life, the sound of hooves had had Sarah running breathlessly to the front door, simply to see the post-boy. None the less, Sarah had seized his arm and almost pulled the poor thing out of the saddle.

"Here," she said, "take this letter to the postmaster. I will give you a shilling to get it to him at once."

The boy gazed at the address, scratching his head. "His Grace the Duke of Richmond, Goodwood, Sussex. That's a mighty long way for i' to gae, Ma'am."

"Never mind that now. Tell me, has your father got a horse and cart?"

"I ha' nae father but I ha' a mam."

"Well, would she drive me to catch a public stage from Berwick? There's a guinea in it for her."

The boy brightened. "Aye, she would tha'."

"Good, on what day does it leave?"

"Thursday, a quarter tae midnight."

"What an ungodly hour! I'd best spend the night before in Berwick. Tell her I'll expect her on that day at noon. Now, here are two shillings for being a good and helpful boy."

And that was how Lady Sarah Bunbury left Scotland, not in a grand carriage but bumping along in a farm cart, her wordly goods in bags around her, her baby daughter held tightly in her arms. The adventure had turned into a farcical escapade, the romantic dream gone sour. She was left with nothing in the world except her marriage portion of £500 which Sir Charles had returned to her and a fatherless baby. At twenty-four years old, Sarah Bunbury had become a hopeless outcast, the sort of woman Polite Society shunned, one who could only look forward to a life of ostracism and isolation.

"They used to walk here," said Sidonie to Alexei.

"And took the time to plant trees, I see."

"Yes, talk about the rose grew round the briar."

"Romantic though."

"Very," and Sidonie snapped a piece from the two hawthorns, each one planted so close to the other that they must inevitably entwine.

"In fact," Alexei went on, "it's so romantic that maybe I do the same thing."

"What do you mean?"

"I think I'll buy a rose tree for your garden to remind you of me."

"When you're back in Russia?"

"When I'm there, when I'm on tour, anywhere really."

"You're lovely," said Sidonie, putting her arms round him. "You knocked every sensible thought out of my head, but you're still terrific."

"Who wants to be sensible?" he answered. "You have all the rest of your life for that. Just think that for ten whole months you've been utterly and delightfully irresponsible."

"And all good things must come to an end?"

"Most unfortunately, I think they probably do."

And it was there, in the place where Lord William Gordon had walked away from his responsibilities, abandoning his mistress and child to their fate, that Alexei Orlov and Sidonie Brooks, despite the fact that they still had a few days left together, took their final leave of one another.

# Twenty-eight

"The art of life," said the Duke of Richmond, crossing one fashionably clad leg over the other, "is never to be caught. And you, Sal, simply hadn't the wit to cover your tracks. You've brought your entire troubles on yourself and so I'll vow to my dying day."

"But what was I to do?" Sarah asked humbly, her head bent, standing before him like a penitent child.

"Have been more discreet about your extramarital liaisons, that's what. You should never have allowed yourself to become the talk of London and most certainly should have foisted Lord William's bastard off onto Bunbury. As for eloping! God save us, but you must have taken total leave of your wits."

"I suppose so, yet I did it all for love, Brother. I thought it wrong to go on using Sir Charles simply as a provider. I also believed I could not live without William and the time had come to act."

"And look what a mess it got you into!"

"I know, I know. I have brought disgrace on everybody through my stupidity."

"The only stupid thing was to be discovered," reiterated Richmond.

A little of Sarah's fire came back. "But you, Sir, have mistresses and bastards all over the place and everyone knows it. *You* have not covered your tracks."

"Men have no real need to do so."

"What?" cried Sarah, incensed at last. "How's that? How could such gross inequality exist?"

"Always has, always will," the Duke answered carelessly. "A randy man will be called a lecher in any age, frowned upon maybe, but never ostracised. A randy woman will be called an old trollop, a draggle-tail, and ignored by women, who will hate her, and by men who, having secured her favours, will no longer wish to be seen with her. 'Tis the way of the world."

He was right, that was the terrible part about it. Listening to his words, Sarah could sense the truth of them.

"Then there's no hope for me," she wailed.

"None at the moment," her brother answered briskly. "The best thing you can do is lie low, keep your nose clean, and hope that the great healer cures your particular malady and eventually people will forgive and forget. With this end in view, I suggest you do not live in the big house with us but go to one of the farmhouses in the Park. Out of sight, out of mind, another old truth I fear."

"I have little choice," Sarah answered bitterly. "I must do as you wish."

The Duke's high-handed tone became more gentle. "It's for the best, Sal, believe me. You really have made the most ghastly blunder, a gaffe to crown them all, and your only course is to try and restore your reputation by living quietly." He came towards her and put his hands on her shoulders. "I know it isn't fair, I know that you did nothing more than I have. But the difference between us is that I stay married to the Lovely, while you ran off. For that crime you will be hounded for years to come."

"What a grim prospect," she said, despairingly.

"Your family will rally behind you, never fear," he answered.

But they had not so far, only her wayward brother, who saw in Sarah's conduct a reflection of his own, rising to the occasion. The Duke of Richmond had gone to London in his largest coach, meeting his sister and her baby off the public stage and escorting them to Goodwood House, overseeing all their pathetic bits and pieces personally. Though he would never have admitted it to Sarah, to whom Richmond felt it his duty to maintain a forceful front, he could have wept at the sight of her, reduced and struggling, with only a spotty crying baby for company.

It had been the Duke's own decision that his sister and her child should take up residence in Halnaker Farm, one of the many dwellings on his estate. Anyone of importance passing through Goodwood made it their business to call and pay their respects to him, and it was thought best, particularly by the Duchess, that Sarah was kept away to avoid embarrassment to either party.

Mercifully, family attention was not focused on her either. Sarah's youngest sister, Lady Cecilia, had contracted consumption and was slowly and painfully travelling to the south of France in the company of Lord and Lady Holland. Compared to the blameless invalid, the healthy sinner became of secondary importance in the eyes of all of them.

Sir Charles, too, knowing what fate had befallen his wife, remained proudly aloof, announcing that he would be seeking a final divorce by Act of Parliament and that there was absolutely no hope of a reconciliation. To put the situation at its most blunt, Sarah was now totally shunned by family, friends and the man to whom she once had been married.

Looking round the simple house where she, as a deserted mistress, would be expected to live her solitary life, the outcast fought back tears. Her days of frivolity, of flirting, of highly charged sexual games, were over for ever. She was a prisoner of the crime of passion and must serve her sentence in full before she could ever enter Polite Society again. A depressingly empty future stretched before her and Sarah Bunbury, having unpacked her things and put her child to bed, sat alone in the shadows on that first night in her new home and wept until darkness came.

Despite the fact that they were parting amicably, that it was agreed and promised they would remain friends for the rest of their days, Sidonie found it hard not to cry. The talented prodigy who had burst into her life like a firecracker, was finally going away. Alexei was off to France to appear on television, give two more concerts and then return, at long last, to Russia. It was goodbye, if not for ever at least for some considerable time.

"I shall miss you, Tovarish," he said, hugging her.

"And me you."

"After my concerts at home I go to America, I think. Perhaps next year. We meet there?"

"It depends on the dates, of course. But it sounds fun."

"Maybe by then you are married. This would not surprise me."

"Who knows, who knows?" Sidonie answered miserably, and turned away so that he would not see the tears which suddenly came welling up. Her life, looked at analytically, seemed to be nothing but a series of meetings and partings; Nigel, Finnan and now Alexei. Feeling very sorry for herself, Sidonie brushed her hand over her eyes and wheeled to look at him once more.

"Give my love to Paris."

"You bet."

"And to Chantal?" It was naughty of her but she couldn't resist it.

Alexei looked slightly discomfited. "She has asked me to stay with her for a few days, yes."

"And why not, indeed? The world's your oyster."

"But you are the pearl," the violinist answered gallantly.

"What an old flatterer you are. Now go on, they're calling your flight."

It was like a replay of the last time they had said goodbye at the airport, only then she had known she would see him again, that it was only a temporary separation.

"Alexei."

"Yes?"

"Thanks for everything, it's been wonderful."

"Thank you."

He bent to kiss her and at that moment a flash bulb went off and Sidonie realised they had been stalked by a couple of press photographers. Knowing that Madame de Chenerilles was still in the country and might well see an evening paper, Sidonie gave him a full-blooded kiss back.

'And why not?' she thought cynically. 'I may as well get the last laugh somewhere along the line.'

"I'm off," said Alexei, tucking his violin case under his arm. "The press might get irritating."

He turned to wave to her at passport control, his face sad, his manner excited.

"See you in America," he called.

"You bet," she answered, imitating him, then turned on her heel and went back to the privacy of her car, away from the journalists, away from his warmth, towards uncertainty.

He was leaving town and making no secret of it, in fact, the unkinder critics said Lord William Gordon was creating a veritable meal of his decision to leave British shores.

*The Scots Magazine* for September, 1770, carried a full report.

> Thursday last, set out for Dover on his journey to Rome, the Rt. Hon. Lord W—— G——, once esteemed by the British Court one of the most accomplished young noblemen of the age. He is gone with a full determination never to return. He has cut his hair close to his head, carries a knapsack on his back, and intends walking to Rome on foot, with no other companion than a very large dog. He was ever remarked for his generosity, and has divided his horses, dogs, etc., among his acquaintances, several to his particular friend, the young Earl of T——lle. He has never appeared in public since the much-talked-of connection between him and a certain lady, by whose friends he was never pardoned, and from their behaviour, he had adopted the extraordinary resolution.

"And so I should damned well think," said Sarah, reading the story and feeling her choler rise. "The air will be fresher to breathe with that creature gone."

In the lonely miserable year she had spent since he had walked away, his mistress had not once seen the father of her child, nor had William offered support, be it moral or financial. He simply had not bothered to contact her in any way. It was just as if Sarah had ceased to exist and she could think of no more heartless thing than for a parent to turn his back on his own child, ignoring the fact that Louisa had ever been born. And now he was going, distributing his wealth amongst his friends rather than to his natural offspring.

"I hate you, William Gordon," she called aloud, throwing the magazine across the room. "You are a poxy cruel bastard whose despicable actions have condemned me to a life of misery. I hope you pay for it one day. Oh, God, I do."

A rush of hatred consumed her, so strong and so severe that a constriction gripped Sarah's chest as a result. Gasping, she went to the front door and leant against the frame for support, breathing in the fresh air in order to calm herself.

It was autumn and the trees in Goodwood Park had already taken on the brave military colours of the season. Deep red, the shade of blood, was overshadowed by the bright high vermilion of soldiers' uniforms, the browns of cavalry horses adding their sombre touches in the fallen leaves. As she watched, a wind eddied these round and round in an airborne whirlpool and Sarah remembered how, in another home park at a time so distant it seemed a century ago, she and the Fox children had chased through the crackling carpet, carefree and careless, not one of them dreaming of the many sadnesses that lay ahead.

Yet the clock could not be turned back. She had behaved both foolishly and recklessly and now must pay the price. Slowly and despondently, Sarah turned to go back indoors. Then, on an impulse she rushed outside again, scooped up an armful of leaves and threw them high in the air, standing beneath the cascade of their fall as if they were drops from a fountain.

"Hurry up, life," she shouted to the blood-red sunset. "Let me serve my penance quickly, and then let something good await me at the end of it all!"

As often happens after a hot summer, the trees were changing colour early, and as Sidonie drove back from Heathrow she noticed the yellowness of the leaves and felt the touch of melancholy that the end of another summer always brings. This, combined with the parting from Alexei, the absolute certainty that their relationship as lovers was over, put her in an introspective mood, a dark shadow hanging over her thoughts, as she wondered grimly where she would go from here, how many more men she would meet and lose before old age finally set in.

She went through her front door knowing that in this frame of mind she would either get drunk or start to play. Acutely aware that the latter course was better for her health by far, Sidonie went down to the music room and hit the keyboard hard, plunging into a work by Soler with what she could only think of as fierce attack.

Her great cure-all worked its usual magic and an hour later the musician was still practising, hardly noticing the time, vaguely aware that the garden had filled with shadow and that the moon was up, the first thin quarter holding the old in its arms. Smiling wryly to herself that she had successfully managed to fight off a fit of depression, Sidonie rewarded herself with a glass of wine, then started a piece by Handel, playing quietly and soothingly, almost in a dream. And it was then that a light was switched on upstairs, throwing a pool of illumination onto her lawn.

Sidonie sat staring at it, suddenly hardly able to breathe, and then very gently, almost furtively, opened the garden door and stepped outside, going into the middle of the garden to look up at the house. The light was on in the flat above hers and somebody was moving about, she could see a shadow thrown against the living-room wall.

'It's his brother, his mother, anybody,' she thought wildly.

And then distinctly, not loudly but clearly, she heard Callas singing "*Casta Diva*".

"Finnan," said Sidonie with certainty, and started to cry properly for the first time since Alexei Orlov had gone.

# Twenty-nine

Adventure always having appealed to him and excitement of one kind or another being the very essence of his life, the blinding white flakes, the frozen ground, the great drifts and icicles and sheet-glass lakes did not deter him from setting off. Wrapping himself warmly, pulling a beaver hat down over his eyes, the Duc de Lauzun set out in the grey dawning, leaving his lodging in Piccadilly on a hired horse, determined to reach Sussex by nightfall.

The Frenchman took the main road to Chichester, conditions being far too hazardous to countenance a shorter route across country. But though he made good time, Lauzun ran into a blizzard at Horsham and was forced to hole up for the night. He found a decent inn by way of consolation and sat down in the inglenook fireplace, a tankard of mulled wine in his hand, contentedly reminiscing about his affair with Sarah, allowing himself the pipe dream that soon it would be rekindled.

He had not seen her for six years, nearly seven in fact, his last glimpse of her when she had stepped over his prostrate form and headed off for Bath, leaving him to the mercy of her startled sister-in-law. But though, after that, he had returned to England only infrequently, gossip had been just as rife on the Duc's side of the Channel, and Lauzun had followed the story of Sarah's decline and fall with fascination. But now, on this particular trip to London, his delight in seeing her get her just desserts had vanished at the description of his ex-mistress's desperate plight.

"They say she does not leave the house for days, except to walk in the park," Lauzun was informed while dining at Almack's.

"Has she no carriage?"

"Apparently not."

"So she is virtually a prisoner?"

"Within the bounds of her brother's estate, yes."

"Damme, she was the belle of Paris when I first met her. How can she bear such a solitary existence?"

"God alone knows: I almost find it in my heart to feel sorry for the stupid woman."

Lauzun had rounded on his companion. "She has been no more stupid than you or I, merely made to suffer publicly for it. It is that bastard Gordon who ruined her life. Why, I swear to God if ever I meet him I shall challenge him to a duel."

His friend had chortled, not in the least offended. "Odds my life, Monsieur, you're a regular firebrand. If you feel that strongly why don't you visit the poor creature? Lift her out of her gloom and so on."

Lauzun's companion had winked and the idea had been born. Sarah's former lover had decided then and there that he would be her saviour, a friend from the past prepared to show his loyalty, and also his love, should she require it! Now the Duc smiled lazily, remembering their times in bed together and how much he had taught her in that respect, and hoped that their affair might soon be reawakened.

He followed in the path of the stagecoach the next morning, glad to see it slowly trundling ahead of him. At one point, just beyond Pulborough, all the passengers had to get out and push, Lauzun assisting, while the coachman and guards eased the horses through the drifts. It was exciting and also gave a glow of health, and the Duc was sorry to leave his companions at the hamlet of Boxgrove and make his way alone up the frosty track which led to Halnaker Farm.

It was dark by now, a scarlet sun having sunk beneath the snows, and Lauzun was extremely conscious of the fear his late arrival might cause to a woman alone. Therefore, as he knocked on the door, he called out the words, "A groom with a message from Lady Holland, my Lady," and was pleased, after a few moments, to hear the bolts being drawn back.

A manservant with a lantern stood in the doorway, peering suspiciously as the Duc repeated his message, adding, "I

would like to see Lady Sarah personally. It's very urgent
that I do."

"She's upstairs in the nursery." And the man jerked his
thumb, standing aside to let Lauzun in.

'A far cry from the old days,' thought the Frenchman wryly
as he made his way up the stairs in the darkness then opened
the first door he came to and gazed into a room flooded with
candlelight.

Sarah was standing with her back to him, feeding her
daughter from a bowl, and Lauzun stood in silence for a
moment taking in the scene. His former mistress looked
stunning, he thought, wearing a simple blue gown, her
dark hair undressed, without powder, hanging loose about
her shoulders, completely *au naturel*.

The child, now five years old by the Duc's reckoning, sat
in a highchair, half feeding herself, half enjoying a spoonful
given by her mother. She looked pleasant enough as children
go but Sarah's breathless beauty and the gloomy romanticism
of her father had clearly eluded the poor creature. Smiling to
himself, Lauzun took a step forward and then Louisa saw him
and started to bellow in fright.

"Who's there?" called Sarah nervously, and wheeled round
to see, her eyes widening in surprise. "My God, it can't be!
Is it really you, Monsieur le Duc?"

"I have come through the dead of winter to be at your
side," he answered flamboyantly, and with that swept the
lovely creature into his arms, ignoring the screams of her
frantic daughter, and giving Sarah a long hugging embrace
which brought the poor lonely woman to the point of tears.

How long she stayed in the dark, staring at the pool of light
flooding her lawn, Sidonie never afterwards knew. She just
sat there, sipping from her wine glass, with every thought in
Christendom, or so it seemed, going simultaneously through
her head. Above all the ideas one stood paramount, that to
kiss and tell was weak, that to burden another with one's
own guilt was the palliative of the immature. Had she
read somewhere, she wondered, that unpleasant secrets
were best carried to the grave? That to force someone to

listen to a story of errors committed was both cowardly and crass?

For now the divine schizophrenia must finally come to an end. Alexei had gone, Finnan had returned, and Sidonie thought of the phrase, "Big girls don't cry," and prepared not so much to lie as not tell all the truth. Then she wondered about the woman who had answered the phone in Canada and whether she could possibly be the reason why Finnan had not yet rung to say he was back.

"Confession cuts both ways," she remarked aloud, and almost smiled at the irony of it all.

But still the phone was silent and Sidonie, after lighting a couple of candles, continued to sit in the gloom until it dawned on her that her number was different, that she had changed it at Alexei's behest before she left for Edinburgh.

"You don't want that Nigel maniac phoning when he feels like it. Get a new number," the Russian had said, almost pleadingly.

"Do you really think it's necessary?"

"I tell you that fat bastard is dangerous."

"Oh, don't be so silly, he just drinks too much."

"Listen to me, Tovarish. He is fruit cake, or whatever it is you say. I beg you to watch your step."

Now she thought, 'Finnan *can't* contact me,' and then immediately countered it with, 'Then why doesn't he come down?'

But one look at the clock answered that question. It was half past eleven, not the hour for one civilised human being to call upon another. Yet, surely, there was no harm in her phoning him just to say welcome back.

'Oh God,' thought Sidonie, standing in her bedroom, the receiver in one hand, 'why this dissembling? I'm guilty and I'm terrified and that's the beginning and end of it. Sidonie Brooks, you are a wimp.' And with that she put the phone down, opened her front door and went softly up the communal staircase.

An opera CD was still playing very quietly in Finnan's flat and she guessed that he was jetlagged, delaying the hour of going to bed as long as possible. Yet even then she lacked that final bit of courage which would enable her to ring the bell.

Sidonie stood there vacillating and it was at exactly that moment that the door opened and Finnan O'Neill, of all the unromantic things in the world, appeared with a black plastic rubbish bag in his hand.

"Jesus!" he exclaimed, jumping visibly. "Is it yourself, darling girl? How long have you been standing there?"

"Hours. I didn't know whether to knock or not."

"Oh sure, and wasn't it always a foolish woman?" he said, terribly stage Irish, and drew her into his arms for a hug that would last her the rest of her lifetime.

They sat talking quietly in the candlelight, two lovers of old grown serious.

"It's been terrible really," said Sarah. "There are simply no other words to describe it."

"But surely, *ma chérie*," answered Lauzun quietly, putting his arm round her protectively, "your family no longer continues to bear a grudge?"

"No, things are much improved on that score. After my poor sister Cecilia died of consumption, Caroline felt that life was too short for us to remain enemies and I was invited back to Holland House. Louisa has forgiven me too. She loved her little namesake too much to stay away for long. As for Emily, she finds it hard to punish the sister she brought up in her household. Only my brother George and his wife remain somewhat distant."

"But what do they matter?"

"They don't really. It is society that matters, Armand. They have exacted their pound of flesh from me. I am not considered fit company to mix with and must remain hiding away, presumably until the day I die."

He who had come to seduce her but whose intentions, on seeing her plight, were now purely honourable, said, "Come to France. You will be welcome there."

"I doubt it. We live in a small world and everyone knows my shame." Sarah turned to him earnestly. "The only thing I beg is that you do not hate my innocent child. She did not ask to be born nor is anything her fault."

"I would consider it an honour to be appointed Louisa's legal guardian, if you would permit me," answered the Duc solemnly.

A flash of the old Sarah reappeared. "I pray that I shall be around a few years yet to care for her."

He smiled and nodded. "I am sure you will, my dearest woman. None the less it would give me pleasure for you to accept."

"Then I shall, gladly. It is a kind gesture."

"It is the least I can do."

"What do you mean?"

Lauzun tightened his hold on her. "When I heard how badly you were being treated I wondered if it was all my fault."

"Do you mean that our affair started me on the road to ruin?" she said, her eyes laughing.

"Well, yes."

"Put it out of your mind. I was looking for love and looking too hard. When you would not elope with me, for good and sensible reasons I see now, I reacted like a spoilt child. Why, I vow and declare that Louisa has more sense than I did then. Please, Monsieur, be assured that if it hadn't been you I would sooner or later have gone astray with someone else."

"Carlisle?"

"More than likely," answered Sarah, and smiled a small secret smile.

"And now, is there anyone?"

She shook her head. "I have put passion behind me. It is too dangerous a fire to play with. I have been alone since William Gordon left me and, believe me, there is a certain satisfaction in it."

"I find that hard to imagine," answered the Duc, thinking that his own behaviour had, if anything, got slightly worse as he grew older.

"Then you must take my word. And for that very reason I think it best if you spend the night at Goodwood House. My brother will be pleased to see you, I know."

"But it is snowing and cold," Lauzun replied, making one final attempt.

"It is less than a mile away and John will escort you with a lantern. Armand, if you have any friendship left for one who treated you so badly, please do as I say. I have sworn to myself that I will do nothing to jeopardise my child's future and any further scandal would be the finish of her. Louisa would become as big an outcast as I."

The Duc got to his feet. "You have grown very beautiful, you realise."

"And why is that?"

"Sorrow, motherhood, who knows? I hope you meet a man one day, Milady, who is of big enough heart to ignore your past and see only the goodness in you."

"Yes, I would like that," she answered quietly.

"What a shame that we cannot be together," Lauzun said wistfully, and sounded almost as if he meant it. "But, alas, my wife is alive and my mistress would object."

"And we mustn't do anything to upset them," answered Sarah, and laughed to herself at his quizzical expression.

They sat in the candlelight, listening to music, not talking, not touching, just being together after such a very long time. The usual politenesses had been exchanged; did the research go well, how marvellous that she had received such rave reviews, were Canadian winters very cold, what was it like to play in a château. All asked and done, and now just a peaceful silence.

"It's late," said Sidonie at last. "I must go to bed."

"So must I or I won't get over my jet lag for days."

"Time's a funny thing," she answered reflectively.

"In every way. Listen, I know we are strangers again. I know that so much water has flowed under so many bridges we could drown in it, but let me say one thing."

"Which is?"

"That even if we had been in each other's company for the last ten months, we wouldn't have stayed the same. No situation is ever static; from day to day things alter. We might well have spent an evening just like this, feeling our way, if we had had some monumental row. Do you see the point I'm trying to make?"

"That even if we'd been together we could still be unknown to one another?"

"Something on those lines, yes."

"That the people we've met we would have met anyway and their influence on us would still have changed us slightly?"

"Probably that too." He smiled at her and Sidonie realised that she had forgotten how green his eyes were, how nice his voice. "Very formally, then, Miss Brooks, may I ask if I can take you out to dinner soon?"

"I think it could be arranged."

"Is that yes?"

"Yes."

"In that case I'll happily say goodnight and sleep well and see you soon."

"Goodnight, Finnan," and she turned to go, hiding her feelings.

"Oh, by the way, how's Sarah Lennox?" he said, as he opened the front door.

"I don't think she's very joyful at the moment."

"Will she be again?"

"Oh, yes, one of these days."

"Your days or her days?"

"Both," said Sidonie, kissing him rapidly on the cheek. And with that she went downstairs, immeasurably glad that Finnan O'Neill was home at last.

# Thirty

The newspaper report was straight to the point and utterly obscene. It was dated 15th February, 1774, and said, "We are able to assure our readers that Lady Sarah Bunbury, née Lennox, at present residing in a dwelling on her brother the Duke of Richmond's estate at Goodwood, is expecting a child fathered by her nephew, Charles James Fox. Lady Sarah will be remembered for her scandalous elopement with Lord William Gordon which resulted in the above named nobleman being forced to leave the country."

As soon as he read it, it being his daily duty to glance through all the papers, the King felt such a tightness in his throat that he thought he would either choke or vomit.

"It can't be true," he moaned silently. "Oh, God, I know it isn't true." And he rang the bell on his desk for an equerry, realising full well that one of his periods of flurry was about to come on.

It was a new young man who stood bowing before His Majesty and George stared at him with some surprise. "Where is Colonel Gilbert?"

"He is indisposed, Sir. I am Major Woodford. I have only recently been appointed to your household."

"Recent or no," answered the King, trembling violently, "I have an urgent mission for you."

"Name it, Sir."

"You must take a letter to the Prime Minister, Lord North, at once, now, immediately."

"Certainly, Sir," answered Woodford, pleased to have such an interesting commission on the very first day at his post.

"And shall I tell you what it says?" said the King, going to his desk.

The Equerry was about to answer that he would not

presume, that it was none of his affair, when he saw to his horror that the King was not only sweating profusely but shaking so badly he could hardly put pen to paper. It was in these moods, these bouts of anxiety, that he had been warned His Majesty should be humoured, so he said instead, "If Your Majesty is so inclined to tell me."

"I'm writing this. 'I can no longer tolerate the attitude of Fox as regards the American colonies in their disputes with their mother country. His behaviour is that of a lout, an abusive rabble rouser, he is as contemptible as he is odious. It is our wish that he be immediately dismissed his place on the Treasury Board.' There, what do you think of that?"

Woodford's first thought was that the King had taken leave of his senses to discuss a matter so delicate with a new member of staff, a johnny nobody, and in fact was puzzled to the extent that he burst out with, "I don't know what to say, Sir. What has Mr Fox done exactly?"

"Made it a policy to torment me all these years and now, this . . ." And the King struck a copy of the *Morning Post* with his hand.

"What is it, Sir?"

"A libel, a calumny, yet another slur on one who is utterly sinned against."

Woodford saw to his horror that His Majesty had tears in his eyes and the instructions of his superiors flashed through his mind. Should the Monarch become agitated in any way he must withdraw quietly and send for a physician to take the royal pulse.

"And who is that, Sir?" asked the Equerry, bowing his way out.

"The most beautiful woman in the world," answered the King, and turned away to look out of the window, quite obviously remembering another, happier time, before depression and fluster had come to plague him.

"Do you know, His Majesty wept," whispered Woodford to his wife, when his tour of duty was temporarily over and he had a short home leave.

"About the story that Sarah Bunbury was expecting a child by her nephew?"

"Yes."

"It's said that he was once in love with her."

"Still is, I reckon. Anyway, Fox got his congé as a result. I overlooked a copy of Lord North's letter, and do you know what he had written?"

"Tell me."

"His Majesty has thought proper to order a new Commission of the Treasury to be made out, in which I do not see your name."

"How utterly cutting," said Woodford's wife, and laughed prodigiously.

Sarah's cup, so bitter for so long, now overflowed with grief. Four months after the vile allegations had appeared in the *Morning Post*, followed almost instantly by Charles James's dismissal from the Treasury, her beloved guardian, Henry Fox, Lord Holland, had died. But as if this were not enough, Caroline, who had adored her husband all her life, followed him to the grave twenty-three days later, after an agonising illness described as cancer.

In view of the salacious slanders being whispered about her, Sarah had fled to Castletown in Ireland to stay with her sister, Louisa Conolly, unable to cope with the added humiliation alone, cut off from human contact as she had been in Halnaker Farm. So it was from Ireland that she caught the packet boat to attend Caroline's funeral, her sister and brother-in-law with her. And it was from the docks that she had travelled to Holland House, vividly reminded of her first journey there all those years ago when she had come from Dublin to take up residence with the Foxes.

And now both of them were gone, Sarah's girlhood companions never to be confided in or advised by again. It was with a heavy heart, her quarrel with the Hollands entirely put behind her, that Sarah returned to Holland House for the wake.

Charles James was there, of course, dressed in black, his mood equally sombre. And as soon as they had a moment alone, he drew Sarah to one side.

"The King's had me dismissed; you know of it?"

"Yes. It's to do with that vile libel, I suppose."

"Ostensibly no. In truth, HM hates me for backing the American colonists, yet I cannot help but think the timing of it all to be highly suspicious."

"You don't suppose he believed what he read, do you?" Sarah asked, her voice suddenly thin.

"God knows. One would hope not."

"After all the filth that's been spread about me I expect people are prepared to accept almost anything."

"Well, I've put it about that when I discover the identity of the author I shall challenge him to a duel."

"I truly wish I could do the same," Sarah sighed sadly.

Charles James patted her hand. "It's devilish hard for you, I know. If only I could do something more than just vigorously deny the calumny."

"When all's said and done, I've brought everything on myself. Give a dog a bad name and so forth." Her voice shook. "I've served my sentence of ostracism four years now. How much longer can it possibly go on, do you think?"

The rogue politician looked at her shrewdly. "When the divorce is over and done people will finally lose interest in you. But until that time I think you'll have to content yourself with being patient."

"I hope to God all this is enriching my soul."

Sarah's nephew barked a laugh. "You can rely on that. They say there's no victory without suffering."

"What a sickening sentiment," she answered, her old self momentarily blazing forth.

"What is?" asked Ste, coming to join them.

"Nothing of importance," Sarah replied, surveying her other nephew with a certain alarm, for the poor creature looked terrible indeed.

Stephen Fox, the new Lord Holland, was now aged twenty-nine, as was Sarah herself, though he appeared to be at least twice that. Enormously fat and even deafer than before, he gave the unfortunate impression of being quite an old man. It was generally believed by the family that under the terms of Caroline's will, Ste's debt to his father's estate, nearly £50,000, would be wiped off. It was also rumoured that Lady Holland had done the same for Charles James who, or so it was said, owed in excess of that! But even this generous bequest could not rid Sarah's eldest nephew of a desperate need to raise money, which resulted in his having a permanently hangdog look about him.

"How are you, my dear?" he asked now, his breathing laboured and wheezy as might be expected in such a very large person.

"Well in health, a little miserable in disposition, I fear."

"As are we all," Ste replied fruitily.

Sarah looked round the black-garbed figures thronging the Gilt Room. "Lady Susan does not appear to be here."

"No, unfortunately both she and Mr O'Brien are very poorly. They sent their deepest regrets, however."

"I would have so loved to see her," Sarah answered wistfully. "Since she returned from America we have met only twice, though we correspond as regularly as ever."

And this fact had been something that Sarah had clung to in her isolated and solitary life. In 1770, Susan and her handsome Irish husband had come back to England from New York, settling at Winterslow, near Salisbury, close by Ste and his wife, Mary, who lived in Winterslow House. Most unfortunately, this mecca of pleasure, to which flocked a constant stream of guests and at which Ste had built a little theatre for the plays they all loved to perform, had been burnt to the ground in January, giving Sarah the uncomfortable feeling that 1774 was going to be a bad year for the Foxes. And so it had proved, the dreadful libel against her being followed by Charles's dismissal and the two tragic deaths. With the fated feeling that the run of bad luck was not yet over, she turned to Ste once more.

"Have you seen Lady Susan's new home yet?"

"No, but we hope to go there shortly."

After the fire, the O'Briens had moved to Stinsford House, near Dorchester, an old manor house belonging to Lady Ilchester, Susan's mother.

"Do report on it when you have visited. And now, if you will excuse me, I'd like to look round a little before I leave."

It was like turning back the clock to walk through the great house, strangely empty and quiet with both the master and mistress newly dead. Treading softly so as not to disturb the silence, Sarah walked its length and breadth. Through the Crimson Drawing Room and the Dining Room, remembering how she had laughed there as a giddy creature as yet unspoilt by the world. Then on along the corridor to the drawing room given over to the young people of the house, then through to the bedrooms, now so empty and still. Finally, having seen enough, Sarah descended the sweeping main staircase to the floor below.

She did not go to the Chapel, where she had married Charles Bunbury what seemed like centuries ago, but went instead to the snugs and private studies in the east wing, coming at last to the den she had once shared with Susan. It was a beautiful room with an arched and decorated ceiling, a mullioned window at the far end, a cushioned seat below it. The window was set in one of the house's many archways in which a door could be closed at night for security. But now the door was open, the light pouring in, and Sarah ran to the seat and knelt up on it as she had done so often in the past. Pressing her hands against the glass, she looked out.

She knew it was not possible, of course, but somehow the carriage sweep, distinctly visible from this vantage point, had gone. And the Inigo Jones portals which had stood so brave and fine at the far end of it had been moved and placed close together at the far end of the courtyard. Horrified, Sarah looked for the elm drive but that, too, had vanished. Furthermore, and this was the most horrid thing, strange people were wandering about in the grounds, grounds so drastically and violently changed that they were scarcely recognisable.

Disbelievingly, Sarah rubbed her hand over her eyes, then stared out once more, and this time shuddered with true fright. For her ghost was standing right outside the window, gazing directly in at her. She had not so much as caught a glimpse of the thing in the last five years, not since the time she had seen it in the snow and fallen down in a faint which had caused her to go into labour. But now, after all this time, the woman who had dogged her footsteps ever since she had first come to Holland House, was there again. Frozen to the marrow, Sarah returned the creature's stare.

And then an incredible thing happened. The woman smiled, the humorous mouth curving, and simultaneously held out her hand. From this one gesture alone Sarah knew that the being was aware of her plight, but did not in the slightest hold her in scorn. On the contrary, the creature seemed to radiate friendship and compassion. Utterly bewitched, Sarah found herself smiling, appreciating a gesture of friendship in a world turned so cold and cruel. She pressed closer to the window to see even more distinctly and the woman leant forward and also put her palms against the glass. And then the vision blurred, as if behind raindrops, and a second later was gone.

Sarah sat on the window seat, bewildered but reassured, no longer afraid of the ghost, or whatever she was, who had made it so clear she posed no threat but offered only kindness and understanding. And then the sound of approaching footsteps brought Sarah back to the present and awareness of her own dire situation came rushing back both to torment and hurt her.

It would have been nice, thought Sidonie, if she and Finnan had been able to pick up exactly where they had left off, if her conscience about Alexei could have left her quietly alone, if life in general could have been a little bit easier. But the truth was that the months spent apart had taken their toll and somehow they had not got back on the same footing.

"Big girls don't cry," Sidonie had repeated to herself, and then wondered if the situation might be easier if she did admit to having had a fling – and what a fling – while the doctor had been away. Yet she could not bring herself to the sticking point and it was only with the greatest reluctance that she finally raised the issue of other friendships during their first meal out together.

"When I was in Russia I met this amazing young violinist," she began, with what she hoped was an extremely casual note in her voice.

"Yes, I read about it in the papers," Finnan answered nonchalantly, completely throwing her off balance.

"How did you manage that?"

"A lot of French Canadians get French newspapers. I read an article about you in *Paris Match*."

Sidonie attempted a careless laugh. "If I remember that one correctly it implied he was my toyboy."

Finnan looked her straight in the eye. "My French isn't that good but I think it gave that impression, yes."

Fate hung in the balance and Sidonie sat silent, unable to utter, aware that to do so might change everything for ever. Finally, Finnan spoke.

"I looked up 'toy' in the dictionary the other day. It said, 'a plaything, a trifle, a thing only for amusement or look, a matter of no importance'."

Sidonie smiled, putting out her hand and covering one of his. "He wasn't exactly of no importance to me. And I suppose he'll be very important to somebody, some day, but I wasn't the somebody and it most certainly wasn't the day."

"I think with very talented people it might be easy to fall in love with the gift rather than the person," Finnan said slowly.

"I love Alexei's talent all right," Sidonie answered truthfully. "He's a genius, it's the only way to describe him. But he's not meant for any one woman, he belongs to *all* women."

Finnan grinned and said Irishly, "That could prove tiring, by God."

The awful moment had passed and would never come back, Sidonie knew it, but still there was one thing left to be said.

"You must feel that love of their talent about your women colleagues. What was the name of the one in your team?"

"Jeannie O'Rourke. Oh, yes, I fell madly in love with her."

"Oh."

"The only trouble was that her husband had a black belt in karate."

He was grinning even more broadly, his eyes twinkling, and it was absolutely impossible to tell whether he was serious or not. Sidonie's brain stepped beyond the situation and thought clearly. To go any further down this path could be destructive for them both. They had reached a J.B. Priestley "Dangerous Corner" and got safely round it. Enough was enough.

"Tricky things, black belts," she answered, "unless they've got suspenders on."

"He didn't wear those, at least not that I know of."

"Well, that's all right then."

It was over, the air was as clear as it was ever going to be. Now they could start to build their friendship again.

"I heard you playing when I got home the other night. It sounded wonderful," Finnan said. "Are you going to tell me how your metamorphosis came about? Was it something to do with Sarah?"

"Oh, yes."

And, just as if they were chatting about an old friend, Sidonie told him about the various sightings in France and how she had stood rapt and attentive, listening to a musician long dead interpreting the music of another age.

"And it really *was* the Earl of Kelly you heard playing?"

"I'm positive of it. He transformed my entire approach."

"My God, what a privilege. You are chosen amongst mortals, Sidonie."

"I know."

"So other than Nigel, it's all been going well?"

"How did you know about him?"

"Your changed phone number; you told me the other night, remember?"

"I do now. Honestly, Finnan, he's getting a bit of a worry. He seems to be obsessed with the idea that we'll get back together. In fact there was a really nasty incident in Bath when he sort of attempted rape."

"What do you mean?"

"He got into my room and leapt upon me, as they say. It was nothing really. He didn't get anywhere."

"Did you report him?"

"I couldn't bear the idea of it."

Finnan looked thoughtful. "I think you should be very

careful. If he comes anywhere near you again you must serve him with an injunction."

"I will, I promise. Now can we talk about something else? To be honest, it depresses me even to think about him."

"All right, on one condition."

"Which is?"

"That you don't let him get away with one more thing."

And with those words said almost severely, Finnan launched into an amusing description of the Canadian way of life, while Sidonie, listening, knew that wonderful lifting of her spirits only experienced in the company of a true and loyal friend.

When she got home and went into her flat, for Finnan and she were far from ready yet to sleep with one another, there was a change in it. Nothing had moved, not a thing had been disturbed, and yet there was a subtle difference in the atmosphere. At first Sidonie thought it was a smell and stood sniffing. And, indeed, there was the faintest lingering of perfume, though that could have been anything, have even blown in from outside.

It was rather more, Sidonie thought, that in some indefinable way the air had been stirred and shaken, to quote Walter de la Mare. There was a change in the very essence of the rooms, particularly the one leading into the garden, Sidonie's music room. It was an eerie feeling and she could have sworn, had it not been for the fact that no door or window had been tampered with, that someone had been in the Garden Flat, looking around.

Yet how could she ring the police or even tell Finnan? Not one thing, not one particle of dust, was out of place. There was no evidence, no proof of any kind of intrusion. Somewhat nervously, Sidonie finally went to bed, only to lie awake, the thought of Nigel and his apparent mania uppermost in her mind until she fell into a dream-ridden sleep.

# Thirty-one

An inexplicable urge to go to Holland House, consciously to seek out Sarah, swept over her so intensely that Sidonie found she could concentrate on nothing else. Usually, music was guaranteed to absorb her completely but on this particular day, having dreamt of Sarah the night before, nothing could alleviate her desperate longing to glimpse the past. Ignoring the fact that it was a Thursday morning and there was a piece by Haydn that Sidonie wanted to rethink, she went out through the garden, pulling the door that led onto Holland Walk firmly closed behind her, for she had been very conscious of security ever since the night she had sensed an intruding presence in her flat.

The delicious smell of autumn was in the air, crisp as apples, the smoke from bonfires in the park wafting and evocative, hinting at colder days to come after the harvest festival and the gathering in of fruit. Despite the distant noise of traffic there was a golden peace about the gardens and Sidonie, strolling, enjoying the warmth of the late September sun, wished she had a jolly laughing child to kick up leaves and feed the birds with. A longing for a baby swept her and, despite the miserable circumstances of her birth, Sidonie at that moment envied Sarah her daughter Louisa Bunbury.

Holland House always looked its best at this time of year, the old bricks turned to amber by the mellow sun, the mullioned windows glistening darts of fire. As was her habit Sidonie eased round the barrier blocking off the courtyard and made for the cloisters in the east wing, walking their length down to the room overlooking the gardens. Of all the rooms left standing, this one above all retained its character, for the original vaulted ceiling was still in place, its lovely lines clearly visible despite the ravages of time and war.

Unable to resist looking at it, Sidonie stared in through the window.

She thought afterwards that in some mysterious way, Sarah must have been calling her, for the hunt was over before it had even begun. Kneeling up on the window seat within, her face deathly white against her black clothes, was the girl Sidonie sought. The centuries rolled away at once, and Sarah Bunbury and Sidonie Brooks were face to face, gazing at one another through a sheet of glass that represented two hundred years.

At this close proximity it was easy to read the Georgian woman's expression, which changed from horribly startled to one of almost tragic gratitude as Sidonie smiled and held out her hand. There was a hunted look about those thin white features, an element of despair within the beautiful eyes. The toll of all she had endured was leaving its visible mark on Sarah, and Sidonie could see at once that the Beauty must now be approaching thirty.

Trying to get even closer, to demonstrate her friendship, Sidonie put her palms flat against the window to cover those of Sarah on the other side of the glass. But, even as she looked, the window seemed to blur, as if water were running down the panes and a second later Sarah had gone and Sidonie was staring into an empty room, only an old cigarette packet showing that the place was still in use in the present century. Suddenly bereft, feeling that she had more to say, more to do to comfort the other woman, Sidonie turned and going back to the end of the arcade, entered the building through the youth hostel fire door.

Holland House was full of people and just for a moment Sidonie gaped at them blankly, wondering which era she was in. But the modern-day uniform, jeans, trainers and sweat shirts, said it all. This was not the age of individualism unlike that other fascinating time she was occasionally privileged to see.

"G'day," said a large friendly Australian, to which Sidonie, attempting to look like a mature student, responded with "Hello."

"New here?"

"Yes."

"Give us a hand with the bags."

Delighted to get a look at Holland House in the twentieth century, Sidonie joined a group enthusiastically hefting backpacks up a flight of stairs, just recognisable as the old east staircase which had ascended behind the principal staircase. And then, loaded with gear, she suddenly found herself in Sarah's bedroom at the back of the house, seeing it full of single beds and bits and pieces of inexpensive furniture. Hardly able to look, Sidonie dumped the bags and would have gone back down the stairs had not a noise caught her ear. She froze, listening intently, and as the babble died away identified the sound as that of a harpsichord.

Suddenly conscious of the absence of voices, Sidonie looked round and saw that she was alone on the east staircase, that the youth hostellers and their luggage had completely disappeared. And as she came down the steps to the ground floor, she realised that Holland House had once again restored itself to its fine splendour with not a modern thing in sight.

Yet for all its grandeur the house was empty of people and as Sidonie crossed the great entrance hall and made her way to the west wing she became conscious of the fact that she had passed no one at all, that the house appeared to be deserted. Yet still the harpsichord played on and opening a door facing her very gently, Sidonie found herself looking into a glorious music room which she had not known existed.

Sarah was there, sitting at an instrument which bore such a striking resemblance to Sidonie's own that she went towards it out of sheer curiosity, all thoughts of caution forgotten. As she drew nearer to the sound, the musician was able to recognise that the Georgian girl was a very competent player indeed, though not a great one. And she also identified, with a laugh, the piece Sarah was performing, her own namesake "Lady Sarah Bunbury", composed by the Earl of Kelly.

But it was the instrument itself which filled the modern woman with awe and a sense of disbelief. For the impossible appeared to have happened. Sidonie was looking at a harpsichord made by Thomas Blasser in London in the year 1745, a harpsichord which, at this very moment, was safely at home in the Garden Flat. Now, at long last, the link between the two women became completely clear to her. The Blasser harpsichord was definitely the property of them both.

Sarah played a wrong note and made a sound of irritation and, looking at her closely, Sidonie saw that in the fifteen or so minutes since she had last seen her, Sarah had grown older. A mature woman in her early thirties was at the keyboard, the mourning clothes gone. Several years had passed for Sarah in what had been a twinkling of Sidonie's eye.

Entranced, Sidonie watched as Sarah stopped playing and pressed a knob in the base of the instrument below the lower manual. A small drawer flew open and, reaching inside, the Georgian woman withdrew a letter. It was dated 25th February, 1761, Sidonie saw over Sarah's shoulder, and about the flourishing signature at the bottom there could be no doubt. It was a love letter from the King of England himself.

My dear Lady Sarah, With what Joy has my Heart been filled since A Very Pretty Lady came from Ireland November twelvemonth. Do You know Who I mean? I send this Pretty Lady a Gift for her Birthday so that she may play the tune Betty Blue, taught me at Twelve Night by Herself. George R.

Smiling yet sighing, Sarah brushed the letter with her lips, then put it back in the secret drawer and returned to the keyboard. But again she made a mistake and Sidonie could no longer resist what she longed to do. Very slowly, she walked into Sarah's line of vision, smiled to reassure the girl, then sat down beside her on the double music stool and, putting her hands to the manuals, played "Lady Sarah Bunbury" correctly.

They could not touch, it was not possible for them to do so, nor could they converse with words. But Sarah turned on her a look of such joy, of such gratitude and delight, that Sidonie felt the tears start into her eyes.

"Oh Sarah, be happy," she said, horribly conscious that the other woman might not hear the words, but longing to reassure her for all that. "I know your future will be bright. Please try to be brave a little longer."

And with that Sidonie rose and walked slowly from the room, more than aware that according to Sarah's journal there was no record of them ever meeting again.

On 19th March, 1776, the London newspaper *Packet* had carried the following announcement. "A Petition of Thomas Charles Bunbury was presented yesterday to the Upper Assembly, praying leave to bring in a Bill to Dissolve his Marriage with Lady Sarah Lennox, his now wife, and to enable him to marry again."

Forlorn and humiliated, Sarah had returned to Goodwood from Castletown in Ireland, aware that though she studiously avoided looking at the newspapers, her servants were most certainly studying them avidly and, no doubt, remarking about her secretly as she sat down at dinner.

In the end this feeling of being sniggered at behind her back had proved too much to tolerate and, in April, Sarah and Louisa had departed for Stoke to stay with Lady Albermarle, her father's sister, being sure of a welcome in that lively old lady's company. Sarah was thirty-two, her aunt seventy-three yet the empathy between them was spoken of respectfully amongst the family. With a great sigh of relief to be away from the renewed gossip, Sarah and Louisa threw themselves into the whirlwind of Lady Albermarle's social life.

It was well known that old Lady Anne liked nothing better than to invite folk to dine and on this particular soft April evening, with spring lambs grazing in the fields beyond the park and the four o'clock sky the colour of irises, six guests arrived by carriage to join the party. There was Squire Thomas, a local landowner, and his wife, and Sir Hugh and Lady Milton, a minor knight and his spouse. But by far the most interesting guest, as far as Sarah was concerned, was Colonel George Napier, introduced to her as a friend of Lord George Lennox, Sarah's brother.

The military man stood well over six foot tall and appeared remarkably handsome and fine in his regimental red coat and white wig, beneath which Sarah could catch a glimpse of crisp curling brown hair. Immediately interested in him as a person, she would have liked to question George Napier about the American colonies, a subject dear to Sarah's heart, but unfortunately the presence of the Colonel's wife Elizabeth, a mousy little thing of about twenty, very slim and demure, put paid to monopolising him in earnest conversation. However, at dinner they were placed next to one another, and Sarah turned to him.

"If I may say so, Sir," she commented, "you look mighty young to be colonel of a regiment."

He smiled, somewhat ruefully. "The truth is, my Lady, the army's desperate with the American colonists causing so much commotion. In fact I'm twenty-five and green for my commission."

'A mere boy,' thought Sarah, but did not say so.

"Tell me," she said, "what are your views on the colonists?"

"I have every sympathy with them. What they are doing is neither treasonous nor rebellious. They are justified in every moral sense."

"But people might get killed," put in Mrs Napier.

"No doubt they will," her husband answered drily.

"I hate war," stated Sarah. "I hate civil war even more. And my flesh creeps at the thought they are fighting on the very spot where recently lived my friend Lady Susan O'Brien. Also my nephew Harry Fox is out there. But, for all that, I sympathise with the poor Americans, I truly do."

She was being too outspoken for the dinner table and knew it.

"Why?" asked Squire Thomas.

"Because they have every right to be independent of us if they so wish."

"The awful thing is," said the Colonel, "I agree with their principles entirely and yet may well be ordered to go out and fight them."

"It's worrying," sighed Elizabeth Napier. She cleared her throat, obviously anxious to change the subject. "I hear you have a little girl called Louisa, Lady Sarah. Pray how old might she be?"

"Eight at the end of this year."

"I, too, have a Louisa, though aged only two."

So the dashing Colonel, boy though he was, was already a family man. Suddenly feeling decidedly middle-aged, Sarah looked at Elizabeth and said, "Then I pray your husband is not called to war. I always feel it is the children of army men who are the ultimate victims."

"Oh yes," answered Mrs Napier with great feeling, "you are so very, very right."

And the two women gave each other a sad smile that neither ever forgot.

It had been the King's reaction to her divorce that had finally broken Sarah's spirit, not the public humiliation nor the shame of having her name bandied about as adulteress. She had stayed at Stoke as long as she dared, getting to know Donny Napier, as the Colonel was nicknamed, and his wife. The more she saw of Elizabeth, the better the older woman liked her. For the girl was a gentle soul, a sea captain's daughter whom Donny had met and married on the beautiful island of Minorca. As for the Colonel himself, he proved, most surprisingly, to be an intellectual. Well read in several languages, versed in both modern and ancient history, the brilliant young man had also studied mathematics, chemistry and engineering. Sarah considered him quite the most attractive and clever creature she had met for years.

But eventually the time had come for her to leave her new friends and the unhappy woman had reluctantly returned to Halnaker Farm to face the inevitable.

The divorce, despite all the sordid publicity, had gone through, and by 24th May had been passed in both the Lords and the Commons and was now ready for the King's assent. But then had come that part of the proceedings which had finally reduced Sarah to a pulp of tears.

"His Majesty is too upset to put his stamp on the Act," the Duke of Richmond had told her, walking over to Halnaker in his shirtsleeves, his face more serious than Sarah could recall seeing it.

"What are you saying?"

461

"That it is rumoured at Court that the King cannot bring himself to be present when your divorce Act is read. That he does not wish to hear your adulterous conduct proclaimed aloud."

"Oh, my God, why?"

"Can't you guess?" answered Richmond harshly. "Have you lost all reasoning power? Surely the matter speaks for itself. The poor devil still has strong feelings for you and refuses to be present when you are publicly shamed."

After her brother had gone, Sarah sat quite alone, going over every detail of her relationship with the man who, for a few crazy months in the summer of 1761, had not only captured her heart but broken it. For the very first time she saw with clarity the pressures he had been put under to let her go, the agony of spirit he must have endured, the disappointment when, with his innate sensuality and love of beauty, he had first cast eyes on his ugly little bride.

"Oh George, George," she murmured, and wept as she never had before. Not only for herself but for the King and Bunbury too, married so that a jilted girl might be seen with the most dandified man in town, not for the right reasons at all. Enormous love welled in her, a love whose basis was compassion. And it was now that she saw herself for what she had been, cheap and reprehensible, an overpainted strumpet who had deserved her fate, asked for it indeed. Yet in getting her just dues another innocent life had been hurt – fatherless Louisa Bunbury, that engaging unpretty girl whose only wish in life was to please, and who caused as little trouble as it was possible for a child to do.

Sarah sank back in her chair drained of everything but the most bitter regrets. What point was there in continuing an existence as worthless and shallow as hers? Then thoughts of Louisa's friendly little face, her wide mouth smiling, twisted her heart. She must go on for the sake of the child she had brought into the world so carelessly. Determined to make a fresh start she stood up, went to her writing desk, picked up her pen and addressed a letter to him who once had loved her so much and who still, in some strange way of his own, obviously continued to do so.

She simply wrote, "Sir, From the bottom of my heart I thank you," and signed it with her maiden name. Whether he would ever see the words she did not know. Perhaps, at some level, an equerry would decide it was not politic for His Majesty to receive such a thing. But she had done it and that was all that mattered. Weeping as if she would never stop, Sarah went into the grounds to find her daughter.

1774 had indeed been an evil year for the Foxes. Starting with the libel against Sarah and Charles James, which had led almost certainly to his dismissal from office, then going on to the deaths of Lord Holland and Caroline, the most tragic event of all had taken place at the end of November. Ste, the second Lord Holland, aged only twenty-nine, had died of dropsy, leaving Mary a grieving young widow with two children.

Money problems had pressed and the bereft Lady Holland had been forced to hold a sale of furniture and books in Holland House conducted by Mr Christie. Walpole, who had been so close to Henry Fox, found himself unable to face the ordeal and wrote to a friend, "The sale of Holland House will produce treasures. I did not go. It would have been a horrid sight to me who lived there so much, but I hear the most common furniture sold as dear as relics."

But one thing that had not been put up for auction was Sarah Lennox's harpsichord. In her first flurry of hatred towards George, she had left it behind when she had gone to live in Suffolk, telling Caroline carelessly that she was welcome to it, that it meant very little to her, in fact was a positive eyesore. But now, with Holland House rented out to Lord Rosebery, for poor little Mary had taken her children and gone to live with her family in the country, Sarah feared for it. Suddenly, because the King had made this final tragic gesture of fondness when no one else seemed to care, she wanted to have the harpsichord he had given her more than anything else in the world.

The divorce had gone through, His Majesty having given his assent to the Bill *in absentia*, and feeling she had no further caste to lose, Sarah had written asking Lord Rosebery for permission to reclaim her possession. A fairly pleasant reply had come back, one which had given her hope that Charles James's prediction that the *beau monde* would eventually pass on to the next source of gossip and forget all about her, might be coming true at last. Accordingly, a carter had been hired and Sarah had gone ahead in one of Richmond's carriages to oversee the removal.

Perhaps she had been too hopeful too soon, Sarah thought, when she finally arrived at the great house. For though the servants were in residence, both his Lordship and her Ladyship were not at home. Pulling a wry little face, Sarah surveyed the silent brooding place which had once been the scene of such gaiety, from Caroline's successful balls and parties to the amateur theatricals which all of them had so greatly adored. Now, Holland House seemed to be haunted by shadows and Sarah knew for certain that a great era had come to an end, the like of which would not be seen again for many years.

"His Lordship said to offer you refreshment, my Lady," the major domo announced grandly as she went into the entrance hall.

"I think I would rather go straight to the music room," Sarah replied with dignity.

"As your Ladyship wishes."

Even here, the ravages of the sale following Ste's death could be seen. Bound books of music were missing and Sarah noticed that Caroline's little spinet had gone, she only hoped to a member of the family rather than at auction. But still there, beautifully polished and as fine as the day it had been given her, stood the King's present for her sixteenth birthday, the Thomas Blasser harpsichord. With a little cry of pleasure, Sarah sat down at the manuals and started to play the tune that the Earl of Kelly had composed for her in France, "Lady Sarah Bunbury".

And then a memory came, of herself as a spoilt little upstart reading the King's birthday message and thrusting it into a secret drawer which she had discovered hidden within the instrument. She had been recovering from her broken leg, then, and had come back to London to catch a

King for bridegroom, to spite Lord Newbattle as much as anything else.

"Lord, what a shallow bitch," Sarah said now and, finding the knob that released it, opened the drawer and took the letter out.

The words made her smile. "With what Joy has my Heart been filled since A Very Pretty Lady came from Ireland November twelvemonth."

If only it could have been different, if only two people who had truly loved one another had been allowed to have their own way. Yet there was no point in dwelling on the past. The only course was to go forward courageously. With a certain determination, Sarah put her hands on the manuals and started to play once more. And then she froze, aware that there was a change in the room, that something had come in that was not quite of the world. Startled to the point where she played a wrong note, Sarah looked up.

The ghost was there, standing as close to her as she had ever been, so close, in fact, that Sarah could have put out her hand and touched her. But she hesitated, not so much afraid as not wanting to disturb the balance of things. As she looked, the beautiful creature smiled at her, and Sarah thought for the first time that they were now much of an age, for, through the years she had seen it, the apparition had remained the same whereas she, Sarah, had grown older.

And then the loveliest thing took place, a thing that she would remember all the days of her life, a thing that seemed to be a turning point, a moment from which Sarah could truly begin to live again. The ghost sat down beside her on the double music stool and played "Lady Sarah Bunbury" so beautifully, so faultlessly, that every hair on the listener's neck stood on end at the quality of sound. Not since the Earl of Kelly had written it for her, had Sarah heard the piece performed so well.

How she longed to be able to speak then, to talk to the mysterious being who had never been far away from her since Sarah first came to Holland House. Yet still some sense of fear stopped her, though the woman was attempting to leap that very chasm, for Sarah could see her lips moving. But the words escaped her, as probably they were meant to do and she had to be content with watching silently as the wondrous creature rose, then went from the room and out of her line of vision.

For a long time Sarah sat staring at the place where the woman had been, before she, too, finally and reluctantly got to her feet. She had the strangest feeling that they would never see one another again, that the link between them was about to break. And yet the harpsichord remained, the harpsichord that the ghost had obviously enjoyed playing so much.

"Perhaps one day," Sarah said slowly, "perhaps one day you will come back to visit me."

And with that, unable to fathom the mystery of it all, she too left the music room behind her.

# Thirty-two

He was there again, Sidonie was certain of it. He was standing in the darkness waiting for her to make a move. For though she had heard no noise, had been awoken by nothing remotely audible, the air of the flat had once more been stirred and disturbed. There was even that faint whiff of perfume she had smelt after the intruder's earlier visit. Filled with stark and instant terror, Sidonie sat bolt upright in bed.

Silence was everywhere, thick and heavy. She thought she had never known such silence and was just wondering how she could quiet her own breathing lest he should hear it, when there was the very faintest of creaks. Straining every muscle, Sidonie attempted to identify from where the sound had come.

It was not in the same room as she was, nor did the noise seem to be on the same floor. With a hideous rush of certainty, Sidonie felt sure that the unknown person who lurked in her flat in the darkness was down in the music room. Very, very cautiously, knowing that somehow she must get to the telephone, Sidonie got out of bed.

She had had an odd two days since the last sad sighting of Sarah Lennox, thrown into a state of elation by finding George III's letter in its original hiding place, then worrying about what she ought to do with it. Furthermore, Finnan was away at a medical conference and the careful reweaving of the threads of their lives was, if only temporarily, back on hold. And now she was alone in the flat, wondering whether the doctor had returned home or not, with a menacing presence in the very room where the precious letter lay concealed.

The telephone was in the hall, recharging overnight, but if she spoke into it she would be overheard, and there lay possible danger. In an agony of indecision, Sidonie sat on

467

the edge of the bed, wondering what to do for the best. And then the sound of the harpsichord being pounded, almost maniacally, drove every other thought from her head, and she rushed out of her bedroom and towards the music room, her one idea to protect the precious instrument.

It was a most creepy and sinister experience for as she started down the small flight of stairs that led to the garden rooms, the violent playing stopped and there was nothing but the sound of her breathing and the knowledge that somebody waited for her in the blackness below. Petrified, Sidonie froze where she stood, caught in the trap that had been set for her. And then, out of nowhere, somebody was upon her, pulling her headlong down the remaining stairs, putting a hand over her mouth so that she could not scream and rending her nightdress. Clutched in a vice-like hold, Sidonie struggled impotently feeling as powerless as a puppet.

But now that he had touched her, she knew who held her captive, knew by his lingering perfume, his body feel. It was Nigel Beltram who gripped her so viciously and, though he said not a single word, Sidonie felt she could guess his intent. The man was high as a steeple on something or other and had come either to rape or murder, perhaps both.

"Don't be a fool," she muttered, forcing her mouth free of his restraining hand. "You'll lose everything. Your career, your future, you'll be ruined."

She couldn't have done worse than to remonstrate, for a stinging blow to the face which really hurt her was the only answer Sidonie got, and she realised that under the influence of whatever substance he had taken, Nigel's violent nature was holding full dominance.

'He's going to kill me,' she thought, and wondered that anyone could hold such a grudge for so long.

All sorts of advice flew through her head; if you knee his crutch you might overbalance, better to take a swing. If he puts his hands round your throat your own hands are free, use them. Go for his eyes, his jugular, anything. It was like a nightmare because all the time she kept thinking of how much he once had loved her and wondering how he could possibly be doing this to her. And then Nigel made his intentions clear as one hand went to his clothing.

Making a ball of her fist she hit him ferociously, and as Nigel's head flew back, she raced up the stairs, out of her front door and up the next flight to Finnan's flat, where she pounded the knocker like a demented thing.

The Irishman came to the door almost immediately and Sidonie guessed that he had only been asleep a short while. But one look at her torn nightdress, her bruised and battered face, was enough to galvanise him into action. Shooting straight past her, Finnan O'Neill careered down the stairs and into the Garden Flat, Sidonie in hot pursuit despite the fact that the relief of finding him at home was starting to make her feel suddenly weak.

But there was no one there. Nigel had gone, not through the front door but via the garden and the door leading onto Holland Walk, which now swung open, a silent testimony to his escape route.

"Right," said Finnan, "you're going into the kitchen for a hot drink. Then we phone the police. I'm afraid I'm not going to clean you up till they've seen you."

"Nurse, the screens," Sidonie managed to say through a rapidly swelling mouth.

"That'll be enough of that, just you behave yourself. Now, what happened for God's sake?"

"It was Nigel. He got in here somehow. I think he must have a key. Anyway, he attacked me again, much more roughly this time."

"How did you get rid of him?"

"A well-aimed punch."

"Barry McGuigan strikes back!" said Finnan and, despite it all, they laughed, giggling like schoolchildren, as much with relief as anything else.

An hour later it was over in every sense. The police had been, had gone to Nigel's flat, only to get him out of bed.

"According to his flatmate he's been there all the time," said the detective sergeant ruefully.

"But it *was* him. I'd swear to it."

"There's nothing we can do with his friend giving him an alibi. It's their word against yours, I'm afraid."

"But somebody attacked Miss Brooks," Finnan put in angrily. "Look at her! She didn't do that to herself."

"Obviously there was an intruder, sir, but the question is did the lady make a mistake. Was it somebody unknown to her."

There was no point in arguing further. Nigel's friend, either believing he was telling the truth or else lying through his teeth, had sworn that they stayed up late watching television, had then gone to bed and, though they had their own rooms, he would have been awoken by the sound of anyone going out.

"That's it," said Sidonie, when the police had gone. "He's got away with it."

"You're positive it was Nigel?"

"Finnan, it *was*. I could smell him. He wears some naff aftershave which is quite distinctive. I've smelt it in here before but I couldn't place what it was."

"You mean he's got in on another occasion?"

"Yes, I believe so, though nothing was touched."

"Then he must have a key. We'd better get the locks changed in the morning."

"The police made light of that point. Do you know what I think?"

"What?"

"That they reckon I had some man in here and we had a quarrel. They kept saying there was no sign of breaking and entering and giving me meaningful looks."

"Oh Jesus and Joseph," exploded Finnan. "Wouldn't it get on your tits!"

"How colourfully you swear."

"Shall I go and break Nigel's head for you?"

"No, I'd hate it. Let him be. The very fact the police went round and saw him may have frightened him off. MP questioned and all that."

"If he does it again, I'll string the bugger up."

"I only hope I'll be alive to see it," Sidonie answered pessimistically.

"You're getting morose. Come on, give me a cuddle."

And that was how she came to spend the night in his arms, her body too bruised for any physical demonstration of passion, but so much warmth and kindness flowing between the two of them that it simply didn't matter. This then, Sidonie thought, must really be what it is all about. To feel as contented as this with not even a kiss must be the height of it.

"I think I love you," she said to Finnan through bruised lips, not caring any more about tactics or frightening him off.

"I *know* I love you," he answered. "In fact I'm bloody certain of it."

"Jeannie O'Rourke?"

"Alexei Orlov?"

"Nuts," answered Sidonie, and pulled him as close as her aching body would permit.

At long last, after so many depressing years, the word contentment had once again entered the vocabulary of that outcast of society, Lady Sarah Lennox. Looking back, she thought the process had begun at Stoke during her stay with Lady Albermarle. Meeting the Napiers, both of whom had treated her in a most civilised fashion despite the fact that her divorce was in the very process of going through, had made Sarah very happy. Then, and she could have kissed him for it, the Duke of Richmond had decided that now his sister was a single woman again, she should have a home of her own. And with that end in view he had asked Sarah to draw up plans of what kind of dwelling she would like, and had set about building her a little house in the grounds of Goodwood Park.

"My house consists of a large staircase of twenty by sixteen," Sarah had written to Susan delightedly, "a housekeeper's room on one side, a pantry on the other with a passage to the offices, which are out of the house, and then to the front. I have a drawing room of twenty-eight by eighteen, and a dining room eighteen square. Above stairs are two bedchambers of eighteen square and a little dressing room, and two smaller bedchambers at the back for servants. You see, nothing can be more compact."

The situation, too, was lovely. A mile from the big house, Sarah's home was to be built in a valley surrounded by wooded hills, sheltered and with a noble prospect. It was all that anyone could desire, the only irritating thing being that the workmen were taking so long about the actual construction. The other annoyance, of course, though this was a major one and affected everybody, was the conflict with America.

Sarah's firm stand on the side of the Colonists had not altered, though she considered the Bostonians to be very bad people, quarrelsome, discontented, hypocritical, enthusiastical liars, or so she told Susan in yet another letter. But though she might hint to her friend that she was violently angry with the King because of his attitude towards the whole wretched war, the thought that, had she been Queen, she could have persuaded George away from this bloody confrontation haunted her constantly. With her by his side as consort, the very history of the world might well have had to be rewritten, or so Sarah Lennox truly believed.

In January, 1779, a letter had arrived from Elizabeth Napier telling Sarah that Donny had left the 25th Regiment to go to the 80th, and had now been ordered to America. Both she and little Louisa were to go with him, a thought which she dreaded as Elizabeth was once again pregnant. Sarah had written back immediately sending her love and giving fond hopes for the safety of all of them, but had posted it with rather a heavy heart. With so many friends and relatives on the other side of the Atlantic, every day brought fresh worries. As much to take her mind off the war as for the reason that her house was still not quite ready, Sarah had set off for London in company with Louisa.

And it was there, during a visit to Lady Albermarle in her town house, that something took place which brought Sarah another step towards the restoration of her happiness. Quite out of the blue a letter had come from Sir Charles Bunbury asking if he might see her. Old feelings of fondness for him returned unbidden and Sarah had written to agree to a meeting.

In fact it transpired they met twice for, on the first occasion, Sarah had burst into such a flood of weeping that her ex-husband had had no choice but to take his leave. But when he called again the next day, Sarah was calm, and they greeted one another with a chaste kiss. She thought he looked well and in excellent spirits, he found her beauty in the full bloom of its maturity, her serenity giving her an inner glow of loveliness.

"No weeping this time then?" Charles said cautiously.

"I'll try not to, I promise," she answered, but still with a shake in her voice.

"There's no need, Sarah, truly. I don't bear any malice."

"How can you say that after all I have done to you?"

"What is past is past. It is my true wish that from now on we can be friends and that you will allow me to call on you whenever I like."

He was so genuine, so kind and generous, that she felt the tears start up again.

"Now don't weep," said Bunbury warningly. "You'll drive me off if you do. If the very sight of me makes you reproach yourself then I'd better keep away."

"No, no, I want you to stay. I can think of nothing better in the world than our being companions. It's just that you are so very good to me."

"Will it ease your mind if I ask a favour?" Charles answered, taking the initiative and settling his elegant frame into a chair. "For there *is* something you can do for me."

"And what is it?" asked Sarah, sitting down beside him, feeling the warmth and comfort of his presence almost with a sense of physical wellbeing.

"I would like to see something of Louisa, to treat her as if she really were my daughter. I have loved her for years, from the moment she was born in fact, and I've missed not watching her grow."

"How sweet you are," said Sarah, and at long, long last meant every word of it.

"It is my belief that every child should have a mother and father where at all possible."

"I do so agree." Sarah frowned. "Oh Charles, I am very worried about poor Ste's children."

"What has happened to them?"

"Well, you know that sad little Mary, his widow, died last year of consumption, still only in her twenties?"

"Yes."

"As a result the two children have been split up. Caroline was sent to live with Lady Warwick, which is a great disappointment to us all as we had hoped she would stay with our side of the family, and Henry, who is a dumpling of a little boy, the image of Ste, has gone to Lord Ossory."

"How tragic."

"It certainly is but it was under the terms of Mary's will, so one cannot argue against it."

"And what of Holland House?"

"Still let to Lord Rosebery and will remain so during Henry's minority, I suppose."

"So everything's changed," said Charles wryly.

"Yes, nothing at all is as it was."

He stood up. "Will you call on me tomorrow and bring Louisa?"

Sarah rose too. "It will be a pleasure. She is no beauty, Charles, being all teeth and very skinny, but has the most amiable, loving disposition."

Bunbury looked away. "Does she ever see her father?"

"Never. He has renounced all interest in her."

"Then I shall take his place and gladly."

And with that he drew Sarah into his arms and kissed her most fondly before he departed.

# Thirty-three

He had floated up out of his body and was hanging suspended somewhere near the ceiling gazing down on it with as much emotion as if it were an old suit of clothes. The room was very bright, full of light and colour, and Elizabeth was there, her face anxious yet angry, and her head shaking no. Leaning over his body was a physician, a handkerchief to his nostrils, and he, too, was shaking his head.

"Gone?" said an army man, standing a little distance from the narrow bed.

"I'm afraid so," the doctor answered.

"Pity, he was a damned fine fellow. And what the devil are we going to do with his child in view of this?"

"There's a survivor?"

"His daughter, a scrap of a thing, about four years old. She'll have to be sent back to England."

"Very sad," and the physician made to draw a sheet over the man's face.

"No, don't," shouted Elizabeth, though neither of them seemed to take any notice of her. "Don't do that, you mustn't leave him. Donny – " she had turned to look at him, floating up beside him so that their eyes were on a level " – you're to go back, do you hear? You can't abandon Louisa like this. Return at once."

"I don't want to," he answered. "I prefer to rest."

"But who'll look after our daughter? Oh, Donny, please." Elizabeth's dear face took on a cunning expression. "Besides, there's a lot of living left to do, and a lot of loving as well."

"Loving?"

"Yes, loving. You're only twenty-eight years old; there's a whole life ahead of you. Now go back."

"Good God!" exclaimed the doctor.

"What?"

"His eyelids flickered and there's a very faint pulse. This man's still alive, the fever's broken."

"Thank the Lord. So the child's not orphaned after all."

"Well, Napier's not out of the wood yet but there's a fighting chance."

"God be praised," said the soldier, and went to inform his commanding officer.

"Gracious me," said old Lady Albermarle, reading the letter which had just arrived in the post-boy's sack.

"What is it?" asked Sarah, looking up from her book.

"It's from Donny Napier. He's sailed into Spithead on a transport ship. But, oh dear, oh dear."

"Bad news?"

"Elizabeth and their baby son both died during the yellow fever epidemic in New York."

"Oh, how tragic! She was such a good sweet soul."

"Apparently he and Louisa also contracted the illness but survived, though Donny wasn't expected to live and his commission was sold to provide money for his daughter in the event of his death. He says he has nothing but the clothes he stands up in – but can he come and see me!"

Despite the gravity of the situation, aunt and niece laughed. "Well, at least he's not pretending. Will you let him come?"

"Of course I shall. Sarah, dear, go and give instructions for two extra bedrooms to be prepared."

"I'll be glad to do so," she answered, and wondered why her feet danced to the doorway at the thought of seeing the intelligent and handsome Donny Napier once more.

It had been an April evening when she had first met Colonel Napier and now it was April again; April, 1780, four years almost to the very day. Looking out of the window of Lady Albermarle's house at Stoke, Sarah Lennox saw an afternoon of quiver and dash, a light wind blowing the daffodils, making the young sheep dance, wetting the coats of the older ones as it blew droplets of water down from the hills. The colours of the day were soft – pale gold, a distant hazy plum, gentle,

gentle English green. And through this pastel landscape, the wild throating of early evening birds rising in a chorus of welcome, came Donny Napier's hired chaise, making its way up Lady Albermarle's long drive, a distant shape that drew ever nearer, carrying Sarah's destiny.

She had never seen two people so altered as he and his child descended from their conveyance. Where he had stood tall and well-made, a fine figure of a man, now he was thin to the point of being skeletal, his deep blue eyes blazing in a face that had known the ravages of fever. As for Louisa, Sarah's heart went out to such a solitary, hollow-eyed little thing.

"Oh, my dear," she said involuntarily, and rushed to take the scrap and hold it tightly in her arms. Over the child's head, Sarah's gaze met Donny's bright stare and she looked quickly away, busying herself with removing Louisa's travelling clothes. And then *her* Louisa came in, all teeth and smiles and the importance of being eleven years old, and took over the charge of her small wan namesake who so desperately needed every friend she could get.

"Well," said Lady Albermarle, "I've a mind to let those two dine together and early so that we can hear all you have to tell us, Donny."

He smiled, though Sarah thought she saw the glint of a tear in his eye. "I've been looking forward to this moment ever since I first knew I was going to pull through. I can't tell you what being here means to me. In my mind I've come through this front door a thousand times." He turned to Sarah. "Sometimes I imagined that you would be present, my Lady, and sometimes not."

"It is pure chance that I am," she answered lightly. "For I have my own house in Goodwood Park these days, very small but very charming. I do hope you and Louisa will visit me there."

"I would regard it as an honour," answered the soldier, and gave a little bow.

They sat late round the dinner table watching the April evening take on the colour of violets before it died quietly away. Then candles were lit and the port was passed and the two women sat in silence while Donny Napier described to them the siege of Charleston in South Carolina and how, when he had returned from there to New York, it had been to find that Elizabeth and her son had both died of yellow fever, alone in a strange country, dead and buried by the time he even heard the news.

"I didn't want to live without her, I'll be honest. But in my delirious state I felt Elizabeth wanted me to stay alive, so I fought for it. But I was actually put on board the transport ship unconscious. My first memory is of coming to at sea."

"What an ordeal for your child; she must have been terrified."

"I sometimes wonder if she will ever recover. Do you know, she often spends days without speaking at all."

"Louisa Bunbury will soon put that right," answered Lady Albermarle with certainty. "She's a regular chatterbox. And now if you two young people will excuse an old lady I'll be off to bed. Please stay up and reminisce. It is good for the soul to talk of one's troubles, Colonel Napier."

"Colonel no longer, I fear. My commander-in-chief sold my commission when he thought I was as good as dead so that Louisa would at least have enough money to get back to England. As I told you in my letter I have no career left and few prospects."

"Then you'll have to do something about it," Sarah remarked certainly, then wondered if she had sounded too peremptory.

Donny flashed a smile and his too thin, hawkish face relaxed visibly. "I'm thinking of going to Ireland to try and raise a regiment so that I can at least get a captain's commission again."

Sarah wondered why disappointment sank within her like a stone. "And will you take Louisa?"

"Yes, of course. My mother's family come from Dublin. I'll lodge her with them."

They had not noticed that Lady Albermarle had quietly left the room.

"Your father is a Scot, is he not?"

"Was, Madam. My nephew is now Lord Napier and head of the family. Anyway Papa was a dour old peer with ten sons and two daughters. He bred us, educated us and sent us out into the world to make our way. I'm afraid there was never any financial help from him."

"Never mind," said Sarah, "you'll just have to achieve success on your own."

Donny leant back in his chair, twirling the stem of his glass between his fingers, staring into its ruby red heart with a smile on his lips.

"How civilised this is."

"What?"

"Sitting here, replete, drinking an excellent port, and hearing words of encouragement from a beautiful woman."

"I didn't realise that I was being encouraging."

"I thought you were going to say you didn't realise you were beautiful."

"I used to be when I was younger, but alas no more. Do you know, Mr Napier – "

"Donny, please."

"Donny, I recently celebrated my thirty-fifth birthday."

"Surely age is only what one looks or feels, nothing else."

Sarah laughed. "But I am beginning to look old."

"On the contrary. I think you are even more beautiful than when I saw you last. You will never be spoiled by the passing years, Lady Sarah. In the words of Shakespeare, 'Age cannot wither her, nor custom stale her infinite variety.'"

There was silence in the room and a log fell in the fireplace sending up a thousand sparks.

"Thank you," said Sarah finally.

"I mean every word," answered Donny Napier, and she saw by the look within his spectacular blue eyes that he spoke nothing but the truth.

The violent assault was like a canker, slowly spreading its poison, affecting Sidonie more dramatically than she would have thought possible. All the practical things had been done at once but they had merely been like papering over cracks. No amount of changed locks, extra bolts, peepholes and chains could ever make her feel the same about the Garden Flat. It was as if Nigel had attempted rape on her home as well as herself, for now its peace, its lovely atmosphere, was gone, rudely shattered by the fact that Sidonie's past had caught up with her present. And the thought that if he could manage to get in once, he could do it again, haunted her constantly.

Her physical hurts had healed quickly under Finnan's sure touch, and that same sure touch had at last brought Sidonie into the full bloom of grown-up love, no toyboys, no fears or tricks, just unashamed happiness in her lover's company and bed. In fact the only thing spoiling an otherwise perfect time for them both was that they were presently away quite a lot, he giving lectures on his Canadian research project, she playing at various music festivals in Britain, France and Italy.

Returning from the airport when the doctor was not at home brought its own kind of nightmare to Sidonie. She would run from her car in the darkness, often carrying a case, rush into her flat, close the front door – then wonder if she was alone. But there had been no sign of Nigel since that terrible night and she guessed that the police visit had worried him, that in his sober moments he could see the terrible trouble he was bringing on himself.

"Is there nothing you can do?" Rod had said when she told him about the incident.

"Not while his friends are going to give him alibis, no."

"You're sure it was him?"

"Don't start that. Yes, I'm positive. Honestly, Rod, I think he's flipped, as they say. He's drinking things and sniffing things and God alone knows what else."

"Can't you threaten to expose him to his constituency party?"

"I thought of that. But until I can actually *prove* something, would they listen?"

Rod had made a face. "No, I suppose not. What a bugger. You need a heavy."

"I can't afford one."

"Then get married. Once you're another man's property our Nige will soon lose interest."

"I shall never be anyone's property as you put it."

"Oh stop being so bloody feminist. You know what I mean."

She had laughed and he had rolled his Italian eyes. "Are those my agent's instructions, to get married?"

"They most certainly are."

"I'll pass the message on."

But she hadn't and just a tiny bit of that old feeling, that old uncertainty about exactly where she and Finnan were going, had returned.

'But I mustn't let it,' she thought. 'Things are so perfect, so blissful, I mustn't allow a single thing to spoil it for me.'

But it was too late. The thought was in her head and there was no way that it would come out again. All she wished was that Finnan would come back from whatever medical conference he was attending so that she could put it to him that the time had come for them to make some kind of decision about the future.

To take her mind off all the things that needed sorting out, Sidonie picked up her much loved copy of *The Life and Letters of Lady Sarah Lennox* and turned to a letter which she always enjoyed reading.

It was from Hove, near Brighthelmstone, 9th April, 1781, and said:

"If my affection for you, my dear Lady Susan, was to be measured by the regularity of my correspondence, *j'aurais mauvaise grace à y prétendre*, but I trust it is not; for I could not very well give any tolerable reason for never writing to you for a whole winter, when I've so very often thought of you and talked of you with my daughter. I have passed this whole winter within two miles of Brighthelmstone for the benefit of sea bathing, partly for Louisa's and my health, but still more out of a desire of being useful to my brother and the Duchess, who have a little *protégée* whom they are mighty fond of, and to whom winter bathing was necessary. As she was too ill to trust her with servants I offered my services, and accordingly have now passed seven months here. I have been very well repaid for my trouble by the pleasure of being of use to the little girl, who is quite recovered, otherwise my *séjour* has not been remarkably pleasant; to a person who like

481

me has no society or acquaintance but her near relations, to be separated from them is the greatest solitude. But although Brighton has had a tolerable number of people in it continually, yet I've never mixed in the society there, and by walking about a great deal I've become personally acquainted with a number of *faces* and *names* whom I know no more of.

My spirits are by no means good but I still prefer the greatest solitude to company I do not *love*; for I must more than *like* my company to be perfectly comfortable."

Sidonie put the book down. Two hundred years earlier, Sarah Lennox had discovered what Sidonie had finally done since Finnan's return. To be perfectly, utterly comfortable with someone it really was necessary to love them.

It had indeed been a long lonely winter by the ocean, in fact the reclusiveness had seemed worse than ever. She and Louisa, together with little Maria Grey, one of the Duke of Richmond's brood of bastards, had gone for long walks along the endless beach, watching the cold sea relentlessly shifting. It had seemed to Sarah as she had gazed out to the distant horizon that she was looking at the rest of her life, stretching on and on, always icy, always the same, and that if it had not been for the company of her charming child, grown no prettier to look at but such a dear good creature, she may as well have thrown herself headlong into that selfsame ocean and allowed it to drag her down to its silent depths.

There had been no word from Donny Napier, doing his best to restore a career in Ireland, other than a letter at Christmas which had been forwarded on from Sarah's home. She had written back, giving her address in Hove, but he had not written further and Sarah had presumed that he had met some solitary Irish widow and thrown in his lot with hers, and wondered why the idea of that plunged her into such gloom.

The one bright thing during those long chilly months had been the joy of watching Louisa develop into a delightful girl. Still only twelve years old, Sarah's daughter was none the less treated as grown-up and received many invitations to visit. At present she was in London staying with Sir Charles Bunbury whom she always addressed as Papa. The love of this child had brought about the final mellowing in his attitude towards his former wife, and Sarah was filled with a great sense of relief that Charles and Mrs Soame, his married sister, were taking Louisa out and about in Society just as if she really were their daughter and niece. Her mother's fears that the innocent child might suffer her same fate of ostracism had been allayed. Yet Louisa's absences made for even lonelier times and Sarah could not wait for the day when the doctors pronounced her small bastard niece finally cured and she could go home to her dear little house.

It was April again, the days bright as a daffodil, the evening sea soft with the shade of bluebells. Walking along the beach, both of them carrying their shoes, Sarah and Maria would look for shells or stop to examine an interesting rock pool, their tiny world totally absorbed with trivia. But destiny was ready now, the wheel of fortune had turned, the time had come at long last for Sarah to be set free.

Looking up from staring at a small crab, Maria said, "There's a man waving at us, Aunt. Look."

She lifted her head and thought she must be dreaming, for Donny Napier, dressed in the uniform of a captain, was striding towards them calling out a greeting. Life flowed into her veins like fire and Sarah, throwing propriety to the winds, started to run to meet him. And he must have been in the same mad mood as she, for as they drew level Donny picked Sarah up by the waist and lifted her high in the air.

"Oh gracious," she said, laughing and breathless, "I am so very pleased to see you."

"And I you, believe me."

"Is this sheer chance, Captain, or had you come to find me?"

"I'm on leave from my regiment. I went to your house but they told me you were still in Hove. The landlady of your lodging directed me to the beach."

"It's wonderful to see you," she said earnestly, taking hold of his arm. "It's been very dull here with only the two young people for company. I should so enjoy a little adult conversation for a change."

"Then will you dine with me tonight? I have booked into a lodging close to yours."

"Louisa's not with you?"

"I left her behind in Dublin, she's very happy there."

"Then provided my landlady can watch over Maria I shall gladly accept."

"Is your Louisa not here?"

"No, she's in London enjoying herself."

"Then let it be hoped her mother can do the same now that I've come to relieve the boredom."

It was just as if they had not parted at all, as though it was the same April evening on which they had originally met.

"Has a whole year passed since last we saw each other?" asked Donny as they walked back to the lodging house.

"About that I believe," Sarah answered, almost casually, not telling him that the past twelve months had seemed like a decade, that she had never in all the time of her penance known the hours drag by so wearily.

"Then I reckon we need to make up for the time we have lost," said Donny Napier and, catching her hand, raised it to his lips.

Maria settled for the evening, they hired a chaise to take them into Brighthelmstone, where they dined in some small, rather deserted, pleasure gardens. But it did not matter, nothing did, because they were laughing together and all the terrible times through which both of them had passed seemed to be diminished by their rekindled friendship.

Each drank a little too much wine in order to overcome their nervousness, but it was Donny, somewhat flushed, who finally said, "You'll never know how hard I've worked to achieve this moment."

"What do you mean?"

"That I strived to get my captaincy not just to give Louisa a future but also that I might come and see you."

"But you could have visited me whatever your position in life."

Donny covered Sarah's hand with his. "May I confess something to you, my Lady?"

"Of course."

"When we first met all those years ago I was a married man."

"Yes, I remember."

"And I had to remind myself of it frequently at the time."

Sarah could feel a slow warmth creeping up her neck and towards her cheeks. Somewhat shakily she said, "I don't follow you."

"I was enormously attracted to you on sight, Lady Sarah. I thought you were the most beautiful, intelligent, vivacious woman I had ever set my eyes on but was hardly in a position to do anything about it."

Sarah gazed at him in silence, her heart quickening its beat.

"If I had been single," Donny went on, the words pouring out now, "I would have fallen in love with you. In fact, though I did love Elizabeth very much, I realised then that my feelings for her were different. She was a warm fire, you were the fireworks. Do you understand what I am saying?"

"I think so."

"But now my circumstances are changed. I am free to speak my mind at last."

"Have you come all the way to England just to say this to me?"

"Yes, by God, I have. When you have been as near to death as I you realise there is precious little time left for any of us. I only waited until I had some position in life, however meagre. But now there isn't a moment to lose. I am here, Lady Sarah, with the express intention of declaring myself."

"Then promise me one thing, I beg you."

"Which is?"

"To study me closely before you commit yourself. I am a woman with a past, Captain Napier. A woman who has been divorced. Before you say another word I want you to think carefully about all of those things."

Donny leant across the table and kissed Sarah on the lips. "I promise to do so."

"Then may we just spend the next few days as friends?"

"Friends or lovers," answered Captain Napier, "just to be in your company is enough for me."

It was hardly possible to believe that Rod Rees was getting married, but the invitation was abundantly clear. "Cressida Cartwright and Roderick Rees invite you to their wedding at Kensington Register Office and afterwards at Rod's flat." There followed addresses and the date.

'And throughout the land there was a multitude of raised eyebrows,' thought Sidonie and, picking up the phone, dialled her agent's number.

"You could have knocked me over with a feather. Rod, who *is* Cressida Cartwright?"

"My fiancée."

"Yes, I realise that. I mean where did you meet her and how long have you known her?"

"The answers are, in the supermarket, and three months."

"Good gracious."

"Our eyes met over some cod steaks as we patiently queued at the fish counter and we got chatting. After that, it was downhill all the way."

"Is she a musician?"

"Heaven forbid! No, she's a lawyer, a barrister to be precise. Australian, very easy-going."

'She'd have to be,' thought Sidonie but refrained from saying so. "Well, I can't wait to meet her. Will you bring her to lunch next Sunday?"

"I will consult her."

"Good. I'll invite Finnan too."

"Have you proposed to him yet?"

"No."

"Then get on with it."

"Cressida Cartwright, Rod's pure delight, right?" Sidonie whispered to the doctor five minutes after the Australian had arrived.

"She's got his number."

"I'll say."

The barrister was large, cheerful, friendly and nearing

forty. She also had the delightful trick of ignoring Rod at his most lunatic, literally not seeming to notice, and was fresh as a daisy on the cynical London scene.

"I adore your flat," she said enthusiastically, doing a tour of inspection. "Hey, Rod, we must get a place like this. It's fantastic. Sidonie, if ever you're moving put me top of your list."

"Yes, I will."

"And so near Holland Park. It's ideal."

"What's wrong with my place?" said her fiancé, slightly hurt.

"It's great for one, sweetie. But the two of us would get stuck if we met in the bathroom, and though I grant you that could prove interesting, how the hell would we get to work?"

"And there you have it in a nutshell," commented Finnan.

"I just love your voice," Cressida answered him enthusiastically. "As far as I'm concerned you could talk all night. Though, on second thoughts, that could eventually get boring."

"You're a tonic," said Sidonie, and was sincere.

After lunch they went for a walk, Rod very reluctantly, while Cressida enthused over Holland Park gardens and what was left of Holland House.

"I bet that was some place in its day."

"Oh, it was. It has a very interesting history."

Cressida gave a large friendly smile. "So have I. I've never been married but I've got a little bastard. A girl aged ten actually."

"Is she with you?"

"Oh, yes. My relies would have taken her but I thought too much of her to let her go. I pay a fortune to nannies but it's worth it."

"Does Rod get on with her?"

"He thinks she's the bee's blooming knees."

"I thought he disliked children."

"He does – all but the ones he's friendly with."

"You," answered Sidonie, meaning every word of it, "are going to do that man a power of good."

"Yes, I think so," Cressida answered artlessly.

After they'd gone and it was getting dark, Sidonie put some more wood on the open fire which she'd had restored in the living room and snuggled onto the sofa, realising that these days she only felt relaxed in the Garden Flat when Finnan was there.

"I think Rod's met his match," she called to where the Irishman was getting a drink.

"Hasn't he just. Funny that, it must be catching."

"What?"

"Meeting one's match. You see, I've recently met the right girl too."

She felt so sick, Sidonie believed she was going to be ill, but she controlled herself and said, "Oh?"

"It happened about three weeks ago."

"At a conference?"

"No."

Thinking it was like a bizarre guessing game, Sidonie said, "I suppose she's come to work at St Mary's."

"No, the truth is she rushed into my flat in the middle of the night with her face knocked to blazes, her tights all torn and her rapier bent, and I suddenly saw her properly for the first time."

Sidonie gazed at him, speechless.

"That was the moment, darling girl, when I knew I really loved you, when, had we lived in a different age, I would have happily shot our fat friend and laughed as I did it. But nothing's for nothing. It took nearly a year apart and a violent assault to show me, fool that I've been, that what's past is past and the future is all one should concentrate on. Sidonie, does your career mean everything to you?"

"No, you silly bugger," she shouted, launching herself at him. "Because I'm greedy, I want it all. You, children, music, the lot. Finnan – " she dropped on one knee, " – will you marry me?"

"By God and the saints on high," he answered, "I thought you'd never ask."

That week together at Hove had, as much as the presence

of young Maria would allow, been a hothouse of suppressed passion. Two people, one of whom had been chaste for many years, the other several, finally made love to one another on their last night together. And what had been so wonderful, so immensely reassuring, was that once that was done both of them knew they could never part again, that magic had been created between them.

"Oh, Sarah," said Donny, stretching the long lean length of him in a contented sigh, "I never realised, innocent that I was, that it could be like this."

"To be honest I had almost forgotten," she answered, her body aching with the joy of long awaited fulfilment.

"This may be the most terrible place to ask but I simply can't help that. Sarah, I have loved you as a person for years, now at long last I love you as a mistress. Will you grant me the greatest favour of all and let me love you as a wife?"

She looked at him very candidly. "Donny, I am seven years older than you are. When you are fifty I shall be staring sixty in the face."

"You look younger than I do and always will, that's my answer to that."

"But neither of us has any money to speak of. We shall be as poor as mice."

"I've endured poverty before. It can't be any worse the second time around."

"But you hardly know me. In all we have probably only met a dozen times."

"It's more than that, I've counted each meeting. But that apart I am acquainted with you well enough to judge your character. You're honest and open and loving and kind. What more could a man ask for?"

"But what about my sordid past?"

"What about our divine future?"

"Listen to me," she answered firmly, "you are about to make a commitment for life. Please think carefully."

"I'll ask you one question," Donny said, propping himself on an elbow the better to look at her. "Do you love me, Lady Sarah?"

"With all my heart, you good sweet man."

"Then if that is so I have not the least doubt of our being happy, come poverty, come age, come every other objection you are trying to put in the way."

"But – "

"No buts. I adore you, you foolish woman. I could never regret marrying you. It is the thing I want most in all the world. And the idea isn't new, you know. In my dreams I've been thinking about it for years. As for your past, to hell with it. Now are you going to marry me or not?"

"Oh yes," she answered, snuggling close to him, feeling the blessed warmth of his body close to hers. "Yes, yes, yes, a hundred times. My brother will be against it, so will Susan, but I don't give a damn."

"There speaks the little renegade of long ago, now grown into the most perfect woman ever to walk the earth."

"Donny Napier, I vow and declare you have become a serpent-toothed flatterer."

"All the better with which to bite the apple," the Captain answered her, and drew the woman he loved into his arms knowing as he did so that both of them had finally sailed into safe harbour.

# Thirty-four

All things considered, the Duke of Richmond had got into mighty high stirrup over the whole affair. Not content with telling Sarah that Captain Napier was far too young for her, he went on to enumerate all the disadvantages of such a disastrous match, the main one of which seemed to be leaving the home that he, the Duke, had built especially for her and launching into the unknown with a penniless soldier. Susan, duly primed, wrote a letter in the same vein using almost the same words, trying Sarah's patience to the full. To her credit she had written back in the most reasonable terms.

"As for me, my dear Lady Susan, my situation is easily understood. I have every advantage by living with my dearest brother that is possible to have, but the affection I have for Mr Napier, the gratitude I feel for his excess of partiality to me, the pleasure of being so sincerely loved, and the hopes of that pleasantest of all societies, which a married person only can enjoy, tempts me to give up the present comfort for the future."

Donny had proposed in May, then had returned to Ireland to fetch his child and wind up his affairs there. It was his intention, now that Sarah had agreed to marry him, to stay by her side until he got her to the altar. However, at the very moment the storm broke, he was away and Sarah was left to face the wrath of her brother alone.

"You're well off, Sal, with a house of your own and everything you could wish for. Why risk all when you may lose all?"

"Because I'm in love, Charles. A sentiment not unknown to yourself surely?"

"Love, pah! Where has love got you in the past, eh? Into nothing but dire trouble."

"But I'm older now."

"Older and no wiser. If you marry Napier you'll live to regret it."

"You are entitled to your opinion."

"Indeed I am, and so strongly do I hold it that I wash my hands of the entire affair."

"But surely you will not try to stop my final bid for happiness?"

"I intend to do nothing, either for or against. Let those of the family fool enough to support you, do so."

And with those words, the Duke of Richmond had turned to the papers on his desk, signalling that the meeting was at an end.

In this way, May 1781 passed rather dismally but early in June Donny and his daughter came back, booking into lodgings near Sarah, and their marriage plans finally began to take shape. It was arranged, as the Duke would not be present at the wedding, that Lady Louisa Conolly would act as head of the family, with Lady Emily and Lady Albermarle lending their support. It was also decided that both daughters ought to be in church and that Sarah should go up the aisle on the arm of her brother-in-law, Thomas. The only thing still to be fixed was the day itself. Donny was all for a date in June but Sarah preferred to leave things until the Duke of Richmond had gone abroad for the summer. This was the only disagreement between two people so happy in each other's company that sheer raw joy communicated itself to everyone else in their presence.

"But why the delay, Sarah? Your brother wouldn't make a scene surely?"

"No, no. It's just that I would feel happier if he were safely out of the way."

"Am I then so detestable to him?"

"He is merely worried about our financial position, that is all."

"He's not alone there," Donny had answered gloomily. "It is *your* family's reaction that is more to the point. I could imagine them shuddering in horror at the thought of your involvement with a woman of my reputation."

"On the contrary. They said, with one voice, that I was old enough and ugly enough to know what I was doing and they wished me all the luck in the world."

"How very refreshing," Sarah had answered with feeling. "The trouble with certain members of my clan, and I include friends amongst that number, is that they are too materialistic. Money is their god."

Donny had grinned, his hawkish face lively. "I would subscribe to the same religion but it's difficult to worship a deity you know nothing about."

"If we talk finances we'll both end up wretched," Sarah had stated, then added impulsively, "so let's go to London for a week and stay with Lady Albermarle in her town house. It would be such fun. We might even visit a theatre or two."

"Agreed," he had answered, just as impetuous as she was. "If you won't marry me at least we can sleep under the same roof."

"And under the same sheets?"

"That remains to be seen."

So they had set off in mid-June, the weather delightful, quite unprepared for the shock to both of them, grown so used to space around them, of seeing how crowded London had become, how dirty and noisy.

"Did I once mingle happily here?" Sarah had asked, almost dazedly.

"You were younger in those days."

"Don't remind me!"

They had laughed then, at terms with the difference in their ages, Donny utterly captivated by this older woman who, for him, embodied all that he found attractive and intriguing in female kind.

"I think," said Sarah certainly, "that we should spend at least one night at an inn in Kensington during this stay. I would so much like you to get a glimpse of Holland House before we leave."

"Your girlhood home?"

"Oh, yes. Donny, it was marvellous, we young people had such glorious larks. There must be so many memories packed within those walls."

"Did you say it was now let out to tenants?"

"Yes, and will remain so until poor little Henry Holland attains his majority."

"And you would prefer not to call?"

"When last I did so Lord Rosebery chose to be out. I would rather we surveyed it from a distance."

"Well, I am prepared to brave them, but if that is your wish."

"It is, my darling, it is."

"Then so be it, Sarah. But know that I am ready to face the world on your behalf."

He loved her so much it was painful to witness and she kissed him for his loyalty.

"Has there ever been a love such as ours?"

"Never since time began," answered Donny, and knew that it was because they had both known so much hardship, so much of life's enormous cruelty, that the fineness of their devotion tasted so very very sweet.

With what alacrity, and indeed with what relief, had Sidonie taken to spending her nights and evenings in the flat upstairs. In a sense, she supposed, she had moved in with the man she was going to marry, it was as simple as that. But in reality she was also taking refuge from the fear of being alone after dark in a place which even now, despite all the precautions, felt vulnerable to Nigel's attack.

Yet, though she might consider herself safe at night, there were the daylight hours for Sidonie to contend with. Her music room, her precious harpsichord, still with the letter from George III hidden inside it, were all in the Garden Flat and, though she might technically be living with Finnan, the very nature of her work took Sidonie back home daily.

His lecture tour was nearing its end, as much as it ever would, initial questions about the Canadian findings having mostly been answered. But still there came the odd time when he had to be away overnight, and it was on these occasions that Sidonie was particularly glad to stop practising early and go upstairs for the rest of the evening. Sometimes she would ask Jannie down for a chat, sometimes she would simply watch television, but mostly Sidonie would just relax in the comfort of Finnan's surroundings, enjoying getting into his bed, even without him in it, just to be close to the essence of him.

Tonight though, with another Wigmore Hall engagement looming up, booked by Rod the moment he had read her French reviews, Sidonie knew that she must steel herself to practise till eight o'clock when, out of courtesy to the neighbours, she would have to stop. So it was with much gritting of teeth, the knowledge that Finnan was in Edinburgh and would not be back till tomorrow nagging in the back of her mind, that she stayed on in the music room trying to ignore the fact that it would be dark by four.

In common with most London parks, Holland Park closed at dusk, but Holland Walk, as a public walkway, remained open, and try as she would Sidonie could not get out of her thoughts the fact that only the garden separated her from the place where anyone could be loitering, that it was through the music room the intruder had made his entry before. To forget her anxieties, to let music consume her to the point where she dismissed everything else, seemed hopeless this evening. There was a pricking at Sidonie's spine, a ghastly feeling of unease she simply couldn't shake off. Determined not to give in to it until she had to, she went to the kitchen and made herself a cup of coffee, then found herself hard put to it to go back down the stairs to the music room.

"Did I ever tell you about the time I met Count Alexei Orlov?" Donny was saying.

"Catherine the Great's lover? No, you didn't."

"I was briefly in St Petersburg with my regiment and encountered him at a dinner party. Well, I am six foot two, as you know, but the Count is so enormous that I could stand upright under his outstretched arm. He's a veritable giant of a fellow."

"No doubt that appeals to Madame the Empress."

"Are you being rude?"

"Yes, very."

"Tut, tut," said Donny, and pulled her close to him.

They had borrowed a vis-à-vis from Lady Albermarle's

stable but, in a highly irregular manner, had dispensed with the services of a coachman and were sitting packed tightly together on the box, the reins in Captain Napier's firm grip. Having left London on the previous day, the couple had spent a leisurely night at an inn in Kensington Village and were now on their way, in the late afternoon, to see Holland House, albeit covertly and from the discreet distance of the drive.

"Are you sure you will not call?" asked Donny for the dozenth time.

"Positive."

"Then how far up the drive should we go?"

"I think to the carriage sweep. We can linger a few moments for you to take in the scene. After all, we are doing no harm."

"But what about the gate keeper?"

"He is still employed by the Holland estate and will certainly open up for us. Here, let me take the reins. He ought to recognise me even after all this time."

"Won't he think it very unorthodox?"

"To see me driving? Oh Donny, don't be so stuffy. Susan and I used to race gigs up and down the elm drive when we had half a chance. He's used to it."

"A far cry from sobersides Scotland," Captain Napier answered wryly.

"If you don't watch out I'll take you up at a canter," warned Sarah as they drew to a halt before the massive gates leading to the house and parklands.

"I'd put nothing past you," sighed her fiancé, feigning despair, yet smiling as Sarah called cheerily to the gate keeper and his wife who bowed and waved with enthusiasm before slowly swinging the mighty portals open.

It had become something of a contest between Sidonie's intellect and intuition. Physically, she knew that there was nothing to fear. She had been round the entire flat checking the windows, each with its own security lock, and putting the chains on the front and music room doors. She had even ventured down the garden, her heart thumping painfully, to make sure that the bolts were shot, the key turned, in the garden door. Yet still, despite all this, feeling like a neurotic New Yorker, Sidonie could not shed the symptoms of fear.

It would have been easier by far to have admitted defeat, to have given up the practice session and gone upstairs but, though she was certain it would eventually come to this, something perverse, something Taurean in her nature would not allow Sidonie to do so until she could not stand the strain a second longer.

"If you give in now you'll never come back," she said to the empty room, and the silence flowed towards her in answering folds.

She had managed to return with her coffee mug and had embarked on Handel, but he had proved too much for her and she had retreated to the Earl of Kelly. Yet her ears were straining over the music she was making and it seemed to her that she could hear the feet of the people moving along Holland Walk, that every sound from the drowsy park had been magnified a million times to ears suddenly sensitive to even a spider's scurry.

And then, above it all, Sidonie heard Nigel's footsteps coming through the park, closing in on her where she waited, trapped and alone. It was impossible, of course, but the impression, ridiculous though it was, was so strong that she jumped to her feet in alarm and would have rushed upstairs to the other flat had the telephone not rung. Thinking it was Finnan, almost weeping with relief, Sidonie went to answer it.

How strange is memory! Tilting her head back to look from the vis-à-vis as it bowled along the elm avenue's impressive length, Sarah could see that the trees were just as fine and noble as she had remembered them, that the approach to the house she held more dear than any other in the world, was indeed the grandest she had ever beheld.

"Do you like it?" she said to Donny.

"It is one of the most beautiful prospects imaginable. What a mighty place. How lucky you are to have spent so many years here before everything came to an end."

"It will live again," she replied certainly. "I feel in my

very bones that the great days of Holland House are not yet over."

"It would be tragic if they were." Captain Napier looked upwards. "I think there's going to be a storm. We'd better hurry."

"Oh, but we must get as near as we can before we go back," Sarah answered him as the first droplets of rain began to fall and a cloud made the day suddenly and ominously dark.

"Yes, I would like to see the house close to," Donny said as the equipage bowled on.

The terrible thing was that one part of his brain continued to function normally, observing all he did in a cold and critical way. Yet, like a trapped prisoner, it was impotent, unable to exercise any control over the other. His censor, for that was how Nigel thought of it, could watch, could even warn, but had no power over all the other teeming emotions released when he had consumed just the right combination of drink and drugs.

He had got into Holland Park by the easiest way of all, simply going down the path leading to the youth hostel then cutting round behind it, making his way past the back of Holland House, bending low so that he wasn't seen by any of the inmates. In a way he was shut into the park, his only exit by the route he had used to come in, but tonight he was in a mood for challenge and Nigel intended to take a circuitous path, ending up in Holland Walk from where he would then go and attend to Sidonie.

He knew that she still wanted him sexually, that all her play-acting about hatred and fear was just to stimulate him even more, to turn him on, to use a vulgarism. And if only she knew how well she had succeeded. He, who had been homosexual at school, bisexual at university, and straight only with her, had never known desire like it. He wanted her so much he could have screamed with the pain of it and believed, though his censor warned him he might be mistaken in this, that one good coupling, one hard roger, was all it would take to bring Sidonie running back to him, gasping for more. Grinning, Nigel rounded the corner of the ruined house, feeling himself beginning to be ready for sex.

It was Jane Brooks on the other end of the line and Sidonie hardly knew how to control her voice.

"Is anything wrong, darling? You sound a bit odd."

"I'm very tired. I think I've been overworking."

"Then take the evening off."

"I'm going to. I'm just on my way upstairs."

"I rang that number but got the answerphone. Is Finnan out?"

"He's away, lecturing in Scotland. He'll be back tomorrow."

"I'm so happy about everything. Daddy and I were most impressed with him, you know."

How to cut her short without hurting her feelings? "Mummy, I think there's someone at the door. I'll have to go. Listen, I'll ring you back in an hour. O.K.?"

"Of course, darling. Take care. See who it is then go and put your feet up."

"I will. 'Bye."

After she had replaced the receiver, Sidonie stood in the hall, listening to the sound of her heart, and then, instead of running for it, went back down to the music room determined that if Nigel were coming for her she would finally trap him, call the police and reveal him for what he really was. Carefully taking the other, the portable phone, from its cradle, Sidonie crept downstairs to lie in wait.

"There," said Sarah triumphantly, "is it not splendid?"

They had stopped in the carriage sweep, the west wicket gate in the railings protecting the house being open, presumably for when Lord Rosebery returned home, and had come close to the steps leading up to the great courtyard.

"Even in the rain it's one of the most magnificent places I've ever seen," Donny answered satisfyingly, and Sarah loved him all the more for his boyish enthusiasm.

But it had begun to pour hard and much as she would have liked to linger it was foolish to stay and risk a soaking.

"Let's head back to the inn," she called over a sudden unexpected clap of thunder.

"Shall I take the reins?"

"No, let me. I know every pothole in the drive. I'll get you there twice as fast."

And with that Sarah swept the carriage round the other side of the half-moon, out through the east wicket and back into the avenue, picking up speed as she went.

"How free I feel," she said impetuously, and, standing up and pulling her hat from her head, Sarah laughed with sheer exhilaration as the horses sped along.

The sleeping park was alive with sounds, the rustle of insects, the call of nightbirds, the ever present traffic from the High Street, and over them all other unidentifiable noises, noises that were just a part of night in London, the vaguely menacing throb of a choking metropolis as darkness covered its many secrets.

Yet though Nigel heard it all, his mind was full of Sidonie and the pleasure that lay ahead when the ecstasy of entry was his. To keep himself high he drank vodka from a hip flask as he proceeded over the green expanse lying in front of the ruined house. It was used for cricket these days, football at the further end, and yet to him, in his drunken state, it seemed like a big lush meadow where he could ride for ever, until time ran out in fact, astride some great black horse that would take him on to the end of the world.

Then suddenly, over all the other sounds, he could hear the creature's hooves and knew that it was coming to meet him, and was glad. He would arrive at Sidonie's door on its back and sweep her up into the saddle and take her with him to a place where he need do nothing but make love from morning till night.

"Oh, God," he murmured, full of violent desire.

The horse was very near now, he could hear its stamp and snort, smell the scent of its harness, its flesh.

"But there are no horses in Holland Park," said Nigel's censor.

"Balls," answered the real Nigel, the powerful Nigel whom

Sidonie loved and always would. But for all that he turned to look.

They were upon him, two stallions, jet dark and powerful, great plumes on their heads, and harnesses gleaming like silver moons. A woman drove them, a woman standing where there should have been a coachman, a woman whose black hair streamed out round her head like that of an avenging angel.

Nigel saw her gaze at him, eyes huge with terror; saw a man in a red coat leap to his feet; saw the great high wheels of a carriage. And then there was nothing except darkness and a profound and incredible silence.

She was driving like the wind, the two black stallions from Lady Albermarle's stable racing down the elm drive almost symbolically, as if they epitomised Sarah's fresh-found energy, her wish to start a new life, her urgent need to escape from all the trappings of the past.

"Go on, go on," she called, the wind whipping her hair – and it was then that she saw something. A man was standing in the tree-lined avenue, the oval of his face turned towards her, his mouth open like a buffoon's, his eyes wide and staring.

"Christ!" said Donny and leapt to his feet, snatching the reins from her hands and pulling back the horses with every ounce of his might. The terrified animals swerved to the right but not before the occupants of the carriage felt the sickening thud of impact and knew that the man in the drive had gone down beneath their wheels.

"Oh, God, oh, God," shrieked Sarah, "what have I done? What have I done?" And she started to scream.

"Control yourself," snapped Captain Napier, and he could have been addressing a field of raw soldiers. "That won't do anyone any good. Get a grip."

There was a grinding crunch as the horses reared to a panting halt, and then Donny jumped down from the box in a leap so swift that Sarah, despite the horror and panic, thought she had never seen anyone quite so agile. Then he was running, away from her and the carriage, back up the drive. With a mighty effort, her heart pounding in great thumps, her legs so weak she could scarcely move, Sarah began to clamber down.

She caught up with the Captain some minutes later, on his hands and knees, crawling amongst the trees, his face ashen with anxiety.

"There's no sign of him," he said, without looking up.

"Was he not lying where we hit him?"

"No, nor was there any indication he'd been there. No blood, nothing. He must have crawled into the undergrowth. Search, Sarah, quickly. The poor bastard needs help."

She dropped to her knees with a will, ripping her dress as she searched through the trees to the east of the drive. But there was no glimpse of anyone and after an hour, during which it grew consistently darker and wetter, Sarah went to look for Donny. He was standing in the drive soaked to the skin, as was she, his hair escaping from its bow, hanging in strands.

"It's a mystery," he said, shaking his head, perplexed. "It's just as if he's vanished, as if he wasn't there at all. Yet a man hit as hard as that couldn't have got far."

"I thought I'd killed him."

"To be honest so did I."

"What should we do?"

"Report the matter to the gate keeper. He can tell them in the big house. They may well want to organise a search tomorrow when it's light."

"We'd better stay in the area for a day or two."

"Quite right," said the military man. "Now come along, my darling. I can't have you catching your death."

She shivered. "Donny, *did* I kill someone today?"

Again he shook his head. "I simply don't know. I could have sworn that there was a man directly in our path and yet it would have been impossible for him to disappear like that. Perhaps we both saw a phantom."

"Perhaps," Sarah said slowly, "he was an echo of another age."

The danger was over, she knew it. Intangibly, indescribably, the atmosphere in the Garden Flat, the stinging, terrifying fear which had come like darts of electricity, had subsided. Even more, the apartment's ambience had returned to what it used to be, harmonious and peaceful, before the night of Nigel's shattering intrusion. Yet in place of Sidonie's terror there had come an overwhelming sadness and for no explicable reason she had found herself compelled to go to the harpsichord and play the most solemn music she knew.

'It's a requiem,' she thought, but could think of no logical reason why.

She must have fallen asleep after that, for the next thing she knew was that the front door bell was ringing, there was daylight flooding through the curtain cracks, and she was curled up on the sofa in front of the television. Blearily, wondering what on earth the time could be, Sidonie went up the music room stairs to answer the door. Two police constables stood there, one male, one female. She gazed at them stupidly, unable to get her thoughts together.

"Miss Sidonie Brooks?" asked the man.

"Yes."

"May we come in a minute, please?"

"Yes. What time is it?"

"Eight o'clock. Sorry to disturb you so early but we have some rather distressing news."

They stood in the hall looking young and Sidonie, catching sight of herself in a mirror, felt old enough to be their mother.

She woke up a little. "Nothing's happened to Dr O'Neill?"

"No, Madam. I believe you are acquainted with a Mr Nigel Beltram."

"He's my ex-husband. Why?"

"Well, he was found in Holland Park earlier this morning. There had been an accident."

"What kind of accident? Is he dead?"

"I'm afraid so."

Suddenly it was very necessary to sit down, not so much because of the shock but because she had known it, had sensed his going, had played for his passing out of life. The arm of the WPC was round her and Sidonie was sitting in the kitchen, her head between her knees, almost before she knew it.

"How did it happen?" she asked faintly.

Officialdom bristled. "The cause of death has not yet been established, Madam. There is to be a post mortem tomorrow."

"But people don't die just like that. Was he mugged?"

"We cannot say at this time. We will keep you informed. You have no plans to leave London?"

This last said very casually but the underlying meaning quite clear.

"No," Sidonie answered with just a hint of bitterness. "I'll be around. If you don't find me here I'll be upstairs with Dr O'Neill. We live together," she added defiantly.

The WPC put her face close to Sidonie's. "Will you be all right now? Have you got a neighbour you could go to?"

"I have but she'll be off to work. No, I'll be fine." A thought struck her. "You won't want me to do the identification, will you?"

"No, Madam. We're asking Mr Beltram's brother to help with that."

"Thank God."

"Yes. Well, good morning."

She saw them out then crawled upstairs and sat in Finnan's living room, willing him to return home soon. Finally, tears came, beautiful releasing tears, washing away all bad thoughts about the man to whom she had once been married, leaving Sidonie with only an enormous sense of sadness that anyone who had once been young and unspoiled, who had come into the world fresh and ready for life, should have ended it all in a park, in the darkness, not very well loved, not even very well liked.

"Oh, Nigel," she wept, "if it was my fault, forgive me please."

But there was no answer from the silent room, the only sound the noise of the world outside going about its business.

"Quite extraordinary," said the pathologist conducting the post mortem.

"What is?" asked the Detective Inspector assigned to investigate the mysterious death of Nigel Beltram MP.

"Those marks on his body. They look just like wheels."

"Are you saying this man was run over?" the Inspector answered in surprise.

"Not exactly. The cause of death is pretty apparent. He had a massive coronary brought on by drink and drugs abuse. I'll get the contents of the stomach analysed but it looks to me as if he'd consumed enough vodka to drown a Russian and he'd obviously been sniffing cocaine. See the state of his nostrils?"

"Then what are the bruises?"

"I've no idea. They're not tyre marks, either car, bicycle or anything else. Yet they certainly do appear to be wheels of some kind."

The detective, who hated post mortems, steeled himself and leant over the body.

"I've never seen anything quite like them. What can have done it?"

"Pass."

"But you can assure me they are not related to the cause of death?"

"Absolutely. Quite bluntly, the silly bugger killed himself with his own cocktail. The human frame isn't built to withstand that kind of punishment."

"Try telling that to the kids on the street."

"They'll never learn."

The detective scratched his chin. "Those marks are worrying me."

"Well, good luck with them. I honestly haven't got a clue."

"I don't suppose I ever will have either."

"No, I shouldn't think so. Fancy a drink?"

"Yes, good idea."

"Fine, I'll just get cleaned up here. See you in the George."

"Right."

But as the Inspector made his way to the pub, the enigmatic marks on the body of the dead man were still in his mind's eye. The knowledge that, because they were not a cause of death it was not strictly necessary for him to find out what they were, did not comfort him at all. For the fact was that his workload and general lack of manpower would never allow him the time to make any further investigation into what was obviously yet another drug-induced death.

# Thirty-five

For the sake of her sanity, for the sake of the rest of her life, the children she might yet bring into the world, Sarah Lennox had tried desperately to put aside the idea that she might have killed a man, albeit accidentally. For though a thorough search of the grounds, extending to the very borders of the park and farmlands, had revealed nothing, the sight of that buffoon's face turned towards her in sheer and apparent disbelief, still would not go away.

"It was an hallucination," Donny had said firmly. "We imagined it, both of us."

"But the impact – how could that have been caused by something that was not there at all?"

He looked puzzled. "That is the one point I cannot quite get over. But then there's the gamekeeper's theory that it was a poacher, that we must have sent him flying and that he scrambled to his feet and ran away in fright."

"Which do you think is right?"

"The poacher."

"Truly?"

"Truly, my darling. Now put the whole incident out of your mind. If you had killed a man we would have found his body."

"I suppose so," Sarah had answered.

But still the memory haunted her until one day, out of the blue, came the idea that the creature, if he were not of flesh and blood, must somehow be connected with her ghost and that Sarah's original thought that he had merely been an echo was the true explanation. If that were the case then she had done nothing wrong, merely witnessed another strange event amongst all the many others she had experienced in her life.

"Do you believe in ghosts?" she had called out to Donny, busy in another room packing his things in preparation for the wedding and the subsequent removal to London.

"No, of course not." He had appeared in the doorway. "Why, do you?"

"You said when we ran over the man that he might have been a phantom."

"I meant a phantom of the brain."

"What is a ghost then?"

"They do not exist."

"Oh boo," she said, as he had turned and gone back to his task. "A ghost is a phantom of the heart."

"What?"

"I said a phantom of the heart, you unfeeling man. And of all the people in the world, believe me, I should know."

For the sake of her sanity, for the sake of the rest of her life, the children she might yet bring into the world, Sidonie Brooks had been forced to put behind her the idea that she might in some way have contributed to Nigel's death. On Finnan's advice, fraught and upset as she was, she had gone for counselling and had indeed felt a great deal better for it. Having been assured that only an inadequate personality would have reacted not only to life but to a wife as her ex-husband had done, that if she had not married him it would have been someone else with whom he would have gone on in precisely the same way, Sidonie began to see things clearly again.

"He was obsessional and that kind of person frequently turns to drink, to drugs, to relieve their tensions. They cannot grasp situations, always seeing them through the wrong end of a telescope."

"Poor creatures."

"They inflict their own wounds, Sidonie. Nobody else does it to them."

"But aren't we all a bit like that? Aren't we all guilty to a certain extent of being our own worst enemy?"

"In varying degrees, yes."

She had gone for a walk after that particular therapy session, and her feet had taken her, without her even noticing, to Holland House. Sidonie had stood in silence looking at the mighty fabric that had withstood so many centuries and thought of all the people who had lived there and how they, too, had been prey to obsessions and fears, to folly and to wisdom, to the million and one pitfalls into which mankind falls daily.

'Nothing changes, nothing ever will,' she thought. 'The most we can possibly hope for is to do our best.'

Had another woman stood on this same spot and thought those thoughts? Had her own beloved ghost philosophised just as she was doing now?

"Oh Sarah, Sarah," whispered Sidonie, "thank you for everything. For introducing me to the Earl of Kelly, for letting me hear how my music really should be played. But most of all, thank you for letting me see you. It has been very special to me."

And Sarah, in the midst of her wedding ceremony, thinking she heard a voice, glanced round at the congregation hoping against hope that she might get a glimpse of red hair. But she saw only old Lady Albermarle nodding contentedly, her sisters Emily and Louisa weeping a little, the two young Louisas clutching their rose petals and rice ready to throw with a will.

But Donny was putting a ring on her finger and she turned to look up at him, smiling, happy beyond words.

"Lady Sarah Napier," he murmured, "my phantom of the heart."

And with that they turned and walked down the ancient aisle of Goodwood Parish Church and out into the August sunshine, the cheers and shouts of their delighted family ringing in their ears.

To escape the cruel glare of the publicity surrounding such harrowing events, they had gone to Ireland at the time of the inquest and subsequent funeral, though Sidonie had sent flowers signed with her initials. Then she had done what she should have done long since and let go of the past, helped back into the present by the warmth and hospitality of the delightful O'Neill family. And, as if this were a signal to fate, when she and Finnan had returned to their respective homes it had been to find that everything had changed, that an entirely new path was opening up before them.

Cressida Cartwright, having transformed Rod into an adoring husband, had been as good as her word and made an offer for the Garden Flat which Sidonie was going to find hard to refuse. A letter from one of the barrister's many solicitor friends was lying on the mat as she walked through the front door. Having read it, Sidonie, somewhat bemused, took it upstairs to show Finnan.

"It's a fabulous offer."

"You'll never see the like again. Let's open some champagne."

"I thought you were saving it for the wedding."

"Plenty more where that came from," he answered. "Listen, I've decided to put my flat on the market too. So, where shall we go to, my pretty Sidonie?"

"Chelsea, Chiswick, anywhere convenient, as long as it's with you."

Finnan refilled her glass. "Prepare for a shock. When I was home something happened to me. I had a severe case of roots. Would living in Ireland suit a classical musician?"

"Perfectly."

"Then I'll start job hunting. If I'm going to change my entire life I might as well go the whole hog."

"What happens if you sell this place quickly?"

"I saw a dear little house to let the other day."

"Where?"

"In Blackheath, on the common itself. It was very romantic and Georgian. I thought it might appeal to you."

"Was it the sort of place Sarah would have lived in?"

"It wouldn't surprise me at all," said Finnan with a laugh, "if it wasn't where she went with her gallant Captain Napier."

"I don't suppose I shall ever find that out."

"Perhaps it's as well not to."

Sidonie sighed. "I shall miss her, you know."

Finnan walked to the window to gaze in the direction of Holland House, then looked back over his shoulder. Sidonie saw that he was smiling.

"I expect that somewhere, even now," he said, "she is missing you too."

# Historical Note

It was in May 1990 that the idea for this book was first suggested to me and, indeed, it started life as a work devoted entirely to George III. However, as I got to know his girlfriend, the irrepressible Lady Sarah Lennox, I grew more and more intrigued with her until, eventually, the balance of the book changed, Sidonie came in and it became Sarah's story rather than the King's.

Sarah's life is well documented through her letters but still one or two questions remain. Firstly, *did* she love George III and, secondly, did he propose to her or not? For the answers we must look to three sources; Henry Fox's account of events, Sarah's letters to Susan and the tale as told by Henry Napier, Sarah's son.

That Sarah was more than capable of lying to Susan is abundantly clear, particularly when she protests too much. A prime example is the letter written when Sarah was expecting a child by Lord William Gordon in which she talks about going on holiday with Sir Charles Bunbury as if nothing was wrong with her marriage.

Bearing this in mind, how much credence should we give Sarah's vehement insistence that she only *liked* the King and did not love him? Furthermore, one gets the impression from Sarah's letters to her best friend that George never actually proposed, whereas Henry Napier tells us, "After her recovery and subsequent appearance in London the King's joy was palpable, his conversations were renewed, his hopes revived, and once again he ventured to say, in allusion to the former conversation, 'I hope you will think of it.' She did so, and accepted him." Which one, we wonder now, is telling us the true facts?

There is no question, however, about the details of Sarah's

promiscuous period, her affairs with Lauzun, Carlisle and Lord William Gordon, her elopement to Scotland, her love child and her divorce are therefore presented in this book exactly as they happened.

Sarah's marriage to Captain the Honourable George Napier (Donny), proved to be a happy one, though throughout their life together they were perpetually short of money. Within the three years following her marriage, Sarah gave birth to three children, Charles, Emily and George. Two years later, William followed, then Richard, Henry, Caroline and Cecilia. Nine children in all, including Louisa Bunbury.

Nothing in Sarah's life was ever quite what she anticipated. She had almost married the King of England and would have probably made a great success of it, but she ended up with a penniless soldier. She was old to start adding to her family when she remarried but had another eight children. Three of her boys became distinguished and heroic soldiers, one was a captain in the navy, another went into the Church and became a Fellow of All Souls. Of her daughters, Emily was adopted by Sarah's childless sister, Louisa Conolly, while three died young; Caroline at the age of nineteen and Cecilia at seventeen, while poor little Louisa Bunbury, she of the big teeth and engaging manner, also died at the age of seventeen years.

And what of the men who loved Sarah? The King, as is well known, became desperately ill, suffering a state described as "madness" but now correctly diagnosed as porphyria by Dr Ida Macalpine and Dr Richard Hunter who published the findings of their extensive research in the *British Medical Journal* in 1966. Porphyria is an hereditary metabolic disorder the onset of which is frequently marked by a heavy cold – the King went down with just such a complaint at the time of Sarah's marriage to Bunbury – and in the worst cases can produce mental aberrations, hallucinations and delusions. The clinching piece of evidence for the two modern doctors was the fact that George III passed urine described as being the colour of port wine or purple, a classic symptom of porphyria, which, they believe, also attacked Mary Stuart, James I, Frederick the Great, George IV, as well as several other of the King's children, and his granddaughter, Princess Charlotte.

Sir Charles Bunbury appointed himself head of the Jockey Club and became immensely influential and genuinely popular. A contemporary wrote of him, "Whatever might be the faults and peccadillos of Sir Charles Bunbury, he was a man naturally benign, of compassionate and friendly disposition, and his plan for treating racehorses, without suffering them to be abused by the whip and spur . . . ought ever to be remembered in his honour." At a meeting at Sir Charles's house on 14th May, 1779, to celebrate the first running of the Oaks, it was decided to start the Derby, the name – a choice between the Derby or Bunbury Stakes – being chosen on the toss of a coin. Sir Charles was one of the few owners to win both the Derby and the Oaks in the same year, 1801.

Lord William Gordon became a fortune-hunter. Having returned from Rome – with or without the very large dog is not recorded – William persuaded his brother, the Duke of Gordon, to take him into his regiment. He then got into Parliament and planned to marry an heiress, a ward in chancery, the Honourable Frances Ingram Stewart. However, the Lord Chancellor ordered Lord William's petition to marry to be dismissed and it was only by making sufficient money through playing faro, thus winning the support of Miss Ingram's mother and sister, that he finally managed to get the bride to the altar. He had one legitimate daughter, Frances, who never married. His illegitimate daughter he never saw again. Interestingly, one of Lord William's kinsmen was George Gordon, Lord Byron.

*The Memoirs of the Duc de Lauzun* were published during Sarah's lifetime, once more bringing scandal in their wake. But Sarah, by this stage, was too old to care. She had outlived Armand, who had taught her about love and introduced her to adultery, his memoirs being published posthumously, presumably by some member of the Duc's intimate circle.

As for Sarah's second husband, George Napier, after years of wandering from home to home in order to accommodate his ever increasing family and with no occupation other than that of a captain on half-pay, he finally came into his own again.

In 1793, the French sent their King, Louis XVI, to the guillotine and Pitt ordered the French Minister to leave the country as England declared war on France. The Honourable George Napier went back on active service, rising through the ranks until in 1794 he once more reached the rank of colonel. After this, Donny remained on duty until his death of "a consumptive complaint" in 1804. Sarah was completely devastated and wrote to Susan that "one week's fever has suddenly destroyed twenty-three years' happiness!"

What became of the others? Louisa Napier, Donny's daughter, remained faithful to Sarah after her father's death but herself died unmarried; Lady Susan O'Brien spent most of her life attempting to find a job for her feckless husband, William, who had tried his hand at everything in America and failed, and had then been filled with an ambition to become a barrister in England, with singular lack of success. Eventually, he became Receiver-General of Taxes for the County of Dorset which no doubt kept everybody happy! William died in 1815 after fifty-one years of unbroken married bliss and equal devotion on both sides, which says a great deal for Susan's patience. She herself followed him in 1827 at the age of eighty-four after only a few days' illness and in full possession of her faculties.

Charles James Fox, after his dismissal in 1774, went into opposition and became leader of the Rockingham Whigs in the House of Commons. His vendetta against George III occupied most of his life, yet no historian I know of appears to have made the connection between the jilting of his youthful aunt, Sarah, and Fox's implacable dislike of the monarch. To me the matter speaks for itself and explains Charles James's Draconian aim to curtail totally the royal power. Fox's alliance with the Prince of Wales, later George IV, who in true Hanoverian tradition was completely at odds with his father, is yet another example of the bitterness the politican felt against the King.

Charles James secretly married his mistress, Mrs Armistead, in 1795. She had been a former lover of the wicked Duke of Dorset, to whose home Knole, near Sevenoaks, Sarah had first fled with Lord William Gordon. In a long parliamentary career, Fox only held high office for less than two years but despite that had two major reforms to his credit, the Libel Act of 1792 and, more importantly, the abolition of the slave trade. A supporter of the American Colonists and the French Revolution, he still thought "both property and rank of great importance". A renegade to the end, Charles James died in 1806.

Sarah outlived all the men who had loved her, including the young Earl of Carlisle, who became Lord Lieutenant of Ireland and later Lord Privy Seal, and died in 1825. She left this world in 1826, completely blind due to a cataract in either eye. Her first love, George, also died blind, also aged eighty-one, in January, 1820. During the previous Christmas he had endured the last onslaught of the royal malady, porphyria, and had talked for a period of fifty-eight consecutive hours without sleeping.

In his excellent biography of George III, Stanley Ayling says, "It may be idle to speculate how differently matters might have turned out if he had allowed himself, or been allowed, to marry his Lady Sarah, that delightful girl who became so charming and intelligent a woman." All one can say, looking back on that pair of fine young people whom destiny brought together then thrust apart so cruelly, is, Who knows?

# Bibliography

*George the Third*, Stanley Ayling.
*Lady Sarah Lennox*, Edith Roelker Curtis.
*Timewarps*, Dr John Gribbin.
*The Life and Letters of Lady Sarah Lennox*, edited by the Countess of Ilchester.
*The Home of the Hollands, 1606–1820*, the Earl of Ilchester.
*The Sword Dance*, Priscilla Napier.
*The Royal Malady*, Charles Chenevix Trench.